D1332629

Items should be returned on or before the last date shown below. Items not already requested by other borrowers may be renewed in person, in writing or by telephone. To renew, please quote the number on the barcode label. To renew online a PIN is required. This can be requested at your local library.
Renew online @ **www.dublincitypubliclibraries.ie**
Fines charged for overdue items will include postage incurred in recovery. Damage to or loss of items will be charged to the borrower.

Leabharlanna Poiblí Chathair Bhaile Átha Cliath
Dublin City Public Libraries

Baile Átha Cliath
Dublin City

Brainse Fhionnglaise   Finglas Library
T: (01) 834 4906 E: finglaslibrary@dublincity.ie

Date Due	Date Due	Date Due
2 0 JUN 2019	14·7·19	2 6 FEB 2019

COPYRIGHT

"This book is a work of fiction, but some works of fiction contain perhaps more truth than first intended, and therein lies the magic."

Copyright © Ben Galley 2015
The right of Ben Galley to be identified as the author of this work has been asserted in accordance with the Copyright, Designs and Patents Act 1988. All rights reserved.

No part of this book may be edited, transmitted in any form or by any means (electronic, mechanical, photocopying, recording or otherwise), or reproduced in any manner without permission except in the case of brief quotations embodied in reviews or articles. It may not be lent, resold, hired out or otherwise circulated without the publisher's permission. Permission can be obtained through www.bengalley.com.

Ben Galley owns the right to use all images and fonts used in this book's cover design and within the book itself.

All characters in this book are fictitious and any resemblance to real persons, living or dead, is purely coincidental.

BRPB1:
ISBN: 978-0-9927871-5-8
1st Edition - Published by BenGalley.com
Cover Design by Teague Fullick
Original Image by John Harrison
Professional Dreaming by Ben Galley
Edited by Kevin Booth

IF YOU ENJOY THIS BOOK

THEN TELL A FRIEND

Reviews and shares are really important to indie authors, so if you enjoy Bloodrush, let somebody know, so they can enjoy it too.

THANKS FOR YOUR SUPPORT!

Brainse Fhionnglaise   Finglas Library
T: (01) 834 4906 E: finglaslibrary@dublincity.ie

ABOUT THE AUTHOR

Ben Galley is a young indie author and purveyor of dark fantasy from rainy old England. Harbouring a near-fanatical love of writing and fantasy, Ben has been scribbling tall tales ever since he can remember. When he's not busy day-dreaming on park benches or arguing the finer points of dragons, he works as a self-publishing consultant, aiding fellow authors achieve their dream of publishing. He also co-runs indie-only ebook store, Libiro.com

For more about Ben, and special Bloodrush content, visit his site:
www.bengalley.com

Simply say hello at:
hello@bengalley.com

Or follow Ben on Twitter and Facebook:
@BenGalley and /BenGalleyAuthor

ALSO BY BEN GALLEY

The Written
Pale Kings
Dead Stars - Part One
Dead Stars - Part Two

SUGGESTED LISTENING

Below are some of the songs that inspired me along my writing journey, and I hope they inspire you too, in any way that they can. Enjoy.

Letters From the Sky
Civil Twilight

F**king Desert, Dude
Khurt

Circles
Ludovico Einaudi & Greta Svabo Bech

Life @ 11
A Day To Remember

Hunger of the Pine
Δ

A Favour House Atlantic
Coheed & Cambria

BomBom - feat. The Teaching
Macklemore & Ryan Lewis

Follaton Wood
Ben Howard

Empire
Alpines

Run
Kill it Kid

Inhaler
Foals

Overdone
Bombay Bicycle Club

Everybody Wants to Rule the World
Lorde

Bleeding Out
Imagine Dragons

Waitress Song
First Aid Kit

Stalemate
Enter Shikari

Ten Tonne Skeleton
Royal Blood

Dreamember
Twin Atlantic

Follow Ben's Bloodrush playlist on Spotify by scanning this QR code with your smartphone:

This book is for the readers, as always.

A special mention also goes out to comedy trio the Sleeping Trees, my friends and fellow mischief-makers, who were the inspiration behind Akway, and will be making an appearance in the second book of this trilogy.

An enormous thank you goes to the great people who helped crowd-fund this book via Pubslush. I'd also like to thank four backers in particular for their level of support. They are:

Michael Ruurds
Paul Dettman
Jacques Smit
and Paul Galley

A PRELUDE

There are many places in this world where we humans are not welcome. Antarticus, for example, has slain explorer after explorer with its wolves and winds so cold and fierce they can cut a man in half. Or the Sandara, plaguing travellers for millennia with its fanged dunes and sandstorms. Or what about the high seas, and the Cape of Black Souls, where the waves swallow ships whole, and never spit them back out? But there are darker places on this earth. Much, much darker places.

These are places that time has forgotten, that *we* have forgotten, now that we've turned our attention to industry, to business, and to science. Our steam and our clockwork may have conquered the globe, but we have built our cities on old and borrowed ground, a ground that knew many creatures and empires before it felt the kiss of our own feet. These were the ages that spawned fairy tale and folklore, dreams and nightmares, the world that we trampled in our march for progress, burying it beneath cobble and railroad.

But stubbornness is a trait of victors, so they say. The vestiges of this old world are still clinging on, hiding in the dark places, lost in the shadows, glaring at us from behind their magic. Oh, they are very much alive, friends, hiding in the cracks of reality, the spaces between your blinks. And woe betide anybody that dares to go hunting for them. You would have better luck in the Sandara.

Of course, you have known this all along. If you have ever felt the hot rush of fear in your stomach when a twig snaps in the twilight woods, then you have known it. If you have ever felt that chill run up your spine every time you cross the old bridge, you have known it.

We humans remember the darkness very well, and how its monsters prowled the edges of our campfires and snatched us into the night. We simply refuse to acknowledge it is anything other than irrational fear. Ghost stories. Boogeymen. Old wives' tales. Nonsense, though we secretly know the truth. So much so that when we read in the newspapers that a man was ripped to shreds by a mysterious assailant in the old dockyards last Thursday, we do not think psychopath, we think *werewolf*. Maybe we would be right.

There are dark things in the shadows, and they are far from fond of us humans.

CHAPTER I

"TO THE LOST"

18th April, 1867

'To the lost.' The surgeon raised his tiny glass with a gloved and rather bony hand.

Tonmerion Hark did the same, though he could only summon the wherewithal to raise it halfway. He let it hover just beneath his chin, as if he were cradling it to his chest. The liquor smelled like cloves. Sickening. However he tried, he couldn't tear his gaze away from the pistol, that sharp-edged contraption of humourless steel and stained oak, lounging in an impossibly clean metal tray at the elbow of his father's body.

'The lost,' he murmured in reply, and flicked the glass as if swatting at a bothersome bluebottle.

A pair of wet slapping sounds broke the sterile, white-tiled silence as the liquor painted a muddy orange streak on the milky vinyl floor. So that was that. What precious little ceremony they must observe was over. Lord Karrigan Bastion Hark, the Bulldog of London, Prime Lord of the Empire of Britannia, Master of the Emerald Benches and widower of the inimitable Lady Hark, had been pronounced dead. As a doornail.

Tonmerion could have told them that from the start, but such was tradition. His gaze inched from the gun to his father's pallid skin, bruised as it was with the blood settling, or so the surgeon had told him as he worked. Tonmerion had decided he did not like surgeons. They were rude; being so bold as to poke around in the visceral depths of other people. Of boys' dead fathers.

Leabharlanna Poibli Chathair Baile Átha Cliath

Dublin City Public Libraries

11

His gaze moved to the neatly sewn-up hole in his father's chest, directly above his heart. The oozing had finally stopped. The puckered and rippled edges of white skin around the black thread were clean. Not a single drop of corpse blood seeped through. Not surprising, thought Tonmerion, seeing as so much of it had been left on the steps of Harker Sheer's western garden.

For a brief moment, the boy's eyes flicked to his father's closed eyelids. He thanked the Almighty that those sharp sapphire eyes were hidden away, not bathing him with disappointment, as was their custom. Even then, in the grip of cold death, Tonmerion could almost feel their gaze piercing those grey eyelids and jabbing him. His own eyes quickly slunk away. Instead, he looked at the surgeon, and was somewhat startled to find the man staring directly back at him, arms folded and waiting patiently.

'And what now?' Tonmerion piped up, his young voice cracking after the silence.

'The constable will be here in a moment, I'm sure.'

'Is he late?' asked Tonmerion, biting the inside of his lip. *The body was so grey ...*

The surgeon looked a smidgeon confused. He pushed the wire-framed rims of his round glasses up the slope of his nose. 'I beg your pardon, Master Hark?'

Tonmerion huffed. 'I said, is he late?'

'No, young Master. Simply finishing the paperwork.'

Tonmerion scratched his neck as he tried to think up something clever and commanding to say. Gruff words echoed through his mind. *Get your chin up. Stand straight. Look them straight in their beady little eyes.*

Words from dead lips.

'Then he must have been late earlier in the day. Why else would he not be here, on time, when I am ready to leave. Instead I am forced to stand here, stuck looking at this ... this ...' His words failed him miserably. His tongue sat fat and useless behind his teeth. He waved his hand irritably. 'This ... *carcass.*'

For that was what it was. *A carcass.* So callous in its truth. Tonmerion could see it in the surgeon's face, the condemning curl in that hairless, sweat-beaded top lip of his.

The surgeon took a sharp breath. 'Of course, Lordling. I shall fetch him for you.' And with that he turned on his heel, making to leave. The leather of his shoe made a little squeak on the white vinyl, but before he could take a step, the sound of heavy boots was heard on the stairs. 'Ah,' the surgeon said, turning back with another squeak. 'Here he comes now. You shall have your escape, young Master Hark.'

'Yes, well,' was all Tonmerion's tongue could muster. He folded his arms and watched the barrel of a constable emerge from the stairwell. The constable's bright blue coat strained at the seams, pinning all its hopes on the polished buttons that glinted in the sterile light of the room. *Now here's a man who has seen too much of a desk and not enough of the cobbles*, his father would have intoned. Tonmerion almost felt like turning and shushing his dead father.

'Master Hark,' boomed the constable, as he shuffled to a halt at the foot of the table. His eyes were fixed on Tonmerion's, but it was easy to see they itched to pull right, yearned to gaze on the body of Tonmerion's father. Tonmerion didn't blame him one inch. It wasn't every day you got to meet a Prime Lord, especially a freshly murdered one.

'My apologies for …' he began, but Tonmerion cut him off.

'Apology accepted, Constable Pagget,' he replied. 'Have you captured my father's murderer yet?'

Pagget shook his head solemnly. 'Not yet, I'm afraid …'

'Well, what is being done about it?'

'Everything that can be done, Master Hark.'

'Well that's not …' Tonmerion began, but it was his turn to be cut off.

'Please, young sir, it's about your father's will.'

Tonmerion threw him a frown. 'What about my father's will? What and where must I sign?'

There was a moment of hesitation, during which the constable's mouth fell slowly open, the ample fat beneath his chin gently cushioning the fall. Not a single sound came forth for quite a while.

'Whatever is the matter?' demanded Tonmerion impatiently.

Constable Pagget summoned the wherewithal to shut his mouth, and soon afterwards he found his voice too. 'It's your father's last wishes, Master Hark, they concern you directly,' he said, his eyes flashing to the surgeon for the briefest of moments.

Tonmerion huffed. 'Well of course they do! I'm the only Hark left. The estate will be left to me,' he replied, trying to ignore the truth in his own words. It frightened him a little too much.

'Not … exactly,' Pagget croaked. 'That is to say … not yet.'

'Yet? What do you mean, *yet*?'

The constable took a step backwards and waved a couple of fat fingers at the stairs. 'You'd better step into my office, I think, young Master Hark. We apparently have much to discuss.'

'This is highly irregular,' Tonmerion began, his father's favourite phrase, spilling out of his mouth. He bit his lip and said no more. Fixing a frown onto his face, the young Hark raised his chin and went to take a step forwards that said everything his traitorous mouth could not: a confident step that said he was inconvenienced, displeased, that he deserved respect, that he was in command here, and not crumbling with worry and fear and disgust and all those other things that lords and generals and heroes don't feel. Sadly, Tonmerion's step forwards was quite the opposite. It was a step so lacking in grace and dignity that Tonmerion would forever shiver at the very thought of it. As his foot hit the floor with a wet slap, not a squeak, Tonmerion realised his mistake. The liquor.

His foot slid away from him, betraying him so casually that his leg, and the rest of him for that matter, were powerless to resist. Tonmerion performed an ungraceful wobble and grabbed the nearest thing his flailing arms could reach … his father's dead arm.

A small wheeze of relief escaped his tight lips as he found himself upright, safe. A similar sound came forth when he realised what exactly it was that had saved him from the most embarrassing fall, though this time it was strangled by horror, and disgust. Tonmerion's gaze slowly tumbled down his arm, from the expensive cloth to his ice-white knuckles, to the dead, bruised, slate-coloured flesh that his fingers were squeezing so tightly. Tonmerion gurgled something and quickly righted himself, red in the face and wide in the eyes. He quickly began to smooth the front of his shirt, but stopped hurriedly when it dawned on him that he had just touched a dead body. He held his hands out in the air instead, neither up nor down, close nor far.

'A cloth,' he murmured. The surgeon obliged him, leaning over to pass him a startlingly white cloth from beneath the bench. Tonmerion dragged it over his knuckles and fingertips, and nodded to the constable. 'Lead the way.'

Pagget had not yet decided whether to stifle a laugh or to share the boy's revulsion. He simply looked on, one eye squinting awkwardly, his face stuck halfway between the two expressions.

'Jimothy?' the surgeon said, and Pagget came to.

'Right! Yes. This way if you please.' He only barely managed to keep from adding, 'Mind your step.'

Tonmerion followed him without a word.

✵

'America.' Tonmerion gave the man a flat stare that spoke a whole world of disbelief.

Witchazel was his name, like the slender shrub, and it was a name that suited him to the very core. He was more stick than man, loosely draped in an ill-fitting suit of the Prussian style, charcoal striped with purple. His hair was thin and jet-black, smeared across his scalp and forehead like an oleaginous paste. Tonmerion had never liked the look of the lawyer. *One with power should dress accordingly.* His father's words, once more.

Witchazel shuffled the wad of papers in his leather-gloved hands and coughed. It meant nothing except a resounding yes. Tonmerion looked at Constable Pagget, but found him idly thumbing the dust from the shelves of his ornate bookcase. Tonmerion looked instead at his knees, and at the woven carpet just beyond them. He tugged at his collar. The constable's office was stifling, heavy with curtains, mahogany, and leather. The news did not help matters, not one bit.

'And this aunt …' he asked.

'Lilain Rennevie,' filled in Witchazel.

'Lives *where* exactly?'

Witchazel's face took on an enthusiastic curve, a look of excitement and wonder, one that had been well-practised in the bedroom mirror, or so it seemed to Tonmerion. 'A charming place, right on the cusp of civilisation, Master Hark,' he said. 'A frontier town, don't you know, going by the bucolic name of Fell Falls. A brand new settlement founded by the railroad teams and the Serped Railroad Company. They're aiming for the west coast, you see, blazing a trail right across the country in search of gold and riches and the Last Ocean. An exciting place, if I may say so, sir. I'm almost envious!' Wichazel grinned.

'Almost,' Tonmerion replied drily.

Witchazel forced his grin to stay and turned to look at the constable, hoping he would chime in. All Pagget did was smile and nod.

Witchazel produced a map from the papers in his hand and slid it across the desk towards the boy. 'Here we are.'

Tonmerion leant forwards and eyed the shapes and lines. 'It looks small.'

Witchazel templed his fingers and hid behind them. 'Yes, but it has so much potential to grow,' he offered.

'Very small.'

'You have to start somewhere!'

'And forty miles from the nearest town.'

'Think of the peace and quiet. Away from the hustle and ...'

'It's literally the end of the line.'

'Not for long, mark my words!'

'And what does this say: desert?'

Witchazel's temple collapsed and he spread his fingers out on the desk instead, wishing the green leather would magically transport him out of this office. What a fate this boy had inherited. Whisked away to Almighty knows where. No mansion. No servants. No money ... Witchazel almost felt sorry for him.

'Desert, yes. It seems that the territory of Wyoming is somewhat *wild*. Deserts and mountains and, oh, what was the word ...' Witchazel clicked his gloved fingers, resulting in a leathery squeak. '*Prairies*, that was it. But surely that's exciting, isn't it?'

Tonmerion had crossed his arms. His eyes were back on the lawyer, trying with all his might to drill right into the man's pupils, to wither him, as he had seen his father do countless times. 'Do I have any say in the matter?'

Witchazel made a show of checking the papers again, even though he already knew the answer. 'I'm afraid the instructions are very specific. You are to remain in the care of your aunt until such time as you are of age to inherit, on your eighteenth birthday. Until then all assets will be frozen in law, under my authority.'

Tonmerion let out a long sigh, ruffling the strands of sandy blonde hair that stubbornly insisted on hanging forwards over his forehead, rather than lying to the sides with the rest of his combed mop. 'And what manner of woman is my aunt?' he asked. He had barely known of her existence until twenty minutes ago. Now he was staring down the barrel of a five-year exile, with her and her alone. He felt a lump in his throat. He tried to swallow it down, but it held fast. 'Is she the mayor? A businesswoman?' he croaked.

Witchazel flipped through a few of his pages. 'She is a businesswoman indeed, you'll be pleased to hear.'

Tonmerion sagged a little in his chair.

Witchazel peered closely at one line in particular. 'It says here that she works as an undertaker.'

The boy came straight back up, stiff as a board.

It was a day for wanton staring, Tonmerion had decided. He may have escaped the body of his dead father in the surgeon's basement, but now he was trapped by the dried pool of blood on the steps of one of the Harker Sheer estate's many vast patios. The stone beneath was a polished white marble, which made the blood, even now that it had dried to a crumbling crust, all the more stark. Tonmerion watched the way it had settled in a thick, rusty crimson slick that dripped down the stairs, one by one, until it found a pool on the third.

When Tonmerion finally wrenched his gaze from his father's blood, he turned instead to the thin fold of paper he clutched so venomously in his left hand. He held the paper up to the cloud-masked sun and scowled: tickets for a boat to a faraway land. Tonmerion didn't know which to hate more: the blood or his looming fate.

'What have I done to deserve this?' he asked aloud. Unable to bring himself to utter a response, and having none to offer, he let the sound of the swaying elms and whispering pines fill the silence.

During the coach ride home, Tonmerion had pondered every avenue of escape. Once his mind had drawn out all the possibilities, like wool spilling off a reel, neither running nor hiding had seemed too fortuitous. He had no money save what he had found in his father's desk: a handful of gold florins, several silver pennies and a smattering of bronzes and coppers. That would not last more than a few weeks. He had given complaining a little thought too, but had come to the decision he'd done enough of that in the constable's office. In truth – in horrid, clanging truth – Tonmerion was stuck.

He was bound for America, the New Kingdom.

That was the source of the hard, brutal lump wedged in his throat. He lifted a hand to massage it and tried to swallow. Neither helped. He took a gulp of air and felt immediately sick. The blood beckoned to him, but Tonmerion steered away from it. He was not keen to repeat the liquor episode.

Remembering the water fountain at the bottom of the steps, he let his shaky legs lead the way. His wobbling reflection in the hissing fountain's pool confirmed that he was indeed paler than a sheet of bleached parchment. Tonmerion put both hands on the marble and dipped his head into the water to let the cold water sting his face. It was refreshing and calming. He took in three deep gulps and felt the coldness slide down into his belly. Wiping his mouth, he stared up at the pinnacles of the pines.

'By the Roots, you're white.'

Upon hearing a voice speak out from the bushes, on an estate that was supposed to be emptier than a beggar's purse, any other person would have jumped, or even squealed with surprise, but not Tonmerion. He did not flinch, for this was nothing out of the ordinary for him.

'He's dead, Rhin,' he muttered, still staring up at the trees.

'Speak up.' The voice was small yet still had all the depth and resonance of a man's voice.

'It's all going to change.' Tonmerion looked over at the blood, stark against the marble, and nodded.

There was a polite and nervous cough, and then: 'I'm sorry, Merion, for your father. I truly am.'

Merion's gaze turned to the marvellous little figure standing in the dirt, half of his body still hidden by the shadow of the ornamental bush –

no, not hidden, *fused* with the bush in some way. Merion did not bat an eyelid.

'It's all changed, just like that,' he clicked his fingers, and the figure stepped out of the shadows.

To say the small gentleman was a fairy would be doing him a great injustice. Contrary to popular belief, there is a great deal of difference between a fairy and a *faerie*. The former are small, silly creatures, more insect than human, and prone to mischief. The latter, however, are a proud and ancient race, the Fae. They are larger, smarter, and infinitely more dangerous than fairies, and bolder. For millennia they have lived unseen in the undergrowth and forgotten forests, just out of the reach of human eyes and fingers. They are now nought but folklore, wives' tales, rubbish for the ears of children. No man, in his right mind, would believe in such a thing as a faerie. But here one stood, as bold and as bright as a summer's day.

Rhin stood just shy of twelve inches tall, big for Fae standards. He was long of limb, but not scrawny. Between the gaps in his pitch-black armour, it was easy to see that the muscles wrapped around his bony frame were like cords, tightly bunched.

Rhin's skin was a mottled bluish grey, though it was not uncommon to see him glowing faintly at night. His eyes were the only bright colour on his person, glowing purple even in the cloudy daylight. The thin metal plates of his Fae armour were jet-black, held in place by brown rat-leather. His boots, rising to just below the knee, were also black.

And of course, there are the wings. Thin, translucent dragonfly wings sprouted from the ridge of Rhin's shoulders and hung down his back, hugging the contours of his armour and body and glistening blue and gold. The Fae lost the power of flight centuries ago. Their wings are weaker now, but they still have their uses.

Four years had passed since Rhin had crawled out of the bushes and straight onto Merion's lap, bleeding and vomiting. Merion had been just a young boy, only nine at the time, and the sight of a strange grey creature with armour and dragonfly wings, sliding in and out of consciousness, would have frightened any child half to death, but not Merion.

Rhin crossed his arms, making the scales of his armour rattle. He tapped his claw-like nails on the metal. It was in need of a polish. 'It's not right, what was done to your father. Roots know I didn't know the man, but he didn't deserve this, and neither do you. Neither do we.' Rhin bowed his head. 'Like I said, I'm sorry, Merion.'

The lump in the young Hark's throat had returned, this time with vengeance. Maybe it was the faerie's condolences, maybe it was the crimson streak in the corner of his eye, or perhaps it was the crumpled fist of papers by his side, Merion didn't know, but he knew his lip was wobbling. He knew it was all suddenly terribly real.

Real men cannot be seen to cry.

More of his father's parting words.

Merion swallowed hard, and tucked his lip under his top teeth, biting down. He nodded and, when he trusted himself to speak without his voice cracking, he said 'Thank you.'

Rhin shuffled his feet and ran an absent hand through his short, wild hair. Jet-black it was, and thick, slicked back and cropped short at the sides. 'Do they know who did it?' he asked quietly.

Merion stamped his foot and paced out a tight, angry circle. 'Pagget doesn't have a clue,' he groused. 'Nobody has any idea.'

'That's …'

'An outrage. Yes, I know. And guess what? That's not even the worst part.'

'Not the worst …? What could be worse than …' the faerie gestured at the slick of blood on the marble steps. '… that?'

Merion turned and brandished the folded paper. '*This*! It's an abomination. A disgrace. An insult!'

Rhin looked worried. 'Yes, but what is it?'

Merion pinched the bridge of his nose and swallowed again. *Say it out loud and, who knows, it just might sound a little better,* he told himself. 'We have to move to America.'

No, no better.

Rhin's lavender eyes grew wide. 'The New Kingdom? Why?'

'My father left instructions, Rhin. All of Harker Sheer, all of his other estates, all of his money. It's mine now, but not until I turn eighteen.' Merion aimed a kick at the base of the fountain. 'And in the meantime I, *we*, have to go live with my aunt, in Wyoming.'

'And where the hell is that?'

'In the western deserts of America, the arse-end of nowhere, to put it plainly. Full of filthy rail workers, peasants, sand, and horses and cows, no doubt.'

Rhin rubbed his chin. 'It sounds perfect,' he said. Merion was about to snort when he realised there hadn't been the faintest tremor of sarcasm in Rhin's words. He stared down at the faerie.

'You're serious?'

Rhin shrugged. 'It's the perfect escape.'

'Yes, for you maybe. I suspected you might like this god-awful fate of mine. Not all of us are runaways and outcasts, Rhin. I'm not in hiding. I have a future *here*, in London. I have a great responsibility to inherit, and a murderer to catch, for Almighty's sake! My father must have justice. The Hark name needs protecting ...' Merion trailed off, flattened by the impossibility of it all. 'I can't just leave. I can't just let it fall to the dogs.'

'You're thirteen, boy.'

Merion flapped his hand. 'But I'm the only one left! It's my duty. And don't call me boy, you know I hate that.'

Rhin took a step forwards, eyes wide. 'You would still have to wait until you were eighteen, even if you father hadn't been killed.'

'Murdered, Rhin. *Murdered.*' The fountain received another kick. 'And no difference, you say? Hah! At least if he was still alive, I could have lived my life in comfort, in society, within reach of the capital. But no, he was *murdered*, and now we have to go live in a shack in some place called Fell Falls. No dinners, no balls, no trips on the rumbleground trains, no visits to the Emerald Benches. Nothing. Sod all.' It was at times like these that Merion wished he'd asked the kitchen staff to teach him more swearwords.

Rhin was not convinced. 'All I heard was no tedious ceremonies, no politics, and no father watching your every move, no offence. We can be *free* in America, Merion. Free to do what we want, safe in the knowledge that you can come back to *this*, to a fortune and a life in high society.'

'In five bloody years!'

'More than enough time to turn you into a proper man, to toughen you up. Not like one of these silk-clad dandies you idolise. A man with rough hands and bristle on his cheeks—ladies would love that.' Rhin dared as much to wink. Merion pulled a face.

'Rubbish.'

'Trust me, I know. Listen to your elders.' Rhin was over two hundred years old. He had a point.

Merion slumped in every possible way a person could slump. He crumpled to his knees and then to his backside, letting his shoulders hang like loose saddlebags and his hands splay across the marble. 'I just don't know. I can't put it into words. The world is upside down.'

Rhin walked forwards to put a small hand on Merion's knee. 'It doesn't have to be a punishment, Merion. It could be an adventure, something that could change you—put some fire into your belly. Five years isn't that long a time.'

Merion snorted. 'Easy for you to say.'

'Are we in agreement. Adventure?' Rhin asked.

With great solemnity, Merion lifted his head and stared up at the roiling grey skies, not a patch or stray thread of blue anywhere to be seen. Merion was going to miss these skies, and their rain, the staple of the Empire. He let the cold breeze run its fingers across his neck and face, savouring that moment. He swallowed one last time, and found that the lump had disappeared—for now, at least.

'I'll let you know when we get there,' replied the young Hark.

CHAPTER II

TAMARASSIE

'I've done it. I've bloody done it. What it'll cost me, I don't yet know. I'm out, but I can hear them shouting. They're still searching. Got the rats out for me, and the moles.'

26th April, 1867

What is remarkable about the human stomach is that, though small, when given the chance to vomit continuously, it can conveniently offer a seemingly endless supply of bile with which to facilitate the act. Merion discovered this fact of biology as he heaved his guts out over the railing for the hundredth time that day. You would have been forgiven for thinking that the sailors would have stopped laughing after the first day, or the second—perhaps even the fourth. But no, it was their sixth day aboard the *Tamarassie*, and the sailors still found his puking the very pinnacle of hilarity. Perhaps it was because he ruined so many of his good clothes.

Merion winced as he felt the acid-burn on the back of his throat. His hands were slimy and his chin wet. Even without looking down, he could tell his rather expensive coat was already soiled. He closed his eyes and pushed himself to try and enjoy the gentle swaying and pitching and rolling … More laughter erupted from the bow as Merion introduced his innards to the sea once more. When he had finally finished, he stared up at the horizon, as Rhin had suggested. It hadn't helped yet, but there was always hope.

The Iron Ocean was a desolate place—a desert in its own right, only one of rolling granite-coloured waves, of whirling foam and drifting, sapphire-blue ice. The day was cold and grey, as it had been since they left Port's Mouth. So cold and bitter was it that the sea spray froze in the blustery air as it rose up to sting Merion's cheeks and knuckles where he hung over the *Tamarassie*'s rusted railing.

Barely more than a converted tramp steamer, the ship was a bucket of rust and poorly-painted metalwork. A pile of iron and varnished wood, she sat low in the ever-heaving waters of the corpse-cold ocean, fat with cargo and passengers seeking fortune on the new continent. She didn't steam so much as waddle towards the city of Boston, far, far away in the hazy, cloud-smeared distance. From where he stood, Merion could hear the slapping and deep resonant churning of the ship's twin paddles, sticking out of the ship's ribs like the fat wheels of a cart, buried to their necks in the water. A jagged-topped funnel sat squat behind the bridge, and the sickly soot-smell of the thick pillar of smoke it belched into the cold air was not helping Merion's stomach one bit.

It seemed his father had left little money for a luxurious voyage in his final will and testament. Perhaps Witchazel had cut a larger-than-normal fee. In any case, the *Tamarassie* was a far cry from the ocean liners Merion had seen in the penny dreadfuls, or rising proudly against the murk of the Thames shipyards.

Merion wiped himself as best he could and tottered across the metal and wood deck towards the door he had left open. He could still hear the tittering mirth of the sailors, who seemed to have spent the whole voyage lounging about on deck. Merion ignored them, and went below to his all-too modest cabin.

Rhin was enjoying a biscuit in his usual spot atop the edge of Merion's largest trunk, where it was piled in the corner with the others. He had shed his armour, but still wore his little knife at his hip, no more than an inch-long shard of black Fae steel. To the innocent bystander, the faerie's blade might have seemed insignificant, a pinprick. But the Fae had learned long ago which arteries, veins and nerves were the ... *tender*

areas of men, when humans had still been young and wild, before their gunpowder and their machinery.

In Rhin's hands the biscuit was as large as a dinner plate, but he was making a considerable dent in the side. Rhin had a sweet tooth— well, more of a sweet fang. Sugar to him was like rum to a sailor. His eyes were half-closed as he chewed and his crystalline wings fluttered.

There was a bang and a thud on the wall outside the cabin, and Rhin fell back into the trunk with a soft thud. As the metal lock started to rattle, Rhin was already half buried in a dark blue shirt, skin and armour shimmering as it became translucent. Faerie skin is a marvellous thing. Its magic delights in tricking the eye, adapting to the colours and light. It is one of the oldest spells of the faeries, and their most coveted. Within moments, he was more shirt than faerie, and his black knife spared not a glint.

'It's me,' said a hoarse voice, thick with phlegm and retching.

There was a quick buzzing, and Rhin hopped up onto the lip of the trunk. 'So it is. Feeling better?'

'Not in the slightest. How long?'

'One thousand two hundred and fifty-six miles to Boston. No, wait. Fifty-five. Four days maybe.'

This particular faerie trick never failed to boggle Merion's mind. Rhin could tell you the distance between any two points on the map as quick as a flash. Rhin had tried to explain it to Merion a dozen times, but the boy could never understand it. All Merion knew was that it actually wasn't magic, as he had originally guessed, but something to do with magnets and poles. An inner compass, so the faerie said.

'I'm going to sleep,' Merion sighed, dropping down into the tiny cot that was fighting for space with his luggage. A broom cupboard would have offered more volume.

'Again?' Rhin asked, rolling his eyes.

'There's nothing else to do on this cursed boat.'

The faerie couldn't argue with that, and he shrugged as Merion covered his face with the dubiously stained blanket that had come with the cot.

Something sharp began to slice through Merion's slumbers and mangle his dreams, shred by shred. He could hear a distant clanging, the muted notes swirling around his head. Slowly but surely, he was dragged from the sucking depths of sleep.

The first thing he saw was Rhin waving to him from the trunk. The biscuit was nowhere to be seen. 'Rise and shine, Lordling.'

'What is that infernal racket?' Merion mumbled, wiping the drool from his face.

Rhin pointed at the wooden ceiling as if the answer was written amongst the flakes of peeling varnish. 'Ship's bells. Better go and have a look.'

The prospect of going back on deck was about as alluring as a sausage from a leper's pocket. Merion sighed, something of which he was quickly making a habit.

'Who knows, it could be important,' Rhin coaxed him.

Merion frowned. 'If you're so bored, then why don't you go and have a look?'

Rhin thought for a moment, and then shrugged. 'Fine by me.'

Merion sat upright and immediately regretted it. He clamped his mouth shut, expecting to be sick, but nothing came. The nap had done him good. 'No, you can't go out there alone. The ship is stuffed to bursting with sailors and passengers. You'll get seen, or tripped over, or …'

Rhin smiled, his sharp white teeth a gleaming contrast to his mottled grey skin. Merion would never have told him, but the colour kept reminding him of his father's pallid body, lying on the sterile white tiles of the surgeon's table. The boy shook his head, pushing that thought into the dark recesses of his mind. 'Then come with me,' said the faerie.

'I believe you mean you should come with *me*,' Merion corrected his friend. 'Let's use the bag.'

One of Tonmerion Harlequin Hark's most prized possessions was, to the untrained eye, a simple rucksack. A relic of his father's days spent exploring the frozen mountains of Indus, Merion had found it in Harker Sheer the summer before last, lodged behind a bookshelf in his father's study. His father had grudgingly allowed him to keep it, just as long as it was put to good use, and kept safe. Merion had done just that. Made from a rough green material, and functional to the core, it was full of pockets and holes and grit. It became immediately and permanently affixed to Merion's shoulders. He would wear it to dinner, and he would wear it to bed, having turned it into the perfect receptacle for smuggling a faerie in.

✶

A crowd of passengers filled the deck: a sea of people all wrapped up in coats and scarves and blankets. They muttered to one another in hushed tones, staring at the man on the *Tamarassie*'s bridge, who was hitting the bell with a hammer every handful of seconds. A fog had fallen on the ocean, muffling the churning of the paddles, which echoed eerily about the ship. Every now and again, a lump of ice would bang loudly against the hull, and cause all the passengers to flinch.

'What's going on?' Merion asked of a woman standing nearby. She was a silver-haired lady in her twilight years, standing bolt upright and proud as though a steel rod had been sewn into her coat. When she turned to face him, Merion could see a glint in her wrinkled eye, the spark of life. She smiled with two rows of very straight and very perfect teeth. A single, lonely scar marred her upper lip, leading from the creased corner of her mouth to her left nostril, weaving a fine, pink path.

'Mist, young'un. And an ice field,' she whispered, in a thick accent Merion had never heard before. He guessed it to be from somewhere deep in America, and he guessed right, though he did not know it. He had never been called 'young'un' before, and he couldn't yet decide what to make of it.

'Are we in danger?' he asked politely.

'Most likely!' she grinned, and rubbed her hands together eagerly.

Suffice it to say Merion did not share the old woman's enthusiasm. He heard Rhin whispering from the rucksack. 'Sounds like this old bag's got a screw loose.'

'Shh,' Merion hushed him.

'What's that?' asked the woman, leaning close.

'Er ... nothing.' Merion coughed. 'Thought I'd heard something.' Even though Merion had lied, at that moment a shout rang out from the bow—a sailor's voice craggy with years of cheap tobacco and even cheaper wine.

'Berg on the port side! To starboard lads, to starboard!'

Merion felt a shudder as the ship's innards clanked and clattered. He could imagine rusty cogs clanked and old cables shimmying from side to side, a strange dance of elderly machinery. He craned his head to look towards the bow. The paddle on the left-hand side—or *starboard* as the sailors stubbornly called it—began to stutter and slow while the paddle on the right-hand side, the *port* side, thrashed the water viciously with its flat iron teeth. Slowly, he felt the *Tamarassie* turn. Merion, his head full of stories and headlines concerning ill-fated matrimonies between ships and ice on the high seas, half-wondered if he was about to meet his watery grave.

The boy was pondering this when a loud gasp fluttered across the deck, cold breath drawn sharply into a hundred or so mouths. The passengers began to move then, some to the railing, others shying away, hurrying to cover the eyes of their children and some of the more fragile women. The crowd split right down the middle, and Merion found himself sliding inexorably towards the railing with the braver half, gaze transfixed on an ethereal mass appearing out of the fog. He was staring goggle-eyed at the bloody crown that graced the peak of that floating mountain of jagged ice.

'Rhin ...' he breathed, 'are my eyes broken?'

'No more than mine, if that's the case,' Rhin hissed. 'By the Roots ...' he said, and then swore in his own tongue.

The old woman was still nearby. She broke off from staring so she could seize the young Hark by the shoulder and drag him closer to the railing, where arms and shoulders and swaddled bodies would not impair his grisly view.

'There, young'un! Take it all in. You don't see this every day. No sir!'

Merion didn't even know what *this* was. Only that it was making him feel sick again. The woman talked in his ear as he took in every tiny, grisly detail.

'Ever been to the deep ice, lad? Me neither, though I heard tales aplenty. Endless ice, they say, far as the eye can see. Not dead though, not at all. It's full of bears and yak and foxes—and people too. Nomads from the mountains. They say a nomad is the only thing in this world that ice can't freeze in one place. And they're vicious folk, as you can see, lad. More animal than man,' the woman waved her arm at the top of the iceberg as it drifted slowly past the ship, as if her jaw had become tired of flapping, and her body needed something else to flap while it rested. A moment of silence passed, punctuated only by curious whispers and the slapping of the paddles. Merion craned his neck and took it all in.

The towering shard of dirty white ice wore a crown of jagged wire and slumped bodies. Half frozen to the ice at their backs, half burnt by the endless, tormenting northern sun, six men had been bound tight to the ice with their legs slashed at the calves. Merion held a hand to his mouth as he thought of how much blood must have pumped when the men were sentenced to their exile, how they must have screamed. They were far from screaming now. What hadn't been picked at by the gulls and petrels now lay, heads yawning at the murky air around about, empty-eyed, but still blissfully sailing the seas.

'What did these men do?' Merion asked in a hollow voice, whilst trying to hold back the crashing wave of nausea surging up his throat.

'Who can tell? They don't look nomad, not in the slightest. Soldiers, by the look of their black fingers. Powder will do that to you, it will, should you play with it long enough. White folks from the places where the wild pines meet the ice and stop dead. Hunting folk. Must have crossed paths with the nomads, then crossed swords. That's what you get when you go wanderin' into nomad territory. They were punished, the fools,' she lectured, almost spitting the last word. But then, in a silent moment of respect, she held her hand to her chest and watched them drift on by, just until they disappeared back into the fog.

Merion shuddered, as if the ghosts of the dead men had tickled his spine. 'I, er, thank you,' was all he could think of to say.

'Welcome, young'un,' she nodded, and then stuffed her hands into a pair of deep, fur-lined pockets. 'So where you headed?'

'Probably back to my cabin …'

The woman laughed then, a harsh cackle, and clapped him heartily on the shoulder. Merion's jolted stomach performed a somersault, and he felt that wave rising again … 'I meant in the motherland, son, the big wide open, the Endless Land.'

Merion scratched his head. 'Wyoming, I believe.'

The woman threw him an odd expression, the bottom half of her face pressing into her neck as her eyes and her ears lifted. A high-pitched hum rose and fell in her throat. 'Been there before, have you?' she asked.

'No.'

'Seems an odd choice, is all, for a young willow like you.'

Merion found himself trying to stand wider, thicker somehow. He failed. 'Trust me, madam, there was no choice in the matter.'

'Don't know many folk from Wyoming. Don't know many heading there neither, 'cept for workers.'

'Should I be worried?'

'I'd be worried about her instead. She's mad as a bucket of smashed crabs,' Rhin hissed, his voice a skinny whisper on the icy wind.

'Gods, no, young'un. I don't suppose you shouldn't,' she shook her head vehemently, but that last sentence stuck like a fishbone in Merion's gullet. *Suppose.* He hoped it was just the old woman's strange drawl, or her astoundingly appalling grammar, that made him start to sweat, even in the cold.

'Well,' the woman said, and clapped her hands. 'Best be back to my supper. Good luck to you, son. Fare well.'

'Madam.' Merion sketched a shallow bow. He abruptly felt a little foolish. Bowing, there on a rusty deck in the middle of the wide Iron Ocean. Well, he may not be in London any more, but he was London-born, a son of a lord, and that meant that it wasn't just blood flowing through his veins, but manners as well, stout, Empire-grown manners.

If you're going to get stabbed, then get stabbed by a gentleman. At least then you get an apology along with his cold length of steel. Merion had heard that whilst hiding under his father's desk during one of his long and stuffy meetings. The young Hark had been unearthed and captured shortly after, unable to stifle a sneeze. His father had beaten him in the garden. Not enough to bruise, but enough to make him think twice the next time.

'You're incorrigible, you blaggard,' Merion snapped at his rucksack, once he was good and alone.

'That one's definitely missing a few tiles from the roof,' Rhin sniggered.

Merion rolled his eyes. 'Let's just go inside before any more nightmares swim past.'

'Right you are.'

As they made their way back to the main stairs, and back to their tiny cabin, Merion scratched his head and asked, 'How many miles, Rhin?'

The faerie didn't even have to count. 'One-thousand, one hundred and ninety-four.'

'What was that particularly colourful word you used that time? When you decided to "spar" with Lord Hafferford's spaniel?'

'Clusterfuck.'

'That's the one.'

CHAPTER III

THE ENDLESS LAND

'It's been three days now since I left. Sift must be furious, but there's no going back. The soldiers keep on coming, spreading wider. Killed two yesterday, but now the sewers are crawling with them, which means I'll have to go over, through the streets. Damn if this isn't heavy.'

30th April, 1867

It was a Tuesday morning when the ship's horn shook the walls of their tiny cabin, shaking their tiny sanctuary down. The *Tamarassie* had reached Boston safe and sound, but the harbour was busier than a brothel on payday, as Rhin had said, looking out of the grimy porthole. Merion did not know enough to comment.

Now the faerie was crouching under the lip of the trusty rucksack, eying the towers and cranes of Boston's sprawling port, which yawned like the maw of some giant stag beetle. Between its jaws, a horde of ships and fractured islands jostled for space in a forest of masts and spars. If Rhin squinted, his keen Fae eyes could make out the clock towers and balloon docks of the city proper, lurking in the thick sea-fog that clung to the shoreline.

Merion was squinting too—not because he wanted to sightsee, but because the rain seemed to be pursuing a vendetta against his eyes. It was that horrid fine kind that soaks you to the bone in minutes. He had been standing on deck for the past hour, watching America crawl out of the fog to greet them, piece by jagged and sea-washed piece.

Boston looked like London from the water, but flatter, as though somebody had flattened the whole city with the back of a colossal frying pan. Its buildings, what few of them he could see through the confounded, blinding drizzle and sea fog, were squat and wood-built. At least by the docks they were. When he blinked, he spied a few lonely towers here and there, in the far distance, but nothing so special as the spires of his home. He felt cold on the inside, and the rain had nought to do with it.

'Boston,' he muttered.

'Looks ... delightful,' Rhin replied, in a whisper.

'An admiral once told me that the only port worth taking the time to ogle at from the water was that of Venezia. Before the sea swallowed it, of course,' Merion said, not knowing where that little scrap of nonsense had bubbled up from. 'And I also remember my father saying something about the docks being the arse-hole of a city. Besides, we aren't staying.'

'Eloquent, that Prime Lord,' Rhin chuckled, then immediately winced. He could even feel Merion's body shift a little, through the straps of the pack. Strangely the boy didn't sag, as he'd expected, but somehow *stiffened*. Rhin bit his lip. 'Sorry. Too soon,' he said. 'You okay?'

Merion nodded. 'Just fine.'

Rhin knew that was a lie, but he didn't push the matter. *Melancholy crumbles, and anger snaps.* He knew that better than anyone. 'Well,' he said, 'that arse-hole better pucker up for our arrival.'

'If we ever get to the wharf, that is,' replied the boy.

Merion was right. There was a long, winding queue of ships between the bow of the *Tamarassie* and the wharfs of Boston's inner harbour. They jostled like rats in a barrel. Merion scowled and pouted, and stuffed his gloved hands deeper into his pockets, trying to dig out some warmth. 'What a foul welcome this is.'

It was then that a familiar voice rang out. 'Hey, son! There he is. C'mere!'

It was the old American woman, swaddled in an oversized sealskin coat with a hood big enough for her head and some extra luggage. She was marching towards him across the slimy deck, beckoning him repeatedly.

Merion prodded himself with his own finger. 'Madam?'

'Don't worry about ma'am-ing me now. C'mon. We're getting off.'

Merion shook his head. 'Pardon me, it sounded as though you said you're *getting off?*'

'That we are. Captain Smout has ordered some boats be dropped, so we don't have to wait for the ship to dock.'

'But my luggage ...'

'See this is why I travel light!' she said, patting her huge coat. 'Don't worry, you can collect your things once the *Tamarassie*'s made port. Give her an hour or so. In the meantime, you're free to roam the docks.'

Merion wasn't sure that he wanted to 'roam' anything, never mind a foreign port, no doubt overrun with scoundrels and thieves. Witchazel's instructions, which, incidentally, were crumpled up in a tight ball in the pocket of his overcoat, were to meet a gentleman by the curious name of Coltswolde Humbersnide. He would be waiting at the *Tamarassie*'s allotted berth, the Union Wharf, just south of where the Charles River met the Mystic River. What an odd name that was, Merion thought, not for the first time since turning his back on London. He wondered if it were Shohari-speak.

'My apologies, madam, but I'm to meet a man at the Union Wharf, you see, and ...'

The old woman simply tutted. 'And so you shall, young'un. Now c'mon!'

And with that she seized his wrist and towed him away, off towards the stern and a rickety boat bobbing up and down on the oil-slicked waters of the harbour. The scents that assailed his nose were quite astounding, and potent too. Merion felt that familiar bile rising in his throat again. But he had no time for puking. The woman practically lifted him onto the rungs of the rope ladder, and down he went.

'Please don't fall. I'm not a fan of drowning,' muttered the faerie in his rucksack.

Merion's heart leapt for a moment as his foot missed one of the slippery wooden rungs. 'Neither am I, now keep your head down.'

'Aye,' Rhin said, as he melted into the shadows.

The boat lurched when he touched it. He felt a rough hand snatch at his flapping coat, and he was yanked down onto a wet bench. A family of three sat opposite him, eyes half-closed, silently enduring the drizzle.

'Good morning.'

'Нет, спасибо,' replied the man, in a language that was utterly foreign.

'Of course.' Merion shook his head and stared at the floor awash with water. *Some inheritance this was turning out to be*, he thought, and instantly the red flush of guilt flooded his cheeks, making his neck itch.

He heard a shout and looked up to see that the old woman was now shimmying down the ladder, and with ease too. The boat rocked hideously as she climbed aboard, making the mother of the foreign family moan rather woefully. Merion could have sworn she was slowly turning green. The father gently patted her shoulder, whispering something in her ear while the son was busying himself with kicking his shoes together.

'Here we all are, then,' announced the woman with a clap. 'Are we off, boys?'

'Yes ma'am,' replied one of the two sailors, as he and another put their hands to the thick oars.

Mercifully, the drizzle became bored and moved south with the same breeze that came to poke at the fog. A little sun pierced the murky morning haze, and Boston was allowed to sparkle for a time. Under the spring sun's eager light, the docks took on a different feel. Colour spilled out of every nook and cranny. The cranes were not made of weathered, ashen wood, as Merion had judged, but of a wood that was a deep crimson mixed with coffee. The ships' banners, which had hung so lifeless in the rain, now shone with bright reds and jolly yellows.

As they swung to and fro between the ships and the pillars of the tall wharfs, Merion caught glimpses of markets and inns and performers poking their heads above the crates and railings. A little something stirred in him then, a boyish lust for vivid colours and noise, and perhaps the slightest hint of danger. He rose slightly from his seat, but the old woman by his side dragged him back down. 'You'll tip the boat, young'un. Be careful now.'

'Of course, madam.' Merion sat back down, but kept his neck craned and his eyes peeled for wondrous things. 'Is it far?' he asked. All thoughts of father and fate had momentarily been banished. Such is the fickle, blessed nature of a thirteen-year-old.

Wharf by mesmerising wharf, they crept north. The current was against them, but the sailors were thick-set like their oars, and they battled on, grunting to each other as they rowed. They could hear the cries from the merchants and shopkeepers over the roar and splash of the port.

'Fish! The freshest fish this side of the Iron Ocean. Kippers, cod, pollock and shark!'

'Glow-worms! Genuine glow-in-the-dark worms! Buy two and I'll make them glow in the day too!'

'Pickled crow eggs for sale!'

'Genuine wolf-skin caps!'

'Roll up, roll up, and feast your eyes on my special …'

'Meat! Every meat under the sun, and under the earth too! Loin of bat, in fresh!'

Merion let himself drown in the noise.

Before long, even the gaps between the big ships became crowded, and they were forced to cut their journey short. The boat's nose was pointed wharfwards, and was soon nudging the cloth fender of a little pontoon. A skinny set of stairs led up to the main promenade.

Merion got to his feet first. As the sailors tied the boat off, he hopped ashore, swiftly followed by the old woman. He followed her up the steps.

'Now, madam, how exactly do we, *I*, get to Union Wharf from …' His words were stolen by the roar as his head cleared the top stair. All too suddenly, he was drowning in a sea of humanity.

The promenade was flooded with people, all heading in seemingly opposite directions. It was a wonder there was no screaming, no injuries. It deafened and blinded him all at once, and it was all he could do to not get swept away in the current. He found the woman's strong grip around his wrist again, hauling him through the river of people and out onto the quieter side of the promenade, where painfully colourful stalls lined the harbour's squat brown buildings.

Merion took a moment to dust himself down, and to check his pack (and faerie) had not been ripped from his shoulders in the stampede. All was safe, and so he turned to his helper. 'My thanks, madam,' he began, but quickly stopped as he noticed she was walking away. 'Erm. Excuse me? Madam?'

Thankfully she stopped, though she only turned her head. 'What is it, young'un?'

'How do I get to Union Wharf, from here?'

'Go thataway,' she raised a hand to point down the promenade. 'And keep on going 'til you see the sign for it. North, understand?'

'Yes.'

'Then good. Fare well, young'un. You keep your skin on, in the wilds,' she said, waving.

And so Merion was left standing alone, sandwiched between the crowds and the merchants, in a foreign city and on the cusp of a strange land—and chilled to the bone by the woman's parting words.

'See?' He could hear Rhin chuckling. 'The bolts are loose.'

'What on earth did she mean by that?' Merion asked, his voice cracking ever so slightly.

'Not a clue, my friend.'

The young Hark scowled. 'Well then, north it is.'

After a few hundred yards of violent jostling, the promenade began to widen, and the crowd thankfully began to thin. The buildings grew taller too, with every step. On the surface, Boston shared a heart-aching number of similarities with faraway London. There were the proud men in their tails and their top hats. There were the high-society ladies, shrouded in servants and tittering between themselves. There were street performers, beggars, and wiry street children, covered in filth from head to toe. Not to mention the whores of course, whistling at every eligible male that passed. Merion couldn't help but stare. One girl, her shirt invitingly unbuttoned, caught his eye and winked. She waggled a finger at him, but Merion's nerve failed him, and he hurried on.

Sadly, no matter how hard Boston pretended to be London, Merion couldn't help but perceive the city's feral undercurrent. The doorway of America was tinged with something wild. Perhaps it was a glint in the eyes of the men who lingered in dark doorways, guns at their belts and hats pulled low over their faces. Perhaps it was the occasional gibbet hanging here and there, cradling a skeleton in an old uniform.

The edges were simply rougher, the polish not as bright. No matter where he looked, or how hard he pretended, there were no towering arches and white pillars, no slender smoke-stacks or shining examples of industry, no scarlet soldiers on patrol, no copper-gold balloons swimming amongst the clouds. And there wasn't a single roast chestnut barrel anywhere to be seen. Merion's stomach growled in anguish.

'Are we close, do you think?' he asked of Rhin, distracting himself with conversation.

The faerie hummed. 'A little further, I think. What's that next sign say?'

Hanging above the arches of each major wharf were boards painted with curling letters. Merion mouthed each of their names as they passed: *Goldrock Wharf, Long Walk Wharf, Ebenezer Wharf, Lincoln Wharf, Union Wharf* ...

'We're here. Thank Almighty,' he said, slightly relieved.

'And the *Tamarassie* is almost here, look.' Merion felt Rhin move in the rucksack, and he turned to face south, where the battered old tub could be seen worming its way between cargo tugs and fishing skiffs.

Merion breathed an almost contented sigh, and began to look around. The wharf was almost empty, save for a rain-soaked blonde man with freckles adorning his cheeks. He was tightly wrapped up in a suit that was too small, even for him, and holding something in his hands.

'That man has a sign with my name on it,' Merion said.

'Better go see what Mr Sign wants, then.'

'I'd hazard a guess at me,' Merion muttered.

Gloved hands still buried deep in his pockets, he strode over to the young man, his chin tilted at just the right angle. 'Good morning, sir,' he called out.

The man beamed and then bowed not once, but twice, as if he hadn't performed it right the first time around.

'Welcome to America,' he said, striding forwards to thrust out a hand. 'Coltswolde Humbersnide, at your service. It's not every day we have a son of the Empire visit, I can tell you that,' he proclaimed, in a crumbling parody of the Empire's tongue. It was as though somebody had punched his accent in the face. Most of his words had the accent of America, yet every now and again one would slip, and the man squawked a word sounding suspiciously British. Perhaps he was stuck between the two.

Merion bowed in return. 'Tonmerion Harlequin Hark, sir. A pleasure. Though I am quite confused: my father always said there was no love for the Empire in America.'

Humbersnide's cheeks flushed with a smidgeon of red. 'Oh, well. No, I suppose there isn't. In any case, I think it's a *downright*,' and here the accent veritably fell over and died, 'pleasure to have you here, in our fine city.'

Merion luckily remembered his manners. 'Thank you, Mr Humbersnide.'

'Please, call me Coltswolde. I work for the same firm as Mr Witchazel, you see, Boston branch. We have been here eleven years now. Our office was the first in the New Kingdom.'

'Fascinating.'

Coltswolde bowed again. 'Thank you, sir. Now, my instructions were to meet you here and put you on a locomotive going west, with these tickets,' he informed the boy, brandishing a sealed envelope.

'Wonderful,' replied Merion, his voice flat.

'Might I enquire where it is that you're going?'

'Wyoming.'

The young man almost dropped his sign. 'Wyoming?' he echoed.

'Yes, that's right. Why, is there a problem?' Merion demanded.

Humbersnide gulped and then cracked an unsteady smile. 'Not at all. I just hear it is rather hot, this time of year. Nice for a holiday, of course. Better than all that *bloody* rain, eh?' He chuckled weakly, and fell silent with a cough.

'I'm not on holiday,' Merion muttered.

It was an uncomfortable hour that passed them by, spattered with polite and mumbled conversation here and there. All the while, the *Tamarassie* crept forwards until her rust-bucket sides were making the fenders moan. Ropes were thrown, planks laid out, and the slow process of unloading began.

As soon as the first few items of luggage hit the deck, an idea blossomed in Merion's head. 'Mr Humbersnide, I hope it's not too bold of me to ask you such a favour, but it seems I have hurt my arm on the boat ride. Would you mind helping me with the luggage? The sailors should point them out.'

Coltswolde's polite smile wavered at the thought of manual labour. He had seen the size of the trunks being unloaded onto the bustling wharf, and he had just remembered he had forgotten to hire a cart. 'Er ...' he croaked. 'Of course.'

As Coltswolde stumbled off down the wharf, busy praying that Merion had travelled lightly, Rhin patted the boy on the back through the rucksack. 'Nice,' he said.

'I think I deserve a little bit of a break, after nine days at sea,' Merion explained with a sigh.

'Damn right,' Rhin replied.

'Five days!' Merion spluttered. 'Just how big *is* this country, Mr Humbersnide?'

While Merion gawped, Humbersnide read through the schedule and totted up the hours. 'New York, and from there to Philadelphia, then Pitt's Berg, Chicago, Cheyenne, and then finally, the brand new railroad to Fell Falls, the last stop. One thousand, two hundred miles ... divided by ... twenty ... Yes sir. five and a half days, it seems. Plus stops for water and coal, so perhaps six.'

'On a train? *This* train?' Merion's eyes switched again to the locomotive that had just sidled up to the platform. His boyish excitement had returned, inconvenient and inappropriate though it may have been.

The locomotive was heart-thumpingly fascinating, he could not deny it. It was a veritable monster straining at the bit, salivating on the gleaming tracks. Steam leaked from its bared teeth, and it dripped water onto the platform. The flanks of its long boilers bristled with wires and cogs and mechanical arms while thin slits cut like gills glowed in places, betraying the fire stoked in its belly.

This locomotive, like the city it seemed so eager to flee, was also feral. Not like the sleek engines of St Vanquish station at which Merion had spent long hours gazing, with their polished silver plates so clear you could see yourself in them. This engine was a wild beast in comparison. Still, there was a part of him that couldn't wait to feel it gallop.

'No, Master Hark, four trains altogether,' added Coltswolde, shrugging casually. 'This is why they call America the Endless Land. Vast, she is. My my.'

'I'm starting to realise that,' Merion groused.

Coltswolde's face had taken on a distant look. 'Vast and endless, that's true, but this railroad will change all of that. Transcontinental, they're calling it. It will forge a path straight across the desert and onto the shores of the Last Ocean, eventually. The Serped Railroad Company have spent years trying to conquer that desert. What with all the trouble from the Shohari and those rai—' Coltswolde realised what he was saying and clamped his mouth shut.

Merion folded his arms. 'Please, don't stop on my account,' he challenged him, but Coltswolde just coughed loudly and busied himself with the luggage instead, manhandling it awkwardly down the platform. Merion would get no more out of him on the matter.

That old lump had returned to stick in his craw, one more worry to add to the pile. During the cold, rumbling nights he had spent on the ship, he had let his mind wander to dark places, spinning fears out of the shadows: *his father's murderer, going unpunished; Harker Sheer being overrun by looters; his father's businesses, taken; Witchazel stealing his inheritance.* Now he had a new grim thread to tug at: the thought of not returning home at all, of succumbing to the dangerous wilds of America. Fear tickled the skin of his back, and laid a cold hand upon his neck.

'Don't listen to him,' Rhin reassured him, whispering as loudly as he dared from the rucksack. 'So far, we've only met two people on this voyage, and both of them have been stark raving mad.'

Merion wasn't convinced. 'I'm starting to think they're all bloody mad.'

'Look, if this land's as wide and as endless as they say, it's probably just all rumour and wives' tales, warped whispers. Wyoming's probably harmless, just too wild for these city boys.' There was more hope than fact in that last sentence, but Rhin didn't let it show. 'Besides, we want to toughen you up, don't we?'

'Even if Coltswolde is right about Wyoming, it isn't as though I have a choice.'

'Maybe not, but even if he is, America's going to have to get through me first.'

Merion felt the warmth of Rhin's friendship quell the cold for a moment. The young Hark stuck out that stiff upper lip of his. 'Well, they say a gentleman never shrinks from his duty,' he mumbled, just loud enough for Rhin to hear. 'It's too late to run away now.'

'That's the spirit. Anyway, we can always get you a gun when we get to Fell Falls.'

'No guns,' Merion snapped abruptly, then softened. 'No guns.'

'A knife then,' Rhin offered.

'Maybe.'

'It won't be Fae steel, but we'll find you some good old fashioned human steel instead,' mused the faerie.

'One knife against the wilds of the Endless Land. Hardly seems fair.'

Rhin chuckled. It was good to see some mirth in the boy. He had heard him tossing and turning in the night, muttering worrisome things. Tonmerion was hurting, that was obvious enough, but the simple fact that he was putting on a brave face was all that mattered for now. There was hope there. Rhin just had to get him to Fell Falls, to that last stop. It would be different there, Merion would see.

'Come on,' said the faerie. 'Let's get moving.'

'Right you are,' Merion cleared his throat and nodded affirmatively. 'Mr Humbersnide, sir!' he shouted.

Coltswolde came shuffling back along the platform. Merion showed him his best smile. 'Yes, Master Hark?'

'I trust I can leave my luggage in your capable hands?'

Humbersnide's face underwent a series of twitches as he deciphered the boy's meaning. 'Er … of course, young sir, in my capable hands.' He even had to look at his hands to check that yes, they were indeed capable.

'Good! My thanks to you, Mr Humbersnide. Now if you'll excuse me, I have a train to catch,' Merion replied, and before Humbersnide could make any comment, or twitch any further, the boy departed, quickly striding across the wooden boards towards his carriage.

'If only we could take him with us,' said a voice from the rucksack.

'True, though I'm sure we'll manage to find another willing helper. My father always said that if a man wasn't a lord, or above a lord, then he must be a servant.'

Rhin winced. 'I'm not too sure the Americans will take kindly to that logic, especially after all the wars and such.'

Merion shrugged again. 'This Kingdom is indebted to us, Rhin. They may not pay their taxes any more, but we built them. And a son should always do what his father asks of him,' he intoned.

Rhin snorted. 'What, like keeping secret faeries in the garden?'

'You found me, not the other way around, friend.'

No answer came from the rucksack.

When he found his allotted carriage, he paused just outside the door for a moment, his hand hovering above the twisted iron railing that sprouted from the rain-spattered wood of the carriage. From there he could lay his eyes along the tracks. Straight as a spear they were, glinting in the sparse light of day. They carved an almost perfect path through the city, and if he looked hard enough, he could just about make out hills, forests, and green fields beyond. *Endless Land, indeed,* he snorted. Everything had to end at some point.

CHAPTER IV

THE BULLDOG'S BOY

'Leg's gone. Fought a cat in the last house. Claw caught me right above the knee, so I've had to wrap it up tight for the night. I'm starting to wonder whether I'll ever see a tree again. This city is all stone and iron. Cold to the bone.

Sift still searches. She's got the Day Watch on my trail. Coil Guards too. It's got to be further east, where the big houses are, the rich houses.'

5th May, 1867

The city was soaked to the bone. A constant pattering of drips filled the air as the drainpipes, arches, lampposts, and even the bricks wept. The day was filled with fog. Interminably thick, it swirled about the streets without a care for the day, filling nooks and crannies until the air was choked and thick. In just the right places, you could stand and watch your limbs turn ghostly, stolen momentarily by the fog. It was an ethereal day. A day to stoke fires, rub hands, and leave the streets to the jealous weather. It was a fine spring day, by any Empire standards.

It was a Sunday, and a lone black carriage rattled through the streets of central London. Pulled by four enormous horses, the carriage was ornate to say the least. Its wheels and axles were gold-trimmed, and a colourful coat of arms adorned each door. If you looked closely, you would have seen an eagle lifting a tiger into a blood-red sky. And if you'd looked any closer, you might have seen the name *Dizali* written in flowing letters. A powerful name indeed, amongst the Emerald Benches.

It wasn't long before the Palace of Ravens loomed out of the thick fog. The two drivers slowed the horses to a gentle trot and aimed their carriage at a pair of giant black gates. The Palace of Ravens was a marvel of architecture—a terrifying one to the average tourist, but a marvel nonetheless. Four giant spires marked its boundaries, and between them thick walls and towering pillars formed the palace proper. It was a humongous box, to put it plainly—a blotch on the face of London. Yet as its detail crystallised out of the fog, it was easy to see that it was grand beyond belief. Each side was a chaotic tumble of glass, turret, balcony and ironwork. The palace glittered in the murk, and through the glowing orange windows, a passerby could glimpse golden chandeliers and vast dining and dancing halls. Ravens cawed in its sharp reaches, watching any passing subjects like worms writhing in the dust.

As the carriage came face to face with the black gates that guarded the entrance to the palace, soldiers poured from the twin guardhouses and surrounded the coach. They had short swords at the hip, shields, and of course, the golden rifles for which they were famous were slung over their backs.

'Papers, if you please,' ordered an officer, the medals pinned to his tall black hat chiming softly as he bobbed his head.

The blackened window of the carriage cracked open an inch, and a thin slice of paper was poked through the gap. The officer stepped up to the coach to grab it. He peered at the scribbled name.

'Your ring, my lord?'

There was a tap of metal on glass as an eagle and tiger-crested ring tasted the misty air, wrapped around a pudgy finger. The officer nodded and clicked his fingers. The soldiers jogged to the gates and began to push. The window was rolled up once more.

A man was waiting for the carriage at the main entrance, hands folded neatly behind his back and eyes low. He wore no hat, only a long coat that bulged in a way that indicated he was carrying a sword. As soon as the carriage had squeaked to a halt on the marble flagstones, the man stepped forwards and opened the door.

High Lord Bremar Dizali practically jumped from the couch to the cold ground. He seemed flustered. Puzzled, and perhaps a touch nervous.

He was right to be so. *Nobody was summoned by Victorius.* Save for Prime Lord Karrigan Hark, that was. But he was dead as a doornail.

Dizali was a broad and tall man, with a sharp face, and ever sharper goatee, dark, like the combed-back hair on his head. There was something rather eagle-like about him, something deep and clever in those narrowed green eyes.

Lord Dizali didn't spare the man a single glance. Not yet. 'Did she say anything, anything at all?'

'Nothing other than to bring you straight here, Milord, nothing at all,' the man smiled, watching Dizali adjust his wide-brimmed hat and grey gloves. He combed his short beard with his fingers and then tucked the stray strands of hair behind his ear. He caught the man's eyes at last, and then his smile soon after.

'You seem to be relishing this, Gavisham.'

'Why ever not, Milord? It's not every day one gets summoned to the Palace of Ravens.'

'No, it is not.'

And with that, Dizali was off, striding up the steps as if they were those of his own home. He would not have admitted it to Gavisham, but he had been waiting for this, waiting for two long weeks. He only prayed he was right.

Floor after floor went by, until he was at the very top of the north wing. Gavisham trailed behind him silently, seeming somewhat deadlier than usual tonight. Dizali could hear his slow, deliberate footsteps several paces behind.

As Dizali's foot found the very topmost step, he took a breath. He turned to his man and pointed a finger at the floor. 'You will wait here, you understand?'

Gavisham bowed low. 'As you wish, Milord.'

After straightening his hat once more, Dizali let his legs lead him to the great door at the end of the hall, the one that shone with gold filigree and jewels. It was etched with scenes of the Lost, from a time before Victorious had risen as their Queen, before she had built herself an empire with wild men and their coin, their blood, and their bodies.

But Dizali was not given time to stare at the beasts and battle-scenes. The soldiers clicked their steel heels and put their shoulders to the magnificent door. It swung inwards into a cavernous hall, one that filled the entire north-eastern spire. Dizali had heard rumours of this room, but now they crumbled to dust in his head.

The room could have accommodated four tall ships piled atop one another, keel to mast, and the topmost pennant would still not have tickled the roof. Dizali felt his ageing bones click as he craned his neck to see the paintings high on the distant plaster, but they were all just one glorious blur at that range. He looked left, then right, and judged it would have taken him almost a minute to run from one side of the room to the other, even without that aching knee of his.

It was the great crimson curtain that impressed him the most. The giant thing cut the room precisely in half, creating a velvet wall over a dozen feet high. Two enormous chains ran across the room and held it aloft and perfectly straight. Its velvet fingers barely brushed the marble floor.

Dizali coughed politely and stepped up to the very centre of the curtain, as he had been instructed to by the messenger earlier that morning. He waited, enduring the silence until it physically ached. When he could take it no more, he bowed low to the marble.

'Your Illustrious Majesty.' His voice sounded minuscule in that giant gold cavern.

Something moved behind the curtain, and Dizali could not help but flinch. There was a distinct rustling, as of papers or leaves, and then a deep thud that echoed about the hall. A voice answered him then, a voice that he had not heard in years, a voice that slithered and rumbled at the same time, a voice from another age.

'What of Hark, High Lord Dizali?' the voice asked him. He could hear the rustling again, and it chilled him.

'He lies dead and buried, my Queen. Buried in Harker Sheer, according to his wishes.' Here, Dizali bowed his head, just in case she was somehow watching. Light spilled from under the curtain as something was moved, and a shadow was thrown flat against the marble. Dizali tried to keep his eyes from following it along the floor. 'A great shame,' he added.

'A good and powerful man.'

'Yes your Majesty,' Dizali bowed his head again. He paused for a moment, and then, 'How may I be of service to my Queen?'

More rustling. More thumping. He swore he could hear a clicking noise, like a clock, or an impatient drumming of nails, or tapping of toes.

'His murderer. Has he been found?'

'No, your Majesty.'

'And his boy,' Victorious rumbled.

'I believe his name is Tonmerion, Majesty.'

'I want him brought to me.'

Dizali bit the inside of his lip, and bit hard. He forced a sad frown, just in case. 'I am afraid, Majesty, that I cannot do that.' There was an angry gurgling from the other side of the curtain, so Dizali just kept on talking. 'It seems that Prime Lord Hark's last will and testament was very specific indeed. He had a relative, it seemed, in the Kingdom of America, and his wishes were for the boy to be sent to live with her.' *Until the age of eighteen, when he may inherit,* or so the lawyer had said. It was amazing what facts can be learnt in the dark corners of taverns.

'Where?'

Dizali made a show of scratching his head. 'I am not sure of the details,' he said, when in fact he knew them back to front, 'but it seems that the young Hark has been sent to the frontier.'

'And what of his estate in the meantime, Dizali?' The way Victorious hissed his name, dragging its vowels out with her serpentine tongue, made him shiver. What made him shiver even more was the thread she was teasing out, the very same thread that he had been trying to wrap around his finger for the last fortnight.

'Sealed by law, your Majesty. Untouchable.'

Victorious took a moment to shuffle around.

'You say that, Dizali,' she said, 'as if you had it in mind to touch it.'

The lord held up a finger. 'Your Majesty, if I may. There was one item of business I was hoping to discuss with you, if I may. It is regarding the Benches, my Queen.'

There was a pause, during which Dizali wondered whether she had turned to stone, or turned into ash, or vanished, or any number of things his queen was rumoured to be capable of. So when she spoke, it almost made him jump out of his suit.

'Speak.'

Dizali took a quick breath to steady himself, and launched into the speech he had been practising in the carriage. 'The lords are talking, my Queen, about Prime Lord Hark. They speak not just of his death, and its suspicious nature, but of his seat and of his own empire. It seems that several members of the opposition feel that now is the time to seize power. Now, as the Second Lord of the Benches, the party falls into my hands. We are united, Majesty, but the opposition talks, and far too loudly for their words to be considered mere disgruntlement. They have become unsteady in the wake of the Bulldog's death. Bold. I believe that there must be direction, and soon, before the opposition begins to get ideas.'

'What ideas are these?'

He took another breath, quick and sharp. 'Ideas such as splitting his estate between the lords, my Queen, or calling for an election, in the middle of Hark's term.'

'Havoc.'

Dizali tried to hide a smile. 'Havoc, my Queen?'

'I do not take kindly to repeating myself in my own chambers, Lord Dizali,' thundered Victorious. 'If Lord Hark is dead, then another must replace him. An election will cause havoc so deep into his term. An Empire with so many wars to fight does not need such distraction at its heart. Yet there is no precedent.'

Politics was a game Dizali had learnt to play very well indeed. 'The party is as much elected as its Prime Lord. There are some who say the power should pass down the party line, to keep the peace.'

More shuffling ensued. Something loomed close against the curtain. Dizali heard the queen breathing. 'And what do you say, High Lord?'

The hidden smile was allowed to flourish, ever so slightly. 'I say, as Second Lord, that such a solution is in the best interests of the party. And as there is no precedent, the royal word is law in this instance.'

'As it has been since the first dawn,' rumbled the queen.

'If I may make bolder, my Queen, such royal words might also deal with the Bulldog's vast estate. I take it your Majesty would prefer to keep it out of the reach of prying hands. Hands that are not as loyal as others,' Dizali said.

Victorious paused to breathe and rattle some more. 'The opposition needs no further fuel for ambition or argument. The Bulldog's boy is to be brought under our wing. I shall leave it in your capable hands.'

Dizali bowed as low as his spine would allow. 'My eternal praise, Queen Victorious.'

A part of the shadow moved then, and though Dizali knew not what part it was, or if it even had a name, he got its meaning. He made a hasty, yet respectful retreat, and hurried back to meet Gavisham at the summit of the stairs. His smile had slipped the moment he had stepped through the doors. Now a firm, tight line had replaced it, accompanied by a hard glint in the man's eye.

'How'd it go, Milord?'

'Well,' hissed Dizali, as he clattered down the steps, Gavisham in tow.

'What's the plan, then?'

Dizali stabbed at the air as he reeled off each command. 'It's time to set the wheels in motion. Prepare the papers. I want the Hark boy, Tonmerion, watched like a hawk. I want reports too, every week. If he sneezes, I want to know of it. Send a wiregram to our good friend and ally. He will know what to do. Understand?'

'Clear as a bell.'

'Then get to it,' Dizali growled. 'I have work of my own to do.'

CHAPTER V

LILAIN

'These creatures are strange. I've never come so close before, not to these ones, with their castles and their slaves and their money. They exude it, flaunt it. The ladies are draped in it. The lords drink it down by the glass, or roll it up and smoke it. It's as if their status depends on how fast they can spend their money.
If I weren't running for my life I would stick around a while longer, and teach them a lesson in frugality.'

6th May, 1867

Steel and iron, that was all that could be heard. Not the chuffing of the colossal engine, not the grating crunch of black shovels on coal, not even the chuckling, or the whispering, or the heated debates of the other passengers. Just iron. Just steel. They battled one another continuously— each creak and bang and thud trying to outdo the next. The clear winner were the wheels, of course, and the sturdy tracks they rolled against continuously.

Merion felt every rivet, every scratch, every little crunch and squeak. It was an incessant clattering that had been hammered into the very bones of his body. He prayed for water and coal stops. He prayed for towns and stray cows. Hell, he even prayed for women tied to the tracks, as he had seen in penny dreadfuls. Anything to quieten the wheels for just a moment, and let him hear the wind, or the trees, or the piercing whistle of the engine, to know there was something else beyond the cacophony.

Days had become knitted together and formed a week. Merion had spent the sunlight hours with his face pressed up against the window, watching every mile roll past. He took in every inch of his new home. No matter how sure he was that he had seen every sight the Kingdom of America had to offer, there was always something new, something different. He felt as though he had seen several kingdoms, not just the one.

In New York, he had seen towering spires the like of which even London could not boast, overlooking a bay of mud and old warships. In Pittsburgh, he had seen wild forests, darker than the woods of home. So dark they appeared, he couldn't fathom how far they must have stretched. In Chicago, he had heard an ocean called a lake, and seen a city so sprawling and stubborn, he wondered whether it would ever end. On the way to Cheyenne, he had rumbled across prairies and grasslands, fenced only by the distant shadows of rolling mountains and the first fingers of desert. Yet still, he hadn't seen it all.

At first, Wyoming didn't seem all that bad. Chugging through the dawn-lit hills outside Cheyenne, Merion had been pleasantly surprised by the amount of green. Sure, there were no forests or trees, nor very many rivers, for that matter, but there were shrubs on the ground, and that's all that mattered. He had heard no more talk of danger or of keeping his skin on above the thundering of the wheels. He even went as far as to enjoy the hot morning sun coming through the dusty window, far hotter than anything he had ever experienced at home. His skin prickled under its rays.

It was then it all started to change—the moment he reached Cheyenne.

It was a small city, compared to Chicago and New York. In fact, it was actually more of a town. But Merion kept that to himself, in case he accidentally offended anyone. He alone stayed on the platform as the locomotive was pulled away to make room for the next. For a while, he wondered if he would have the carriage to himself, but as he stood there sweating in the hot sun, his fellow passengers began to arrive, one by one.

The first didn't give Merion any real cause for concern. Neither did the second. However, by the third, Merion was starting to notice a pattern, and it was a pattern that began to make him rather nervous indeed.

No women. He noticed that first. The passengers lining up alongside him were all men. And, to Merion's delight, they were the sort of men that looked very fond of dark doorways and sharp implements. That much was evident from the things attached or hanging from their bullet-studded belts. Guns and knives and other such tools built for bodily harm.

Their hats were dark and low, and their clothes dusty and ragged. Some wore dungarees, others riding gear. All of them wore heavy, thudding boots. It made Merion cast a self-conscious eye over his own choice of footwear. Comfortable leather shoes with their laces tied in almost-perfect bows. They even had a velvet lining. Merion wiggled his feet to remind himself.

I am either going to be the height of fashion, or the court jester, Merion told himself. Only time would tell which.

Merion kept his eyes low and his mouth shut. Instead he bathed in the rough grumblings of the men around him. He could not hear much, but what he heard both confused and swiftly demolished that slight shred of hope he and Rhin had savoured before Cheyenne. In truth, their words terrified him.

'Sullyvan's got all the men sleeping together at night ...'

'Well, what in Maker's name is that gonna do, huh?'

'Just makes us a bigger target, is all.'

'Makes us a buffet.'

'Digger's right. Ain't nothing to be done, 'cept build us somethin' solid. Quarters. Barracks. Anything.'

'Pah! Only guards get quarters. They're the ones watching over our hides all the live-long day.'

'And we're the ones bending our backs all day, putting iron in the ground.'

'Heard Yule got bit last week?'

'*Bit?* Man got ripped in half!'

'Down the middle.'

'Wife only knew him 'cause of a mole he had on his right cheek.'

And so their hushed conversations went. Some of them must have noticed him, after a spell, but it did not make them speak any quieter.

'No good pretendin' it ain't happened,' as one of the workers so eloquently put it.

Truth hurts, and the frontier was full of it. *Welcome to the wild west,* he thought. *Last stop before Hell.*

The locomotive that came to fetch them was considerably less impressive than the one he had first seen in Boston, and the other two that had come after it.

If those three had been princes, here was the pauper.

Merion scowled as it pulled into the station, belching oily steam. This locomotive was smaller, for one thing, and covered by at least an inch of dust. There were six carriages, but only two were for passengers. These carriages had large portholes instead of windows, no doubt pilfered from some downed air balloon. In fact, the whole train looked stolen, borrowed, or otherwise improvised.

The men on the platform didn't seem to mind. They stepped right up to the lip of the platform and waited for the doors to stop in front of them. Some even made quick bets as to where the doors were going to stop, and who would be closer. Gold and copper glinted in the sunlight.

Merion was the last to board. He shuffled on in the wake of the workers, guards, and other riffraff, his legs like molten lead. His luggage was thankfully being loaded for him, alongside barrels and boxes of tools and supplies, headed for Fell Falls.

'Maybe we should get you a gun after all,' whispered Rhin.

Merion did not dignify that with a response. The men would have heard him, in any case.

He found a seat near the door and put the rucksack on his lap. He could feel Rhin moving around so that he could peer out at the carriage interior. The men sprawled about, as though they had already done their day's worth of hard work.

As soon as all the luggage and supplies had been transferred from the other train by the station workers, the locomotive released its breaks, and the whole carriage shuddered.

The men chatted idly, this time of women, gambling, and stories of the war. Rumour had it some were still fighting in the misty swamps of the deep south. Renegades, Merion heard them called. One man said they were all doomed, once the steam warships of Washington got there, with Red King Lincoln standing on the bow of the *Black Rosa*.

'With his trusty axe,' another added, and the men thumped the seats patriotically until dust filled the carriage.

Soon the talk turned to the wild Shohari, and Merion couldn't help but lend an ear. He closed his eyes, pretending to be asleep, and let his body rock with the rickety train.

'Shohari are gettin' braver.'

'Coming further south every summer.'

'I heard they already overrun some of the northern towns. Landsing was razed to the ground not this winter gone. Heard they took some of the women too. Men've gone looking now the snows have thawed. Damn shame, ain't that right.'

More thumping of seats.

'I heard they own the nor-western mountains to rights. Ain't nobody that'll venture into them woods.'

'Nor the canyons neither.'

'Lord Serped will 'ave somethin' to say if they come near Fell Falls. With his lordsguards and gatlings.'

Merion's ears pricked up at the sound of the word 'lord'. *What was a lord doing all the way out here?*

'What're you talking about 'bout, Hummage? You know they been seen already. On the ridges.'

'Shit. Scouts is all.'

'Ain't just scouts from what I hear. Got war parties roaming as far south as Shamrok Hills.'

'Can't the patrols from Kaspar pick 'em off?'

'They are, sure as hell. But they're too many.'

A deep voice echoed in the far corner of the carriage, one Merion hadn't heard yet. 'I heard they brought their shamans too,' it said, and there was a silence. 'You ever seen a shaman in real life? Any of you?'

More silence. 'Those Shohari are somethin' else. They got proper magic running through their veins, mark my words. I heard men say they can peel the flesh right off your bones at a hundred paces. Turn the steel of your rifle hot as hell, 'til it burns your hands or explodes. Take your soul, too, if they lay hands on you. A little chanting, a little blood, and you're theirs.

Merion's own voice surprised him, so much so he could not help but squeak halfway through his last sentence, so that it came out as more of a question than a fact. 'My father said that magic is only what science can't yet explain. That it's all a trick.' He heard Rhin muttering something derogatory in the pack, and immediately wished he had kept his mouth shut. Perhaps it was his nerves, or the need to be noticed that had made him squawk. He did not even agree with his father. He had a faerie for a best friend, after all.

The laughter started slowly at first. A few chuckles here and there to get the ball rolling. One man started wheezing, and slowly but surely the carriage erupted into uproar. Merion looked at the floor and wished he would melt. He wished he had Rhin's powers.

As the laughter finally died away, one of the nearest men slapped his hand on his thigh. 'Shit, son, your father's got some balls. All a trick, hah!'

Merion was not sure what the ownership of a pair of testicles had to do with the matter, but he nodded anyway.

'Just wait until he meets his first railwraith!' somebody else cackled.

'Or sandstrike!'

And the laughter began afresh.

In the pack, Rhin winced as the men yelled out each individual peril of the wilds. He swore he could feel Merion trembling with fear through the cloth walls of his little sanctuary. The faerie racked his brains for something useful to say, but he couldn't think of a single word. He only had words for himself.

'Poor lad,' he mumbled.

One by one, the green shrubs that had brightened Merion's morning died away until there was barely anything but rock, sand, and brown scrub. Merion sighed. Even the terrain wanted him to feel unwelcome.

As the train reverberated around him and made his teeth jiggle, Merion's mind once again turned to its dark corners. He wondered what he had done to his father to deserve this. He wondered whether he should start cursing his name, whether it would make any difference.

Merion had left London in a muggy cloud of confusion and disbelief, almost as if he were still dreaming. But with every mile west he'd crawled, that disbelief had melted away and left something very solid in its place. His father had been murdered, and he had been banished to live with his aunt, the undertaker. His whole life hung in suspended animation, ripe for greedy claws to pick at. That disbelief had become a very chilling reality.

The young Hark may have been trembling, but he had no tears to shed. Along with the fear there came a burning, indignant anger. And as we all know, anger must have an escape route, otherwise it boils up into something a little more dangerous. So it was that Merion's anger gave him an idea, a purpose to shield him from this awful new reality of his. He swirled it around inside his head, and let it keep him warm.

As they steered a course north and west, the scenery swapped between the unbearably flat and the worryingly steep and craggy. Merion had one thing to say for the cobbled-together locomotive: it was as strong as the sea. During the ten hours between Cheyenne and Fell Falls, it never broke pace once, not even on the hills. It was an unstoppable force that dragged him ever-onwards.

The sun was just setting when they crested a hill only a handful of miles from Fell Falls. For a moment, Merion couldn't bring himself to look, before he remembered some more of his father's cold words: *We must always stare our opponents square in the face, whether in the street, the ring, or amongst the Benches.*

'So be it,' Merion spat, and turned, daring Fell Falls to inch closer. And so it did.

Close up, the town looked like a monster, sprawling and leaking charcoal smoke from its pores. Its veins were dusty streets scarred with the pockmarks of hooves and wheel-ruts. Its tentacles were wandering, misshapen buildings and ambling paths. Its skin was made of wooden slats, jagged and tortured like every true monster's skin, and like every true monster, it was being harried and attacked.

The freshly beaten railroad from the east pierced the monster's side like a silver spear and ran it clean through. Roads snaked in from the north and south, looking for all the world like ropes lassoing the creature's wooden limbs. As the light faded and the shadows grew long, Merion could almost imagine the town thrashing and flailing as sunset made the sky ripple. With every twist of the track they came closer. The locomotive aimed its nose right for the heart of the town and chugged towards it. The men in his carriage had grown silent. Merion just pressed his face harder against the glass.

The black skeleton of a church lay on Fell Falls' eastern outskirts, as though it had somehow escaped the tentacled clutches of the sprawling monster yet had paid the price with fire and flame. In the scorched soil of its graveyard, stood a congregation of sun-bleached crosses, creaking in the desert breeze. Some were dressed in dusty hats with holes, others adorned with pickaxes and tools, still others with garlands of wild flowers, either fresh or dried and crumbling. Some crosses bore no gifts at all. Merion tried to count them as they rumbled past.

On the locomotive's other side, to what Merion assumed was the north, a great barn stood alone in the desert. Flags flapped from several poles on its roof, each bearing colours and shapes, but at that distance Merion couldn't make out their specifics. To his squinting eyes, it almost looked like a coat of arms of some sort.

No matter where Merion looked, how far he craned his neck, or how much he squinted, he could not spot a single drop of water. Unless they were to be found in the surrounding low hills, it seemed that Fell Falls actually had no falls at all; the name was a lame joke at the town's expense.

As the locomotive pulled into the station (if a jumble of wooden decking, a glorified shed, and a small outhouse can be considered a station), the sun was just about to set. The vast sky had turned a deep, furnace-orange, and it made Fell Falls glow.

There was barely a brick building in sight. The whole of the town seemed to be constructed of a grim grey wood. Thankfully, its citizens had gone to some effort with their paintbrushes, and there were plenty of colours on the insides of the monster. There were plenty of citizens too. The dusty streets were abuzz with men and women. Workers, guards, farmers, shop girls, stableboys, the lot. Merion watched them as they wandered to and fro, some drinking, others laughing. Some even sang. He wondered how there could be so much merriment in a place as dangerous as this. *Why weren't these people in their homes, behind locked doors?* He wondered.

What Merion did not know, and would soon find out, is that it took a special type of person to exist out here, on the edge of the world: the sort of person that knows, as we all do, that copious amounts of alcohol and laughter are brilliant methods of keeping the heavy weight of mortality and an occasional disembowelling off your back.

Once the train had come lurching to a halt, the men filed off one by one, rubbing their hands at the thought of whiskey and women. So eager were they, in fact, that Merion was soon left alone. He had a grim look on his face.

Rhin's head poked out from beneath the flap of the rucksack. 'Are you ready?' he asked slowly, as if it were a dangerous question to be asking.

'I am. But trust me, Rhin, we won't be here long,' growled the boy.

Rhin narrowed his eyes. 'What are you on about?'

Merion shook his head. 'I'll tell you later.'

'Right you are, but don't do anything stupid in the meantime, like running into the desert. I don't feel too good about deserts.'

'Stop worrying,' Merion replied, and with that he got to his feet, and forced himself out onto the platform.

Merion was carrying Rhin and the rucksack in his arms now, rather than on his shoulders. After checking that his luggage was being unloaded, he wandered down a short set of steps and onto the dusty earth of the town.

Both boy and faerie peered around. The light was fading fast and not all the street-lamps had been lit. Aside from the station workers, the platform was empty. All the passengers had disappeared, already barging their way into the first tavern they could find.

'Your aunt should be meeting us, am I right?' Rhin asked.

'Yes. Aunt Lilain.'

'*Aunt Lilain*. Sounds so plain next to "Karrigan".'

Merion had to admit the faerie was right. 'Well, she's a Hark nonetheless.'

Rhin sighed. 'Hark or not, it looks like she didn't get the wiregram about picking you up.'

Merion stared back at the sign hanging above the platform. 'Fell Falls', it said, in bright blue lettering. Merion found a nearby barrel and perched on top of it. 'Nice place,' he muttered.

Rhin shuffled out of the pack so he could see Merion's face. The boy's face was expressionless now, deadpan. 'Could be worse, from what the men were saying.'

All Merion had to do was look left, to the west, where a few rugged hills stood stark against the red of the dying sun. 'This is the frontier, Rhin. All of those things that the men talked about, they're just out there. Barely a stone's throw away.'

Rhin unsheathed his knife and waved it around, slicing at the air. 'Well, they can come try their luck. They're not the only ones that are magic,' he hissed to the darkness. Nothing replied. Nothing moved and, secretly, they were both very glad.

'See?' Rhin sheathed his knife.

A moment passed, and Merion huffed sharply. 'Where on earth is that aunt of mine?'

Rhin looked about. He pointed towards the milling crowds of the town. 'I don't suppose it could be that crazy woman sprinting towards us, could it?'

'I think I've had my fill of crazy,' Merion sighed as he turned.

There was indeed a woman coming towards them, and she was indeed sprinting. If you have ever had a stranger run as fast as they can towards you, with little or no explanation, then you will know how nervous Merion suddenly felt. Rhin even went as far as to unsheathe his knife again, poised inside the rucksack.

'Thank the Maker!' cried the woman, as she skidded to a halt barely a foot from Merion. He coughed as her dust cloud enveloped his face.

The woman patted him on the shoulder and smiled broadly. His aunt was all wire and tanned skin, quite obviously as strong as a mule, and not nearly so old as Merion had expected. In fact, there was barely a wrinkle on her face, just a smattering of well-used laughter and frown lines. Her hair, the trademark Hark blonde, was scraped and tied back into a long ponytail that ended somewhere above her hips. She had a brown mole beneath her left eye, almost like a lost teardrop.

It was her clothing that gave Merion the most cause for concern. Instead of the graceful frocks and dresses in which he was used to seeing women, his aunt dressed somewhat like a man. She wore dark jeans held up by a thick buckled belt, and a checked shirt rolled up to the elbows—very informal indeed.

'Sorry about that. I thought I'd missed you! Don't want you wandering off on your first day here. Somebody could have shot you!' she looked about furtively, as if checking for snipers.

The look on Merion's face told her that he did not get the joke, if it could even be called one. She patted him on the shoulder again and smiled even wider. Merion was just grateful she still had all her teeth.

'I'm joking, nephew. One good thing about Fell Falls is that we're too busy shooting other things to be shooting ourselves. In a way, it's the friendliest place on earth,' Lilain said.

Merion looked around and decided that his aunt was a liar. In the street ahead, tucked into an alleyway, he could see a man urinating on his own boots. 'Doesn't look too friendly to me,' he muttered.

'You'll see,' Lilain winked. The gesture reminded him of the old woman on the barge, and he wondered if his aunt was just as crazy as she had been. 'Now, where are my manners?' she asked herself, and all of a sudden she was transformed into a different person. She stood straighter, taller, and her hands came to rest gently in front of her. She clasped her fingers and curtseyed, looking for all the world as though she had just entered the dining hall of Humming Tower. 'My nephew,' she said. 'It is a pleasure to see you again.'

Merion was desperately thankful for the touch of refinement. Perhaps his aunt had been joking all along. 'Tonmerion Harlequin Hark of Harker Sheer, at your service,' Merion replied, bowing low. *Always lower for family, no matter how distant.*

His aunt curtseyed again, and introduced herself. 'Lady Lilain Hark of Fell Falls, formerly Lilain Rennevie, socialite, citizen, crack-shot, and town undertak– Oh, hah! I can't do it! Can't stand all that pomp and ceremony, dearie me. Left all that behind long ago. Still got it though, eh?' she snorted, her veneer crumbling to ash in front of Merion's eyes. As she chuckled away, he began to boil.

'Anyway, Tonmerion, that reminds me. Before we get you settled in and talk about anything else, I need your help. I've got a body that came in just this afternoon. The workers have already gone to the saloons, so it's just me. And dear me if he isn't a big fella. You look like a strong young lad—fancy giving your aunt a hand?' Lilain asked, cheerful as could be, as though she had just asked him to help pick strawberries.

Merion's voice was flat, but nowhere near calm. 'You want *me* to help *you* move a dead body.' It wasn't even a question, the way he said it. 'A *dead* body.'

'Yes, just over to the Runnels, back to the north.' Lilain jabbed a thumb in the air and smiled again. 'Fancy it?'

Before he could answer she had already turned and begun to walk away. 'It's this way,' she chimed, in that eroded Brit accent of hers.

It was then that Merion chose to explode, with no warning or apology.

'Now, just wait one … bloody … SECOND!' He had not really meant to yell, but he had, and now it was too late to take it back. He dumped his rucksack in the dust and squared up to his aunt. He brandished a finger as if he meant to poke her with it, but he could not quite summon the tenacity. Instead he just vented, as he had wanted to since getting on that blasted locomotive in Boston.

'In case Mr Witchazel has proven thoroughly incompetent, and you are not aware of what I have been through, the last three weeks of my life have been utter torture. My father—*your* brother—has been murdered. My home has been taken away from me. My life has been torn apart at the seams. I spent two weeks in a tiny cabin on a ship more rust than metal. I have thrown up more times than I can bear to count, and several of those times through my nose, which until then I hadn't even thought possible. I have seen icebergs decorated with dead soldiers. I was battered senseless by the crowds of Boston and nearly bored to death by a lawyer's assistant. And to top it all off, I have just spent the last week on a variety of trains travelling across this godforsaken country of yours, only to be made aware that my final destination, my last hope for refuge, is a meagre scratch in the middle of a desert, surrounded by creatures that want to tear me in half, and shamans who want to peel the skin off my bones at a hundred yards. So in summary, Aunt Lilain, please *do* excuse me if I don't currently have the stomach for carrying dead bodies around in the dark! I would have thought my own aunt, my father's sister, would be a little more sympathetic to my plight! I half-expected this nightmare to end in Fell Falls, not begin anew!'

Merion suddenly realised he had not taken a breath in quite a while. He decided to remedy that before he passed out. His head swam. Aunt Lilain had crossed her arms about halfway through his tirade, and now she just stood there, staring, a nothing expression on her tanned face. Merion decided to throw caution to the wind and just carry on. 'Now, if you will point me in the right direction, I would like to find whatever bed you've prepared for me, and go to sleep in it. I will be leaving in the morning.'

Lilain answered so quickly she nearly snipped off the end of his sentence. 'Is that so?' she retorted.

'Yes, it is.'

The two stared at each other for a moment, until Merion realised that his aunt was the sort of person who needed to be asked twice. 'If you could show me which way to go, please, it would be very much appreciated.'

Lilain's only reply was to brush past him and reach for his abandoned rucksack, which was leaning against the side of the barrel. Merion chased after her, but she had a head start. The sack was on her shoulder by the time he could interfere.

'That's my rucksack …' he said as he reached out to grab it.

'Oh, no problem. You've had a hard couple of weeks. I've got it,' she replied, striding towards the centre of town. Merion had no choice but to hurry along in the wake of her long, loping strides. Rhin winked from under the lip of the rucksack. Merion could see his purple eyes glowing softly.

'Are you taking me to the body, or your house?' Merion enquired, hoping it was the latter.

'The house,' his aunt replied. He sighed in relief. 'Via the body.'

'Did you not hear what …'

This time, Lilain did cut him off. 'Oh, I heard just fine, thank you. It's a left here.' Lilain swung into a short alleyway, and then out along a hip-high fence that guarded patches of vegetables. A goat bleated somewhere in the shadows.

'Do you live out on the edges of town?'

'Last house in the Runnels. It's where they always put people like me.'

'People like you?'

'Undertakers. They like our business, but don't want to see it on their doorstep ... especially not in a town like this.'

Merion wasn't quite sure he got her meaning, but he mumbled an 'I see' all the same. She was leading him up a very gentle rise now. The houses, or shacks in some cases, were thinning out. The road became less defined and more rugged. Soon enough, they came to a long cart, its handles propped up on the arm of a fence so it lay almost flat. On it lay a macabre object covered by a sack. Merion gulped.

'Come on out, Eugin. Boy's not interested in games,' Lilain called to the darkness.

Merion's heart stopped for a brief moment as the sack moved. A pair of arms groped for air. Lilain grabbed the corner of the sacking and yanked it free, revealing a portly man with a pair of spectacles hanging on his grime-smeared nose. He looked at the boy, then at Lilain.

'What? Why?'

'Tired.'

'Oh. Well, Boston is almost two thousand miles away, as the crow flies. Boy has come a long way.'

'At least somebody realises that,' Merion said. He had not really meant to say that out loud. *Why did that keep happening?*

'Don't encourage him, Eugin. Go home. I want to see you working on that cooler bright and early. No slacking, you hear?'

'Yes, ma'am.' Eugin sloped off, waving a hand at Merion as he scuttled away.

Lilain snapped her fingers and shouted over her shoulder, 'Oh, and Eugin?'

'Yes, ma'am?'

'Is the body on the table?'

'Both halves, ma'am,' came the reply.

Merion's stomach churned. He looked around him, peering into the darkness, as if he were trying to root out this offensive table. In truth, he was considering whether he could make a break for it, as if running might solve all his problems, but this desert all looked the same: dark, empty, and dangerous. Lilain called to him, and he froze.

'You coming or not?'

Merion bit the inside of his lip again, nursing the perpetual scab that had formed there thanks to his new habit. 'Do I have to sleep near the body?'

'Well that depends on where you're sleepin', doesn't it?'

Lilain's house was slightly larger than the other houses, and a little more ornate. It definitely was not a shack, as Merion had feared. It looked like there might have been some money under its pillows and floorboards once, but no longer. It appeared young and yet old. Even in the dark, Merion could see the flaking paint, the little crack in the window to the left of the door, the missing roof-tiles. Lilain thrust her key into a lock, and waved. She still had the bag over her shoulders. 'Come on, do you want to see your options?'

Merion shrugged then. It was a tiny movement, but it spoke volumes. It was a shrug for the world and everything in it, for fate and destiny too, for all the blasted things that had brought him here, and for his father's murderer. It told them that tonight, they had won, but tomorrow might be different. *One night couldn't hurt*, he told himself, as he stepped over the threshold into his new, if not temporary, life.

CHAPTER VI

SEVENTY-FIVE THOUSAND

'She's persistent. Two weeks now, and I'm still running, still being chased. She'll have my head on a spike if it's the last thing she does. There's no going back now. Onwards.'

7th May, 1867

In the bustling core of London, to the west of its beating heart, was Jekyll Park. It was a sprawling carpet of green fields and huddled trees, stretching from the backside of Bucking Tower, all the way up to Kensing Town Gardens. In fact, Jekyll Park was so vast, that if you stood at its very centre, just to the west of the Long Water, and ignored the towering spires of Knightsbridge and Westminster—and the cloying smog—you wouldn't have a clue you were standing in the middle of the largest city on earth.

In the park's southwest corner, in the very centre of a square field of grass, sat a copse of old oak and elm. The trees were so tightly packed together that it was nigh on impossible to see the old well at its centre. A hundred years ago, a boy had drowned in it. He was one of the gardener's lads, and a sad funeral it was. The father almost tore the well to pieces, but the other gardeners had calmed him down, and planted a ring of saplings around it to keep other children from meeting a similar end.

Within seven years the wood had swallowed up the well and the darkness between the trees had become thick and impenetrable. A rumour spread that the copse was cursed. This reputation stuck. Even a century later, it still had the power to rattle teeth. Nobody ever went near the copse nowadays; not even waifs or strays slept nearby. This was a wise decision to make.

✭

Dawn was starting to claw its way across the bruised sky. Jekyll Park was empty. The air was dead and silent, and not a single breath of air stirred the trees. And yet, at the foot of one infamous copse, the grass was shivering, writhing to and fro as quick feet sought a bit of rest.

It had been a long walk—a very long walk, in fact. From the misty Bodmin moors into London is not a jolly in the country by any stretch of the imagination. These faerie feet were worn sore and blistered. They were tired of flitting about and using their magic. It was time for a fire and some nectar, by their master's reckoning.

One by one the faeries reached the base of the old well, and one by one they materialised out of thin air, hooded and hollow-eyed. Thirteen altogether. The tallest one waved a hand in an upwards motion and without a word they began to ascend the crumbling face of the old well. The faeries didn't make a sound as they grabbed the old granite. Their wings didn't even twitch beneath their cloaks.

The rope was there, as they'd been promised, hanging from an arch of wood and pointing down into a deep chasm. It was completely out of faerie reach. The tall fellow, their leader it seemed, looked about for a bucket, platform or lever, but there was nothing. So, he shrugged and leapt into mid-air to catch the fine, silver rope.

'Onwards,' he hissed, and his crew followed suit.

Soon enough they were all sliding down the rope using only their bare hands. Had they paused to sniff, it might have smelled like burning rubber. For what seemed like an age they descended, hand over hand and with ankles pressed against the rope. The darkness was soft at first. The rope could still be seen as well as felt. The little coin of morning light still hovered above them. But then the darkness became absolute, and all-consuming. It lasted so long they began to wonder whether they had been cursed with blindness, but then the first outpost appeared.

Built straight into the walls of the well-shaft, the outpost glowed a greenish-blue thanks to its myriad glow-worm lanterns. It was a fuzzy sort of light, the kind that looked like you could stroke it if you tried hard enough. Dark eyes and grim faces peered out at them from between arrow slits.

As soon as the first outpost had faded into the darkness, the second appeared, chased by the third. Soon enough, garrisons and guard houses encircled the whole circumference of the well shaft, so that the faeries descended through hoops and rings of glowing blue.

And then they saw it: the fortress of Shanarh, capital of Undering, last Fae stronghold of London. It glittered like a thousand burning sapphires on a thick dark carpet of stone and black faerie steel. The silver rope held them high over its sharp ramparts and pointed turrets. A lesser creature might have wailed and come to a scrabbling halt on the rope, but not these. As they descended, the faeries silently and calmly noted their destination: a wide courtyard set deep into the twisting spire that was the Coil of Cela'h Dor, home of the Fae Queen.

It was only when the thirteenth pair of feet graced the brown marble that the doors at the far end of the courtyard were flung open. Three shadows emerged from the bright blue light of the spire's innards, becoming faeries as they marched into the half-dark of the courtyard. The upper world, now drenched in morning, was nothing but a speck in the darkness. Undering's Lonely Star, for that is what the people of Shanarh had come to call it.

The lead man was shouting before he was even halfway to reaching them. 'At long last! The White Wit and his Black Fingers finally decide to answer our call. It has been two weeks since—'

Finrig Everwit, infamously dubbed the White Wit, leader of his crew, the Black Fingers, stood even taller than normal, and beneath his cloak his wings buzzed angrily. His hair was white as snow, and long, so that it curled out from underneath his hood and hung against his neck. Finrig cut the faerie's sentence off coldly. 'Listen here, Magistrate. Two hundred and thirty-eight miles it is, to this hole in the ground from Bodmin country. Two days it's taken us. Two days for your messenger to get to us. Four days for us to prepare. That's eight days by my count, Magistrate, just over one whole week, nothing like two weeks. Hear that!' he said, in a deep voice for a faerie. Rumours had it this Finrig

Everwit had a smidgeon of dwarf running through his veins, from long ago.

The magistrate stopped so close to Finrig that their noses almost touched. He waved a sharp-clawed finger in his ear. 'Hear this: Sift is livid. She is beside herself with rage, I will have you know. The job wasn't done right, Finrig.'

'Come again?'

'The job wasn't done right, I said!' The magistrate was brave for a short faerie. He stood over a whole head shorter than Finrig. From his height, Finrig could stare right down at the magistrate's bald little head, and imagine cracking it against the side of a hot pan to make an omelette. These cave-dwellers were paler than a sheet of parchment, that was for sure—almost as pale as he was.

Finrig folded his arms, conveniently nudging the magistrate back a step. The shorter faerie responded by ruffling his long black coat and adjusting his collar authoritatively. He glanced at each of his guards, and they took a step forwards, standing at the magistrate's shoulders. It only made him look smaller.

Finrig was not one for shouting. 'Calm down,' he said, 'before I lose my temper. What exactly are you accusing us of?'

The magistrate shook his fists. 'He's gone, Finrig. Gone, I tell you. He did not return with the … *item* as you yourself assured us he would. We wanted him marched back here, not given an option! Now he's gone, and the item with him.'

'By the bloody Roots! Gone where?'

'Over the bloody sea is where! America.'

'His boy took him?'

'Of course! His father? Murdered. Human problems by the looks of it. The boy was sent to the Endless Land, or so our spies tell us.'

'So you know where he is?'

'Yes.'

'And you have spies?'

'Yes, of course, but …!'

Finrig slowly bent forwards until his eyes were perfectly level with the magistrate's. He couldn't help but relish the way the other faerie recoiled. 'Then why the fuck have you summoned us? Surely you have other Fae that are capable. We were right in the middle of another job.'

Brainse Fhionnglaise   Finglas Library
T: (01) 834 4906 E: finglaslibrary@dublincity.ie

The magistrate bared his sharp teeth and held on tightly to the collar of his long coat. 'Don't you dare use those filthy human words in my presence, you hear me? You've spent too long on the fringes, dallying with *them*. You're in danger of becoming like Rhin.' The magistrate narrowed his eyes until it almost looked as if he was asleep, in the midst of an angry dream. 'You are here, Finrig Everwit, because *she* demanded it. You are still Fae, are you not? Then you answer to Queen Sift! You and your men. You left the job half done, took your gold and left. It's time to set it right!'

Finrig raised a hand, but one of the guards batted it away, his armour clanking. The faerie growled, and said no more.

'Take them inside,' ordered the magistrate, in a voice a little higher-pitched than he would have liked. The Wit brushed past him, nearly knocking him to the floor.

Inside the Coil, the halls were blindingly bright. There was a glow-worm lantern every five paces, and together they painted the inside of the twisted spire a deep, electric blue, the sort of colour that would play havoc with human eyes.

The faeries did not even notice it. Such were the habits of an underground race. They had learnt to live with the glowing, the slithering, and the scuttling, and whatever else the dirt kept as its own.

The Wit and his Fingers were marched up a spiralling set of steps and ushered into the very peak of the Coil. The guards made sure not to step too close. They had all heard the rumours. They didn't dare poke their guests, didn't dare hurry them. Feeling more like captives than guards, they were entranced by the mere reputation of this giant of a faerie they followed up the endless steps.

At long last, they came to the Queen's quarters, and the magistrate barged his way through the crowd of gathered courtlings to knock on Sift's door. He did so with great ceremony, waving his hand about in a circular motion before knocking once, twice, thrice. There was a brief pause, and then a shrill voice commanded them to enter. Finrig took a breath, and pulled his hood down, as did his men, and the guards gawped on.

When the door was shut, and the whispering guards locked out, Queen Sift of the Fae emerged from behind a desk piled high with scrolls and walked with long slow paces to a small, but regal chair made of stag beetle horn. It sat very much alone, compared to the other furniture in the grand room. As the Wit, the Fingers, and the magistrate shuffled forwards to bow, she waved a hand, and took a seat upon her thorny throne.

'Finrig,' she spoke his name as if weighing it. Her voice was deep for a female, even for the husky tones of faerie women. It had an echo to it, a strange quality that Finrig, much to his annoyance, had never been able to fathom. But it was her face that never failed to make his wings shiver. He raised his head to meet her bright golden eyes, and found words to say.

'Your Majesty.'

The only splash of colour to mar Sift's pure ashen skin were the thin veins of dark crimson that circled her ears and temples. Her frame was tall and long yet wiry, like a coiled fangworm, always ready to strike. Her ears were devilishly pointed, and her teeth, when she smiled, were needle-like daggers. Finring, a faerie who had successfully fought and killed almost everything the wild had to throw at him, could not help but quail slightly in her presence.

Sift drummed her sharp nails on the antlers of her throne for a moment, while she thought. It was an uncomfortable sound.

'Do you know why I have called you back here, Finrig?'

Finrig cleared his throat. 'I have just been informed, your Majesty …'

Sift flicked her gaze to the magistrate, who quailed also. 'Did you tell him everything, Rinold?'

Magistrate Rinold nodded feverishly. 'Yes, your Majesty.'

'Then you know where he is, Finrig?'

Finrig nodded. 'I do, Queen Sift.'

Sift drummed her nails some more. 'Now please, Finrig,' and here she paused to pick a little something from under her nail, 'could you be a dear and tell me exactly *why* Rhin Rehn'ar is currently residing in the Endless Lands?'

'It appears that he didn't take our threat very seriously, your Majesty.'

Sift leant forwards and the throne creaked. It was a sound as ominous as the creaking of a gallows. 'It appears that he didn't take it very seriously at all, Finrig. What, pray, made you so damn confident that you thought a simple threat could do the job? Are you that smug in your reputation?'

Finrig swallowed. 'He keeps a boy, your Majesty, the son of a wealthy lord. Rhin was bound to him, loyal as a dog, and hence easy to find. We threatened the boy, and painted a very ... *vibrant* picture for him.'

'Not vibrant enough, it seems.'

Finrig did not like what he had to do to, but he knew it was the only way to walk out of that room with his limbs still attached. The faerie bowed again. There would be laughing around the campfire later if they managed to keep their skin on. 'I sincerely apologise, your Majesty, for this mistake. If there is any way I could be of ass——'

'Leave us!' Sift shouted, making her audience flinch as one. 'Rinold, Finrig, you stay. The rest of you Fingers, even the guards, leave now.'

There was a nervous scuttling that didn't achieve much. The queen soon hurried it up. 'NOW!' she screeched, and the scuttling became a stampede towards the door. It was hurriedly locked and barred.

Now that they were alone, Sift got up from her throne and began to walk slow circles around the two faeries. It was so intimidating she might as well have taken out a set of carving knives and begun to sharpen them. It was as if fear leaked from her pores and enveloped them, like some bewitching perfume. Whatever it was, it worked. Finrig shuddered as she spoke.

'We never told you what Rhin stole, did we?' Sift asked.

'No, your Majesty, I don't believe you did.'

'Perhaps if we had ...' and here Sift's eyes darted to stare at the magistrate. Rinold felt like a mouse in her shadow. She was even taller than Finrig. '... told you more of the details, you might have realised beforehand that a simple threat was nothing short of a preposterous solution.'

Rinold shuddered.

'However, I am prepared to enlighten you now.'

Finrig had never longed for a chair so much in his entire life. 'I'm listening, your Majesty.'

'Rhin stole the Hoard, Finrig. The *Hoard*.'

Here we shall briefly digress, as the ways and words of the Fae can be confusing on the first encounter. Let us allow a few moments for an explanation. The Hoard, or the *Haor 'n*, as it is known in the very old tongues, is the Fae's fortune, the gold at the end of the rainbow, so to speak. For some reason or other, in human literature this has been attributed to the hole-dwelling leprechaun instead. This is yet another reason why the Fae dislike us, but actually the misunderstanding has worked to their advantage. Nobody goes looking for creatures who don't possess pots of gold.

The interesting thing about the Hoard is that it is not at all what you would imagine an enormous pile of Fae gold, collected over countless decades, to look like. No. Faeries are much smarter than this. Piling all that gold up in one place means two things: it's easy to skim a little off the top, and it's hell for the accountants. Faeries have spells for this sort of thing.

The Hoard can take any shape, and be of any size: that of a pocket; or a safe; even a hat, in some cases, which is never wise if you intend to wear it. In Sift's case, she had stored her kingdom's wealth in a large leather purse—a purse that Rhin Rehn'ar stole from her, four years before.

Finrig was speechless for a spell, until Sift clicked her fingers and snapped him out of it. 'The whole thing?' he asked.

'Of course the whole thing,' hissed Rinold.

Sift whirled on him. 'Did he direct that question at *you*, Magistrate?'

Rinold collapsed into a bow. 'No, my Queen.'

'Then keep your miserable mouth shut before I personally stitch it up for you!' she screamed. Spit decorated Rinold's face. He was not sure if answering would be a direct contravention of her last command, so he just whimpered instead. Sift seemed satisfied. She turned back to Finrig, much to his delight. Sift's golden eyes roved over his thick and fraying black cloak, over the dark red mud on his grey boots, at the slight hint of a dagger in his pocket. The man was wilder than the badgers that plagued the north tunnels, she thought.

'I will make it worth your while.' Sift's voice slipped a little lower. A lone finger reached out and prodded Finrig in the chest. The faerie could have sworn it felt cold, even through his clothes. 'When the Hoard is once again in my safe keeping, you will be rewarded, handsomely: fifty thousand florins, for both you and your men, new clothes, new weapons, women, estates … whatever you like.' Each word was another prod.

Finrig swallowed even though his throat was dry. *Fifty thousand* … 'For doing what, your Majesty?'

'Why …' her finger crept up until it lifted his chin, '… for fetching Rhin Rehn'ar for me. I want him and the Hoard brought back and placed right here, where you are standing, Finrig. Dead or alive, I do not care,' Sift spat. 'So long as he returns with the Hoard. Do I make myself clear, *Wit*?' She stared at him and he stared right back. He had found a little courage in the depths of his stomach. There was a reason why it was he who stood there, and not one of his competitors. He was the best, and—despite his mistake—Sift needed him.

'Crystal, your Majesty,' he replied.

'Then we have an agreement?'

Finrig's courage burnt bright. 'Forgive me for speaking plainly, your Majesty, but I don't believe I have a choice.'

Sift's lip twitched. She narrowed her golden eyes at him, but before she could speak, or hiss, or bury her fangs into his neck, he went on, praying he was not being too bold.

'How could I refuse the offer of Queen Sift? I would be a fool to choose otherwise.'

Sift relaxed ever so slightly. 'I am pleased.'

Finrig held up a finger. 'However,' he began, tugging at his clothes, 'My men are in an even worse condition than I, and the voyage to America, for our kind, will be long and difficult, dangerous even. Might I humbly suggest doubling the fee you so kindly offered?'

Sift simmered for a moment before answering. 'Seventy-five thousand, and not a florin more.'

Finrig bowed so quickly he though his neck would snap. 'Thank you, your Majesty. We will leave at once.'

'You are dismissed.'

Finrig couldn't resist tossing Magistrate Rinold one last venomous look before he swivelled on his heel and left. Rinold looked terrified. Finrig did not blame him, but he did care either. He merely focused on keeping his pace somewhere between a polite retreat and an all-out scramble.

When the doors were locked and barred behind him, Finrig took a breath. The hallway was empty save for one guard. 'My Fingers?' Finrig asked of him.

One of the guards nodded, helmet rattling. 'In the courtyard, waiting for you. Is Rinold still in there?'

Finrig nodded. 'He is indeed, and she isn't in a good mood.'

The guard looked at the door. 'Oh dear.'

'Enjoy the clean-up.' Finrig patted the man on the shoulder and headed for the stairs. He barely made it one floor before the screaming started.

In the courtyard, his crew were sullen and wary. They eyed their leader suspiciously as he sauntered up to them.

'What are you lot glaring at?' he challenged. His second-in-command, Kawn, cleared his throat. He was a veritable brick of a faerie.

'What did you speak of, Wit?' he asked.

Finrig's face cracked into a wide smile. 'Florins, lads. Florins aplenty.' There wasn't as much cheering as he had expected. In fact, most of his crew just swapped curious glances.

'Aye?' asked Kawn. 'In exchange for what?'

'For going to fetch Rhin Rehn'ar back, dead or alive.'

Kawn snorted. 'That snivelling prick? But he's in America now. How many florins has that que …'

'Seventy-five thousand,' Finrig said, before fixing Kawn with a sour stare. 'Seventy-five thousand florins.'

Finrig's crew, the throat-cutting, beggar-slaying lot of them, stared at him in silence.

Kawn stamped his foot. 'Ain't no land of the Fae, America. Our kind have never had a foothold there. How dare Sift ask us to do …'

'You know what seventy-five thousand florins means, lads?' Finrig muttered absently, making a show of playing with his fingernails. 'Any clues? It means homes. Wives. Crops. An honest life …' The look in Finrig's eyes was faraway and hopeful. His hands were now clasped as though he were praying, and he tilted his head to the Lonely Star. But the Wit had never been able to hold a straight face for long, and he was soon grinning and cackling. He winked at his crew. 'And by that, lads, I mean dirty great big houses with big bastard tables laden with meat. I mean all the wine you can guzzle and all the faerie-tail you can fuck. I mean retirement, lads! At last!'

Some of the crew began to smile, then grin, then rub their hands together. Even Kawn began to look tempted.

'One dead body is the cost of crossing the river to paradise, isn't that what they say? Well in this case it won't be any of our bodies. It'll be that of Rhin Rehn'ar's.'

This time there was plenty of cheering.

CHAPTER VII

WELCOME TO FELL FALLS

'They found me. I have no idea how. I buried the bandages. Haven't bled in days, but somehow they picked up my scent. Must have moles. Got an arrow through my side but I can still run. Need to find water ...' [the rest of this page is smothered in blood]

7th May, 1867

It was very quickly apparent to Merion that his aunt's definition of 'options' differed quite a lot from his. His sleeping options, as they currently stood, were: a cupboard on the uneven landing; a corner of the study where his aunt apparently used to sit and paint; the notorious basement; or a small square room a smidgeon larger than his cabin on the *Tamarassie*. He chose the latter.

'I've arranged for your luggage to be delivered in the morning,' his aunt was saying, her voice penetrating Merion's daze of dissatisfaction. She put her hands on her hips, and watched Merion lower his rucksack to the floor. His eyes roved over the rickety old bed that took up most of the small room.

'I'll get some cutters and nip off that popped spring in the morning. In the meantime, don't impale yourself,' she said, with a hint of a smile. 'I'm joking.'

Eyeing the dust on the headboard and the windowsill behind it, he knew it was a dumb question, but he asked it anyway. 'Do you have any servants?'

Lilain nodded. 'Fourteen of them.'

Merion's head had already snapped around before he realised she was joking. Yet again. He sighed. 'Why are you not angry with me?'

Lilain threw him a confused look. 'Should I be?'

'I shouted at you.'

Lilain threw her hands up in the air. 'And you had a right to. I make too many jokes. I know that. Should have known you'd want to blow off some steam. Spend enough time on the rail, you start to think you're a locomotive,' she told him. 'Now, we good here?' Lilain thumbed at the door.

Merion was still churning over his aunt's answer. 'But children are not to shout at grown-ups,' he replied, automatically reciting one of his father's many lessons.

Lilain stepped forwards and laid a hand on his shoulder. 'Nephew, you're in Fell Falls, Wyoming. All children are grown-ups here, the moment they set foot on that dusty platform. You'll see. If you stay, that is.'

Merion sniffed. 'I'm sorry to disappoint you.'

Lilain eyed the rucksack with her grey eyes. 'We'll talk about that in the morning. I have to … you know.' His aunt jabbed another thumb at the door. She was so unlike his father, Merion thought. *How could this animated, chatty undertaker be a Hark?*

'Carve up a dead body,' he said flatly.

Lilain shrugged. 'There's also a dog, but that's a favour for a friend. It can wait 'til morning,' she replied, and then added, 'Right, off to work. Sleep well, Merion. It truly is a pleasure to have you here.' Lilain paused for a moment, her hand resting on the doorframe. She fixed him with a stare. Had it not been for her smile, Merion would have found it rather intimidating. 'I have so much to tell you,' she said.

Merion just bowed, and said goodnight.

Only after his aunt had shut the door, and he had heard her footsteps on the basement steps, did he unfasten the flap of the rucksack. Rhin stood on a folded jumper, tapping his foot and grinning. 'I like her,' he said.

'You would. She's an exile. Just like you.'

'Hey,' Rhin glared. 'I was thinking more along the lines of a free spirit. You should listen to her, Merion. Give her a chance, at least for a little while.'

The faerie had never seen the boy's face so resolute, so hard. 'No, Rhin,' he said, 'my father's murderer must be found, and I have to get back to London. I'm not going to argue about it. My mind's made up.'

Rhin shrugged and hopped onto the lip of the pack. 'Fine. Then I'm staying here.'

Merion mirrored his shrug and looked away. He found himself staring at the door. 'Have it your way,' he told the faerie.

Rhin began to rummage under the bed, where he found an old suitcase with a gaping hole in its side. 'Almost as though she knew I were coming,' he chuckled, rubbing his hands. He poked his head inside and hummed. 'Needs a clean, but otherwise perfect.'

'Glad somebody is happy here.'

'Why don't you unpack? Take your mind off it,' Rhin advised, from somewhere inside the suitcase.

Merion thought about it, but the thought of finding places for his things made the situation seem a touch too permanent for his liking. *He wouldn't be here long, after all.*

Merion suddenly had an idea. He put his hand on the doorknob and muttered more to himself than to Rhin. 'I think I might get some answers while I'm here.'

'Sure you can stomach it? I've seen you go green before, you know. Remember that dead bird? With the maggots?'

'Stop it.'

Rhin just chuckled to himself.

'Just don't break anything while I'm gone. The same rules apply here as they did at Harker Sheer, understand? Nobody else knows,' Merion lectured him as he stepped through the door and out into the hall.

'I know, I know.'

'Good boy,' Merion added, just before the door closed. Rhin could have sworn he saw the lad wink sarcastically. He growled and strangled the life out of an old sock.

★

Somebody was singing. It wasn't the septic smell that reminded him so much of his father's autopsy, nor the dripping of old pipes, nor the carts with shapes hidden under old blankets, lying up against the earthen walls that disturbed him. It was just the singing. It was Lilain of course, warbling away at some strange old tune whilst she went about her work, pulling bits out of one cavity and sewing up another.

It wasn't long before she noticed him, hovering in the shadows. 'Come to stare at the dead?' she asked, in a low voice. It sent a shiver running down Merion's spine, and was quickly followed by another as his aunt lifted up the corpse's head so its dead eyes could look at him. He immediately clamped a hand over his mouth.

Lilain stifled a giggle and laid the head back down. 'Bucket's in the corner, Tonmerion.'

Merion found it just in time. He spewed his guts until he had no more to give, and then sat with the bucket cradled in his lap for another few minutes.

'You okay?' Lilain asked, in her singsong voice.

Merion belched. 'His face,' he whispered.

'Half of it is missing, yes. Railwraiths have a thing for tongues, so they say. They go for that first, but they're not the most precise of creatures, not with bits of railroad spike and twisted iron for fingers.'

Merion looked up to see if his aunt was smiling. She wasn't. 'Have you ever seen one?' he asked, making quotes with his fingers. 'A railwraith?'

'Two. From a distance, thank the Maker.'

'Are they big?' Merion felt his natural boyish curiosity creeping out, despite the nausea.

'Some can be twelve feet, maybe more. Most are nine or so.'

'And they hunt us?'

'That they do.'

'Why?'

'Because we're building a great big railroad straight through their territory, so the scientists say, and the wraiths apparently like the taste of railroad worker. And guard too. Pretty much anything with two legs, two arms, a face, and boots on.'

Merion couldn't help himself. 'And what are they, exactly?'

Lilain laughed, and put down her scalpel for a moment. 'My, you've got a mouth full of questions, Tonmerion. Why the sudden interest in the wraiths?'

Merion pushed himself up from the cold floor and staged over to the table. He thanked the Almighty his stomach was already empty. He gagged all the same. Lying upon the table was a man of two halves, split from left shoulder to right hip. Half his insides were gone, and the rest of him was a torn-up mess. Sand and bits of iron filled his wounds. His tongue was missing, of course, along with the rest of his face. Merion couldn't take his eyes off the gaping hole in the man's head.

'You, erm. You said you had a lot to tell me?'

Lilain laughed, and Merion watched as she deftly used her scalpel to remove a scrap of lung. She dropped it into a porcelain bowl. 'Well, I don't just have stories of railwraiths, that's for sure. I could tell you so many stories, Merion, but not all of them can be told in one night.' She glanced at him as she hacked at something similar to bone. 'I was hoping you might stay, so I could tell you all of them.'

Merion watched the dark blood leaking from the areas her scalpel had kissed. His stomach gurgled again. 'Only my friends call me Merion,' he said.

Lilain huffed. 'And what about family?'

Merion pulled a face. 'My dad always called me Tonmerion. Or sometimes Harlequin.'

'Yeah, but I'm your aunt, and aunts always have nicknames for their nephews, or so I'm told. Merion it is. Could you pass me that saw, please? The longer one?' she asked. Merion followed the direction of her pointing finger and found the saw sitting on a wooden tray at the end of the bench. It shone dully in the bright lantern light. Merion handed his aunt the saw, and took the opportunity to look around the room as she began to remove the man's head from his shoulders.

The room was sparse, and smelled of death. And sick too, but Merion suspected that was his own. Here and there, intricate instruments sat on trays and bathed in bowls. A pile of towels and bloodied blankets sat next to a sink, ready to be washed. A mop leant on a bookcase in the corner, a bookcase filled with jars and vials of all different sizes and colours. Some of the larger jars held little pieces of human paraphernalia: an ear; a heart; an eyeball in some cases, floating in a greenish soup. The colours of the assorted vials offered the rainbow. Merion was starting to give some serious credence to the idea that his aunt might not be sane. The odds, at the moment, were stacked high against her.

Lilain was pointing again, waving her finger about. 'Now the syringe, Merion. No, the little one. That's it. And the vial too.'

Merion watched her as she worked. She had found what was left of the heart, or so she told him, and wanted to take a sample of blood. Once again his stomach gurgled at him, urging him to go back to his room, but Merion was a stubborn fellow, and he forced himself to watch. Lilain lifted the vial up to the light and swirled the thick, dark blood around. She was muttering something, something that sounded distinctly foreign to his ears. Whatever it was, he couldn't make it out. She put the vial on a nearby table and went back to work with her scalpel. Even though Merion detested her profession, he had to admit she was good at her job. She worked quickly and deftly, slicing little pieces from the heart and placing them in little wooden dishes that were laid out in a row on the side of the table.

'What are you doing?' Merion asked.

Lilain smiled. 'Glad you asked! Samples. See if we can find out more about the railwraith.'

Merion spied a chance to resume his interrogation. 'Do railwraiths bleed?'

Lilain's smile grew very wide indeed. She gave him that stare again. 'Everything bleeds, Merion.'

It took no less, but no more, than an hour to finish with the body. In the end, Merion had to hold one half of the corpse as Lilain sewed the man back together, ready for burial. Merion mentally vowed to burn his clothes. He couldn't even bring himself to look down at the crimson stains he knew for sure were now decorating the front of his white shirt.

Merion caught his aunt winking at him. 'You'd make a great apprentice. I do have an opening, if you're interested?'

'No, I am not,' Merion tersely replied. He found himself instantly regretting the sharpness of his tone.

Lilain laughed his guilt away. 'Position's always open,' she said, and then swiftly changed the subject. 'So Tonmerion Harlequin Hark? What's that short for?' There was a hint of a smile on her face.

Tonmerion furrowed his brows quizzically. 'I don't believe I follow,' he replied.

'Oh never mind,' Lilain tittered. She brushed a strand of blonde hair behind her ear, daubing herself with blood. Merion blanched, but his aunt didn't seem to notice, never mind care. She just hummed to herself and carried right on. Merion thought about mentioning it, but decided to press on with questions instead. It was time to get some real answers.

'So,' he said nonchalantly, 'why here?'

Lilain looked up and sighed. 'Well ain't that a question of many halves. Do you mean to ask me why I live here, and not in the Empire? Or are you asking why I live on this side of town? Or perhaps you meant why it is that *you* are here? Or, do you want to know why we, as a race, are here in the desert, and therefore, why *he*,' and here she waved the scalpel at the mangled body, 'is here? So, young nephew, which one is it to be?'

Once Merion had finished digesting his aunt's words, he looked around for something to sit upon and found a wooden stool sitting in the corner. Once he had placed himself on its worn seat which, mercifully, was quite far away from any tools, tables, or corpses, he placed his hands upon his knees. 'All of them, I suppose,' he replied.

Lilain cast her gaze over the body, and muttered something to herself. 'Fair enough. Mister Travish will take a lot of needle and twine, by my reckoning. You not tired?'

'Father used to say a boy is never tired when there are questions to be asked.'

Lilain mulled that one over. 'Never heard him say that. Wish I had now …' She stole a moment to wink at him before continuing. 'Well then. Why am I here, in Fell Falls.'

As Lilain talked, she worked. The scalpel danced in time to her tongue as she probed and cleaned and borrowed. When she was finished with an area, her bony hands would fish out the needle and sew the ruptured wounds shut as best they could. All the while she bent close to the body, her soft grey eyes keeping her bloodied fingers in check. Her voice was quiet but clear, and the way her words tumbled out gave her tales melody and emotion. Merion was instantly absorbed. Nobody, especially young gentlemen like Merion, can resist a natural-born storyteller.

'Karrigan and I were always two sides of the same coin. We were brother and sister, and yet we couldn't have been more different, believe me. Karrigan was serious and taciturn. I was annoying and irritating. He was drinking tea and wearing suits while I was still playing with paint and dirt. As we grew older, we just grew further apart. It ain't uncommon, in siblings.

'While Karrigan spent his time with father, learning the ways of business and politics, and of bending his fellow man to his will, I spent my time training myself in nature, learning the plants and creatures and the olden stories. He used to call me Molefingers, did you know that? But father had lessons for me too, as well as his son. He lectured me about all sorts. Medicines and herbs, just like his father had taught him. Old friends began to arrive at the door, men of biology and history. Father had them hold private classes just for me. Rats, mice, frogs, birds, fish … we dissected everything, just to learn. So guess what? Molefingers soon became Bloodfingers. It was a wonderful time. Until your father made it to those Emerald Benches, at least. Now listen close, Merion.'

Merion listened very closely indeed.

'When Karrigan was made an Emerald Lord in his own right, father decided it was time to bestow on his son all his titles and businesses, to step back, and retire with mother. Unfortunately, their version of retiring meant buying a steamship and sailing it straight into the Cape of No Hope. Their bodies were never found. I was devastated when we received the wiregram. You know the first thing your father did, nephew?'

'No?'

'He cut me off. Overnight. Said if my science and magic wasn't going to bring in any revenue, I had to move out of Harker Sheer.'

Merion's expression grew cold and icy. 'You're lying,' he accused her.

'Am I? Your father was a ruthless businessman, was he not?'

'Yes, but …'

'Trust me on this one, nephew. I'm not trying to soil his name. It was his way of challenging me, see, of getting this olden nonsense out of my head so I could help him run his precious Empire. But I had no taste for it.' Merion almost missed it, but at that precise moment, Lilain's hands paused in their work, for just a second. The moment vanished, and the hands kept moving. 'So I did Karrigan a favour and got myself good and lost. The embarrassing sister, vanished into the wilds, leaving nothing but a note saying "Farewell."' Lilain snorted. 'In truth all I did was get on a locomotive and head to Prussia, but that's another story. By chance and circumstance, I wound up here in Fell Falls.'

'But how?'

'Little over a year ago, I was living in Chicago—'

Merion couldn't help but interrupt. 'Undertaking?'

'Amongst other things.'

'Like what?'

'Like exploring the wilderness, and hunting down strange and wonderful creatures. Undertaker by day, amateur scientist by night.'

'But it's night now, and you're ... undertaking.'

'It's just an expression.'

'You mentioned my father saying science and magic. Did my grandfather's friends teach you that too? Can you do magic?'

Lilain looked up from the corpse for the very first time, and smiled that trademark smile of hers. 'Of sorts,' she replied, almost in a whisper. 'For instance, I can make the blade of this scalpel disappear.' Lilain waved her hands around the dirty blade and whistled.

The stool creaked as Merion leant forwards ever so slightly. He couldn't help it.

'Watch very closely,' she told him. The stool creaked again.

With more hand-waving and finger-twiddling, Lilain slowly raised the scalpel high above her head. Then, after a smattering of so-called magic words, she brought it down. There was a thud as the flash of silver buried itself in the dead man's ribcage. 'See?'

Merion was not amused. He crossed his arms while Lilain chuckled to herself. Anyway,' she continued, 'the contract ran out on my job, and they didn't need me anymore. The war had moved south, and the gangs were getting bored of fighting each other. Chicago had more undertakers than bakers, so they said. I decided it was time to go where the bodies were. Took what was left of my savings, and moved myself to the frontier.'

'Here, in Fell Falls?'

'Right you are, and to skip a question or two, this town was built here because the Serped Railroad Company has been hired by good King Lincoln to forge a path to the Last Ocean. The towns move with the rail. When the rail moves too far away from the last town. A new one is built and the frontier moves. Except the rail ain't moved more than a couple of miles in a year and a half. Now Mr Tavish here,' Lilain slapped her client's ruined chest, 'is lying on my table because he strayed into the desert to take a piss. Strayed too far and paid the highest price. The railwraith had dragged him half over the hill by the time the sheriffsmen caught up with it.'

'Did they kill it?'

'Gosh, no. Just scared it off with guns and nitroglycerin. Now,' and it was here that she began to work faster, reaching more for the needle now. Merion could tell question time was nearly up. Like any good story-teller, Lilain was holding something back, and the urge to uncover it almost made Merion squirm.

'Now, to tell you why I am here at the edge of town means I have to explain a little bit about American superstition. What do you think of when we talk of magic?'

Merion scratched his head. 'Rabbits in hats. Doves. Cards,' he said.

'Now, that's magic. What about magick, with a k?'

'I would say you have atrocious spelling.'

Lilain clicked her fingers. 'Ha, well, young nephew, it's actually the olden spelling. Differentiates between the magic of stage magicians and con artists, and real magic, the stuff of wizards and shamans.'

'What is this olden you keep mentioning?'

'Ever heard somebody say "in the olden days"?'

'Yes. Margrit, one of the servants in the house. Never stops saying it. *Stopped*.'

'Well, once again, modern times have twisted our view of things. Olden days doesn't just mean a few decades ago, it means centuries ago, when humans were young and new to the world.'

'You mean, when we lived in caves?'

'Sort of. These are what we true historians call the days of olden, the time that myths and legends come from. Olden ways and olden stories. They've both been lost over the years, as we've grown up. We don't believe in such things any more, do we, nephew? We don't burn witches at the stake and we don't believe in fairies. We believe in the Almighty and all his creation. Right?'

Merion thanked the very Almighty in question that Lilain did not see him flinch at the mention of the Fae. He just went along with it. 'The stuff of fairy tales and bedtime stories.'

'Bingo.'

Merion didn't know what bingo was, but he assumed it meant he was right.

'Well, the olden days aren't all that olden here, not in the west. Magic is spelt with a k here, nephew, don't forget that. This is the sort of place where the stuff of fairy tales breaks down your door at night and skins you from tip to toe, the sort of place where monsters really do have a penchant for sleeping under the bed, and where wives' tales always end with the wives being eaten alive. America hasn't had time to forget the olden days, nephew. They're still very much alive and kicking.'

Merion felt the blood draining to his toes. 'I thought you were trying to convince me to stay?'

'I am! Isn't it exciting? All that history, all these creatures. It's incredible.'

Merion rolled his eyes. It was like being invited to a knife fight on the premise of it 'being a laugh'. 'You sound like a woman I met on the ship. Forgive me if I don't share your enthusiasm, Aunt Lilain.'

'You'll see soon enough,' she told him. 'And so in summary, I live out here on the edges of town because the others are afraid of ghosts and zombies and other such undead creatures.'

'And …' Merion couldn't help but stammer at the mere mention of the undead. They scared him more than he liked to admit. '… are they right to be worried?'

Lilain hooted with laughter as she closed up the last of Mr Tavish's gruesome wounds. 'Hah! Not in the slightest. Human spirits aren't strong enough to maintain ghost-like form, never mind manipulate anything. Older spirits can though. Zombies?' And here she shrugged. 'Possibly. But I always take my precautions.'

'Pre— precautions?'

Lilain tied off the final loop of thread, and Merion's heart sank a little when the scalpel cut it clean. 'A little sprinkle of the right kind of dust here and there does the trick,' she mumbled to herself. With a sigh, she stood upright and put her hands together. 'And I believe that brings us to the very last of your questions, doesn't it?'

'It does.'

Lilain took a moment to walk around the table, so she could lean against it whilst facing her nephew. She crossed her arms and looked at him. 'So, why do you think you are here?' she asked.

Merion knew this one. 'Because somebody murdered my father,' he replied flatly, begrudging saying it aloud.

Lilain shook her head solemnly. 'No that's the answer to the question of why my brother is dead. Why are you *here*?'

The young Hark sighed. He despised guessing games. 'Because my father thought it would be a good idea to ship me off to the edge of the world for five years, leaving my inheritance protected only by law and open to the pilfering of thieves and jealous lords?'

'Wrong again.' Seeing the colour growing in his cheeks, Lilain decided to put him out of his misery. 'You're here, nephew, because I just happen to be the only family you have left on this earth. My father and mother were both only children, like their parents before them. No aunts, no uncles, and no cousins. Why, Karrigan could have left you in the care of the party, or the law, but from what little I know of politics and the thieves you talk about, that would have been a very bad idea indeed. No, you're here because this is the best place for you. Your father wanted you here. Not out of spite, nor lack of love, but out of design.'

Merion took several slow and long breaths. It all seemed logical, but he still didn't like it one bit. 'You may see a design in all of this, Aunt Lilain, but all I see is a mistake,' he said, almost growling his words.

'With all due respect, Tonmerion Hark, you ain't seen shit yet,' she replied, grinning wide. She knew then she had possibly pushed him too far.

Merion got down from his stool and straightened his shirt. He wrinkled his lip when his fingers rediscovered the sticky bloodstains he'd forgotten about. Merion looked past her as he spoke, at the stairs in the shadows beyond. He could not quite meet her twinkling eyes.

'This all seems rather like a joke to you, Aunt. I was expecting the sister of my dead father to be a little more ... *upset* at her brother's murder.'

Lilain's face fell into the very picture of gravity. 'I have done my grieving, nephew. I won't let anybody tell me different,' she replied. There wasn't a single trace of humour in her voice. 'Duty's done.'

Merion didn't reply. He was already halfway to the stairs. Lilain didn't stop him. Instead she let him go, waiting until his feet disappeared from view to call out. 'The way I see it, I may have lost a brother, but I've gained a nephew. The Maker's ever fair, in my eyes.'

She received no reply, save for the creaking of the basement door. Lilain brushed that offending strand of hair from her face once more, and clapped her hands against her thighs with a sigh. 'Well, Mr Tavish. Let's get you to bed, shall we? I've got a dog to see to.'

Mr Tavish didn't complain one bit. He just smiled his awful smile up at the brick ceiling as he was wheeled into the cold darkness of the basement.

CHAPTER VIII
THE MAN AND THE MAGPIE

Must keep running. I'm not letting that fucking Queen win this. I'm not going to die on her terms.

7th May, 1867

For the first time in over a fortnight, Merion awoke to find his bed was not trembling. That is, his head was comfortably wedged on a friendly pillow, rather than a stranger's lap, and neither was it numb from being pressed against a rattling window. A scraping noise had awoken him. It was coming from under the bed. Merion opened his eyes and immediately regretted it. The light was streaming throughout the holes in his curtains and making his room glow. It was too bright and cheery for his liking. He reached for the blanket and pulled it over his face. It smelled like mothballs.

'Must you always sharpen your sword this early in the morning?' he asked in a muffled voice.

'Best time to do it,' came the equally muffled reply. Merion felt Rhin's words reverberate in the centre of his back. 'Never know what'll happen after breakfast.

The very mention of food stoked a fire in Merion's belly. He was ravenous after emptying his stomach into the bucket the night before. The whiff of eggs and bacon sneaking through the cracks in his door did not help matters. If he concentrated, he could hear his aunt whistling in the kitchen. Before Merion braved the sunlight, he turned his mind to his day and what he would accomplish. Was he sure he wanted to do this, to brave the rail and the high seas all over again? Merion was not truly sure, but that sounded all too much like giving in—and Harks did not give in. The only way out was through. Merion spent the next five minutes with his eyes scrunched up tight, devising a plan, tiptoeing along the edges of slumber at the same time.

Rhin's voice brought him abruptly back to reality. 'You getting up or not?' he asked.

'Yes indeed.' Merion said, and via his strength of purpose and hunger, he threw himself out of bed and onto the wooden floor. He was surprised to find the planks were warm under his bare feet, in contrast to the cold rug and marble of his vast bedroom in Harker Sheer. Merion grumbled as he reached for his shoes.

Rhin poked his head out from under the bed. 'Bacon and eggs. Sounds great.'

'Yes, yes, I'll see what I can do. You just worry about your sword,' Merion said, mumbling around a yawn.

'And beans too, if there are any. I hear Americans like their beans.'

'And just where did you hear that?'

'On the train.'

Merion shrugged. They had heard a lot of things on the train. 'Fine. Keep quiet.'

'Aye aye, sir.'

Merion opened the door and was instantly enveloped in a wall of grey smoke. He grimaced and put a hand to his mouth. 'Aunt Lilain?' he yelled. 'Something appears to be on fire!'

'Only me!' came the reply, from the right. He could see a shape moving about in the smoke. 'Now, I don't normally cook, so my apologies if it ain't what you're used to.'

Merion's stomach didn't care. It dragged him forwards into the smoke and into a chair at the small round table in the centre of the kitchen. Lilain busied about the room, checking pans and stirring the contents of assorted bowls. A plate landed in front of him. Its edges were so hot they burnt Merion's fingers when he tried to move it closer. The breakfast came slowly at first, in little bits and pieces, splatters and splotches. Soon enough it became a landslide. Bowls began to gather around his plate, full of porridge and jam and milk and sauces. Sausages rained. Beans spread like oil slicks. Slices of toast began to tower around him. Merion could barely get his fork in edgeways as the food kept coming. It wasn't long before he was staring at a fortress of a plate. Merion didn't even know where to start.

'Er ...' was all he could muster.

'Enjoy,' Lilain clasped her hands together. She was beaming. 'I can rustle us up some more toast if you—'

'No, thank you.' Merion held up a hand, busy examining an intersection of mushrooms and fried onion. 'I think this may be enough.'

If the sheer quantity of the breakfast didn't kill him, he suspected its quality might just finish him off. Some of the sausages were more charcoal than meat, the egg nearest to him looked as though it could be employed as a plate, and it actually seemed as though the beans were trying to run away, rather than just wanting to see the world. An eager Aunt Lilain watched on as Merion gingerly raised his fork. He couldn't decide which morsel to stab first. The closer his fork got to the mountain of food, the more Lilain leant over the table, and the tighter she clasped her hands.

But it seemed that today Merion had some good fortune, for once. There came a loud knocking at the kitchen door, and then in burst the rotund Eugin. His face was redder than a beetroot and sweat dripped from his chin in great globules. Merion found his hunger suddenly waning.

'Lilain! Has there been a fire?' he gasped, noting the smoke.

'No, I'm just cooking! What on earth is it?'

'Another dead on the railroad.'

'You joking with me, barrel-boy.'

Merion barely suppressed a laugh.

'Lordsguard's honour, ma'am.'

'That only works if you're a lordsguard, Eugin.' Lilain thumbed her nose. 'Two in two days. That ain't normal.'

'Workers won't go back out there today. Whole town's full of them. Unofficial holiday, they're calling it.'

'Yeah, 'cept for those who have to look after the bodies.'

'Are you coming, Mister Hark?' asked Eugin.

Lilain shushed him as she reached for her hat and gloves. 'Don't be silly, Eugin. Boy's just sat down for breakfast. Leave him be,' she said, and promptly pushed him out of the door. She turned back to

Merion. 'By all means, go wandering, but promise me three things. Don't wander outside the town limits. Don't go into any taverns, and don't get on a locomotive. If you are going to leave, then it'll be me seeing you off, you hear me?'

Merion nodded, pretending his mouth was full of food.

'Good. Oh, and don't go downstairs.'

He nodded again.

'And your luggage will be dropped at the door at noon.'

More nodding.

Lilain stared at him a bit more, narrowing her grey eyes. There was a slight sheen of bacon grease on her nose. 'You do understand me, don't you, Merion?'

One last nod.

'Good. Then I'll see you back at the house this afternoon if not earlier.'

The door slammed, and Merion was left alone. Several seconds passed before Merion put down his fork and got up from the table. He could no longer hear Lilain's footsteps or Eugin's panting. He was well and truly alone. And as all children do when they suddenly find themselves alone, Merion went exploring.

The old house was, simply put, far from special. The upstairs was a creaking mess, where the bare floorboards were strewn with clothes and bits of paper. There was a small study over the kitchen, full of ageing furniture covered with books and old scrolls. Merion let his fingers wander their pages, tracing the lines of the detailed drawings, sketches of dissected eels and body parts. He grimaced, and moved on.

The main bedroom was equally untidy. The curtains were thick cotton, and they transformed the room into a dark cave. A single bed sat in one corner, a chest of drawers in another. More books were on the floor, along with more clothes.

The outhouse, which Merion found at the bottom of a dusty garden, was almost not worth mentioning. It was a tall wooden box standing upright in the ground, looking more like a coffin than a privy.

He opened the creaking door and the smell hit him in the face like a brick. There was a seat and a hole, and that was it. A few sheaves of soft paper had been folded and left on the side.

Back in the house, the ground floor consisted of the kitchen, a set of grimy stairs, a storeroom full of stretchers and shovels, and his measly bedroom. All in all it was a shambles, but the heat of the morning sun and a glimpse of the town had doused his disappointment and disgust. Merion itched to see the rest of this doomed little town, to come face to face with whatever fates he had been lumped with.

Merion found Rhin waiting patiently on his bed. The sheets had been folded and the pillows punched. 'We're not staying, remember.'

Rhin just smiled. 'I'll believe it when I see it.'

'Don't do that,' Merion scowled as he rummaged through the rucksack for a fresh shirt. 'Don't just smile me aside like Lilain does, as if I'm joking. I assure you, I am deadly serious.'

Rhin snorted and drummed a quick rhythm on his knees. 'So, did you get the answers you wanted?'

'Some, but not all. She's holding something back, I can tell.'

'What did she say?'

'She told me about my father, and why she lives here. Kept talking about olden days as well.'

Rhin tilted his head. 'Did she now?'

Merion clapped. 'I knew that would interest you! Why haven't you ever told me about these olden days? She told me she got lessons on the subject when she was my age.'

'Because such times go by a different name to the Fae. The golden days, not olden. A few of your kind have kept the stories alive; singing the old songs all these years. Maybe she was taught by them.'

Merion shimmied out of his shirt as he thought aloud. 'But why would my grandfather care about such things?' he asked.

Rhun shrugged. 'Looks like you need to ask some more questions. In the meantime, let's go exploring.'

'*I'm* going exploring. You are staying here.'

Rhin's face fell. 'What?'

'It's too dangerous with you in the rucksack. I'll go alone and scout it out. In return, you can have my breakfast.'

This seemed to get Rhin's attention. The faerie was a greedy sort. 'You don't want it?'

Merion nodded and pointed to the kitchen. 'Aunt Lilain's quite the … er, *cook*, but I'm not in the mood for eating.'

Rhin hopped down from the bed and looked around the doorframe. He spotted the pile of steaming, smoking food instantly. 'Have fun in town,' he muttered, as he strode towards his newly acquired feast.

Merion paused on the doormat, door half-open, the heat from the morning already spilling inside the dark house. 'Don't eat too much and pass out again. Remember last time?'

'Never fear. I'm not keen on going through that again.'

Rhin was already murdering the first sausage before the door closed.

Blast if it wasn't hot. The sun had barely risen over the eastern hills and already the ground was shimmering underfoot. Merion could feel the moisture pouring out of him with every step he took down the rocky, dusty trail into town. He was genuinely concerned that his boots would fill up with so much sweat he would have to empty them by the side of the road. Wouldn't that be embarrassing, his first day in town? But it could also possibly be his last.

He soon came to a small row of dusty gardens and a familiar alleyway. It was mercifully cool between the houses. Merion leant against the wall while he caught his breath. He could hear the hustle and bustle of a main street at the end of the curving alleyway. It sounded hot and dusty, and, he guiltily confessed, rather exciting. Merion followed the alleyway and stepped out into the heat once more. He was almost instantly knocked down by a large man carrying a heavy sack.

'Watch it, boy!' he barked, as he sauntered on down the street, hat low and beard bushy.

Merion did indeed 'watch it'. He watched it as carefully as he could for the next few hours.

The streets of Fell Falls were not the streets of London; that was clear. They were simply tamed stretches of bare desert, kept in line by buildings and fences. But they teemed and buzzed and thundered like London's; that was for sure. The combined hubbub of hooves and carts and feet churned the air, making Merion's heart pound. Conversation was rife. Large groups of people had congealed on the steps of each and every building, busy swapping hot words. Everybody was talking, and death was the topic of the day.

'Two deaths in two days.'

Merion heard those words repeated over and over as he roamed the streets, dodging men on horseback and rumbling carts full of iron and wood. He took a short break between two piebald horses so that he could watch the world pass by, and take it all in. If Merion thought he had seen the wildest bunch of people that America had to offer, he was instantly proved wrong by the citizens of Fell Falls. He had never seen such a stranger breed of stranger.

From the men with brimmed hats and triple-barrelled guns at their belts, to those covered in dust and hauling heavy sacks to and fro, the citizenry both thrilled and scared the young Hark. Once again, it seemed that no town could be without its whores. Those that were not leaning out of high windows and whistling at men stood in the alleyways and doorways, chatting idly to passers-by. Like the taverns that dominated every corner Merion could see, they served to keep mankind distracted from the fear of the wild, of the unknown. He was starting to realise that now.

It seemed that business had also managed to find a toehold at the edge of the world. People needed to shop, of course, no matter how many fanged and terrifying beasts lay just over the hills. Blacksmiths, butchers, tailors, farriers, jewellers, stables, banks, barbers, general stores, and even a pet shop; the streets bristled with their signs. It did not take Merion long to find the post office. It had been thoughtfully placed at the very centre of town, and had even been painted a bright blue to help it stand out. He marched right up its steps and pushed through the swinging doors.

Now, unfortunately for Tonmerion Hark, there is a certain method behind using a swinging door, and he was completely unaware of it. The basic mechanics involve pushing the door forward, stepping through aforementioned door, and then releasing it, remembering to step clear of its return swing, lest you get struck in the back. Some of the more vicious swinging doors have been known to do this.

So it was that Merion followed steps one through three of this method to the letter, but sadly failed to remember step four. The door sent him staggering forwards to sprawl rather ungracefully over the post desk.

As Merion regained his balance, he heard somebody sniggering. He looked up to find a short bald man sat behind the counter. He was wearing a clerk's uniform so bleached by the sun it was almost grey, and for some reason he had thought it a good idea to cultivate a moustache under the balloon-like growth he called a nose. Merion wasn't surprised to see that he was lacking several of his teeth.

'I want to send a letter,' Merion stated.

The clerk regained his composure and laid his hairy hands flat on the counter. 'Well, you're in the right place for it. Where's this letter of yours going to?'

'To London, please. To Constable Pagget's office on Gibbet Street.'

The clerk puckered his lips and emitted a low whistle. 'Empire-born, are you? Gonna cost you.'

This man was already beginning to irritate him intensely. Merion took a breath. 'I imagined it might. How much?'

Now the clerk began to suck at his teeth. Merion wondered how many more annoying noises he had in his repertoire.

'One sil'erbit,' he said.

Merion shook his head. 'I don't know what one of those is.'

The clerk laughed so hard and so suddenly that he wheezed instead. Merion clenched his fists and forced himself to be polite. *Manners.*

'A silver bit, son. A silver coin with Lincoln's face on it.'

'I don't have one of those ...' Merion mumbled as he dug into his pockets.

'Well then, we ain't sending your letter now, are we?'

'... but I do have one with the sigil of Queen Victorious on it.' Merion held a silver coin up to the sunlight streaming through the windows and then placed it on the counter. He left his finger on it, pointing straight down at the queen's mark.

The clerk sniffed, and coughed, and then shuffled in his seat. 'Don't normally make a habit of taking Empire coin,' he finally said. 'It'll have to be two.'

'But you just said ...' Merion spluttered.

The clerk just shrugged. 'Exchange rate,' was his only excuse.

'Fine.' Merion dug out another silver coin and slid it across the desk to sit beside the other. A finger was placed on that sigil too. 'How long?' he asked.

'How long what?'

'How long does it take to get there?'

'A month, at best.'

Merion rubbed his forehead. 'Do you have a pen or a quill?'

The clerk sniffed again. 'One sil'erbit.'

'Not to buy! To borrow.'

The clerk shook his head, trying to give his mouth an officious slant. 'We ain't in the habit of loanin' pens to strangers. 'Specially Empire ones.'

Merion wanted to take a pen and shove it up the man's nose, but he managed to stay calm. Well, almost. 'I'm not a stranger,' he snapped. 'I am Lilain Rennevie's nephew, I'll have you know.'

The clerk raised his greasy eyebrows. 'Are you indeed?'

Merion nodded firmly. 'I am. Now, may I have a pen?'

An ink-stained finger was waved at the doorway. 'Over there. On the desk.'

Merion scowled. 'I'll be back momentarily.'

The clerk sniffed once again. 'Very well then, I'll see you, *momentarily.*'

With his shoulders well and truly hunched, the boy stalked over to the desk and snatched the pen from its little glass jar. He stuck a hand inside his shirt and pulled out a few of the blank sheets of paper he had swiped from his aunt's floor. With purpose, and a dwindling supply of ink, Merion bent over the paper and scribbled until his arm ached. He recounted his whole journey, going into detail on the conditions of his past and current accommodation, and making sure to convey exactly how dissatisfied he was with the transfer of information from London to America. Finally, just as the pen offered up its last obsidian drops, he demanded to be updated on the capture of his father's murderer, and insisted on being sent a return ticket.

When Merion was finished, he held the paper up to the light of a high window, like a trophy of his utter dissatisfaction with the world.

'You done?' grumbled the bald dolt behind the counter.

'Yes,' Merion replied. 'Yes, I am.' He returned to find his two silver coins had been already been pocketed. 'To the office of Constable Jimothy Pagget, Gibbet Street, London, the Empire of Britannia.'

'Here,' said the clerk, sliding an envelope across the counter. 'Write it yourself. That'll cost you a copper dime by the way,' he sniffed, as Merion pulled a bronze penny from his pocket. 'Don't send many letters over the Iron Ocean.'

Merion looked the man square in the eye. 'Well, from now on it will be a regular occurrence,' he told him, and then glanced back at the desk. 'That pen needs more ink.'

The clerk gave him a look that seemed to suggest Merion had just asked for a pouch of gold nuggets instead of a pot of ink. He shook his head, tutted, and produced a fresh bottle from underneath the counter. 'Don't be using it all up now.'

Merion had half a mind to spill the ink on the floor as he made his way back to the desk. He scratched out the address as quick as he could, and then pressed the letter into the clerk's palm, along with another copper coin. 'So it gets there a little faster,' said Merion, puffing out his chest.

'Hmph,' replied the clerk, and as Merion gingerly slid through the swinging doors, he added, 'You'll be lucky.'

But Merion did not hear him. He was too focused on his next task: he had business at the train station.

✦

'*How much?*' Merion shouted over the deafening hissing of the locomotive. A fresh batch of workers had just arrived, adding to the chaos that gripped the town. 'It sounded like you said fifty gold florins!'

'That's right, sixty gold florins!'

'*Sixty?*'

The driver, whose name badge said 'Eldrew', was a big pile of lard topped off with a big black beard that was thicker than a hedge. His face, what little of it could be seen, was smeared with engine grease and coal dust. His eyes twinkled in the sun as he gazed at his beast of a machine. He could have been staring at one of the street whores, the way he eyed her up and down. Taking a grubby hand from his pocket, he flashed five fingers, then one. 'Sixty!' he shouted again.

Merion's heart sank. *Sixty gold florins.*

'Somebody has paid a lot of money for me to be here,' he whispered to himself, his words lost in the hissing of the engine. People milled around him. There was the occasional shove, or casual elbow. Merion didn't feel a thing. He just stared at the great big jets of steam erupting from the locomotive's jagged vents and wondered how he could ever gather together such a large amount of money. His mind tumbled over a wandering path of logic, aching for a plan, a scheme, anything that could get him all the way to the ocean and beyond. All the while he thumbed the few coins he had in his pockets.

How did people make such vast sums of money?

Business!

But what do businesses depend on? His mind wandered back to his lessons with Lord Danker Crumb, and his fabulously boring lectures on the commercial structure of the Empire.

Product!

But what could he sell? All he had was his luggage.

Luggage!

Merion's fingers flashed in front of him as he mentally totted up the worth of his personal effects, his only earthly possessions save for the clothes on his back. He soon became irritated. Not enough.

What else could he sell? What else was there, aside from products?

Skills!

But wait just one moment. He couldn't bake worth a damn. He couldn't hammer a nail or tend a garden. He couldn't work a railroad. He couldn't sing, nor play any instrument besides a smattering of the celloine, and he couldn't imagine the wild west being very tolerant of such a thing. He couldn't paint. He couldn't write, and besides, he found authors to be whinging, pompous creatures, their heads far too full of nonsense. All in all, his list of skills was wearing pretty thin.

There was one thing he was good at, however, and that was sneaking. Merion's thoughts progressed from sneaking to burglary, as all desperate minds are wanton to do. He did know a certain faerie who could turn invisible, after all. Then he heard his father's voice in the hall, and remembered watching from behind the banister as his father berated a police constable for letting a notorious art thief escape. *Thieves,* he had bellowed, *are the scum of this society, sir. A blight not to be taken lightly! They thieve not because they are unskilled, sir, but because they are simply too lazy! They feed off the very men that might have employed them in the first place, and gnaw at the foundations of this great Empire!*

It was then that Merion realised the locomotive had run out of spit and vigour, and was now squatting contentedly on the tracks. He also noticed that the driver was now staring at him, as he had been for the last few minutes. A pair of grubby fingers clicked in front of his nose, and he shook himself out of his daze.

'I said, you alright, sonny?'

Merion nodded vigorously, more to shake the cobwebs from his eyes than anything. 'Yes. perfectly fine, thank you.'

'Looked like you'd been cursed for a moment there. Done near scared me to hell.'

Merion bowed. 'My apologies. I wonder if I could ask you one more question, if I may?'

The driver went right back to staring at his beloved locomotive. 'Shoot.'

Merion put on one of his best smiles, one that said, 'I'm a very hard worker', as well as screaming 'Please, please help me'.

'You wouldn't happen to be looking for any more staff, would you?' he asked.

Some of you, whether once upon a time or very recently, might have had the pleasure of meeting a man of the girth similar to our good locomotive driver. A man of, and let's try to be polite here, *gargantuan* proportions. If you've met such a man, you may also be aware of a certain phrase: 'The bigger the man, the bigger the laugh'.

So it was that the driver's braying roars of laughter followed Merion all the way down the steps of the platform, and all the way to the next street. But Merion was not deterred.

Jobs. Jobs. Jobs. He scanned every window and doorway as he swerved his way through the milling crowds. The addition of another fifty or so workers had done wonders for the level of conversation. The rushing noise of gossip and chatter was now so loud that it gave Merion a headache. No blacksmith, bank, or apothecary wanted a young lordling fresh from the Empire. Some laughed like the driver. Others just grumbled rudely. He refused to try the post office, and couldn't even get near the taverns. And if that wasn't hopeless enough, the owner of the only general store he found didn't speak the common, and every single one of the stables played havoc with his sinuses.

And so, after a truly dejecting morning, Merion found himself trudging up the hill into the Runnels. He found his aunt's house where he had left it, but it was what he found on her sun-bleached porch that made him jump.

'Mornin',' grunted the stranger, tipping his wide-brimmed hat, and then dragging it even lower over his grizzled face. He was sat on the only bench available, lounging against one of its rickety arms. The man was dark-skinned, and seemingly made of scars and leather. Merion followed the winding lines through his stubble, wandering down to his neck. The rest of the man was covered in brown, desert-worn leather. From his thick gloves to his spurred boots, to his hat and necklace of lizard's teeth, only his neck and his face braved the hot air. Most curious of all, however, was the company he kept.

A small magpie perched on his left shoulder. It stared at Merion with its one good eye, the one that was still jet-black and bottomless, rather than shrivelled and misty. The bird clacked his beak together once, twice, three times.

The man lifted a gloved hand to stroke the magpie's chest. 'Easy there,' he rumbled in a low voice. 'He don't like new people.'

Merion climbed the last few steps onto the porch. He could see more of the stranger's face from there. A once-broken nose, an ear sporting more than a few notches, and a cheek spread thick with salt and pepper stubble. 'I think I am beginning to feel the same,' murmured the boy.

'Everyone's new at some point or other.' The man shrugged, and went back to stroking his magpie, which still had its beady eye fixed on Merion, as the boy lingered by the front door.

It was then that the man began to sniff. It was gentle at first; Merion barely noticed it. Then he saw the man's nostrils moving faster, wider, until he was snorting loudly. Merion was just about to ask whether he was having sort of fit when the man suddenly fell still. His lip began to curl.

'Empire.'

Merion rolled his eyes. 'Half the town could tell that from my accent.'

'London.'

'Again, it's not a hard guess.'

'West of the Palace.'

Merion opened his mouth to say something, but the words died on his tongue. *Was this a little taste of magic?* He could not help but wonder. 'Go on,' he said.

'You had pines where you lived. Big old place too, I bet. By the dust in you.'

Merion was too spellbound to talk. He just urged the stranger on with his eyes.

'Come on a train, and via the sea too. Can tell you only been here a day too. You ain't got the stink for it. You will though.' The man took another quick sniff. 'Got another smell on you too … though one I'll be damned if I recognise …' The stranger bent almost imperceptibly forwards from the old bench.

Merion quickly put an end to the trick. 'So can I help you with anything at all?' he asked.

'Just fine here, thank you.' The stranger leant back, and even had the audacity to put his boots up on the porch's creaking railing. 'Your aunt should be back soon. She knows me.'

'How well?'

The stranger tipped his hat again. 'Well enough,' he said. His magpie squawked in agreement.

'What a comforting answer,' Merion grumbled. 'Where is my aunt, anyway?'

The man pointed a leather finger back down into town, and then west, towards the brown hills in the distance, where the view shivered in the roasting heat of the desert. 'Halfway down the rail, so I hear. Tending to a body. Latest in a long line.'

'With that Eugin fellow?'

The stranger slapped his knee and cackled, making Merion jump. 'That fat tub of lard. He's slower than a mule. She ought to get a fresher understudy, that's for sure.'

Had the stranger been looking, he might have seen Merion's ears prick up. An idea slowly crawled out into the open of his mind. It wasn't the finest idea mankind had ever witnessed, but it was better than some of the worst. Merion made his excuses and started down the wooden steps. 'I trust you will not burgle the house while I'm gone. You and your magpie?'

The stranger tipped his hat once more. 'You got my word, son,' he said.

'I wonder how much that is worth,' Merion whispered to himself as he trudged back down the trail.

CHAPTER IX

OF MAGICK WITH A K

'Leg's opened up again. Found some pine sap to bind it, though I don't know how long it'll last. I think I've lost them for now. Need to disappear, need to keep moving. It's getting heavier, I swear. And colder. Damn winter. There's a house ahead.'

7th May, 1867

'Hand me that short shovel, Eugin. No, the shovel, not the pickaxe, you lump,' Lilain scolded as Eugin bumbled about. 'Go stand over there. See if the sheriffsmen want a hand with the rail-bones.' Lilain pointed to where a group of blue-coated men stood in a tight circle around a ball of crushed iron that resembled a wide grinning skull. She shivered momentarily.

Eugin shook his head. 'No chance of that, Lilain,' he replied. 'None'll touch 'em. Bad luck, they're sayin'.'

Lilain pulled a face. 'Nothing wrong with rail-bones. They're just bits of dead iron now,' she asserted. Lilain had found the shovel, and she was now digging it into the space between a knuckle of bent iron rail and the dead man's hip. 'Now get over there and stay away from this body.'

'Yes, ma'am.' Suitably scolded, Eugin bobbed his head and then scuttled away towards the sheriffsmen.

Lilain mumbled to herself as she prized the knuckle of rail free of the corpse's crushed pelvis. With her knee, she manoeuvred the body a little to the right, and then let the rail fall back into the sand. 'Maker, is it hot today! How and *ow!'* she hissed suddenly, catching her finger on the sharp edge of the rail. She ripped a little gauze from the roll she kept in her pocket and wound it around her finger until she couldn't see blood.

'Never lose a drop,' she whispered, then shook her head and smiled.

'Are you hurt?' said a young, foreign voice.

Lilain whirled around to face him. 'Merion,' she stated flatly. 'What are you doing here?'

'I came to find you.'

'You should have stayed at the house.' She sounded annoyed, upset even. Merion was a little surprised to say the least. 'It's dangerous on the railroad.'

'But there are so many people …' Merion turned to look at the tangled clumps of people stretching from the bloody spot on the rails all the way back to the station, the squat blotch in the distance. 'The workers seem furious.'

Lilain rubbed her chin. Like any Hark, she didn't like to be proved wrong, however trivial the matter. 'Hmm, you're right, I suppose. Besides, you might be more useful than my current assistant.'

Merion turned around to look at Eugin, and found the young man staring right back at him. He thought about waving, but tried an awkward smile instead. 'As long as I don't have to touch any blood,' he said to his aunt.

Lilain raised her eyebrows at that. Merion tried to gauge what she was thinking. She was surprised, that was for sure, but she soon blinked the expression away, and shrugged. 'Well, I can't promise you that. As you can see, the deceased is rather … beside himself.' Lilain pointed to both halves of the dead man. This one had been severed at the waist, and the two halves had come to rest several feet apart, trailing Almighty knows what across the sand. Merion wished he hadn't looked. His eyes had been avoiding the carnage until now.

Gulp.

There it was, the bile, that old friend, rising up to burn his throat and make his chest heave.

'Close your eyes and swallow hard,' Lilain wagged an advisory finger. 'And if that don't work, make sure to spew somewhere other than here.'

Merion did as he was told, scrunching his eyes up tight and pushing back the bile as hard as he could. 'It worked,' he gasped, as the urge to vomit slowly faded. 'Where were you on the *Tamarassie?*'

'The what?'

Merion pointed back east, as if the ocean lay just over the rolling hills. 'The ship I sailed on to get here.'

'Ah. You'll have to tell me all about that. How about tonight? Over my famous pork chops. That is, if you're not leaving us just yet?'

Merion bit the inside of his lip. 'The train was delayed.' The excuse sounded stupid, but it was all he had. Lilain nodded, and a warm smile spread across her cheeks.

'Well I'm glad it was,' she replied, then quickly got to her feet. 'Now then, let's get this poor old fellow onto the cart, agreed?'

Merion sighed. 'I am assuming I don't have a choice.'

Lilain chuckled and rested a hand on his shoulder. 'If you're to be my helper, then no.'

'Do I get paid?'

'Just like your father. Tell you what, let's call this a trial run. You do a good job, I'll see what I can rustle up.'

Merion beamed, but then crumbled as he remembered something. 'Oh. There's a man on your porch.'

Lilain had moved to the lower half of the man, and was reaching for his ankles. 'Did he have a magpie on his shoulder? Here, give me a hand,' she asked, as casually as though she were asking for a match.

Merion took a look at the man's bloodied and booted feet and felt that bile rising. *Eyes. Swallow.* He repeated it over and over until he felt almost normal again. At least as normal as you can be, whilst grabbing at the blood-encrusted jeans of half a rail worker. He could smell fear on the man, as well as the dank, soiled smell of a messy death.

'Yes he did. However did you know?' Merion grunted as he tried not to take in too much of the foul air. The body lurched as they pulled on it. It left in its wake things that Merion dearly hoped he would never have to see again. *The pay better be good.*

Lilain chuckled. 'Oh, that's just Lurker. He's a friend.'

'Lurker? What an odd name.'

'Well, he does have a tendency to lurk, as you've probably seen. He looks mean but he's a big pushover really.'

Eugin hovered around them as they dragged the half-corpse to the sun-bleached bed of the cart, angled as it was like a ramp.

'Eugin, the cart.'

'Yes ma'am.' Eugin scuttled forward, eager to be of use again. Merion could have sworn that he muttered something as he hurried past, but he could not be sure.

Once both halves of the worker were securely in position and a blanket had been spread over the cart, Lilain pushed a shovel into Eugin's sweaty palms.

'Would you look after the mess, Eugin? Merion and I will take Mr Gowl here to the table. Thank you. And remember to get those three sil'erbits from the sheriffsmen too. I won't let 'em forget that I don't do this out of the kindness of my own heart.'

Eugin worked his gums for a while, and then finally just nodded.

'Good,' she said, and then gestured for Merion to take one of the cart's handles. 'We've got an appointment in the basement, haven't we Mr Gowl?' she remarked jovially to the blank face of the corpse. With a grunt and a shove, the cart bumbled out of its rut and began to follow them across the baked dirt and sand towards the heart of town.

Merion was already sweating buckets. 'I do wish you wouldn't be so ...'

'So what?'

'... *casual* about the dead.'

Lilain pulled that face of hers again, the one she had mocked him with at the station the night before, her feigned lady of the court. 'One has to be casual around the dead, Merion, so that one can avoid succumbing to the dreadful melancholy,' she chuckled. 'You'd do well to remember that one, trust me.'

Merion could feel the eyes of the townspeople and workers on them. It made him sweat even more. 'Why are they staring?'

'People like to think there's a big invisible wall around Fell Falls. They like to think it keeps the wild out and them safe behind their doors. But as I told you last night, that ain't true.' Lilain wrinkled her nose and shook her head. She made sure to keep her voice low so that only he could hear. 'So when they see the victims of the wild carted through town for all to see, it reminds them of what's just a stone's throw away, and for a moment it shakes their stubborn trailblazer's spirit. Just for a moment,' she opined wryly.

Merion pondered the faces of the crowd as it parted for them. Some were blank of expression. Others sobbed. Some even looked angry, staring at the body then off into the wild, as if promising vengeance. Others just looked plain scared, chewing on second thoughts. He was grateful in a way, that his aunt was not wrapping the reality of Fell Falls in cotton wool for him. It just made him want to leave that much quicker.

Merion missed the narrowed eyes, hidden deep in the crowd, eying him up and down, and mentally making notes. Eyes that watched him like a hawk.

✭

The stranger was in the exact same position as Merion had left him, nearly an hour ago now. His boots were still on the railing and the magpie was still on his shoulder. Once again, it fixed Merion with its beady eye, and followed him all the way to the steps of the porch. Only then did this Lurker fellow click his fingers at the bird. 'Hey,' he spoke softly. 'Let him be now.'

Merion was thankful, but he did not mention it. *Lurker.* What kind of a name was that anyway?

As his aunt climbed the steps, the stranger got to his feet. Merion had gauged him to be tall, but not *that* tall. Even as stooped as his posture was, he had to be nudging six and a half feet, maybe even seven. 'Lil,' he said, tugging at the brim of his hat.

Lilain waved her bloody hands and smiled. 'Lurker, always a pleasure.'

There was a moment of silence between the two adults, during which Merion tapped his foot and Lurker sniffed. Lilain put a hand on the boy's shoulder. 'Merion, why don't you go into the house? Lurker can help me with Mr Gowl.'

'Sure,' Merion replied, and gladly went into the house, eager to be out of the hot sun and out from under the stare of the strange man and his magpie. He went straight to his room.

Upon opening the door he found Rhin splayed out under the edge of the bed, groaning. At first Merion thought he'd been attacked, or had an accident of some kind. Then he noticed the faerie's stomach; the round ball that was now trying so very hard to escape from between the buttons of his leather shirt.

'Unnnghh,' wailed the faerie. 'I ate the whole thing.'

'The whole of ...' Merion stuttered. 'The breakfast?'

'It took me an hour.'

'Almighty ...'

'He can't help me now. By the Roots, I'm stuffed. And thirsty too.'

'Bacon will do that to you.'

Rhin groaned at the very mention of the meat. 'How was the town?'

'Bloody,' Merion replied, holding up his crimson hands for the faerie to see. Rhin tried to sit up but immediately regretted his decision. 'Yours?' he gasped.

'No. Mr Gowl's.'

'Who?'

Merion held up a pair of empty hands. 'Some worker, eaten by a railwraith. He's in two bits. Maybe three, I didn't want to check.'

Rhin stared wide-eyed at the mangled springs of the bed. 'Almighty indeed,' he said thoughtfully. 'Was it close to town?'

'On the very outskirts.'

'Did you see it?'

Merion raised an eyebrow. 'If I didn't know any better, Rhin, I'd say you were intrigued.'

The faerie slapped his hands on the floorboards. 'Of course I'm interested. I'm trying to embrace the wild, as you should be. Facing up to being a man, or whatever it is you humans do.'

But Merion shook his head and thrust out his jaw. 'No, I refuse. I will be leaving this place very shortly.'

Rhin sighed. 'So your little excursion went well, did it? Got a train ticket, have we?'

Merion puckered his lips. 'No, not yet.'

This time, Rhin managed to prop himself up on his elbows and swivel so he could see Merion's face, as he stood cross-armed in the middle of the room. 'Go on. How much?'

Merion muttered something incomprehensible.

Rhin put a mottled hand to one of his pointy ears. 'Sorry? Didn't quite catch that.'

Merion practically snarled the answer. 'Sixty florins!'

'Roots, boy, no need to shout.'

'Don't call me boy. Not today. Besides, I sent a letter. To Constable Pagget, demanding passage home and the capture of my father's murderer.'

Rhin nodded. 'Well then, not a complete waste of a day,' he quietly replied.

'I want that bastard caught. Caught and hung for his crimes.' Merion clenched a fist and considered sending it barrelling into the wall. He clenched his fist to his chest, and thought better of it.

'So who's the fellow on the porch?' Rhin asked.

Merion scowled. 'Some friend of my aunt's. A man called Lurker.'

'Lurker?'

'That's right.'

'Sounds pleasant. So where are they now?'

'Putting the body on the table, I suppose.'

'Well, do you know what he does, where he's from? You said there was something fishy about your aunt. Could be talking about you,' Rhin suggested.

Merion bit his lip. 'Why would they be talking about me?' he asked.

Rhin shrugged, leather shoulders and gossamer wings squeaking softly on the wood. 'Well, you could always go find out. In the basement, you said. Nice and dark down there, I imagine.' Rhin even threw in a wink for good measure.

'You have a way with words, Master Fae.'

'And your aunt has a way with meat and pans. Now get going, before I pass out from the strain of talking.'

'Gluttonous beast,' Merion muttered as he snuck out of the door and into the corridor.

✫

The basement steps were shrouded in darkness, just how he liked it. Merion tiptoed down the dusty steps, careful to stick close to the wall or the railing so the old wood would not creak. He could hear the soft pattering of conversation at the far end of the basement, near the table. Inch by careful inch, Merion crept forward, straining to pick words out of the jumble of hushed voices. Whatever they were talking about, they did not even trust the dead. For some reason, Mr Gowl had the blanket bundled up around his head.

He could hear Lilain talking. Even though she was whispering, he could sense the frustration in her voice. 'How can you trust them? They send worker after worker to the front, hoping that sheer numbers will get this railroad of theirs built. Greed, over men's lives. More and more are going to die when he gets here, believe me. He'll bring them down by the carriage-load. It'll be a buffet for the wraiths.'

'More work for you.'

'Like I need that. Grim enough as it is.'

'You got a boy to support now, Lil. Ain't no stopping progress. Lord Serped will get this railroad built if it kills him.'

There was that name again. Merion cupped a hand behind his ear.

'Word has it another line's being driven into the ground to the north, Spelltown, just out of the Shohari killing grounds. Say they're going to break even by winter, at the rate they're going.'

'No wraiths?'

'Not a peep. Got bears though. Rockbears. Even a ghostbear or two, if my ears ain't fooled me.'

From the shadows, Merion watched his aunt sigh and let her head roll back so she could stare at the ceiling. 'How I would love to get my hands on one of those.'

'For your collection?'

'Whyever else? Come on, what news of your Shohari friends?'

'Still intent on moving south.'

'Serped won't like that.'

'War parties have already reached Shamrok. Some say Kaspar City's in danger.'

'Pah. Serped ain't the only lord in that town.'

'What is it with you Empire lot?'

Lilain chuckled drily. 'Like to be in charge is all. Believe it's a birthright. We, *they*, rule two thirds of the world, and what they don't rule they infiltrate with business and industry. Anyways, enough of this talk, I need to get dissecting Missus Hanniver's cat.'

'Cats again?'

'Popular stuff, Lurker.'

'Thanks, again.'

'Always a pleasure.'

Merion froze as Lurker turned on his heel and marched towards the stairs. Merion pressed himself tightly to the brick wall and hoped the shadows would help him. The sound of Lurker's boots grew loud, and Merion watched the tall figure pace past him in the darkness. The magpie squawked accusingly, but Lurker simply touched his fingers to the brim of his hat, and kept on walking. Not a word was said.

Merion let go of the breath he had been holding and felt his body sag. *That was close, too close.*

It was then that Lilain's voice rang out, clear as a bell.

'I do not abide sneaking in this house, young man.'

Merion quickly got to his feet and tried to make it look as though he had just passed Lurker on the stairs. 'I was not sneaking, Aunt Lilain,' he asserted haughtily. 'I don't sneak.'

Lilain looked him up and down slowly. She scowled, though with her smiling creases it was hard to tell if she was serious or not. 'You're a boy, aren't you?' she asked. 'All boys sneak. So says Lurker.'

Merion carefully slipped around the side of the table and found his favourite stool, right where he had left it. As he approached, something on the wood of the seat caught the light and sparkled momentarily. Merion leant down so he could peer at the glittering culprit. He ran a cursory finger across the wood and then held a sparkling fingertip up to the light.

Lilain waved a hand. 'Gold dust. Lurker was sat there.' As she spoke, she gathered her tools and instruments: several vials, a syringe, and half a dozen tarnished instruments that sported a dazzling array of blades, prongs, and other such sharp edges.

Once Merion had finished wiping his seat down with the sleeve of his shirt, he took a seat 'So he's a gold miner then?' he guessed.

Lilain smiled, a hint of pride there, or so Merion thought. 'A prospector. The very best. People say the gold dried up a year ago, but somehow Lurker keeps sniffing it out,' she cast him a glance then, as if to watch his reaction.

Merion wore a puzzled look. 'Sniff it out,' was all he said. Now that he was sat down, he found that he was extremely tired. Far too tired to ponder riddles and strange prospectors. 'And what about that magpie?'

'Jake? Ha, an old friend.'

'Why do you keep such strange company out here in the west?'

Lilain looked up from cleaning her blades and raised an eyebrow. 'Do you not keep strange company, Merion?'

Merion could feel the damned guilty heat rising in his cheeks. 'What do you mean?' he whispered. *Surely she could not know ...*

Then her serious face cracked into a smile, and Merion knew he was safe. He smiled back shakily. 'You're one of us now, aren't you? We are your strange company,' she said.

'Ha, quite,' Merion replied, wondering how long he could wear his smile for. It was already starting to slip. 'So, a cat?' he asked, hopping subjects.

'A cat indeed!' Lilain manoeuvred a small tray onto her infamous table. On it sat a small object hidden under a little square blanket. 'Do you like cats?'

Merion shook his head vehemently. 'Not in the slightest.'

'Good, so you won't cry when I cut up puss then,' Lilain chuckled, dragging the blanket off 'puss'. It was a mangy tabby, dead as a doornail and slack as a flag on a windless day. Its eyes, which of course were staring right at Merion, were a deep oaken brown. Empty, and flat.

'Real men cannot be seen to cry,' Merion told her, sitting a little straighter.

Lilain snorted as she lifted her scalpel. 'Another of my brother's gems? Thought so,' she replied. She waved her blade about in mid-air as her eyes roved over the cat, looking for a spot to strike. But she didn't move, not for a while. Instead, she looked up at her nephew, still twirling the scalpel, and said, 'So then. What shall we talk about tonight?'

Merion cocked his head to one side. 'I'm happy to listen if you're happy to talk.'

Lilain nodded. 'That I am. There's a lot to talk about, Merion, that's for sure,' she said. 'Can I take it this means you're staying?'

Merion pursed his lips, trying to keep the words from coming out until he had mulled them over first. He didn't like the sound of them one bit, but they were all he had. 'For a while,' he muttered.

Lilain winked at him. 'Good,' she replied, obviously thrilled to hear it. 'Now,' she said, with a flourish of her scalpel, 'let's get on with the job.'

Job.

Merion held up a finger. 'Speaking of jobs, Aunt Lilain,' he began, trying to sound as authoritative and business-like as humanly possible, 'I was wondering whether we could discuss the prospect of mine.'

'Ah yes,' Lilain said, as she slid her blade along the belly of the cat. 'Now I have to say, you did a good job today. No complaints. Did the work. Few too many questions, but we'll deal with that. So what do you say? Want to learn what I do?'

Merion forced himself to nod. 'And my salary?'

'Ah, *salary*. Now, let's see. Eugin get's a sil'erbit and four copper dimes for every body. You'll have to share a few shifts with him first. Can't let him go right away, now can I? One sil'erbit a body, for the next week. What d'you say to that?' Lilain raised her bloody fingers, and smiled. Merion stared into the dead eyes of the cat while he did his sums.

The boy practically sagged under the weight of the numbers as they climbed and climbed. Unless the entire populace of Fell Falls caught the plague and perished overnight, it would take years to raise those damned sixty florins.

'However, there will be a little rent to pay,' added Lilain.

Merion met Lilain's eyes, finding not a trace of humour in them. No wink in sight. 'What?' he gasped.

Lilain shrugged casually, ignoring Merion's fuming gaze. 'You're living under my roof now, Merion. Food and keep cost money in places like this. Got bills to pay.'

'*Bills?*' Merion found himself spluttering as he hopped down from the stool. 'What bills? You live in a desert. You don't even have running water.'

Lilain put her hands on her hips. 'I don't have heating either. Don't forget about that. I've got an extra mouth to feed now, don't forget. And there's equipment, supplies, taxes.'

'Taxes?'

'The world runs on taxes, Merion. You of all people should know that.'

Merion, of all people, knew one thing and one thing only: 'This is unbelievable,' he hissed, as he stormed off in the direction of the stairs.

'You stop right there, Tonmerion!' Lilain barked in a voice that Merion not heard before, one that stopped him rather forcefully in his tracks. It had that Hark ring to it, that commanding tone he longed to hear in his own unbroken voice. He slowly turned around to find Lilain walking slowly towards him. The scalpel was thankfully on the table where it belonged. Her arms were crossed, but even so, Merion could still tell that her fists were clenched. 'Now don't you go shouting at me because you can't have what you want. So life ain't fair, and you got dealt a bad hand of cards. I feel for you, but life rarely is fair, and we play with the hand we're dealt. Nothing you can do to change that. So don't you go yelling and snapping at me, the woman, the *aunt*, who's putting you up and taking you in, who's given you a job that don't involve dancing with railwraiths. You understand?'

'Yes,' Merion whispered.

His aunt leant closer and cupped a hand behind her ear. 'Do you understand me?' she repeated.

'Yes,' Merion said again, louder this time.

A firm hand directed him back to his stool. 'Good. Now, fire away,' Lilain ordered him, and all sternness crumbled away by the time she had returned to her scalpel and her dead cat.

Merion was a little bamboozled, to say the least. 'What?'

'Questions. I know you've got 'em, so fire away.'

Merion shuffled on the stool, making it creak. 'Erm,' he said, wiping his brow. 'Alright. Lurker. What's his game?'

Lilain had already begun stripping the fur from the cat. 'Gold, nephew, and lots of it. Now before you start thinking about loans and favours, forget it. The man would never lend you a dime. Not a selfish man, by any means. No. He just squirrels it away for some reason.'

'Don't people ever try and rob him?'

His aunt laughed loudly at that. 'Oh, they try alright, the fools that don't know who he is. You've seen how big he is, right? But that ain't all. Lurker's got magick in him.'

'With a k?'

'Most definitely a k, young nephew.'

Merion couldn't help but let his eyes grow wide. *Almighty damn this woman and her stories, and this land and its magic too*, he cursed quietly to himself.

Lilain went on, working in her usual calm and precise way. Once again, Merion couldn't help but watch. 'He spent some time in the south, or so he's said. Fighting for Lincoln in the great forests of Missipine. Doesn't talk about it much. He's a quiet man, and I know he's seen things he'd give all his gold to forget. Apparently he ran into the Shohari down there, and they don't take too kindly to us humans.'

'You say it like they're not ...'

'Not what?'

'Human.'

Lilain wagged her scalpel and tutted. 'That's because they're not. Different physiology. Had a look inside one in Chicago, and believe you me, their bodies are almost more animal than humans. Long necks, big shoulders, long limbs, chiselled features, greenish skin, and blood so dark it might as well be called black. But they are wise, and old, and they have had magick in their blood since the earth was young. It's kept them wild and fierce.'

'Animals then?' suggested Merion.

'No, you'd be wrong to think so. They're an intelligent race, Merion, make no mistake. They know more about this earth than all the historians and scientists of America and the Empire combined.'

'So what did these creatures do to him? Is that why his face is scarred?'

Lilain flashed him a smile. 'No, they let him go. Something about him stayed their knives. He's been able to walk their hunting grounds ever since. So, you can imagine the gossip. That's why he keeps himself to himself.'

'Why?'

His aunt nodded. 'Shohari saw the magick in him. Got it from his mother, I hear. They let him go because of that. Rumour has it he comes from an old line of wilder-walkers—explorers and trailblazers to you and me—and the story is that they might have had Shohari blood running in their veins.'

Merion put a hand to his nose. 'Is that how he does his sniffing thing?'

Lilain nodded, flicking a strand of yellow hair from her eyes.

Merion was not about to waste any time mulling over the answers. He launched straight into his next question. 'So who's this Lord Serped?' he asked.

Lilain hummed as she opened up the cat and bared its organs to the lantern's light. She was looking for something now, her fingers inching towards the syringe and the empty vial at her elbow. 'So you were eavesdropping.'

Merion shuffled around. 'No, actually. I heard his name mentioned today, in town.'

Lilain fired off question after question. 'By whom?'

Merion answered as fast as he could think. 'A man.'

'Where?'

'At the station. He was complaining about the railroad.'

Lilain wasn't buying what Merion was selling, not for one moment. 'Was he now?' she mused. 'Lord Serped,' she began, and here she made a little sound of disgust as she reached for the heart of the cat. Merion leant forwards so he could watch her deftly slicing the connecting arteries and veins. It was gruesomely fascinating, he had to admit. 'Lord Serped is Empire-born, no doubt an affiliate of your father's at some time or another. His business is transport. His father designed the roads of Washingtown, so he's got some big boots to fill, where Lincoln is concerned. So what better way to prove himself than driving a railroad straight to the shores of the Last Ocean, taking upon himself a task that no ship nor horse nor pair of feet has ever succeeded in doing.'

'Has he bitten off more than he can chew?'

Lilain smirked at that. 'Probably, but he's a stubborn bastard. And stinking rich. He'll see it through.'

Merion hummed. 'I'm starting to get the impression that you might not like the man.'

'I'm not overly fond of the kind of men who exploit the desperation of others for profit, throwing the lives of men aside like old handkerchiefs whilst blindingly surging forwards into the unknown without due care, attention, or respect. So no, Lord Serped won't be invited to sit at my table in the near future.'

Merion couldn't help but ask. 'An Empire man, you say?'

Lilain threw him a sour look. 'Getting more ideas about leaving are we?'

Merion shook his head and looked back at the cat. Its heart now lay in a porcelain dish at the tail-end of the table. Lilain's hands hovered above it, the needle of the syringe dancing over the organ's puckered chambers. Lilain's lips began to move, slowly at first, then faster. Merion watched as she gently slid the needle into the heart and drew back on the plunger. Dark red blood gurgled into the syringe's glass chamber. There wasn't much to be had, but Lilain got every last drop. She did not rest until the syringe was over half full.

With a level of gracefulness and precision that bordered on the reverent, Lilain gently decanted the contents of the syringe into the conical vial. When every drop had been squeezed from it, Lilain laid it down, put a tiny cork in the mouth of the vial, and held it up to the nearest lantern.

'What are you looking for?' Merion asked. His words shattered the silence, and he felt for all the world as though he had just farted loudly during a church service.

'Purity,' Lilain whispered.

Merion pulled a face. 'Are you ... *collecting* that?'

Lilain licked her lips and put the vial down. 'Let me ask you a question,' she said, placing her hands on the edge of the table and leaning forwards so she could look Merion clear in the eyes. 'Have you mourned for your father?'

Merion was quite taken aback. '*Excuse me*?' he spluttered.

Lilain kept on at him. 'Have you mourned for him, Merion, since leaving the Empire's shores?'

'I fail to see why this is any of your bus—'

His aunt's face was like flint, hard and unflinching. 'Because it's important, Merion, even though real men cannot be seen to cry, they are *allowed* to cry. Do you understand me? I guess what I'm asking is, have you wept for your father since he died?'

Merion once again hopped down from the stool, bristling with anger. That old fire was back and burning bright. His aunt had most certainly struck a nerve this time, and a raw one at that. 'That is none of your business! I wouldn't dare ask anybody such a question!'

Lilain slapped her hands on the edge of the table. 'But if you did, I would answer yes, Merion, that I *have* wept for my dead brother. Because it's necessary for getting the anger and frustration and hurt out. Trust me on this one, Merion.'

But Merion had been pushed too far. 'I don't want to trust you,' he snapped. 'And I don't want to talk about this!'

'Merion …!' Lilain called after him, but the young Hark was already halfway to the stairs. 'Tonmerion!'

'No!' came the reply, swiftly followed by the sound of a slamming door.

Lilain grit her teeth and thumped a palm against the table. 'Shit!' she hissed.

'And what's the matter with you?' Rhin asked as Merion stormed into the bedroom. The door almost burst from its hinges he shut it so hard.

Merion paced like there was no tomorrow. 'That aunt of mine, that *woman*, dared to talk to me about father. Asked me if I'd cried for him, as if that was of any importance!'

Rhin shuffled out from under the bed and leant against one of its legs. He seemed a little more comfortable now. A few inches had disappeared from his swollen belly.

'Well, have you?' Rhin asked.

Merion threw his hands up into the air in exasperation. 'You as well?'

The faerie quickly surrendered. 'Enough said, lad. Pay me no heed.'

The young Hark pressed his hands to his face. 'That blasted woman …' he could be heard muttering. When he pulled his hands away he sighed. 'I'm exhausted. And tired of today. I'm going to bed.'

Rhin looked out of the window to check that yes, the sun was still firmly stuck in the azure sky. 'But it's barely evening, Merion.'

'Like I said,' mumbled the boy as he flopped onto the bed. His breathing had already slowed and deepened. Rhin climbed onto the bed and watched his chest rising and falling.

'That you apparently are,' he replied. He walked across the bed to where a second pillow sat scrunched up next to Merion's head. Rhin fluttered his wings and then sat down. *It was definitely a lot comfier than his suitcase*, he thought, as he shuffled around, all the while sinking deeper into the pillow. When he was comfortable, he crossed his arms and took a few contemplative breaths. 'So what's the plan?'

'Gold,' mumbled the boy, already drifting into the land of sleep. 'Magic. Failing those, a rich lord of the Empire.'

Rhin pinched the bridge of his nose between his claws. 'Right you are then,' he said in reply. Visions of what the next few weeks might entail passed before his squinting eyes. Torn was the faerie, torn between being a boy's only friend in a foreign land, and a selfish, singular desire that he had come secretly to harbour. He had stored it away in the deepest, darkest recesses of his faerie mind, along with all the other secrets. He knew that if he uttered it, it would have crushed the young Hark to an emotional pulp. Rhin did not want to go home.

CHAPTER X

THE SHOHARI

'I must be mad. I must have lost too much blood to be thinking this
... *[some illegible scribbling here]*
The boy. That impetuous little sod.'

12th May, 1867

Another three bodies graced Lilain Rennevie's mortuary table before the week met its end. And what a scorching week it was. Every day seemed hotter than the last. The ground cracked and the home-grown trees in yards and gardens splintered. No wind. Just the dust, and the dry prickling heat to contend with.

But then Sunday arrived, and with it came rolling black clouds of wind and lightning and deafening thunder. The merciless storm battered Fell Falls into a muddy pulp for a whole afternoon. Merion spent it gawping at the forks of lightning and the strange flashes of green and blue that ran through the black clouds whenever the thunder rolled. The town was soaked to the bone by the time the thunderclouds grew bored, and slipped to the west. Merion was sad to see them go. He had been able to close his eyes and hear the Empire in the pattering of the raindrops.

All in all, it had been a deeply dissatisfying week. The young Hark's days had been spent roaming the town, sleeping through his boredom, or kicking cans across the graveyard while he stewed in his anger and thirst for home.

Evenings had been a completely different kettle of fish. Lilain was an owl. Her work filled the twilight hours. She barely slept more than a few hours a night. Merion would have dropped from exhaustion, but it never seemed to slow her down. Not one bit. Bodies were easier when they were kept cool, or so she said. Night was perfect for that. Merion tried not to form an opinion on the matter.

The railwraiths had struck twice during that blistering week. One was a prospector, found dead and ripped to bloody shreds at the end of the line. There were many different things to carry to the cart that day. Nobody knew his name. Lilain just kept calling him Mr Doe.

The second was another worker, an older gentleman with a face full of creases. Some of the other workers had called him Ole Pa, and he had been like a father to more than a few of them. Lilain had known him as Old Jaspar. The wraiths had kindly ripped his head from his shoulders and left it a hundred yards down the track, almost like a warning.

It was the third body that caused the greatest uproar. A scout by the name of Jeeber had been sent from Kaspar City to prepare the town for Lord Serped's arrival. Unfortunately, he never made it. He was found on the north trail, barely ten miles from the fringes of Fell Falls, a long arrow driven straight through his heart. An arrow fletched with blue and purple feathers. Shohari colours.

All Scout Jeeber's death did was ignite even more anger and fear in the citizens of Fell Falls. With the town swollen with workers and guards, there was gossip aplenty. Emotions were running high. On Merion's long walks and trips to the post office, he had seen more than a few black eyes and missing teeth, and kicked the shattered necks of many a broken bottle with his dusty shoes.

Lilain refrained from sharing her thoughts on the matter, never echoing the gossip. Perhaps it was due to the silver coins that jangled in her pockets, or maybe she simply wanted him to make up his own mind, Merion was not sure. In any case, he felt the fear of the town, and shared it.

By the Almighty, did they talk! Once Merion had firmly asserted to Lilain that the subject of his dead father was not, under any circumstances, to be a part of their conversations, and once Lilain had kindly suggested to Merion that if he was going to make a habit out of laying down rules, he might want to look into the architecture and methods of building a suggestion box, they formed a pact. Merion would get the answers he had begun to thirst for (and what meagre pay his aunt could offer whilst Eugin was slowly yet firmly ousted from her gainful employ), and Lilain got an ear to bend, and a helper to boot.

And so while Merion helped carry limbs and severed heads, and helped clean the tools and table, Lilain let her tongue wag. The work was revolting, but the stories and answers took his mind off the murderous little town, giving him ideas, and therefore hope. There was always a little sting of secrecy in each one of her tales, as though she were still skirting around a truth she was not ready to share.

It was exceedingly curious the way Aunt Lilain harped on about blood. She seemed fascinated by the stuff. In between her stories, his aunt would ramble on about how blood works, and how it sustains life. Honestly, Merion could not have cared less. But he let her prattle on, hoping she would soon get back on topic. What was even more curious, was that she only spoke of blood when she was busy dissecting the variety of dead dogs, cats and rats that Fell Falls had to offer—without forgetting the wild animals that found themselves trapped in fences or drowned in wells. All sorts of strange things found their way onto Lilain's scrubbed table: three-horned goats; desert foxes of a smoky blue colour; beetles as big as Merion's head; dragonflies that actually resembled, well, dragons, even down to their tiny scales and little pin-like teeth. And every time one of these creatures graced her table, the faithful syringe and empty vial were standing ready at her elbow, waiting to be filled.

All this talk of blood posed quite a problem for her young nephew. While his aunt was coldly professional about the whole business, utterly oblivious to the gore she handled so skilfully, blood was the one aspect of a dead body that turned his stomach the most. Merion did not truly know why; all he knew was that the way it dripped, or dribbled, or seeped ... made him shiver. She was too distant, too cold for Merion's liking. He did not want to be like her. The disgust and incredibly strong urge to vomit he felt reminded him he was still normal.

Merion thought it all highly irregular, and wondered whether his aunt were a collector of sorts. Perhaps it was just some strange science, maybe another burial ritual. Merion didn't know, and didn't care.

✦

Fell Falls felt subdued after the rain. The gossipers and minglers had retreated to the saloons and bars, and there they remained. The streets were empty but for a few stubborn sheriffsmen on horseback, churning the wheel ruts and bootprints into mud.

Rhin peeked out at them from under the flap of the rucksack, skin shimmering, half-vanished. Their faces were grim and their beards trimmed short. They were grim yet somehow reassuring, a sign that law and order still held sway at the edges of the world; that even in a place like Fell Falls there were men dedicated to patrolling, and watching, and guarding. Rhin stared at their blue coats and white stripes, and at the triple-barrelled rifles balanced across their laps.

As they trudged deeper into town, it soon became apparent to Rhin that alcohol was very important to the citizenry of Fell Falls. He had lost count of the number of saloons he had already seen. He shrugged. Tough times and alcohol were never far apart. As Merion's quickly deteriorating shoes squelched through the mud, the faerie noted down the places he would explore at another time. The apothecary was high on the list. You could never go wrong with an apothecary. The blacksmith's, that was another stop—he could sharpen his blades nicely if he got a chance. And the stables; it had been a long time since Rhin had last spoken with a horse; they were dumb creatures with a simple tongue, but like faeries, they never refused a chance to gossip. Rhin rubbed his hands in anticipation.

'Where are we going?' he called up to Merion.

'Post office.'

Rhin rolled his eyes. 'Letters. Fun.'

He could hear Merion tutting from above. 'Have some respect. I'm waiting to hear from Pagget.'

'About what?'

Merion elbowed the bag sharply. 'About my father, idiot!'

'Of course.' Rhin bit his lip. 'How long have you been waiting?'

'Almost a week. And last time I had to bicker with an utter dolt behind the counter. You'll see what I mean.'

Rhin didn't know what to say to that, so he just stayed quiet and watched the painted post office emerge from behind a corner. Soon enough, he was being tucked under a counter and poked with a foot. Rhin listened to the clerk shuffle his way out of his well-used chair, heard the crackle of saliva as his lip curled.

'Ah, the little lordlin' returns. That's right, I heard all about you, I did,' said the clerk. Rhin quickly realised that Merion had been right. The man was quite obviously an insufferable little shite.

Merion ignored the clerk's jibes like a trooper. 'Are there any letters for me yet?'

'Not a scrap of paper for you, Lordling.'

'Can you at least look?'

'Of course, your Majesty!' the clerk crowed. Rhin wondered if the clerk would still feel like making jokes if he dug his black knife into his thigh. Rhin's slender hand strayed to the scabbard at his belt, twitching.

There was a moment of rustling and commotion as the clerk made a show of looking through every single pigeonhole and poking his crooked nose under piles of paper and envelopes. He was muttering something about the Empire, that much could be heard. Rhin began to reach for the lip of the rucksack.

'See? Nothin'. Next train won't be in 'til tomorrow, just before the Serpeds arrive. Won't get no mail 'til then. Go away and come back tomorrow, *Lordling*.'

'Tomorrow,' muttered the young Hark as he slipped carefully between the swinging doors. He dragged his rucksack behind him like a broken shield, head low and eyes frustrated.

Merion trudged down the steps, across the street, and down a side-alley, thankful for the coolness of the dark, narrow space, damp and sodden after the rain. The rusted pipes running above his head dripped solemnly. A light mist had begun to rise from the dirt.

The boy shook the rucksack. 'See what I mean? Intolerable.'

No answer came.

'Rhin?' Merion asked again, reaching for the flap.

If you have ever experienced that awful moment where you are on the cusp of falling asleep, mind already wreathed in the first inklings of dreams, and abruptly find yourself falling or tripping. Then you know that lurching ache in your stomach, the flash of dizziness, that thin sliver of panic puncturing your heart. You will know all too well what drove

Merion to his knees, and made his fingers tear frantically at the rucksack's fastenings.

'Rhin!' Merion cried. There wasn't a scrap of armour to be seen. No angry buzzing of wings. No grey skin and purple eyes. The pack was empty.

Merion had always been prone to nightmares. Even before his father's murder, he had often spent his nights shivering at the foot of his bed, trying to shake the monsters from his wide eyes while Rhin patrolled the corners and shadows, knives drawn and wings buzzing. The faerie had always been there to keep him safe. And so it was that his darkest nightmare of all was losing the only true friend he had ever known.

Merion pushed himself to his feet and scrambled towards the post office. 'He must have fallen out,' he muttered frantically to himself. 'Must've snuck off. Damn him!' *Please no. Please, Almighty, no.*

Merion practically sprinted the yards to the swinging doors, but just as he was about to barrel through them, he heard a sharp yelp and a howl from inside. Merion skidded to a halt and threw himself hard against the doorframe instead, edging sideways so he could peek inside.

The clerk had befallen some sort of accident it seemed, an injury of some sort. Merion could not help but smile at the justice. He watched the clerk hopping about madly on one foot, both hands clamped to his thigh. He seemed to have cut himself; blood was creeping into the cracks and creases of his interlocking fingers. His face was the very picture of agony and his tongue was busy painting the air the very definition of blue in between his high-pitched howls. Merion felt as though he were back in the kitchens of Harker Sheer, listening to the potwash men banter over hot murky water and slippery plates.

'Man howls like a rat on a spit,' said a voice down beside him.

Merion was immediately torn between melting into a puddle of eternal gratitude or booting the faerie over the nearest rooftop. Instead, he whirled around and gawped at the semi-transparent faerie, leaning casually against the wall and flicking the last few drops of blood from his black knife. He was smirking.

Merion made a vague strangling noise in his throat. 'You …!'

Rhin instantly noticed the red in Merion's eyes, the white pinch of his cheeks. 'What's wrong?'

'I thought you were gone!' Merion hissed, eyes feverishly scanning the streets for any watchful eyes. 'I thought I'd lost you!'

Rhin nodded. 'Ah. I was actually teaching our rude friend a lesson,' Rhin pointed past Merion, to the doorway. The clerk was delving deep into his arsenal of expletives now. Rhin could hear him banging his hand on the desk in time with his words.

Bang!

'... a shit-swilling, piss-guzzling, mother-fu—'

Bang!

'... Maker-damned, knuckle-dick whore-ass—'

Bang!

'I think that's what the eastern men call "karma",' said the faerie, suppressing another smile. 'Thought you might appreciate it.'

Merion threw his hands up and slapped his forehead. 'You can't wander off without telling me.

Rhin shrugged. 'But I'm fine,' he offered. 'Nothing happened.'

Merion tugged at his hair, blowing loudly though his mouth. He sounded like a trumpet.

Rhin jabbed another finger at the doorway. 'Look, I only wanted to teach that dolt a lesson. Don't you find it funny?' Rhin asked. 'Come on, Merion. I'm safe, as always. Stop worrying. Got my lucky coin, after all.' Rhin patted his chest.

Merion looked to the sky for patience. After a few more moments of counter-banging and scintillatingly descriptive language, Merion threw up his hands and sighed. 'Fine,' he said, unable to keep his face from breaking into a mischievous smile. He held open the rucksack and quickly scooped the faerie up, then returned to the doorway to enjoy a little more of that sweet vengeance. The clerk was sprawled on the counter now, trying to see what the hell it was that stuck him.

'Did you give him the whole blade?' Merion whispered.

Rhin's voice was tight with amusement. 'No, but I think I might have accidentally caught something important in the process.'

Merion had to clamp a hand over his mouth to keep from braying with laughter. Inch by inch, he dragged himself away from Rhin's glorious mischief, and back onto the muddy street.

'Home?' asked Rhin. He was half out of the pack, clinging onto the fraying straps, bold now that the day's light was failing.

Merion's sniggering came swiftly to a stop. 'Don't call it that,' he said.

'Alright. Your aunt's house?'

'Yes.'

Merion headed back to the side-alley and for the north side of the dripping town. The thick, rising mist was now so thick it tried to swallow his boots. Merion kicked out his legs and watched the mist swirl. The alley was darker now that evening was slowly yet inexorably falling. There was a chill in the air, the like of which he had not yet felt in that blistering desert. It sent a shiver up his spine.

Merion flinched when he noticed the figure at the end of the alley, sat against the corner of the building; a hunched-over, cross-legged pile of rags and threadbare sacks. Man or woman, Merion couldn't tell. It was currently bent over the mouth of a drainpipe, making loud slurping noises. Merion slowed his pace, treading softy through the muck. The beggar had yet to notice him, and was still busy with dusty water dribbling from the cracked pipe. One of Merion's boots sunk noisily into a puddle and the beggar looked up. Merion bit his lip, and silently cursed the damned mist.

When the beggar spoke, it was with a voice split with age, use, and harsh drink. A man then, by its depth, and his tone was shaky, weak, and fraying at the edges. 'Spare a coin for an old soldier?' he asked, holding out a dripping hand.

Merion shook his head, but when the beggar did not move, he answered with a firm 'No thank you,' and made to move past. The man stank of sweat and mould. It tickled Merion's nose in a way he did not like at all.

'Just look me in the eye, son, so I know I ain't invisible.'

What a decidedly odd thing to ask, thought Merion. He was about to politely decline once again, but found that his legs were moving of their own volition, dragging him towards the dishevelled heap of a man. He tried to stop himself, but there was something about the man that pulled him in, in the way that a freak at a circus might—that strange voyeuristic urge to stare at those so different from ourselves, and to measure our worlds against theirs.

Merion leant down to meet the man's eyes, hidden as they were under the lip of a filthy hat. He caught a glimpse of a pair of scabbed lips, then a slim broken nose, but before he could reach the eyes, the beggar flicked his head up. Merion couldn't help but flinch, and then again when he realised his gaze was met not by pupils, but by puckered recesses of grey flesh.

'Hehe,' the beggar chuckled, hearing the boy gasp. 'Gets them every time.'

Merion could not stop himself from asking. 'What happened?' he blurted, and then quickly remembered his manners. 'If you don't mind me asking?'

'I would tell you all, for a coin or two,' whispered the beggar, licking his cracked lips with a thin tongue.

Even though he felt Rhin punch him through the canvas of the rucksack, Merion delved into his pocket and pulled out a copper dime. 'Here,' he said, and placed it in the beggar's palm.

The beggar looked around, as if he secretly had eyes after all, and then motioned for the boy to lean closer. 'Ever heard of the Shohari, son?'

Merion's heart beat out a fast patter of excitement and intrigue. 'I have. Did they do this to you?'

The beggar nodded. He frowned, his scars managing to take on a forlorn look. 'And many other things too, son. Many things,' he said. 'Blood and pride.'

'But why?' asked Merion.

Once more, the beggar looked around, as if to check if they were alone. 'Fought them up in the high mountains,' he said, when he was satisfied. 'Back east, years ago, before we pushed the Shohari back out here. They're devils, I tell you. Know a hundred ways to skin a man alive, and they take great pleasure in doing it. The man don't die, see, while they're doing it. They could be wearing him as a coat before they put him out of his misery.' The beggar shuddered then, as if chilled by some awful memory.

'That's horrible,' Merion was revolted.

The beggar nodded sombrely. 'That it is, son. But they're mighty fascinated with us, that they are. Don't stop at the skin, no. Their shamans like to get their paws on as much of us as possible. Brains, liver, tongue, and eyes, of course. Fascinated with our blood too. Say they use us for their spell-making, they do. We've got power in our veins, I think, and they want it.'

Merion bent down to a crouch and leant closer to the man. Curiosity, battling with the stench. 'What kind of power? Like magick?' he asked.

The beggar took a breath before answering. He did not seem to share Merion's excitement, it had to be said. He looked distant and pale, still wrapped up in whatever haunted history he kept. 'You're damn right, son. Damn right. I saw them with my own eyes, right before they spooned them out of my face. Casting lightning and fire from their hands as if it was nothin'. All chanting and dust, and dancing too. Magick makes 'em shake like crazy. And the blood ... Everywhere ... Everywhere ... Everywhere ...' The man began to rock back and forth, rags rustling.

Merion quickly thought up a lie to interrupt the beggar's recitation. 'I heard they can tell the future? That they can tell you the truth of anything?'

The wet hand darted out again. 'Another coin to refresh my old memory, son?'

Merion fished out another penny and dropped it into the man's palm. He felt another fist in his back, and coughed.

The beggar frowned at him. 'Why'd you want to know, son? What have you heard.'

Merion raised an eyebrow. *Whatever had he just stumbled across?* 'I'm just curious, that's all.'

'You heard about their witch then, huh, and her magicks?'

'No, but are you saying she can ...'

That seemed to be the wrong answer. The beggar rocked faster and faster. 'Forget you ever heard it, son. Man doesn't need to know his future. Pray you never meet her. I do, every night. I shouldn't have joined the fuckin' army in the first place. Should have stayed at home. Had a wife there. Pretty thing ... Shit.'

Merion slowly backed away, sensing his pennies were good and spent. The beggar did not even notice. He just rocked back and forth, countering away to himself.

But when Merion turned his back, a sharp cry froze him.

'Son!' snapped the beggar.

Merion didn't move. 'Yes?' he asked, shakily.

'Blood ain't just for bleeding, you hear me?' he hissed. 'You hear me?'

'I hear you.'

The beggar went right back to his muttering. His words faded into the mist as Merion wasted no time in escaping. 'Ain't just for ... blood. So much blood ... Their lips ...'

Merion walked in silence, utterly confused and yet infuriated by the beggar's cryptic words. The Shohari witch. Could she really tell a man's future, or was it simply a case of too much whiskey and too much sun? Was he just a mad old tramp or a man of truth? *Blood ain't just for bleeding.* What did that even mean?

In the half-dark, his aunt's house sat like a guardhouse at the edge of the town, its back defiantly, or perhaps even foolishly, turned on the wilderness and the distant hills.

When the door was securely latched behind him, Merion bent down to peel his muddy shoes from his wet feet. There were voices coming from the kitchen. The door was closed, letting only a thin blade of candlelight and a few whispers escape.

Merion crept forward. One of the voices was Lilain, that was for sure. The other was deeper, darker. A man, no doubt. Merion crept closer still.

With each and careful step, the murmuring began to sharpen into syllables, then words, then finally sentences. Merion hooked a finger behind his ear and leant close to the crack in the door.

'... when I say he's ready, dammit! Not before. He's already been through enough.'

'Time's as good as any. He can put all that anger of his into it. He's got a right...'

'*No*, Lurker, I said no. I don't want to break him. Karrigan's death still pains him, I can see it. Throwing him headfirst into all of ...'

Lilain's words dwindled away, and there was a moment of aching silence. Merion froze like a wincing statue.

'Of what, Lil? Speak your mind.'

'Shh, Lurker. Did you hear the door a moment ago?'

Merion was already backing away when the orange light began to flicker. Seconds later it spilled into the corridor, tumbling around the sharp shadow that was his Aunt Lilain. Her shadowed face was that of flint.

'Merion,' she stated. 'Eavesdropping again.'

Merion adjusted his coat and lifted his chin. 'It is not eavesdropping if I have a right to know whatever it was you're talking about.'

'And what gives you the right?'

'Because you're talking about me, of course.'

Lilain tilted her head like an owl measuring up a mouse. 'Were we indeed?'

'You were talking about my father, saying I've already been through enough!'

'I don't think we were, were we, Lurker?' Lilain turned, revealing the towering form of the prospector standing behind her, near the table. His magpie was strangely absent.

All Lurker did was grunt, tip his hat, and make for the kitchen door.

'I'll see you in a week or so, Lil,' he grumbled before he left.

Lilain fixed her nephew with an icy stare. 'I think you'd better go to bed, boy,' she said.

'I told you, I heard what you were say—'

Lilain snapped her fingers and Merion clamped his mouth shut. 'And I told you that I don't abide sneaking in my house! Now get to bed, before I make you sleep in the outhouse!'

Merion was aghast. 'You wouldn't dare!'

Lilain made as if to grab him by the collar, but Merion skipped away, storming off to slam his bedroom door. Lilain shouted after him. 'I'd dare alright, nephew, now get!'

Behind his closed boor, Merion held his shoulder against the wood, waiting for the telltale thud of the basement door. He put a fist against his forehead and bared his teeth. 'There's something going on here, Rhin. I need to find out what it is. I need answers,' he hissed.

Rhin snorted. 'Oh yes? From who? It doesn't sound like your aunt is going to be very forthcoming.'

Merion swung the rucksack off his shoulders and shook the faerie out of it. 'Then I'll get them from Lurker. Did you hear him? He wants me to know. I'm going to follow him.'

'You can't be serious?' Rhin said, wide-eyed, as he watched Merion stuff the rucksack with clothes and various other things that sat pretty low on the scale of usefulness in the desert.

'Get your sword,' Merion ordered the faerie.

'Merion, hang on,' Rhin said, holding up a pair of grey hands. 'We can't just leave. What about Lilain, and your job?' Merion stood up so he could tower over him. He put his hands on his hips.

'Get your sword, I said.'

Rhin had seen that look in Merion's eyes before, and he knew better than to argue with it. At least this wasn't *technically* leaving, he thought. They weren't getting on a train just yet. He shook his head. 'Fine,' he replied. 'Nobody else is going to protect you.'

Once the faerie had strapped his scabbard and black longsword to his belt, he rubbed his hands. 'What's your plan?'

Merion punched a space in the contents of the rucksack and held the flap open. Rhin's wings thrummed as he jumped in. 'Follow Lurker and ask him what in the name of the Almighty is going on, what my aunt is hiding, and who killed my father. If he knows the Shohari, then he might know of the witch.'

Rhin pulled a face. He hunkered down as Merion tied the straps and swung the pack over his shoulders. 'You want to find this witch? Didn't you hear the bit about wearing skin coats?'

'All I want to do is ask Lurker. Take a shot. Are you with me or not?' Merion demanded.

'Fair enough,' Rhin mumbled. 'I am.'

'Are you ready?' Merion asked.

Rhin paused for a moment before he answered. 'Are you?'

Merion shrugged the question off, like a cobweb in the attic. 'Of course,' he replied, and with that he gently unlatched the door and tiptoed out into the hallway. He could hear the gentle scratching of Lilain's bone saw in the basement. She was good and busy.

Merion slipped quietly out of the kitchen door, blinking to shake the bright candlelight from his eyes. He peered into the darkness, trying to glimpse Lurker's hatted shape. He couldn't see a thing. 'Rhin?' he asked, and within moments the faerie had climbed up to his shoulder. He put a hand flat against the bridge of his nose, and began to scan the empty night. There wasn't a single star to be seen behind the hazy veil of clouds that trailed in the wake of the now-distant storm. There was no moon. Merion crossed his fingers and trusted in the eyes of the Fae. He was right to.

'There.' Rhin pointed to a faint lump lumbering along the road to the north.

'Right you are. Now, into the rucksack with you.'

Merion broke into a run and tore off down the gentle hill towards the muddy road leading out of the town. The cold air felt good in his lungs. It felt dangerous and yet exciting. It felt like escape, and progress most of all. Merion sucked it in and savoured it, along with the burn in his legs.

By the time he caught up with Lurker, the prospector was sat on a rock by the roadside, smoking a badly rolled cigarette. His magpie, Jake, had returned, and it perched on his knee. As always, it stared at Merion. But the boy's heart was pumping too hard for him to notice.

'Lurker,' he gasped, his lungs aflame.

Lurker shook his head and waved the snout of his pipe. 'Take a moment, Merion. Put your hands on your knees and bend over. Long breaths, now.'

Merion did as he was told, and instantly felt better.

Whilst the boy caught his breath, Lurker struck a match on the rock and relit his cigarette. He took a long drag and then held it, eyes closed. When he finally exhaled, there was barely any smoke at all. 'I know why you're here,' he rumbled, flicking the glowing embers. The tobacco smelled sweet and sickly at the same time.

'You do?' he asked.

'Mhm,' Lurker nodded, pausing to smoke some more of his pipe. He sniffed. 'Lil ain't got the goods, so to speak, the answers that you need. Am I right?'

Merion nodded. 'That you are.'

Lurker waved his cigarette about as he spoke. 'Strange things, answers. Most times, you want them so badly, but when you get 'em, you wish for anything that you could forget 'em. Lose them somehow. Hmph.' Here he shrugged, then pointed the pipe at Merion. 'And you came runnin' after me because you think I'll give them to you.'

'Right again.'

Lurker snorted rudely, crushing Merion's hopes in one fell swoop. 'Then you're a fool, Tonmerion Hark. I wouldn't cross your aunt if my life depended on it. No. If she says you ain't ready, then you ain't ready.'

Merion wore a pained look. 'But I *am*. I promise you. My aunt is wrong. I'm ready to know what's going on here. I need to know who killed my father. I need to know how to get home! It's killing me, don't you understand? And I know you want to tell me the answers. I heard you saying so to my aunt. She doesn't know me, but I know I'm ready for the truth, Lurker. I *need* it, before I go insane!'

Lurker looked up at the clouds and sniffed. 'Boy does have a right to know the truth. Who are we to keep it from him?'

Jake squawked at him. Lurker gave the bird a stern look. 'Don't you take that tone with me, sir. I know what I'm doing.' His grey eyes flicked back to the boy. 'Tell me again. How old are you?'

'Thirteen.'

'See? Thirteen. I was already working fields by then. You weren't even an egg,' he said to the magpie. Jake flapped his wings and squawked no more.

Merion sighed. He was exhausted, and he knew it. He decided to make one last desperate plea, to see if he could appeal to this prospector's moral side, if such a thing existed. Merion threw his hands up in the air and then let them fall to slap against his thighs. 'Look, Lurker. Will you do what's right and help me find out the truth?'

Lurker sniffed the cold air for a spell, and then leant forward. Merion could barely see his eyes, thanks to the shadow of his hat. 'No,' he said.

Merion's heart fell like a stone. But it was then that Lurker stood up, and the boy's heart rose back up with him. 'But if you ain't going to leave me alone, then so be it. I'll take you to those who can,' he said quietly. 'But bear in mind, you asked for this, not me.'

Merion pushed his luck. 'Are you taking me to the witch? The Shohari witch?'

Lurker narrowed his dark eyes and growled. 'Who told you about her?'

'A beggar in an alleyway. An old soldier who fought the Shohari.'

'Ugh,' Lurker grunted. 'Then he's a fool.' The prospector crossed his arms and sighed. 'If you're to travel with me, then you travel by my rules. You stop when I stop, you eat when I eat, and you shit when I shit, understand?'

'I ... er, yes,' Merion nodded.

'Good,' he said, and with that, he turned his back on the boy and began to walk north. Merion followed eagerly.

'So it is the witch you're taking me to see,' Merion guessed.

Lurker flicked his cigarette to the dust irritably. 'You'll see soon enough. No more questions for tonight. I like to travel quiet.'

Merion fidgeted as he followed Lurker's footsteps through the mud. 'Then ... could I just ask one more of you? I'll promise I'll be quiet after.'

Lurker sighed. 'Speak then, boy.'

'What exactly is a knuckle-dick?'

CHAPTER XI

OF BUFFALO AND BEANS

'The boy. That impetuous little sod, he did it. I think I'm in the house. Smells like dust, sweat, and blood, though that's all mine. This is the first time he's left me alone. He doesn't say much. Don't know how old he is, but his eyes are older than the rest of him, that's for sure. He just keeps staring at me, and I can tell he's drumming up the nerve to ask: What the hell am I?'

13th May, 1867

His feet burned. The miles had fallen away, step by painful step. Miles and miles of sun-drenched desert, flaked and rippled like the puckered skin of some over-baked goldfish, already dry as a bone despite the recent storm.

His knees ached. The poor excuse for a path that they followed wandered between fields of red sand and patches of prairie scrub bristling with twisted cacti. Not a soul walked the path with them, neither ahead nor behind them.

His lips were raw. In fact, the only living things Merion had seen on their silent, wearisome journey were the sort that slithered, or scuttled, or soared on the rising thermals and squawked at the wind. Merion didn't have to look up to know the vultures were still circling above them. He could almost feel their keen eyes on the back of his pink neck; he could almost imagine them licking their beaks and praying to whatever feathery god they believed in for a fatal trip or a sudden and vicious heart attack. Merion would give them no such satisfaction.

His eyes throbbed. If the truth be told, Merion was already doubting his decision to follow Lurker into the wilds. Hell, he had been thinking it since noon, and he wagered it was now closer to three.

At first he had been terrified. The cold, dark hours of the desert night had been full of squealing and snarling. Shadows had flitted back and forth, just out of reach of Lurker's dusty lantern, far too close for Merion's liking. But then dawn had broken, and what little excitement and anticipation he could summon had quickly been dampened by the ceaseless trudging, the countless stubbing of toes, and the dogged heat.

With every sluggish step, and with every flicker of hot pain that came from his feet, Merion's determination had crumbled. Even the tempting gleam of precious answers was starting to wane. Such was the curse of impetuousness. It goes hand in hand with fickleness. Simply put, Tonmerion Hark was exhausted.

'Why …' Merion took a moment to gasp as he felt the cracks in his dry lips widen when he spoke, '… on earth do you not own a horse, man?'

Lurker went as far as shrugging. That seemed to be about the entirety of his answer.

'Did you hear me?' Merion thought he heard a sigh.

'Never liked the beasts,' Lurker replied. 'Don't smell right, by my reckoning. Too much blood, not a big enough brain.'

Merion frowned. 'Am I supposed to know what that means?'

There was a familiar squeak of leather as Lurker shrugged again. Merion wondered whether it was too late to turn back. He wondered how angry Aunt Lilain would be, and whether it would actually be better to let her cool down for a few days.

'When do we make camp?'

Lurker turned his head just a little. His dark skin shone with sweat. 'Why? You tired, boy?'

'No,' Merion lied. 'Just don't want to spend another night treading through hell with nothing but a lantern and a magpie.'

Lurker could be heard chuckling. He tugged a hand out of his pocket for the first time in what must have been twelve straight hours and reached under his cloak to the small of his back. Merion heard a metal *snap*, and before he knew it, Lurker was holding a gun aloft, pointing it at the vultures. They knew well enough to flap higher. The contraption was enormous for a handgun. The thing had six long barrels, all neatly and tightly bound together in a ring, surrounded by ornate steel bands. Where their slick, black steel met the dark wood of the gun's thick handle, a huge hammer sat, gently kissing the backs of the barrels, poised to rear and strike like a rattlesnake.

'Kolt. Never leave home without it.'

Merion shook his head. 'It's vulgar.'

Lurker didn't seem to care. He drummed his fingers against its handle and watched it shine in the hot sun. 'That it may be, but Big Betsy here hits like a sledgehammer. She can blow a hole through a cow with one shot,' he boasted.

'Please don't tell me you know that from experience?'

Lurker snorted, which apparently meant *no*.

Merion shook his head. 'So when are we making camp?'

'Several hours or so, when the sun starts to drop.'

Several hours …

Merion shuddered at the thought of another hour, never mind a few. 'Can we at least …' he sputtered. 'Can we just …'

Lurker stopped and turned. 'Spit it out, boy.'

Merion held up his hands while he took a moment to gulp down some well-deserved air. 'I know I stop when you stop, and all of that, but can you just, please, *stop* for one moment? I feel like my feet are going to fall off.'

'I highly doubt that,' Lurker grunted. Jake croaked in agreement.

'One minute, please.'

Lurker looked around, surveying their roasting surroundings. Jake followed his gaze with his one good eye, every flick and turn. He held up a finger and felt the breeze, what little of it there was in this damned desert, and sniffed several times. Merion was too busy to notice what Lurker was up to, and in too much pain to really care. He simply sagged to the floor and stretched out his legs, hissing partly in pleasure, partly in pain. It felt as though his feet were slowly stewing in their own juices.

'Aaaaaaaalmighty, that bloody hurts.'

Lurker was now staring far into the distance, to the northeast, where the dark smudges of hilltops could be seen above the wavering horizon. 'When the blisters pop, your skin'll harden,' the man muttered. The blasted fool was still wearing his heavy coat and his wide hat. He must have been roasting under all that leather, along with the belts and the luggage … *Madness.*

'I think they've already popped,' Merion grimaced as he prodded his toes. He had to count all his toenails just to be sure none had taken a mind to wander off.

'Well then,' Lurker sniffed. 'You could always piss in your shoes.'

Merion looked up, horrified. 'I could *what?*'

'They're leather, ain't they?'

'Yes.'

'Then piss in them. Soften's em up. Stops the rot.' Lurker waggled his foot. 'Pissed in these the first few days I got 'em. Never had a blister since.'

I wondered what the smell was, Merion thought, involuntarily wrinkling his nose. Besides, judging by the way Lurker could stride mercilessly on without ever breaking pace, Merion would have bet Lurker's feet were made more of hoof, or iron, than bone and skin.

'I am not going to piss in my shoes.' Merion could swear he heard a poorly stifled chuckle coming from his rucksack. He barely resisted the urge to elbow it. He caught Jake's eye, and the bird clacked his beak. Merion narrowed his eyes. 'That's even more vulgar than that cannon of yours.' Merion sighed, and turned his attention to gently peeling off his shoes. 'Ahhhh,' he couldn't help but wince as each throbbing foot came free.

'Not a fan of guns, boy? Might be a problem 'round these parts.'

'Has Lilain not told you anything?'

Lurker threw him a cold look. Merion wilted slightly. 'She told me enough.'

Merion gently massaged his feet. He could have sworn that steam was emanating from the insides of his shoes. 'Then you'll know it was a gun that killed my father. So no, Mr Lurker, I am not a fan of guns.'

'Makes sense. Question is, you a fan of buffalo?'

Merion's head jolted up. 'Buffalo?' Aunt Lilain had spoken of them, of their horns and hooves. He had yearned to see one then, and he could not help but yearn now, despite how damn tired he was.

'Whole herd, coming in from the north. Look here.'

Merion rolled onto his knees and shuffled, rather gracefully, it has to be said, through the sand and grit to where Lurker was standing with one foot on a small, knobbly rock. He pointed with an arm, and Merion squinted into the haze.

'I don't see anything,' he said, the disappointment clear in his dry voice.

'Look harder.'

'Well that helps. I really don't—Wait.'

A dark line had appeared in the shivering heat waves, a line that reached for miles across the horizon. It was then that Merion felt the fear in the ground, the nervous trembling of the sand around his knees. Hooves. Thousands upon thousands of hooves, battering the earth in thunderous unison. The dark line grew thicker as the mighty heard came closer. Merion could hear them now: a low rumble in the air, interrupted by the occasional trumpeting bellow. Merion began to pick out the galloping shapes of the faster beasts, the ones outstripping the rest and leading the way. With every bone-shattering stride, the buffalo drew nearer, until Merion's heart began to jolt along with their frenzied rumble.

For one stomach-churning moment, it looked as though the herd would swing towards them, but then they turned again, and veered east and away from them, down into a slight dip in the land.

The buffalo were enormous. Taller and wider than a carriage, and veritably dripping with muscle. Their shaggy black manes danced and streamed behind them, flecked with white spit from their heaving, slavering mouths. They seemed like furious, skin-wrapped steam engines for all their snorting and grunting. Merion wagered that had it been cold, they would have looked the part as well. It was the buffalos' horns that thrilled him the most. Curved, long, and deadly, they looked to be made of iron instead of simple horn, even going so far as to glint in the sun, as any metal worth its salt would.

Lurker waited until the very last wheezing buffalo had hobbled past before he spoke, almost as though his words might have ruined the spectacle. 'Don't ever want to get on the wrong side of a buffalo, boy, trust me on that one.'

'And trust me, I don't intend to,' Merion said, putting a hand to his chest to steady his heart.

Lurker snorted, and took the opportunity to fish out his pipe and a fresh pinch of tobacco. 'Full o' strange old wonders, this part of the world,' he mumbled around the mouthpiece of his pipe.

Merion shuffled back to his shoes. He eyed them as a passer-by might look at a soiled, drunken tramp on the street. He wanted to spit on them, never mind piss on them. As he painfully eased them back on, he noticed that they were rapidly falling apart. He cursed under his breath.

'Are those things lined with velvet, Hark?'

Merion rolled his eyes. 'Indeed they are,' he muttered.

'Shit, boy. And worn down to a thread, I see. You'd better pray we meet a roamin' trader on the way; otherwise you'll be walking the desert in your socks. That ain't something I would go recommendin'.'

Merion didn't exactly relish the thought either. 'Wonderful,' he grunted.

He could smell the earthy tang of the leather, the dusty scent of paper and books. He ran his hands over the dark wood of his father's desk, watching how his fingers changed colour under the sunlight pouring through the towering stained-glass windows. Blue, green, red, and every colour in between, broken only by the tall shadow standing mere feet away, staring at the kaleidoscopic world outside the cavernous study.

Merion lifted a fist to his mouth and coughed politely. The shadow turned slightly. A stern, angular face looked back over the stark line of a muscled shoulder. Merion waved.

'Hullo father,' he said, his voice sounding sluggish and faint in the dream.

'Have you found him yet?' asked Karrigan. His lips had barely moved. His voice sounded faraway and on the brink of being lost.

Merion furrowed his brow. 'Pardon me?'

'My murderer, Tonmerion.'

The younger Hark shook his head, flushing red. 'I'm trying my best, father. This man, Lurker … he's taking me to—'

'It's not good enough.'

Merion's eyes itched as they began to water. He forced himself not to reach up and rub them. *A sign of weakness.* 'Father ... please,' he whispered. 'I will find him, I promised you.'

Karrigan turned back to the paned glass and sighed. 'Beans, Merion.'

'Father?'

'Beans.'

'I don't understand...'

'Beans I said, you listenin', boy?'

Merion's eyes snapped open, letting reality flood back into them. His head lolled as he shook off the dizziness of the dream.

Lurker was brandishing a dirty wooden spoon at him. A little cluster of brown beans clung to it for dear life. 'Don't you be fallin' asleep on me yet. You eat when I eat, remember? Got to get some food in your stomach before your head hits the pillow. This ain't the sort of place you want to wake up hungry. Here, have some beans.'

Merion rubbed his eyes with the palms of his dusty, dirty hands and blinked the sleep out of his eyes. He peered down into the bubbling pot Lurker had suspended over the timidly crackling flames. Beans, indeed. 'Is there any bread?'

'No sir.'

'No bacon?'

Lurker just chuckled at that.

Merion's stomach rumbled painfully. 'Any meat at all?' he whined.

Lurker looked up from stirring his pot. There was a hint of a scowl on his face. Little did Merion know that beans were very important to a man like Lurker. Beans could be counted upon. Beans could warm a soul as well as a stomach. Beans could turn a rough day on the road right around.

And here was Merion, turning his nose up at them.

'Well, seeing as my ole pap's recipe ain't good enough for you...' Lurker paused to thrust a hand into his nearby pack. There was a moment of rummaging, during which Merion's stomach rumbled with hope as well as hunger, and then Lurker threw something at him, a little slab of something hard and no-doubt chewy, wrapped up in grease paper and string. '...you can have what's left of my jerky. Carve off a piece, go on.'

'I don't have a—'

Steel flashed as a knife spun over the flames and landed in the sand inches from Merion's knee. The boy tried to quell the shaking in his hand as he tugged the blade free. 'Thank you,' he whispered.

'Welcome.'

A bowl was filled with beans and passed across the fire. The beans were big and soft, and the sauce they swam in was thick and rich, deep with spices and smoke. Merion was instantly apologetic. 'These beans are incredible, Lurker.'

Lurker didn't look up. He just kept slipping beans into his mouth, one by one, eating like a grizzled old turtle might. He managed a brief, 'Thank you,' between spoonfuls.

The jerky was tongue-numbingly salty, but it too was rich and spicy. Merion had never tasted anything like it. It was like chewing on a boot, sure, but a tasty boot at that. The boy soon gave up on the knife and simply just started tearing chunks off with his teeth.

Three bowls of beans and half the jerky later, (some of which was surreptitiously slipped into his rucksack), Merion was once again dancing along the edges of a deep sleep. Lurker had already packed away the pot and stoked up the fire, and while Merion pulled his blanket tighter around his shoulders and rocked back and forth, fighting sleep, Lurker began to work on something. It was difficult to see, but it was definitely something to do with Merion's shoes. Lurker looked to be attacking them with his knife.

'Are we safe here?' Merion asked, gazing around dazedly at the little wind-cut horseshoe of red rock they had made camp in. They were halfway up a sharp hill, all chiselled at the sides, and hidden away quite nicely in a hollow. Rhin was stowed away in the rucksack and kept close at hand beside Merion's right knee. Jake was curled up in a black feathery ball on the left-hand side of the fire, snoring in little hissing gasps.

Lurker nodded as he worked. 'Safer than most, that's for sure,' he replied, distracted.

'That's hardly comforting,' Merion mumbled.

'Last night we had the protection of the town. The bigger things are drawn further west, to where the railroad and the worker camp is. We sort of snuck out the back.'

'But we're nowhere near the town now.'

'No, we're closer to Seragho River, off to the east, see? If we'd a moon tonight you'd see it lie like a silver snake, curving through the hills.' Lurker waved his little blade at the ragged horizon and speckled heavens.

Merion took another peek at the night sky, and not for the last time that evening shook his head at the sheer number of stars and dusty swirls it had to offer. He had never seen a sky like this in London. It was alien and other-worldly, as if the *Tamarassie* had taken him to the moon instead of the New Kingdom. The night breeze blew cold, and Merion shivered.

'I'd wager that Lord Serped is chugging along it right now in that grand riverboat of his, on his way to Fell Falls.'

That woke Merion up a bit. 'Right now?' he asked. He had forgotten all about the Serpeds in his rush to follow Lurker. But his momentary excitement sank almost as quickly as it had surfaced. There was nothing he could do about them now. They could be a back-up plan, he decided, and nodded affirmatively to himself, inwardly congratulating himself on his shrewdness. Father would be proud.

He *will* be proud.

Lurker was still chuntering away. Merion had not imagined such a stoic and silent fellow to be so talkative around a campfire. Perhaps it was simply more comfortable for him out here, with a ceiling of stars, a rock for a bed, and a belly full of beans.

'... but this ain't wraith country no more, so don't you worry 'bout them. Not yet, anyway.'

'Again, comforting.'

'It's the little things you got to watch out for, in these parts,' Lurker looked up and met Merion's eyes. 'The things that don't look harmless until they bite you. Half the time you don't know you've been bitten until the bastards have sucked a pint of blood out of you.' Lurker stared, and Merion stared right back. The boy suddenly felt itchy, as though he could already feel tiny teeth testing his skin, or little claws climbing under his clothes. He involuntarily shivered.

'You mean like insects?' Merion scratched at his neck.

Lurker broke eye contact and went back to whatever he was doing. 'Among other things. The sort of things Lil likes to collect.'

Merion could not help but put a hand on his rucksack. 'What exactly *is* her fascination with cutting up strange animals?'

Lurker tugged at the brim of his hat. 'I'll let Lil tell you all about that when we get back.'

'And here I was thinking I was actually going to find some answers in this desert.'

'In a few days, you'll have them,' mumbled Lurker, and there was a finality in his voice that made Merion hold his tongue for once. He hunkered down, ignoring how cold his back was compared to his roasting front, and tried to ignore the lack of feeling in his legs. Sleep clawed at him, dragging him down. Tiredness seeped into his bones and muscles and pulled at his eyelids. The fire began to grow blurry, then disappeared altogether into darkness and vacuous silence.

Merion ran his hands across the dark wood of the desk, and wiggled his fingers in the stained light...

Lurker waited, his head slumped on his chest, until the boy was snoring soundly. He tongued his yellow teeth thoughtfully while he stared over the ochre flames. Jake had awoken, and was now looking between his master and Merion. If a magpie could have tutted, Jake did.

Lurker threw him a look. 'Don't you be judging me now, bird,' he whispered.

Jake ruffled his feathers and clacked his beak disapprovingly.

Lurker shook his head. 'Cantankerous magpie,' he muttered. He spent a little while drumming his fingers on his knee before reaching for his battered old flask. He shook it, making it gurgle, then fished a small corked vial out of a pocket deep in his coat, half-full of a dark crimson liquid. Jake watched with his beady black eyes as Lurker pulled the cork out with his teeth and a dribbled a few drops of the thick liquid into the flask.

'Not too much, not too little,' Lurker told himself.

Jake clacked his beak again.

'Lil ain't the only bloodletter in Wyoming, Jake. You know that. And no, it ain't for me, 'afore you ask,' Lurker replied as he shook the flask.

A squawk this time. Lurker shushed him. 'I know what I'm doing. Boy's got his father's blood in him, I'm sure of it. Unlike you, I don't have to see it to believe it.'

The seemingly one-sided conversation was apparently over. Jake said no more. He tucked his beak under one wing and closed his good eye, shutting all this nonsense out. Lurker tucked the flask under his knee and patted it. 'You'll see, bird. He'll be fine,' he muttered, and then reached again for his knife, to continue working on Merion's shoes.

CHAPTER XII

SPIT AND VIGOUR

'I don't know how long it's been now. A week? Two? The boy's found his tongue, but mine is still dry as parchment. Hurts to speak, and he doesn't understand my scrawling ...'

14th May, 1867

It was early when the sun arose to burn the cold of the night away, to chase the timid mists back into the splintered ground, far too early for Merion's liking. He cracked his eyelids open a smidgeon and winced as the brightness made his eyes hurt. This desert was insufferable.

'Mornin',' muttered Lurker. Merion could have sworn that he hadn't moved an inch in the night. He was exactly as he had left him: sat cross-legged, head down, and busy with Merion's shoes. Lurker was just about finished with them. Now, in the morning light, Merion could see the results.

Two patchwork shoes of borrowed leather and brightly-coloured cloth sat side-by-side in the red sand. His own shoes had been cut and ripped to shreds, spliced with a pair of what Merion would later learn were called *noa'sins*. Shohari shoes. Lurker had even managed to save some of that velvet lining, putting it to good use around the heels. They weren't what Merion might have chosen for walking down the cobbles of Kensing Town, but he—along with his battered and blistered feet— was very grateful for them.

'You made those for me?' Merion croaked, his throat raspy from his deep slumber. He had slept like the dead.

With his thumb and his blade, Lurker cut free the final loose thread. He flicked it into the fire and sighed. 'Done,' he said, then tossed the shoes to Merion, who caught them awkwardly.

The big man didn't look like the sort of man who was fond of sleep (the black rings around his deep brown eyes were testament to that fact), but Merion had to ask. 'Were you up all night making these?' he enquired.

Lurker shrugged. 'Way I see it, I can sleep when I'm dead.'

The logic was brutal, but sound. Merion shrugged right back and turned the shoes over in his hands. They were rough; Lurker was no tinker, but they seemed solid enough. Merion gently slipped them on to his aching feet, biting his lip as his blisters complained. It was painful, but he managed it. The shoes were tight, but for some reason that felt like a good thing.

Merion said as much. 'They're tight,' he remarked, but then realised his manners. 'I mean, thank you, Lurker.'

'Welcome,' replied the man. He was sat with his legs drawn into his chest, his thick leather-clad arms resting on his knees.

In truth, Merion was not accustomed to random acts of kindness, especially from a man such as Lurker. Merion did not know quite what to offer in return besides a few spare socks or a handshake, so he decided to show a little interest in the man.

'So I take it Lurker isn't your real name?' he asked.

Lurker's stare moved to the ashes of the dead fire. 'No, it ain't. But I don't mind it. Suits me, so Lil says. I'm more Lurker now than anybody else.'

Merion nodded. Lurker's matter-of-fact way of speaking was strange, but Merion found that he couldn't help but agree. There was a wisdom that emanated from him, and Merion was fascinated by it, perhaps because on some level he knew it was a wisdom born from toil and hardship, from struggle and tribulation. There was a deep and dark history behind those brown eyes, behind those scars, and Merion was suddenly very eager to dig it out.

'So, what is your name, if you don't mind me asking?'

Lurker scratched his grizzled chin, his nails rasping on his wiry stubble. It was clear he wasn't one for laying his cards out for all to see, but he answered all the same. 'Well,' he said, 'ain't nobody asked that in a while. I used to be called John, John Hobble. Before some whiskey-sick rail worker accused me of lurking in a saloon one day. It was busy. He was loud. Name kinda stuck. Don't go to many saloons no more.'

'Well thank you again, John Hobble.' Merion's rumbling stomach interrupted any further questions, so he mentally tucked them away for later and asked an altogether more important question instead. 'So, what's for breakfast?'

Lurker sniffed and looked out at the desert. Now that the sun was up, Merion could see the Seragho curling around the hills to the east. If he'd looked a little closer, he might have spied the white blotch of a grand riverboat eagerly chuffing and splashing its way towards Fell Falls. 'Sand and sweat,' Lurker replied.

Merion grimaced. 'That doesn't sound too appetising.'

Lurker was already on his feet. 'Don't make time for breakfast. We got to get moving, afore it gets hot.'

'But...' Merion's stomach gurgled away in disappointment. Merion had secretly hoped, just a little, that today would be better than yesterday. *Fat chance of that*, he thought.

'Here,' Lurker said, brandishing a beaten-up old flask. 'Drink this.'

Merion eyed it suspiciously. To his left, Jake cackled away to himself. The bird sounded grumpy, if that were possible. 'What is it?' Merion asked.

'Water, boy. Clear the sand out of your throat and let's get goin',' Lurker threw the flask and Merion narrowly avoided knocking himself out with it as he caught it clumsily.

Merion gave the water a cautionary sniff. It smelled like water. He took a little sip. It tasted like water. In fact, it tasted like the best water he had ever tasted. Merion hadn't realised how thirsty he was.

'I ... er ...' Merion held the empty flask upside down and winced. 'Did you want some?'

Lurker snorted but then patted his coat pocket. 'Got my own. You keep that. We'll be hittin' a spring by noon.'

Merion slowly got to his aching feet, half-expecting to be bludgeoned by searing pain at any moment, but little came. He emitted a few gasps and hisses here and there, as he took the first few tentative steps, but his new patchwork shoes performed marvellously. 'That's much better,' he said.

'Good,' Lurker replied as he gathered up his things. Jake flapped his iridescent wings and returned to his favourite spot on Lurker's left shoulder. He cawed when he noticed Merion hadn't moved. The boy was swaying slightly, and he was resting a hand on his belly.

'You okay, boy? Something wrong?'

Merion held up a finger and took a few long breaths. That seemed to fix it. He blinked and sighed. 'Fine. Just felt a little queasy, is all.' *Probably from the lack of breakfast,* he silently added.

Lurker had a strange look on his face. 'Sure?'

Merion swallowed, and nodded. His stomach was still rumbling, but the wave of nausea had passed. 'Sure. I feel fine.'

As it turned out, Merion felt *great*. Maybe it was the fact that he had new shoes. Or, maybe it was because his body was giving him one last spurt of energy before it completely fell apart from starvation, he didn't know. What he did know was that food was the last thing on his mind at that particular moment. Merion just wanted to walk. The miles fell away like the wilted petals of a long-dead flower. Yes, his stomach still gurgled away. Yes, his feet still hurt. Yes, his legs ached, but Merion could not fight his own momentum. He just wanted to keep moving, to feel the sand fall away beneath his determined stride. In fact, he had to concentrate on holding himself back, lest he overtook Lurker and sped off into the desert in a cloud of dust and sweat.

And his tongue. It had spent the whole morning wagging, and still it didn't want to stop. Merion rattled off comment after question like rounds from a gun. Some Lurker deigned to answer, others just ricocheted into the wilderness, to annoy the rocks and rodents and vultures instead.

'And so that means it has to be political. Now I don't know much about the Benches, but I know my father was a famous man. A ruthless man. I mean, you can't make everybody like you, can you?' Merion prattled on.

Unseen by Merion, Lurker rolled his eyes. 'No, you can't.'

There was a sharp snap as Merion clicked his fingers. 'Exactly.'

He felt a sharp nudge in his back and tiny, almost inaudible 'Shhh!' from the rucksack.

'Don't shush me,' Merion blurted, and then instantly caught himself. He clamped his mouth shut.

Lurker stopped dead in his tracks and turned around. He was sniffing the air. 'I didn't shush you. Not that I don't want to, boy. You've talked the morning to death and it looks like the afternoon will be buried right alongside it. You talk for the Empire, I told you I walk in silence. I like the peace and quiet, so you'd best focus on holding your tongue for the next hour at least. But I know one thing, that I didn't shush you. Who you talkin' to?' he asked, sniffing at the air.

Merion crossed his arms, then scratched his head. He coughed and stared at the nearest hill. Damn it if he wasn't finding it hard to stay still. His legs wouldn't stop shaking. 'I thought I heard … It doesn't matter,' Merion made his excuses, hoping he was convincing enough.

Lurker squinted, looking the boy up and down. 'You are jittery, ain't you?' he said, then a smile began to spread over his dark lips. Jake cawed and launched himself into the air. Lurker chuckled as he watched the bird go. 'Told you,' he muttered.

Now Merion was confused. 'Told me what?'

'Nothin'. Now you shut your trap?'

Merion hopped from one foot to the other. 'But … But I wanted to know more about the war you mentioned … and …' He trailed off. Getting answers from Lurker had been like trying to bleed a boulder. Though he had been rewarded with a few, a few was never enough for a thirteen-year-old. He had never really known the meaning of 'few'.

Lurker shook his head sternly. 'Wars are for fighting, not talkin' about. Nobody got anything good to say about the war. You don't want to hear it.'

But Merion really did. Boys and talk of war went together like rain and the Empire. 'Can we talk about my Aunt Lilain?'

Lurker almost fell for it. 'What about Lil …? No, I said no more questions. When the sun goes down, you can talk. For now, you just put those jittery legs into good use and walk. You hear?'

'Fine,' Merion mumbled. Lurker turned back around and the young Hark couldn't help but twitch and jerk forward, his legs pining for the movement. 'But can I just say—'

'No.'

'—that the reason you probably walk in silence all the time is because you walk alone all the time.'

There was a grunt and Lurker tipped his hat. 'I got Jake.'

'But he can't talk.'

'That's what you think.'

'You have a talking magpie?'

'I thought I said silence? Shut it!'

And shut it Merion did. Even when they stopped for water at a small spring hidden in the armpit of several tall, striped rocks, the boy said nothing. It almost killed him to do so, but he held his tongue, letting it just flap about on its own behind tightly-gritted teeth. Lurker simply plodded along, sniffing the air every couple of minutes or so. Merion busied himself with watching Lurker's pack bob up and down as he walked. Every now and again, Merion would glimpse a flash of metal through gaps in the seams of Lurker's battered leather coat, and his mind would turn to thoughts of guns, and white porcelain tiles.

As they trudged further and further north, the country began to bunch up, like a carpet shoved into a corner. The sand rose and fell beneath them, and the constant undulation started to put dents into Merion's strange burst of energy. The terrain remained the same for the most part. Just dull and dusty, bare and scorched a rusty colour. If their feet did not hit sand, they found bare earth or rock instead, or a shrivelled plant. It was tough going, and matters were not helped by the merciless sun beating down on them. But as every sun must rise, it must also fall, and so it was that the sun finally gave up its near-unbearable assault and began to slink away to the west, eager for fresher prey.

The path took them deeper into the rocky, tabletop hills, where at last the earth turned a little greener. Brave little plants and anaemic shrubs clung tightly to the shadows between the juts of stone and rocky outcrops. Some even had the audacity to sport a few bright flowers: whites, yellows, even a few blues. Merion tried to count each and every one, as if somehow a lofty enough total would reassure him that there was still life in this barren wasteland of a country.

By the time they found their campsite, Merion couldn't wait to sit down. The sandy hollow looked so inviting it might have been covered in velvet and strewn with duck-feather pillows. Merion slumped into an undignified heap and let the rucksack slip from his shoulders. Even though Rhin was usually as light as a feather, even with all his armour, at that moment the faerie felt as heavy as rubble. Merion sighed as he felt the cold evening air soothing the sweaty warm patch across his spine. Merion was spent.

'What happened to all that spit and vigour o' yours, then?' Lurker smirked.

Merion shrugged. He couldn't bring himself to move. 'Evaporated, apparently. Must be that cursed sun.'

Lurker gazed off to the west, where the bruised sky still glowed defiantly orange. 'Yep, she's a harsh mistress.'

Merion rolled his eyes. 'That's one way to put it,' he mumbled, then abruptly clicked his fingers. 'And speaking of suns, I do believe ours has set for the day. Which means I get to carry on talking, does it not?'

Lurker churned his tongue around his teeth for a spell. 'S'pose. I did say.'

'And they say a man's word is his bond.'

'That's more a lie than a truth in these parts, boy. Do well to remember that.'

Merion sighed. 'That may be so, John, if I may call you John ...?'

'Don't sound right to me.'

'That may be so, Lurker, but I'd wager you were a man of his word.'

Lurker spat. 'Shit.'

Merion, despite his tiredness, had to grin. *There was always more digging to be done.* 'I'll take that as a yes, shall I?'

But Lurker wagged a finger. 'Dinner first, then you can talk. Don't want you havin' t' shout over my grumblin' belly.'

Merion huffed, but Lurker's stomach wasn't the only one growling. Merion rolled onto his side. 'And what is the menu tonight? Salmon? Boar sausages? Prussian potatoes?'

'Beans.'

Merion slapped his hand on the ground. 'Beans! Of course.'

Two days, and already Merion never wanted to see another bean in his life.

Sadly, Lurker was in charge of the pot. And as Merion was quickly learning, when Lurker is in charge, you'd better be ready for beans. As Lurker caressed and nurtured his bubbling pot, waving the spoon to and fro like an artist delicately crafting a masterpiece, Merion wondered if the man knew how to cook anything else, but he held his tongue, and silently awaited his bean-laden fate, busying himself by ordering his questions in order of importance. His fingers drummed a little impatient rhythm on his knees.

Jake was hopping around the small fire, eying Merion with his single black eye. At first, he ignored the strange magpie (which seemed more and more human by the day, might he add), but each time the magpie passed, he paused a little longer, staring up at Merion as if straining to set fire to Merion's hair with his good eye.

Another minute went by, and Merion snapped. 'Agh!' he cried, clapping his hands at the magpie. Jake could not fight his instincts. He leapt to the other side of the campfire, a thrashing, cawing ball of frantic feathers.

'Why'd you go do that for?' Lurker sounded a touch angry. Merion couldn't help but be slightly taken aback by it.

'He...' Merion began, suddenly tasting how childish his words sounded. 'He keeps looking at me.'

'He's a bird. Every bird has a bit of an issue with staring. Can't help it.'

Merion wrapped his arms around his legs and glared at the magpie, who was hovering just to the right of the fire, opposite Merion's rucksack. For the moment, he stayed where he was. Still staring, of course, but motionless, nonetheless. 'But it's like he's accusing me of something. He doesn't like me.'

Lurker snorted. 'Jake don't like many folks. Barely tolerates me.'

'Hmph,' was all Merion could say to that.

'Here, grab a bowl.'

'Joy,' Merion whispered under his breath.

His reluctance lasted just until he put the hot spoonful into his mouth, and felt the rich, dark sauce spreading over his tongue. It was delicious, and without waiting to swallow the first mouthful, Merion began to gobble the contents of the bowl, spoon after overflowing spoon.

Merion wolfed down two bowls and still beat Lurker to the end of his one. Lurker seemed to eat one bean at a time, taking his time, savouring each mouthful like a man who had never tasted food before. Spending so much time in the desert will do that to a man.

'So,' Merion began his inquisition, 'you said my Aunt Lilain hasn't told you much about my father's death?'

'No sir.'

Merion ticked off his mental notes on his fingers. 'Just that he was shot, and the killer is still on the loose.'

'Mhm.'

'Then what do you know about Aunt Lilain?'

Lurker sniffed, keeping his eyes on his beans. 'Lots, and then not a lot, if you know what I mean.'

Merion sighed. 'No, not really.'

'She tells a lot of stories. I know about her and the three-week-old pig she found in a swamp. I know about her ex-husband, and how she likes to joke about striking him stone-cold dead with a hammer. I know all the stuff on the surface very well indeed, but then again I don't know much about what's underneath. She's a very private woman, your Aunt Lil.'

'But why undertaking?'

'That's not all she does, boy. Your aunt has a brilliant mind, don't you forget that. One of them scientists, no doubt about it. She knows more about bodies and blood than anyone I've ever met.'

'So what exactly is she hiding? What does she know about my father's death that I do not?'

Lurker shook his head. Merion caught a glimpse of movement to his right, but when he looked, Jake was standing as still as a little statue, beady eye once again firmly glued to the young Hark. The boy scowled.

'That's not for me to say, boy. You'll find out in a day or two, no doubt,' the prospector was saying.

Merion sagged. 'But you said *that* a day or two ago. Where exactly are you taking me, anyway? You still haven't told me,' he whined.

Lurker glared at him then. Now that night had fallen, his dark eyes had been reduced to mere flecks of firelight, glinting in the shadow of his wide-brimmed hat. Merion shivered. 'You'll see,' was all Lurker offered by way of a reply.

'Fine,' Merion retorted. 'Then tell me this: why does she collect animal blood? Why would a person do such a thing?'

Lurker smirked. 'Why indeed, boy,' he said. 'It's partly a job, partly a hobby. She's got a thirst for it, strong and deep. When she's not taking them to bits, she's out there hunting, or trading.'

'Trading for what?'

'Anything she can get her hands on. Got a thing for fish at the moment, and a fish is a hard thing to find out here in the desert.' Lurker thumbed his jaw. 'Gets 'em from the river, or so she says. Obsession, some might call it. It's why she moved out here, to this devil's crotch of a country.' Lurker spared a moment to sip a little something from his flask, and then held up three fingers. 'Lil always says there are three things she's yet to get on her table, "in whole or in part" as she puts it.'

Merion leant forward. 'And what are they exactly?'

Lurker prodded each of his fingers in turn as he counted. 'A dragon.'

Merion scoffed. 'Really?'

'A mermaid.'

Now this was preposterous. 'She cannot be serious.'

'And a faerie.'

The silence that followed ached. Merion literally had to push the words out of his mouth with his tongue. 'I see.'

Lurker sniffed and nodded slowly.

'And what exactly would she do with a ... with one of these monsters?'

'Bleed them, most likely. Explore 'em on the inside.'

Merion's lip curled with his curt reply. 'Vulgar.'

A finger was levelled at the boy. 'Necessary,' Lurker corrected him. 'Like I jus' said: part hobby, part *job*.'

Merion rubbed his eyes for a moment, knuckling away the sting of acrid smoke. The young Hark hadn't had the pleasure of sitting at the edge of many campfires.

To his right, Jake hopped a little closer to the boy's rucksack. Only Lurker saw, and he kept his lips tighter than a hatful of witches, or so he might have said.

'And what is it about blood that fascinates her? Why is she so obsessed with it?' Merion asked.

Lurker withdrew his finger and tapped it against the side of his nose. 'Curious stuff is blood. There's all different types, did you know that, boy?'

'I would have guessed as mu—'

Lurker cut him off. 'Not just from beast to beast, boy. Each and every one of us has a different sort o' crimson flowing through our veins. You and me, we can't share blood ...' It was here that Merion wondered why on earth he might want to do such a thing, '... we ain't—how'd Lilain put it?—*Compatible*.'

Lurker shuffled around on his arse for a moment before continuing. 'Way I heard it, Lil never saw eye to eye with your father,' the prospector rumbled gruffly. 'Now he and she might have been of the same blood, in the family sense, but that's as far as it went.' Lurker sniffed. 'A thoroughbred, your father, Merion. As thoroughbred as they come. Different sort of crimson altogether. What was it they called him again? In the Empire?'

Merion swallowed. 'The Bulldog. Bulldog of London.'

Lurker whistled. 'See now ain't that a title. And why exactly did they call him that?'

Merion did not feel comfortable now that the inquisition had been turned around on him. But sometimes you have to give a little to get a little more. 'Because he was stubborn. Because he was proud, and because once he gave up barking and bit down, he wouldn't let go until you begged him.' Although it was painful to speak in the past tense,

Merion felt pride flowing through him as he waxed boastful about his father.

'When my grandfather handed over control of the Hark empire to my father, he ripped it to shreds and rebuilt it even stronger. There wasn't a single industry he didn't dominate, and his reach didn't just stop at the borders of London. "The world may speak many languages, but the only language that is completely and universally understood is the language of power", so he used to tell me. But that's enough about me. I'm supposed to be asking the questions, not you.'

Those darkly glinting eyes of Lurker's flashed. 'I said I'd answer *some*. I'm taking you to those who can answer the rest. Ain't that enough boy?'

Merion's face was becoming flushed. 'Please, can you stop calling me "boy"?'

'Well that's what you are, ain't it?'

'Why don't you just tell me what I want to know now, so we don't have to keep traipsing through this barren wasteland any longer?' Merion whined.

But Lurker was firm. 'I told you, *Merion*, it ain't for me to tell you. Promise is a promise.'

'Oh come on!' Merion spluttered. 'I don't want another day of burning sun, of dusty shoes, and … and … *beans*! Just tell me!' Merion's whining had taken on an angry tone, and it was one that Lurker did not like. Nobody spoke ill of his beans.

Lurker leant forwards and the firelight played in the cracks and creases of his grizzled face, like wizened wood. 'I said no, boy. And that's the end of it.'

Merion's mouth flapped wordlessly for a moment before it was shut, and sealed, and the words grumpily stowed away. Merion frowned so hard he gave himself a headache. He sighed, and rubbed his eyes. *Almighty damn this smoke!*

It was rather unfortunate that he chose that moment in particular to knead his eyes … the very same moment that Jake chose to pounce on his rucksack.

There was a horrendous screech as the magpie ripped the flap free and dove inside, his wings flapping madly, claws thrashing and beak clacking. Merion jumped in shock, and upon witnessing what was going on, immediately lunged for the rucksack as it hopped and skittered across the sand. He screamed for the bird to stop. Lurker stayed silent as he got to his feet to tower over the sudden chaos.

Now, it is wise to learn at this juncture that the common faerie is blessed with rather incredible reactions. Being much, much smaller than a human, and having wings very similar to that of a dragonfly, faeries are forever being mislabelled as a delicious snack by the feathered creatures of this world. For birds have canny eyes, and some, given the right light, can see straight through a faerie's spell. Corvids, as Lil would have lectured, such as Jake, have such a skill. This is why birds and faeries clash more often than you might think. Sadly for the birds, the Fae have had centuries to practise.

The screeching ceased abruptly, replaced by a harsh shout, and the sound of fabric-wrapped struggling. Within seconds a small boot kicked open the flap, and in a flurry of dishevelled feathers, Jake reappeared, held tightly by a fearsome, hissing faerie, wings proud and thrumming, sword held gently against the magpie's iridescent neck.

Rhin had the bird in a clever hold, using his body and strong left arm to pin Jake's wings behind his back. For all intents and purposes, the magpie might as well have been bound with iron. The faerie's black blade glittered like coal in the firelight.

Lurker was having none of it. In a flash of leather and steel, his gun was drawn, levelled barely three feet from Rhin's head.

'Let that bird go, or lose your fuckin' head. Your choice,' growled the prospector.

Rhin bared his sharp teeth. 'Not a chance. Lower that cannon of yours or I'll slit this *klasch*'s throat like butter.'

Merion was frozen with a paralysing mixture of shock, awe, and terror. He had to physically force the words out of his throat. It was like shoving boulders up a pipe. 'Stop it! Lurker, John, put that thing down. And Rhin, let that feathered bastard go and step back. Please, just do it.'

Rhin threw him a glance, fierce and defiant, but Merion stared him down. Rhin flickered purple with anger, and then shoved Jake away from him, recoiling into a crouch, blade up and ready.

'Lurker … Lower your weapon!' Merion hissed, and Lurker did as he was told. The gaping barrels of the monstrous Big Betsy slowly fell away, dropping to nuzzle the lip of Lurker's right boot moodily.

'Fine,' Lurker grunted. He was furious, Merion could tell. His gloves creaked as he clenched his fists, tight as could be. 'You stay there Jake,' he barked. 'Keep your eyes on that reptile 'til I've had my words. Unnerstand?'

Jake squawked, sharing his master's fury He veritably shook with anger, feathers puffed to ridiculous degrees.

'Now see here, Lurker…' Merion began.

Lurker took one giant step over the crackling fire and cuffed the young Hark around the ear. Merion yelped, falling to the sand. Rhin was by his side in a blur of black faerie steel. Jake was aiming to pounce, hopping around behind him.

'Enough!' Lurker shouted, and the chaotic scene stopped dead. 'Get up,' Lurker pulled Merion upright, keeping his eyes on the faerie. Merion sullenly came level. His ear stung like nobody's business, and his body refused to stop shivering.

Lurker prodded him in the chest with a damning finger. 'I think it's you that owes some answers. And I intend to get 'em.'

Merion shook his head free of his dizzy spell and motioned for Rhin to back down. The faerie did as he was told, but his eyes still burned all the same.

Merion crouched down in the sand, and Rhin followed suit. 'What do you want from me? How dare you and your diseased bird—'

'Oh we dare alright. A man has a right to know who or what he's sharing a campfire with. I don't know you one bit, but I took a chance seeing as you're Lil's nephew, and you're in a fuckin' sorry situation. Now that you've decided to return my kindness with lyin', I know you even less, and a care about as much.'

Merion flushed red. 'I didn't lie!'

'Hiding is the same as lyin', in my book! You should have told me you were smuggling this dangerous little shit around.'

'Why?! It's my secret, not yours.'

Rhin snapped his teeth together. 'And I am a faerie, you ignorant fuck. One of the Fae, so mind your tongue when you're talking to me.'

Lurker squatted down on his heels and rested the gun on his knees, pointing away into the night. He titled his hat back so that Merion could get a good, close look at the stone-hard certainty in his eyes. If Merion had not been so full of rage and indignity, he would have had to fight to meet that gaze. 'Look, boy,' Lurker said in a low voice, 'the secret's out. I ain't going just to ignore the fact you got a faerie ridin' 'round in your rucksack. That don't sit well with me. That ain't exactly a regular everyday occurrence, you hear me? It ain't normal, and that, boy, demands answers.' Lurker paused to hawk some spit into the sand. 'Shit, until ten seconds ago, I always thought Lil was joking when she said faeries. I knew I smelled something on you, from that first moment on the porch.'

The boy spoke slowly, fighting to keep his voice level. 'And that's exactly why she cannot know. I do not want my best friend bled and dissected in some basement.'

Lurker thought about that for a second. He chewed his lip, and then nodded. 'I can unnerstand that.'

Merion narrowed his eyes as he stuck out his hand. 'Then do we have an accord?'

Lurker shook firmly. The leather of his gloves was painfully rough. 'We do,' he said, 'and now you need to tell me what the hell is going on here.'

Merion sighed. By his knee, Rhin rolled his eyes and waved a hand. He dug his blade into the sand and levelled his gaze at Jake, who was more than delighted to return it. Merion spoke slowly, but firmly. 'Rhin is an outcast. His people, the Fae, exiled him as punishment for a crime he didn't commit,' Merion began.

'What crime?'

Rhin spoke, his voice like stones clacking together. 'Stealing the Hoard.'

'The what?'

'The Hoard,' Merion answered. 'An entire kingdom's fortune in gold, held in whatever shape you want it to be. A room. A trunk. A cave. Queen Sift chose a small purple and gold purse, right?'

Rhin nodded solemnly. 'Always one for irony, that maniacal bitch.'

It was marvellously evident in Lurker's face that he was struggling to believe this story, even despite the obvious fact that he was actually sharing a campfire with a faerie. Merion went on.

'Rhin managed to escape the Fae and ran for his life. Three weeks, he spent dodging hansom cabs and Rottweilers and the soldiers that had hunted him. He finally found his way to Harker Sheer, my home.' Merion's eyes glazed over as the scenes replayed themselves in his mind. 'The best hiding spot was always the rhododendron.'

'What's one of those?'

Merion sniffed. Perhaps rhododendrons were not all that common in the desert. 'A big plant, with big, waxy-green leaves. Gunderton could never find me there. One of the under-butlers. Fat as a pig and as dumb as one too.'

'I always hid opposite the kitchens, so I could run in if he got too close. Never did though. One October day, I was lying on my stomach, peeking out behind two fat leaves, watching Gunderton run in circles around the grounds, when I heard a choking sound from behind me. There was this little grey thing, Rhin, crawling out of the bushes towards me, half-dead and with a hole through his side. He managed to say "arrow" before he passed out against my leg. He was white like parchment, and covered in his own vomit. His eyes were just two pools of black blood, and he was shaking like a leaf.' Merion looked at Rhin, who was drumming his lithe fingers against the crossbar of his sword.

'Took him two weeks to speak again. I hid him in a suitcase under my bed and fed him anything I could steal from dinner or pinch from the kitchen. Father almost found him once, whilst I was dragging the suitcase into the attic of the northeast tower. That's where I put him, so he didn't have to live in a suitcase for months on end.'

'There was a long rope to the trees on the northeast corner. Always one step from the woods.' Rhin almost managed to sound wistful.

'Not a soul went up there,' Merion continued. 'That was four years ago, just before my father began his campaign for the seat of the Prime Lord. I've been hiding you ever since.'

'And I've been keeping you safe ever since.' This was directed more at Lurker than anybody else.

Lurker sniffed several times before he answered. 'Your own guardian faerie, Merion.'

Rhin nodded. 'You could say that.'

'An' you came all the way to the Endless Land to protect this boy?'

Rhin shrugged, as if it was simply nothing. 'He is my friend. Somebody's got to look out for him. Besides,' and here he scowled, 'I doubt the Fae have ever forgotten me.

Merion wore a quizzical expression. 'I thought you said they had stopped looking for you? That you were safe.'

Rhin shook his head. 'The Fae never forget a wrong. Especially Sift. They can hold a grudge for centuries. That's the downside to having enemies that think middle age is about three hundred years old.'

Lurker whistled at that. 'Forty-two years have been plenty enough for me.'

Merion smelled out a chance to turn the conversation around. 'Oh really? How so?'

Lurker narrowed his eyes. 'Now just because you told your story don't mean I forgot you lied to me.'

'So you get to know my secrets, but I don't get to know yours? Outrageous,' Merion groused.

'I'm done with talking,' Lurker asserted with a wave of his hand. He laid his gun by his side and sought out his pack for a makeshift pillow. 'Our tongues have wagged enough for one night. I'm bidding you a goodnight now, so I have the energy to walk tomorrow.'

'Fine,' Merion replied, bubbling with irritation at the stubborn prospector. He vowed to try again in the morning.

Merion reached out for the trusty, though now rather battered, rucksack and shoved it under his stinging ear so he could put his back to the faerie and the fire—and to Lurker. Rhin sat back against the boy's spine and watched Jake retreat to a similar position. 'It's going to be a long night,' the faerie whispered to himself.

It was only as Merion teetered on the precipice of deep, dream-chased darkness that Lurker chose to have the final word. 'Make sure to sleep sound, boy. Tomorrow you meet the Shohari. And if we're real lucky, they won't decide to kill us. Goodnight now,' he said, as nonchalant as could be.

CHAPTER XIII
NEW ARRIVALS

'I don't know if this boy is fearless or just plain mad. Then again, I'm not too used to nine-year-old human young. I told him what I was and he just nodded as if I had told him the day of the week. He hasn't stopped asking questions since I croaked a few days ago. Most humans just scream or faint. This one seems utterly delighted to have a faerie under his bed. Maybe he is mad. Who cares? I think I'm finally safe.'

15th May, 1867

'Almighty's balls, boy. Not in the bloody toolbox! Spew somewhere else, you idiot! Bloody hell! It's on the spanners and everything,' yelled Master Bowder, the flushed and balding man screaming from the floor, body half-swallowed under a piece of machinery that looked so complex, it gave Juspin a headache just looking at it.

'Sorry,' he said, half-mumbling as he wiped his mouth. Now that the ship had come to a halt, the pitching and yawing was even worse. It was playing havoc with his stomach.

'I'm starting to wonder why I listened to your grandmother, and apprenticed you. If she hadn't helped raise my ma, then...' The end of Master Bowder's sentence was a violent shaking of his fists, greasy knuckles and all.

The engineer shimmied out from under the machine and sighed at his soiled tools. 'Bloody hell!' he spat.

Juspin had decided the Iron Ocean did not like him. Ever since he had been manhandled on board the *Amitie* in Plymouth, the waves had rolled and the wind had howled. The angry sky hadn't spared a scrap of sunlight, and the sea had battered the prow and flanks of the steamship day and night.

It must have despised him almost as much as his master at that very moment. Juspin shuffled awkwardly and made a show of squinting at the cogs and tubes and greasy cogs. 'So ... what's wrong with it?' he asked, quietly.

'Needs a whole new set of gears is what's wrong with it, lad,' huffed Bowder. The man was interminably irritable. 'Got spares, luck has it, but not the bolts. They're in the for'ard hold, right in the bow. Square-headed, 'bout yay long.'

Juspin nodded, but his legs didn't move. Bowder looked him up and down as he would one of his great steam engines, as if to check to see if he was still functional. 'Well, lad, get to it!' he bellowed, panicking Juspin into flight.

The boy skidded through the doorway of the engine room and trotted down the hallway, trying desperately to dig out his internal map of the ship. Four days, and already he was expected to know where everything was on this lurching, dripping ship. A wave of nausea rose and fell, and Juspin swallowed hard as he pressed on, mumbling directions to himself and worrying his carrot-hue hair with nervous fingers. He was desperate not to mess this task up. Just one would be nice.

After another few anxious minutes of jogging through dark corridors, sparsely lit by twitching lanterns, he finally came to a heavy door secured by a wheel. Juspin almost winded himself trying to loosen it, but finally, with a horrendous screech, it came free and spun for him.

The hold was darker than the corridors. In a stroke of brilliance, Juspin fetched a lantern from its hook and thrust it into the shadows. A dozen boxes wrapped in brown sheets greeted him, nothing more. The floor was thick with grime and crusted salt. Juspin held his breath as he wandered deeper into the hold, though he knew not exactly why. More crates, more boxes, more brown sheets. Juspin was starting to wonder whether he had made a wrong turn when he saw the curve of the bulkhead in front of him, and heard the dull crashing of the waves over the drone of the powerful engines. *Those confusing bloody engines.*

Where the deck met the bulkhead, he saw a little tower of small boxes stacked against crates bursting with cogs and sprockets and all manner of spare parts. Juspin punched the air and ran to the boxes.

The lantern was put on the deck while Juspin delved into the first few boxes. The first was full of washers, the second screws. The third, to his delight, were the bolts Master Bowder had described: square-headed and the length of his hand.

He did not notice the pain at first, only a cold pinch in the back of his legs, just above his ankle. Then he felt the blood seeping into his borrowed, oversized boots, and the pain began to surge. Fae steel cuts deep. With a squeal, Juspin collapsed to the floor and clutched at his leg. His foot flapped uselessly in the air. Blood dripped down his trousers.

'What in—?' Juspin gasped.

A cold needle of black steel rested on his forehead, and he fell instantly still. The lad blinked furiously. To his tear-stung eyes, it looked as though a strange white creature with black armour and crystal wings stood by his head, staring down at him with a terrifyingly confident smirk.

'We've caught a rat, Kawn,' said the creature, in the Queen's common. Juspin began to howl again, but the steel tapped him sharply. 'Easy now, rat.'

Another creature loomed out of the shadows, and poked something bloody at his ribs. Juspin whined. 'And what are we going to do with this rat, Wit?'

'Can't have this *caelk* squeaking, can we?' said the Wit, cocking his head to the side to get a better view of his prey, sweating profusely as it was, its tears mingled with its sweat.

'Take him below for the Fingers. See if he gives any sport. If not, throw him in the bilge,' the Wit ordered, calm and cold as an iceberg. It was then that he lent forward, and offered the poor boy a consoling shrug. 'Sorry, my lad. Looks like you boarded the wrong ship,' he said.

As the other faerie clicked his fingers, just before the bag was thrust onto his head, Juspin found himself wholeheartedly agreeing with the murderous little beast.

✪

'And the two onions, that'll be fine,' Lilain smiled and pointed at the last surviving onions on the market stall. The deliveries had been sparse. Trouble on the line, they said. Though that didn't do much to stop the shoving and yelling earlier that day.

'No fish today, ma'am? Got sardines in.'

Lilain's ears pricked up. 'Fresh?'

'No ma'am, in brine.'

Lilain frowned. 'Spoils the meat,' she said.

'Yes ma'am.'

Lilain paid and cast around for her next objective: the sheriff's office, to see if there had been word of that damned Merion. The boy would not have gone far. He must be hiding in the town somewhere. Lilain couldn't wait to give him a hiding when she saw him. She didn't trust herself to dally with the other thoughts, the dark alternatives. Lilain put a little more kick in her urgent stride, eager to weave a little faster through the crowds. The streets were choked and excitable. Lilain slowed a little, watching how the tide of townspeople moved against her, surging slowly yet inexorably towards the railway line.

Clutching her bag of vegetables and dried meats close to her chest, Lilain decided to follow the flow, and let herself join the rank and file of the curious crowds. Together they kept moving until they reached the platform, and found it already awash with crowds and clumps of people. Green and yellow pennants fluttered here and there, twitching with anticipation. Lilain bent her ear to some of the surrounding gossip, and soon found herself frowning.

'Lord Serped and his whole family!'

'Come to sort this wraith nonsense out, I hear.'

'For once and for all.'

'I'll drink to that.'

'I'll believe it when I see it,' said the last, a sullen-looking worker.

Lilain found herself slowing to a crawl, and letting the others nudge and brush past. There she waited. Slowly but confidently, the whispers began to grow and grow. Lilain stood on her tiptoes to see, but the press on the platform was too thick. As the thick-knitted crowd on the platform began to cheer, others surged forwards to catch a glimpse.

Whether they were there to grin or to glower, everybody wanted to see the Serpeds up close. Even Lilain crept forward, partly because it was futile to push against the flow of the crowd. Soon enough, she glimpsed a pale hand waving above the crowds, stiff and stoic. Lilain raised herself on tiptoes to drink it all in.

Lord Serped stood tall in his open-top carriage, decked with silver and painted coat of arms: a green wyrm, coiled casually around a silver spinning-top. The ladies Serped sat upright and prim on either side of their lord and master, surveying the dusty crowds with carefully drawn smiles. The mother, Ferida, and her daughter, Calidae, were copies, mere decades apart.

Their clothes were fine enough to draw some grumbles from a scattering of workers in the crowd. The lordsguards, trotting proudly on their horses and decked out in black cloth and mail, kept a watchful eye for any trouble. Sheriffsmen walked between the gaps in the crowd, their narrowed eyes vigilant.

Lilain sneered. *Pomp and ceremony, purely for the inflation of the bastard's ego,* she thought to herself. It was then that she caught it; the space between the elbows and waving arms, forging a clear channel for her to stare down, straight into Castor Serped's eyes. Lilain froze for the briefest moments, and then made sure to glare right back as his gaze locked on hers. For all the shortness of the moment, the space in the crowd, enough silent words were said. Then Serped's eyes were lost in the throng of hands and faces, and Lilain turned away, to glare at the dust instead. As she waded her way out of the crowd, she could not help but shiver at the chill that ran down her spine. The boiling sunshine failed to warm her.

CHAPTER XIV

RAILWRAITH

'The boy's name is Merion, for short, and today he officially welcomed me to his home as a permanent guest. I'm not sure the boy's father would be so welcoming. He's a powerful man. You can tell just by the way he walks. And men of power don't have time for flights of fancy. He's stern, but he seems wise.) (There's a scent on him I can't figure.)'

15th May, 1867

If you have ever been roughly or rudely awoken, you will know exactly how unpleasant and jarring it is to be dragged from the soft, amorphous haze of your dreams and thrown into the light of day without so much as an 'excuse me'. Panic and confusion, both at once, do not a joyous experience make.

Tonmerion found two rough leather hands grabbing at his shirt collar, shaking him violently. His eyes snapped open, and he instantly wished they hadn't. Lurker's weather-worn face was an inch from his. Merion could almost taste his stale, tobacco-stained breath. So very different from the smell of fresh bread and spitting sausages wafting up the stairwells of Harker Sheer that he had been dreaming of.

'Get up!' Lurker hissed, voice strangled with urgency. Merion had never heard Lurker so panicked, and that kept the boy's mouth shut and his body obedient. Something really must have been wrong.

'An' tell that bloody faerie of yours to back down, afore I make him,' Lurker snapped, eying Rhin, who was hard-eyed and hovering by Merion's side, blade half-drawn from his grey scabbard.

'Rhin,' Merion croaked, and Rhin shoved the blade away.

'Follow me, fast and quiet. No shoutin', no arguin', no questions. Lest you want to end up as dead meat for the vultures.'

Merion didn't speak a word as Lurker pushed his head low and led him in a scrambling run over the lip of their hollow and down onto the hillside. He did not take them far. He found them a boulder to hide behind and shoved Merion up against it. Merion desperately wanted to know what was going on, but he was too scared to talk. Lurker was rattled, and seeing him so fidgety and wide-eyed kept Merion's lips tightly sealed. He watched the big man creep to the edge of the boulder. A dull bang echoed through the crisp morning air. It was barely an hour past sunrise, and already the heat was beginning to creep into the air. Merion flinched as another thud shook his still-sleepy bones.

'Am I the only one who wants to know what the hell is going on?' Rhin whispered, his words barely audible. Lurker waved a hand at him to be silent.

Rhin's question was soon answered. After several more ominous bangs, the stomach-clenching form of a hulking railwraith emerged at the foot of the slope, and paused to scratch its face. Even from half a mile away, they could hear the screeching of ragged claws on iron cheekbones.

The railwraith was quite the monster. It must have been ten feet tall, and even then it was hunched over, glaring at the wasteland. Twisted iron rails formed its bones and frame. Greased bolts and shards of wood gave it tooth, skin, and sinew. Railspikes gave it claws and spines to decorate its shoulders. Its eyes were simple: black and empty holes bored in the tortured iron. It was a monster from the darkest of nightmares. By the backside of the Almighty did Merion want to run! Only fear pinned him down.

The three of them froze as the railwraith turned its hollow gaze to the higher hillside. Sunlight flirted with its sharp features, danced on its dusty claws.

Rhin was the only one who dared to move. He reached out and touched both Merion and Lurker with his hands. Then he began to shake.

His eyes became tightly-scrunched whorls of grey skin, and his sharp nails dug at their clothing. Merion had to bite his tongue to keep himself from yelling. Gradually, they began to fade. Not completely, for that would have made Rhin's eyes bleed, but enough for them to look like rock and pebble rather than two quivering humans. It worked a charm. The railwraith's gaze passed them by, and the creature looked to the east instead. With a screech of metal, the monster lumbered off, its footsteps thundering across the desert.

An hour, they waited for those footsteps to die away. Railwraiths can be fast, when there are fresh rail workers to be ripped apart, but this one had been in no rush. It took yet another hour for Merion's heart to calm itself to a normal patter. His neck already ached from the amount of times he had looked over his shoulder, praying not to see a railwraith lurching after them. Only when he felt safe did he dare to break his silence. Lurker was ahead, as usual, though today his pace was a little faster than normal. Merion did not blame him. He was happy to keep up.

'That was a … I mean, it had to be … a railwraith, right?'

'Strange,' Lurker murmured, 'for one to come so far north, where there ain't no action to be had.'

'Maybe it got lost?'

Lurker mused. 'Maybe. Strong to come this far in that shape.'

'What do you mean, in *that shape*?' asked Rhin.

In his haste and worry, Lurker had almost forgotten Rhin was there. The prospector threw a dark look over his shoulder to confirm that yes, indeed, that *was* a faerie walking beside the child, as real as a slap in the face.

'Thanks. For earlier,' said Lurker gruffly, tipping his hat.

Rhin sketched a quick bow mid-stride. 'Welcome.'

'Railwraiths are only railwraiths when they come across some rail, see? Before we came to the desert, they just kept to the woods and the hills, building themselves up out o' trees and rocks whenever a traveller wandered along. What do you think tumbleweeds and dust devils are? Lesser wraiths, just bored, is all. But then along came the Serped Rail Company, and gave 'em summin' stronger. Iron. Steel. Steam-machined wood. Railspikes. A *boofay* of hardcore shit for them to rip up and bend into bone and claw.' Lurker sniffed. 'Seems ironic to me, like we're being punished for our damn brazen ambition.'

Merion hadn't expected such a loquacious answer, but he was not about to argue. 'So you think the Almighty, or Maker, is punishing us for trying to build a railroad across a desert?'

'God's got nothing to do with it, and he ain't my Maker. If he is, then he did a horse-shit job of it, and I won't be worshipping his craftsmanship. I don't want to believe in a god that gives us the keys to the world, says "enjoy", but then forgets to take the evil with him afore he leaves. We're too much for our own selves, boy. Though we try to forget we're animals, on the inside, it can't help break out when it gets an excuse.'

Merion furrowed his brow. This was all getting rather a bit too theological for his liking, touching on the blasphemous. Merion tried to steer the conversation elsewhere.

'Are you talking about the war?'

Lurker grunted. 'I suppose I am.'

'What was it about?'

Lurker stopped dead but did not turn. 'You don't know?' he grunted.

Merion shook his head. 'No. We had our own wars, in Indus and Ashanti.'

'Hundreds of thousands dead, and you never heard.'

'My father told me of the war, but only because it was damaging trade.'

'Damaging trade. All heart, that Karrigan.'

Merion raised a finger. 'Now see here—' he began, but Lurker dismissed him with a snort.

'The south wanted to be its own kingdom, separate from a united America. The north wanted the south to release its slaves as freemen. Now, at the time, as a slave myself, I found myself agreein' with the north. But as a Karolin slave I didn't have much choice in the matter. Deep south, boy, where swamps go on for miles and miles—that was my home, and it's about as north as a crab's ass.'

Merion suddenly felt very awkward indeed. He had guessed that Lurker might have had such a history. The scars and his skin certainly indicated so. Merion winced as he thought of how he had spoken about Gunderton, the under-butler, the night before.

'You were a slave?' Merion asked, timidly.

'Six years. Taken as a free man, I was. Put to work in the clockwork factories near Severed Creek. Kept my head low and my manners nice. That's when I found my knack for ... finding things. Precious stones mainly, gold, silver, that sort of thing. Could sniff 'em out.' Lurker sniffed then, as if to prove the point. 'Masters took a liking to my talent and kept me close. But then when the war started, and Lincoln blockaded the ports, it got tough. Several of us escaped one night, when the guards were fighting, and made off into the swamps. Miracle we made it to the border, never mind Virginia. Seven of us left the camp that night, and only two made it through to Lincoln's blues. Me, and one man.' There was a rasping as Lurker rubbed his chin. 'Don't remember his name. Didn't say much.'

'So you fought for Red King Lincoln?'

Lurker grunted again. 'Never liked that name for him. It's lost all meanin' to folks. He was called "Red" because of all the bloodshed he put a stop to, and "King" was somethin' we slaves called him, to be ironic. The south wanted a king, you get it? Just kind of stuck. Makes him sound like a butcher.'

'But what about that famous bloody axe of his?'

'He knew how t' swing a blade, that was for sure. I saw him once, in a puddle of blood and guts outside Peter's Burg, swinging an axe like nobody's business. Cannon firing right past his ear. Hat on tight. Always insisted he fight alongside his men.'

'What was it like? In the war?' Merion could not help but ask. He was only a boy, after all.

'You don't want to know, boy. Believe me when I say that. Like I said, all men are animals on the inside, and war is the perfect excuse to show your true colours. I've seen slaughter on a scale that would make you want to tear your eyes out.' More chin-rubbing. More rasping. 'What happens 'tween men on the battlefield should stay right there, down with the piss and the shit and the blood. And let's not forget the mud. I was glad to be rid of it.'

'When was that?'

'Three years now, thanks to Lincoln. Enough time for me to find myself a different kind of sorrow, but that's another story for another day. Quiet now. We're coming into Shohari country, by my reckonin'. Keep your head down and don't talk.'

But Merion did not want to keep his head down, and his tongue still. 'Now just wait one minute,' he said, coming to a halt. Hands had already met hips. 'Do you think I'm just going to follow on, after what you said last night? How do I know you're not leading us to our deaths? I didn't come out here to die, I just want my answers.'

Lurker turned to look at him. 'Fought alongside many a Shohari in the war. And their wilder cousins. They were kind enough to teach me some of their ways, a little of their tongue, here and there. The Shohari know me. Least, a few of them do. We just have to hope we run into some friends.'

Merion sighed. 'How very comforting,' he said.

Rhin piped up. 'And what about me, hmm? Are the Shohari particularly adverse to the Fae?'

Lurker tipped his hat backwards. 'Now, that I don't know, so I think we oughta put you back in that rucksack, Rhin, and then we'll be on our way.'

And so it was. Under the baking heat of the midday sun, they trudged northwards, curving slightly west as the sun slipped from its zenith. They stopped only once to sip water and nibble at salty jerky, and then they were on their way. The country was bare, deserted as a desert can be. Here and there sheer-sided towers of red rock thrust up out of the scrub, like abandoned fortresses, scoured clean by the hot wind. It felt hotter today than it had before, and the bludgeoning, endless anger of the sun made him want to curl up in a ball and pray for sunset.

'Is it far now?' he croaked, somewhere around half-past three.

Lurker whispered over his shoulder. 'No, but quiet. We got eyes on us. Don't look!'

But Merion couldn't help it. His head jerked up involuntarily. Before he caught himself and brought his gaze back down, he spied two silhouettes atop a flat-topped hill to the west, black against the deep blue of the big, wide sky. They were on horseback, and they held spears, or long guns maybe; Merion couldn't tell. Pennants streamed from them. Merion's heart thudded.

'How long?' he asked.

'Hour maybe, once they see us keep on going straight. They're watching to see if we'll turn. Marking their territory like a hound pisses on a stump. You stay good and quiet now.'

Merion, did exactly as he was told. Ten minutes passed, and still the two silhouettes watched on. Lurker guided them further west, hardly heading north at all now. He was making a statement. Another ten minutes slid achingly by, and when Merion snuck another glance at the hilltop, he saw the Shohari had gone. His heart dropped like a stone.

'They're gone,' he whispered, focusing on his boots.

'Not quite, boy.'

Lurker pulled Merion close as the first horses galloped over the rise ahead of them. Merion held his breath. The Shohari were the very definition of wild. From the tips of their black and braided scalps to the unshod hooves of their slavering, piebald steeds, they dripped with savage energy. They were tall, very tall indeed, and lithe and wiry. Their strong arms and legs looked like bunched cords wrapped in dark, sun-drenched skin. Their jawlines were as sharp as the spears strapped alongside their long, stolen rifles, and their eyes were hooded with heavy, proud brows. Their faintly greenish skin was aged with more than just pitted lines and creases, but with ageless knowledge, perhaps, and the confidence that comes with it.

The Shohari wore close to nothing. Their only garments were leather wraps around their groins and coloured beads around their necks. A few wore waistcoats of fur, others wore bright ribbons of blue or purple fabric tied around their foreheads. They all had small axes and knives at their belts.

The riders hissed as they encircled them, almost twenty in all, and Merion was left praying that this was just a traditional, friendly Shohari greeting. Lurker seemed to think otherwise, and wrapped another arm around the boy, tucking him closer into his side. The prospector looked for the tallest rider, and met his stern gaze.

'*Wa, sh'ana see,*' Lurker said, making little circular movements with a cupped hand.

The Shohari he spoke to did not seem too impressed. '*Ah eshe gauk! Wah me' heera. Sam tee!*' he challenged. His talk was slow, his words deep and sonorous.

Lurker shook his head. '*Ot a she, mik,*' he replied, his tone rising and falling as though he were half-singing his words. The language was garbled and fractured, barely sounding like language at all. His gloved hands added whatever words he did not say out loud.

'*Zah e'nalta.*'

'*Tus ah o'nalta.*'

The Shohari rider moved his jaw from side to side as he thought. '*Wa, a'bash?*' he asked, finally.

'*Mayut.*'

'*Mayut, seh?*'

'*Seh.*'

The Shohari hissed and levelled a spear at Lurker. The other riders began to murmur and chant. Merion shivered, even in the heat. '*Seh? Eh, pe n'ash!*'

'*Seh!*' Lurker barked.

'*Te'ah!*' shouted the rider. The circle of Shohari and horses fell deathly quiet. '*Me, a teh,*' he told them, and then pointed, just to make sure they got whatever point he was making. Merion wished dearly to know what it was.

'*Mayut,*' Lurker nodded. The rider clicked his tongue and pulled at the reins of his piebald horse. One by one, the Shohari riders began to peel away and form a line. A space cleared at its centre, and Lurker and Merion were told curtly to fill it. Whatever the prospector had said had worked, but it was evident these Shohari were not happy in the slightest.

Merion tapped Lurker on the back. 'Where are they taking us?'

'To see the Buffalo Snake if we're lucky, and they don't change their mind. Chief Mayut. A friend, of sorts.'

'And are we to walk the entire way? Hardly fair when they have horses. How far is it?'

'Ten or so miles, maybe more. They move around.'

'But it will be night-time by the time we get there.'

Lurker turned around to wink. 'Just in time for the party, then.'

Merion's eyes widened, enough to inform Lurker he was curious, possibly even excited. 'The party?' he echoed.

'It's almost a full moon. Feastin' time. Tonight, we'll eat like Shohari. They'll be mighty interested in you. Told them you'd come from across the sea to meet them.'

'Well I suppose that's true…' Merion paused to think. 'Does this mean we don't have to eat beans tonight then? No offence.'

'Offence taken, but no beans.'

Small mercies, Merion thought.

CHAPTER XV

DEADOAK

'Tested the leg today and it seems to be working. Magick is back too, now that I've regained my strength. I've developed an unhealthy obsession with following this father around. Turns out he's set to be the highest lord of the Empire, second only to their Queen. Of all the houses I crawled into ... The man literally oozes secrets. It's fascinating.'

15th May, 1867

The camp appeared first as a glittering swarm of orange fireflies floating between two sharp hills. The pounding of the drums came next. Deep, thumping beats reverberated through the ground and made Merion's heart dance. Step by step, the camp materialised out of the night. First a makeshift pen for ponies, then the sheer sides of a tall and lonesome tent, held together by long poles and braided ropes. The camp was awash with yellow and red, painted by torchlight. Long-limbed figures slid between the shadows and patches of light, ominous, in the way they loped.

There was no road through the camp, and the small party of riders and foreigners had to weave between the guide-ropes and cooking fires to reach the epicentre, where the drums thundered away and yet-unseen mouths screeched and cawed at the star-speckled sky. Merion could smell food. His nose was certain of it. Corn bread. Meat. Sizzling fat. He could picture it dripping from spits and gurgling in pans. His stomach twisted in a knot.

It was then he glimpsed the dancers, spinning in concentric circles around a great pyre, piled high with blazing logs and bundles of dead desert weeds. Its heat was impressive. Merion could feel his face prickling even from a hundred feet away. The dancers must have been roasting in their skins. There were hundreds of Shohari gathered there, and countless more beyond the glare of the great fire. They sat in wide circles around cooking fires or bunched together in tight groups. Some hammered at drums. Others sang. A few capered around and whistled away on odd, flat flutes.

The riders had abandoned them, and Lurker and Merion were left at the edges of the crowds to watch the frenzied, half-naked (and in some groin-stirring cases, utterly naked) revelry, and wonder where the hell they were going to sit. It was very quickly evident that they had no real choice in the matter.

The Shohari rider Lurker had argued with was pushing his way back through the crowds towards them. He had come from the direction of the big fire, and whatever he'd found there had apparently put him in a very bad mood indeed. His dark eyes were locked on Lurker.

'*Me, at'eh!*' he shouted, when he was barely a dozen feet away. His harsh voice cut through the noise and heads began to turn in their direction. It did not take long for a hush to spread over the immediate vicinity. It took even less time for the quiet to spread to the other side of the pyre. Soon enough, the whole crowd was staring at them. It was terribly eerie, in the wake of the ear-splitting din. Merion could feel a single bead of sweat dribble down his forehead and onto his nose. He desperately wanted to wipe it away, but he was petrified that any movement would break the muttering silence and bring the whole tribe swarming towards them.

'Not ... a ... word,' Lurker breathed. Merion had no arguments with that.

The silence stretched on and on, getting tenser all the time, like the string of a celloine being tightened and teased out. The snap would come at any moment, Merion knew it. With every aching second that passed, he curled tighter and tighter into himself.

A shout rang out over the hundreds, clear as a desert day. 'Lurker!'

Merion could see the speaker now; a large man standing in front of the pyre, looking for all the world like a shadow ablaze. 'Lurker! *Kam as'a nahwa!'* he called, beckoning to the two strangers. Lurker gave Merion a shove.

'You heard the man,' he said, with a sniff.

Merion began to negotiate the crowds, praying that with every step his feet would land on earth, and not a hand, or a torso, or somebody's dinner. He did not fancy starting a very violent and very short war through a clumsy misstep.

'Easy does it,' he muttered to himself as he snaked through the throngs of Shohari. They smelled like the earth after rain, but with a tang of sweat thrown in. Every now and again he passed a female, and his head would spin as he breathed in the overpowering perfume, thick with spice and floral notes that hit him like a hammer.

At long last, they reached the centre of the party, where the air was hot, and tinged with a strange animal scent. The crowds had thinned out to make way for the dancers. The large man stood alone, his arms outstretched and welcoming, fingers beckoning. He had a wide smile on his wrinkled face. To call him fat would have done him a disservice. He was simply *big*. And in every sense of the word; from his tree-trunk legs to his bear-like shoulders. This man was one big slab of greenish meat. Beads dangled in huge quantities from his forearms, neck, and even his ankles. He wore nothing but a kilt of fur and a knife at his waist. White feathers had been braided into his long and matted hair. A polished vulture's beak balanced gently on his forehead. This was the chief. There was no doubt about it.

This may have been why Merion was so gobsmacked when the first thing Lurker decided to do was punch the man square in the jaw.

'Agh!' Lurker grunted as he cradled his wrist, flexing his fingers and shaking out the sting.

Merion nearly fell to his knees. All this way, all this tension, all that relief, and now Lurker had to go and seal their fates with one stupid punch. 'Why?!' he gasped, eyes wide, lip shaking.

But the chief, despite nursing his jaw, was chuckling. He had reeled back under the blow, but now he had straightened up and was wiping a dab of dark, almost black, blood from his lip. 'Getting old,' he smirked, and then with a grunt of his own, he returned the favour.

The chief moved like lightning. Lurker took the strike like a champion. Eyes shut and jaw clenched, the chief's fist caught him just in front of the ear. Lurker dropped to one knee as stars and fireworks exploded before his eyes. No flexing of fingers for the chief. No cradling of wrists. He simply waited for Lurker to rise with a wide smile.

But Lurker didn't rise. He stayed right where he was, with one knee buried in the hot sand, one hand held up in surrender. He too began to chuckle, and it was then that the crowd began to cheer and whoop and holler for their chief.

'*A'seh.* Maybe I am, Mayut. Maybe I am.'

The chief, Mayut, then turned to Merion and fixed him with a twinkling stare. 'And him?' he asked, curtly. His knowledge of the common must have been limited. 'A warrior?'

Before Lurker could answer, Merion bowed low, as low as his spine would allow. 'No sir, I am no warrior. I am Tonmerion Hark, sir, son of Prime Lord Karrigan Hark. It is an honour,' he said, in his most formal tone.

When Merion rose up, the chief was looking to Lurker, that same glint still stuck in his dark eyes. Lurker snorted. 'A warrior in training.'

'Ah.' The chief nodded, scratching his bloody lip as if mulling it all over. He bent a hand towards Merion, and the boy stepped forward.

'Look at your friend,' the chief ordered in a slow and ponderous voice.

Merion looked, and the chief swung. Hard.

The last thing Merion heard before his nose met the dust and sand was laughter, erupting all around like a volcano of hilarity. *Figures*, he thought, before sliding from the pain into darkness.

✣

'Yes, but you didn't *have* to say I was a warrior, now did you? You knew what a warriors' greeting was. You'd just bloody taken one, for Almighty's sake,' Merion grumbled around a mouthful of greasy meat. 'That chief is fast, for his size.'

'That's why they call him the Buffalo Snake. Big, but quick as a rattler.'

Merion just grumbled at that.

By the gracious Almighty himself, this food was good. Dried meat, roasted meat, fried meat, and meat chopped and diced into stews; there was more meat than Merion could have ever dreamed of. He did not dare enquire as to what he was munching. He didn't want to know. It could have been his fellow man for all he cared. His eager stomach welcomed all. Had Merion the testicular fortitude to enquire about the history of his supper, he would have learnt that the Shohari had caught and cooked a cornucopia of desert fare: rat, fox, lizard, vulture, goat, buffalo, snake—it was all there, sizzling away in various places around the great pyre.

And the fruit: Merion had never tasted such things. He couldn't help but wonder where on earth the Shohari had managed to find fruit in the desert, but once again, he was happy being blissfully ignorant. There were sweet pears with soft spikes on their skins. There were little berries that partially resembled wrinkled strawberries, except for the fact they were blue; Apricots that soured the tongue; plums that burst in the mouth —Merion tried them all.

It would have been culinary paradise, had his face not ached. Every time he chewed his jaw cried out in agony. He had bitten his numb tongue too, and it complained every time he reached for another apricot.

'You want them to give you answers? You act like one of them,' Lurker shrugged, half-hiding a smile. 'Wise move anyway.'

'What was?'

Lurker's smile grew a little wider. 'Going down like a sack of boulders like you did. Passing out. Always wise to let the chief win.'

Merion flicked him a look. 'Shut up.'

The chief in question was sitting six feet away, holding court with several of his advisors, or so Merion guessed. Several of them had a few feathers tied in their hair, but none as many as Chief Mayut, the Buffalo Snake himself. They gestured wildly as they chattered, their clipped and jittering words coming out in streams. At the edge of their group sat the rider from earlier. He hadn't touched a crumb, nor a drop of drink. He just stared at Lurker and Merion with a pair of narrowed eyes. He was Mayut's nephew, his *Ton'a*, as it had turned out, and a staunch loather of humans.

There was one other figure sitting across from them. This one also stared, and yet did not. In the bright light of the fire, Merion could see that the woman's eyes were milky and dead. She was blind as a mole, and yet somehow Merion could not help but feel she was looking *directly* at him. No matter how hard he tried to distract himself with food and an ever-growing belly, he could not shake off the feeling of those eyes. A suspicion began to grow.

Finally, Merion asked Lurker. 'Who's that, sitting by the chief, on the far side from our friend?' he enquired, and then leant closer. 'Oh, is that the witch?'

Lurker sniffed. 'You'll see, soon enough.'

'It feels like she's staring at me. I mean, she looks blind, but I can't help but think … You know?' Merion shrugged, his words sounding more and more foolish as each fell off his tongue.

'No,' Lurker shook his head.

And still the woman stared. Merion snuck quick glances over his hands as he wiped his greasy face.

The witch was made of leather, for all Merion could tell. Her dark greenish skin wore the lines of a hundred different creases, like the scribblings on an old map. Toothless, she mumbled to herself, mashing her wrinkled lips together in sequences that Merion had no hope of discerning. Whatever it was that she said, he could not hear it over the hubbub. Her hair hung in long, thick braids over most of her face. They coiled around her neck and spilt onto her lap. Some even lay in the sand, like black snakes basking in the warmth of the fire. In her hands she held a skinny staff of pine, bleached by the sun and all wrapped up in cloth and hair. Its tip held a rattling nest of bones, stolen from dead mice, rats, and chickens—a little ankle bone here, a pierced skull there, all wrapped up in wire. That alone sent a chill down Merion's back, never mind the rings of bones hanging from around her neck.

'See the blood,' Lurker broke the boy's reverie. He pointed, making Merion flinch. There, hanging from hoops in the hem of the woman's ragged skirt, were little crystal vials of various colours: some yellow, some dark red, others black.

Merion squinted at the strange little vials. Somehow, he recognised them. 'Just like the ones Aunt—'

'Mayut!' Lurker called out, cutting him off. '*Wa ham eshe. See to 'm as ana,*' the pointing finger curled back to Merion.

'What did you just say?' Merion hissed as the chief got up from his bench and walked over to sit cross-legged in front of his guests. Lurker motioned for Merion to follow suit, and together they shifted from their pillows and slid onto the warm sand, sitting almost knee to knee with the chief. Mayut pointed at the dark bruises already blossoming across Merion's cheek and laughed.

Lurker held up his hands and made a wide gesture. 'Merion has come to ask a favour of you, a favour of the Shohari.'

Mayut nodded sombrely, and then turned to face the boy. Merion could sense there was ceremony behind this. 'Why?' Mayut asked. *Not 'what'. Strange.*

Merion spoke loudly and clearly. 'Because I am told you are the only ones who can give me the answers I need.'

Mayut spoke almost as much with his hands as he did with his mouth. With every word of broken common came a gesture; a circling motion, a jab of his fingers, a wave to the spark-flecked sky. 'We know answers to many questions, little warrior. Some cost nothing. Some cost more.'

'Cost?' Merion's heart fell a little. He made a show of patting his pocket. 'I have nothing to offer.'

Mayut shook his head vehemently. 'The cost lies in truth you seek.' The chief saw Merion's confused expression and gestured to Lurker.

The prospector sniffed. 'He means that sometimes you don't want to know the answers, once you have 'em. Wished you hadn't asked at all. That's the cost.'

Merion shook his head. 'Whatever it takes, I need to know the truth,' he urged.

Mayut leant close. There was meat between Mayut's teeth, Merion could see that, but he could also see the earnest fire in the chief's big eyes. Merion felt like melting under that gaze. 'Sure?' Mayut asked.

Merion ignored the almost imperceptible kick from the inside of his rucksack and nodded. 'I am,' he replied, firm and final.

Mayut clapped his hands together and pressed them against Merion's chest. It was much better than a punch, that much was for sure. 'Not for me to decide,' replied the chief.

'Who then?' Merion asked.

Mayut signalled behind him, and Merion craned his neck to see. 'Khora,' said the chief.

'Who?' Merion asked, although he already knew. He could already hear the rattling bones. Mayut rose and moved aside.

The blind witch shuffled forward, raising not a hand to steady or guide herself. Her staff was apparently for holding, not to aid her walking.

Khora. Merion was not sure if that was her name or her title. But he kept his mouth shut and his questions at bay. It was all he could do just to smile politely as she approached him. He was painfully aware of the stares from those around him, even Lurker.

Khora didn't speak. She held her staff aloft and rattled the bones above Merion's head. Then, with deliberate slowness and agonising precision, she reached up and plucked four sharp bones from her matted hair.

One.

Two.

Three.

Four. They landed in the sand. Two crossed each other like two swords on a coat of arms. The other two ignored each other.

Khora began to thump her chest then, a slow beat that sounded quite ominous to Merion. The others around them sat as still as skeletons, watching the little ritual. Khora muttered away to herself. Mayut seemed to be following her words closely, mimicking her words with his own silent lips. Merion ached to know what she was saying.

When finally Mayut turned back to him, there was a grave look on his face, one that worried Merion deeply. Khora was beating her chest faster and faster now. She began to pace back and forth, throwing the young Hark narrowed, squinting looks, made all the more haunting by her milky, dead eyes. Just before Merion could open his mouth to enquire what it was exactly that was causing all the fuss, the chief spoke.

'You hide something from us,' he said, low and dangerous. 'We not help those who lie, human. Even one who is friends of Lurker.'

Merion's cheeks flushed red. He prayed that it was not noticeable in the hot glow of the fire. 'Hiding something?' he echoed, weakly. Lurker nudged him sharply with an elbow. His dark look said everything. 'Yes,' Merion added. 'Of course.'

While Khora fidgeted and pranced about, getting closer and closer all the time, Merion reached for his rucksack. He could already feel Rhin stirring within.

As he tackled the buckle and strap, Khora danced forwards to paw at the fabric of the bag, picking at it with skeletal hands and long nails. Merion had to fight not to recoil. He did not want to anger the Shohari any more than he apparently already had.

'He's in here,' he muttered. Merion tipped the bag up and Rhin came striding out, chin high and chest puffed, every bone and muscle in his little grey body stretching so he could stand that precious half an inch taller. His iridescent wings were spread and proud, and his right hand rested calmly on the hilt of his black sword.

'May I present Rhin Rehn'ar, of the Fae. My friend and … faerie.'

'And a fellow warrior,' Lurker added. Both Rhin and Merion threw him an acidic look. Neither wanted to witness Rhin having to trade blows with Chief Mayut.

Mayut approached them, his pace slow and yet again ponderous. '*Jejeh'na,*' he announced, and whispers scampered around the ever-growing circle of Shohari around them.

'Pardon me?' Merion asked.

'*Jejeh'na!*' shouted the chief, making Merion jump. 'He who knows the name of the forest. Winged devils. Black needles. Our fathers told their stories of them, when Shohari lived north, where greenwood grows tall and dark. Story and legend. They both stand before my eyes,' Mayut said, reaching up to touch his brows and his vulture's skull.

Rhin decided that now was a very good moment to bow. Hoping all the while that he was not about to receive a heavy blow to the face, he delivered his finest, most regal bow, reserved only for kings, queens, and great Fae lords—and the occasional princess, of course. 'Chief Mayut. It is an honour to sit at your fire, as I imagine our ancestors once did, when the moon was a little brighter than it is now,' said Rhin. This was the first he had ever heard of the Fae in the Endless Land, but this was not the time for history lessons.

Mayut raised an eyebrow. '*Jejeh'na.* Wise beasts of silver-tongue.'

Rhin nodded.

Mayut glanced towards Merion. 'Why you follow this little warrior?' he asked.

Rhin answered quickly. 'He once saved my life, and now he is my friend.'

Mayut nodded. This was logic he could understand, universal in its simplicity. 'And you do not have his answers?'

Rhin bowed his head. 'I wish I did.'

'Khora! *Mayu n'sasah!*' Mayut barked to his shaman. Khora sprang to life, snatching her bones from the ground and rattling them around in her cupped hands, humming some odd little tune.

Merion's heart began to beat, faster and faster. Was this the moment he had been longing for, since that day he had stared at the blood on the steps? Was this it? Would he finally be able to fit the scattered pieces together? He was already writing the letter in his mind. *Dear Constable Pagget ...*

The bones rattled on and on. Khora's sweaty face rippled with straining veins. With a cry she released her charms, and they scattered in the sand. Merion's mouth had gone dry. His fists were beginning to ache from clenching.

'What do they say?' he blurted.

'Silence,' Mayut hissed. Khora look up at him and made several motions with her hands, drawing squiggly lines in the air. Merion's chest thumped.

'*Res ahm? Te Akway?*' Mayut whispered. Khora nodded. She looked drained, and strangely confused, as if her bones had fallen uselessly A dull ache began to spread across the young Hark's ribs.

Mayut rubbed his hands together. 'Khora has spoken. You sleep here tonight. In the morning we leave.'

Merion cocked his head. 'Leave? Leave for where? Do you know who killed my father?' he asked.

Mayut shook his head. 'To know this, you first know other answers. To questions you not ask. Bones give Khora no more tonight. We take you to Akway. He will hear your questions.'

Merion was one lip quiver away from whimpering. 'And this Akway will know who murdered my father?'

Mayut shrugged. 'He might,' he replied. 'But might not. We will see. Tomorrow. Now, we dance. Do you dance, Merion?'

But it was all getting too much for the boy. This constant oscillation between hope and hopelessness, between thumping fear and downright exhaustion, was becoming unbearable. Merion just wanted it to be over.

Merion shook his head, declined politely, and then promptly slumped to the ground. Lurker led Mayut away, whispering in his ear. Rhin came over to thump Merion on the leg. 'What's wrong with you, Hark?'

Merion threw up his hands and let them fall onto his legs. 'Will this ever end?'

'That sounded like progress to me.' Rhin tried on a smile, but somehow it didn't fit.

Merion stared at the whirling dervish of bare flesh that spun around the fire. Rhin put a hand on his knee.

'You sure you want to do this, Merion? Sure you want to know the answers? Mayut could be right, you know. About the consequences.'

'You sound more scared than I do.'

Rhin shook his head solemnly. 'I'm scared for you, Merion. You've got a heavy burden to bear as it is. Can you really stand it being any heavier?'

But Merion seemed resolute. Hearing his own doubts in the faerie's words somehow bolstered his stubbornness. 'The answers will lighten that burden, not make it heavier. Why do you think I crave them so much? Why do you think I'm here, in this Almighty-forsaken desert?'

Rhin winced. 'I'm not so sure you've considered what—'

Merion glared. 'Well it's not you that has to be sure, now is it?'

The faerie held up his hands and backed away. He had seen enough tantrums in his time, seen the silver spoon spat across the room on many an occasion. 'Fine,' he said calmly. 'Now come and watch the dancers. Distract yourself until tomorrow. Nothing needs doing until then.'

Merion huffed, but the faerie was right. Merion got to his feet and sauntered to where Lurker and the chief were now sitting, at the edge of the crowd, inches from the spinning, convulsing dancers.

His backside found a warm spot to Lurker's left, on the opposite side from the chief. Rhin settled down next to him and whistled. 'I think you're too young for this, Merion.'

Merion found it hard to argue with that.

You could say one thing for the Shohari, that they are far from shy.

Merion could not help but stare as he watched the Shohari girls twirling around in front of him, barely a scrap of material between them, their only coverings bright splashes and stripes of purple and blue paint.

There were men too, of course, dressed with masks made from the furs and feathers of desert cats and huge vultures. But it seemed that this dance was a female's domain, that the rhythmic pounding of the drums and wailing of the strange instruments was for the women, not the men.

Their dance was mesmerising. Feral to the core, they swayed and danced and yelped. It was hypnotic, the way their long limbs moved, as if they had no bones at all. Like shadows, they moved, black against the light of the huge pyre, shaking all the while as if possessed by maniac spirits.

Merion's eyes widened as a group of women moved closer, eager to please the chief and the strangers from the south. They flashed their sharp teeth and howled as their serpentine bodies moved to the drums. Merion's jaw hung agape. He found himself blushing as he caught their wild eyes, one at a time. He would never have admitted it, not in a thousand years, but Merion couldn't deny the stirrings in his groin, the swirling of sudden emotions. Manners faded away. There were no fathers here, no watchful aunts.

It was then that Merion noticed Lurker was averting his eyes, staring at the sand instead of the naked display. He could see the downward angle of the man's hat in his peripheral vision.

Lurker spared not a glance for the female form. His eyes were fixed at a spot just inches from his legs, and far away from the dark, sweaty skin only a few feet from him. There was a shadow over his face, but Merion could tell he felt uncomfortable.

'Lurker?' Merion asked.

Lurker sniffed and cleared his throat. 'Miles away, boy. Never you mind me.'

'Is it the dancers?'

'No, they're fine. Too fine for me, perhaps.'

Merion had to admit that he did not follow.

Lurker tutted. 'Too familiar then,' he said, with a sigh. 'Had me a Shohari wife once, for a spell. Year maybe. Maybe less. House fire put an end to that.'

Whatever it was, something had loosened Lurker's tongue a little. Perhaps he felt safe here, surrounded by the wild, strange Shohari. Perhaps he'd sipped more of his hipflask than usual. Whatever it was, Merion did not complain.

Lurker kept talking. 'Was after the war, and we was livin' out in the sticks outside of a tiny town called Hopeoak, near Denn's Folly in Ohio. Folk in the town weren't right in the head, not so soon after the war. Blamed my sort for a lot of things, and weren't too keen on Shohari neither. What a couple we must of made to them. We were just two demons living on their outskirts, and they didn't like that.' Here Lurker took a breath. 'Went up to Crickshaw one day to fetch some new pickaxes. Took me hours to get there, it was so damn hot. I'd been in a fight the week before, and a busted knee still hadn't healed right. I was slow as a drunk mule.

Lurker paused here to sniff and stare at the dust some more. 'I saw the flames from the next hill. Thought it a brush fire or somethin'. But no, it was our house. It was all rubble and cinders by the time I hobbled to it. Lehlana was dead inside. I didn't need to see her all healthy and soft again to know her throat had been cut before the fire. The fucker that did it left the knife on the table.'

'Who?'

Lurker rubbed his nose. 'I don't rightly know, but I must have killed him at some point or another…'

Merion was puzzled. 'But … then how do you know?'

Lurker met Merion's eyes then. His voice was cold and half-dead. 'Because I went down to that town and killed every last man I could lay hands on. Gun. Knife. Rock. Whatever my fingers found, I used. Spilt blood in every saloon, store and outhouse that shit-creek town had to offer. I got every one of those murderous bastards, and when I was done I marched right out of there and didn't stop running for two days. Came west and never looked back.' Lurker broke off his stare, and Merion finally took a breath. He was starting to understand what the chief had meant about the cost of the truth. The truth was that Merion was rubbing elbows with a mass murderer.

'I hear they call it Deadoak now.' Lurker didn't sound proud, but then again he didn't exactly sound apologetic. Merion tried to see it from his perspective, and wondered what he might do if he had a dead wife, and a townful of murderers to hand. Merion found himself nodding. 'My father would likely have called that justice.'

'As would the Fae,' Rhin said.

Lurker sniffed again. 'And that's what I tell myself,' he said. 'And so now you know about me, and what I've done. Will that shut you up for a while?'

Merion nodded. 'I suppose it might. For tonight at least.'

'Well, fortunately for me, you got other ears to scorch tomorrow, besides mine. Though good luck getting answers out of these mouths,' Lurker chuckled. 'Here, have some of this.'

With a tired groan and a creak of leather, he leant across the chief and grabbed a clay bottle. Mayut grinned at Merion while Lurker uncorked it.

'Is it alcohol?' he asked, sort of hoping it was.

Lurker disappointed him. 'No, no. Just a mix of herbs, oils, and other things. It's good. Everybody here is drinkin' it,' he said, motioning at the whirling lines of dancers.

'I shall not be dancing.'

'Don't worry, just drink.'

And there they were, those famous, everlasting words of wisdom. Words usually and liberally dispensed by those already well down the river of drunkenness themselves. This drink was altogether more *interesting* than alcohol. It was *sho'aka*, an old Shohari recipe, and it was potent stuff. Merion felt it hit him almost instantly; little tendrils of warmth worked their way up his spine and into his shoulders. He liked it.

After a few more gulps he wiped his hand across his mouth and passed the bottle back to Lurker, who also took a few swigs. Together they sighed and turned to watch the dancers, and slowly the sho'aka wormed its way into their skulls, and began to work its magick.

Merion felt warm, that was for sure. There was a fire in his stomach, bubbling up his throat and into his cheeks. His eyes felt dry. They kept snagging on his eyelids, every time he moved them. They were heavy too, like musket balls. Why was his mouth so wet? Was he hungry? He had to keep swallowing to avoid drowning in his own spit. His teeth felt rough.

The hooks of irreality slid under his skin, and gradually his night began to warp and change. Colours burst in the fire. The dancers became taller, and darker, like strange shadows dancing before a funeral pyre. One moment he was standing. The next he was sat down, Rhin grinning at him. Time hopped back and forth like a sluggish toad, and somewhere in that swirling, muddy soup of moments and images, Lurker got up to dance.

It was not a moment of drunken hilarity. Nor was it a moment of cheering and yelling. It was a moment that only Merion seemed to notice, as he lay there supine in the sand, one eye half-closed and the other blinking continuously. The young Hark rolled his head to one side, watching Lurker walk on the side of the world. His steps were slow but determined. The closer he drew to the fire, the darker he became, until his form danced and wavered like the others spinning around him. It was then that Lurker did a strange thing.

Button by button, garment by garment, Lurker began to undress. Merion squinted. In the flashes of light, and as Lurker turned from side to side, he saw the marks.

There were scores of them. Thick red lines, criss-crossing his back in a web of torture, as though the man's back had once been flayed apart and then woven back together. Merion found himself sucking on his teeth as he imagined the pain, the screaming.

'John,' he whispered, even though he knew Lurker couldn't hear him. He soon lost sight of him in amongst the naked bodies.

Merion turned back to the dark sky and let it spin. He was melting into the sand, he could feel it. Rhin would have to come dig him out in the morning. In between the nonsensical ramblings of his addled mind, Merion found himself mumbling a word over and over again, like a charm to keep his questions at bay. Sleep had started to paw at him, and he was more than ready to let it drag him off. He was starting to feel rather sick.

'Tomorrow,' he whispered. 'Tomorrow.'

Tomorrow he would get to the bottom of all this. Truth be damned.

CHAPTER XVI

ANSWERS FROM AKWAY

'Close. Far too close for my liking. We were headed for the stairs to the northeast tower. I was in the suitcase, all wrapped up. His father came out of nowhere. Demanded to know what the boy was doing. Got to hand it to the lad, he spun out the yarn. Karrigan's suspicious now though.

Merion's spent the night in his room. I've spent it up here, with the pigeons and curious spiders. At least I've got something to eat.'

16th May, 1867

Sweating was once again the order of the day, though this time, Merion thankfully did not have to walk. The grogginess of whatever he had imbibed the previous night still hadn't quite worn off. Twice he had emptied his stomach, much to the amusement of the Shohari. Though the fresh air had set him right again, thank the Almighty.

By midmorning, he had decided that the little piebald pony he had been allotted needed a name, and that name was to be *Gorm*. It dribbled. It wheezed. It constantly wandered off the beaten trail. It spent long minutes just staring at the grass in front of its long nose: Gorm by name, gormless by nature. He was nothing like the ponies and small horses Merion had ridden in Caravel, on the dark beaches of the west coast.

Gorm's only redeeming feature was the fact that Merion could ride him. Even though his back was bony, and he had to be constantly kept in check with sharp tugs of the reins, by the time the Shohari stopped for water Merion's feet had not touched the sandy earth for almost four hours. It was blissful, and his aching feet thanked him.

The countryside rolled past, changing gradually as they moved from the hills and onto open, empty plain. The ground was greener here. Small emerald shrubs abounded. Cacti waved them past with rigid, bristling arms. Herds of buffalo could be seen milling about in the distance. Mice ran under the hooves of the horses, and jackals yowled at them from their dens. In only half a day's travel, Wyoming had come alive, and Merion soaked up every drop of it.

Every one of his senses was on fire. The twittering of little finches filled his ears. The blossom of the shrubs and the sour-sweet scent of the cacti bombarded his nose. He could taste every little bit of grit on his tongue. He knew every hair and bead of sweat on his skin. Even the light had its way with him; stinging his eyes and making the colours of the plains pop and shimmer.

'When does this stuff wear off?' he asked moodily. Lurker rode just up ahead. His head had been bowed most of the day. Riding horseback apparently made him feel sick.

'Noon. You'll feel right as rain,' he grunted.

'Rain would be very welcome right now.'

Lurker snorted. 'You'd be lucky, now we're slippin' into summer. You picked one hell of a time to come to Wyoming, boy.'

And *hell* was the perfect word for it.

By noon, the air shivered over the prairie. Even there, amongst the green shrubs and cacti, the heat was oppressive. Sweat ran down his face in little rivers, making his eyes sting all the more. Every inch of him burned, almost as though he could actually feel his skin cooking, bit by bit. It seemed as though their journey would never end, that the plains would stretch on for eternity, but then a miracle appeared on the horizon.

First, it came in the shape of a long, dark smudge, punctuated only by a few hills and a dusty canyon carving a chunk out of its right flank. Halfway through the searing afternoon, it was a thick band of deep green, gently swaying in the heat-waves coming off the plains. Then at last, as the day crumbled to evening, Merion realised what it was. He shook Rhin, who had fallen asleep on Gorm's neck. 'It's a forest, Rhin. Wake up.'

And what a forest it was. The trees stood like an impenetrable wall, hundreds of feet high, battlements bursting with deep green bristles and knotted branches. *Nothing is small here,* thought Merion to himself, craning to look upward, daring his neck to snap.

The Shohari made no signs of halting to gawp. They plunged straight into the forest without so much as a word. The dust-brown tree trunks they rode between were like the pillars of the sky itself. They must have been a hundred paces around, at least. Big red berries glistened in the lower branches, hiding amongst the sage green of the fir. Creepers tussled with their thick, wandering roots. The air was thick with the smell of acid-sweet resin. Their path led them a merry dance through the undergrowth and down into a small ravine made sheer by slick granite rocks. Water trickled under-hoof. The going was slow, but steady. Still the Shohari made no noise. They were deadly silent to the very last. At the bottom of the ravine they followed its walls deeper into the forest. The day was on its death-bed, and with the towering trees and dark granite, it was unnervingly dark in the ravine.

After an hour of silent trudging, they came to an opening in the rock. The sheer walls peeled away and formed a wide, teardrop-shaped hollow in the earth. A small lake had gathered there, ringed in ivy and shadow. One solitary island sat on its glass-like surface like a broken crown. One tree grew alone on the little spur of rock, and one tree only. Even from the little grey beach at the edge of the hollow, Merion could see it was stunted and crippled. Its pale-leafed boughs stuck out at odd, tortured angles, and it seemed to sway, even though there was no breeze.

'The Sleeping Tree,' murmured Lurker, from behind him.

On the beach, a small and no-doubt ancient canoe was pulled up. 'Akway,' announced Mayut, pointing at the dusty vessel. 'He waits for you, little warrior.'

Merion scrambled off Gorm and stepped forward. 'I go alone?'

Mayut shook his head, scowling as if that were preposterous. 'No. I with you, and Lurker too. Maybe.'

'He can come,' Merion replied, with a sideways glance at the prospector. Lurker just shrugged. 'And Rhin,' he added, letting Rhin climb back into the rucksack.

'Then let us go,' Mayut nodded, and with a flick of his knife the chief cut the rope holding the canoe on the beach. Together the three pushed it across the shingle and into the cold water. Lurker and Mayut took the paddles, and with deep, strong strokes they powered the creaking canoe towards the island. Merion sat in the middle, staring at the water. The lake was like liquid glass. Even in the gloom, Merion could see fish at its bottom.

The young Hark felt terribly nervous and yet excited at the same time. He wondered what Akway would look like, and how he managed to stay alive on his odd island. *Perhaps he caught the fish with a spear, and lived in the branches of this 'sleeping tree' ...* Merion spun himself a little fantasy while the two men paddled.

With a thud, the nose of the canoe struck rock, and Merion was jolted forwards.

Mayut wrapped a scrap of rope around a protrusion of rock and then grunted at Merion. 'Little warrior. Up there,' he said, and pointed. Merion noticed his voice was softer now, gentler, as if he were afraid to wake something. It made Merion's heart beat even faster. *This is it*, he told himself.

Merion hopped onto the rock, narrowly avoiding dunking one entire shoe in the water. With Lurker in tow, he scrambled up a little path to where the ancient tree clung to the rocks with thick, gnarled roots. There was no dirt here for its tentacles, only rock. He wondered how it had survived all these years.

Breathing slightly heavier than usual, Merion stood before the Sleeping Tree, and took in all of its twisted beauty. Every inch of its bark was contorted and warped into whorls, zigzags and spiderwebs. Even its leaves were curved or coiled, as though some great force had reached up inside its trunk one day and pulled out its insides, sucked everything inward. Even though there was no breeze, its leaves rustled, and Merion found himself transfixed by their sighing.

The boy looked all around, up and down, but there was no sign of any Akway, shaman or wise man, nor any other strange, old or malnourished soothsayers. Merion was beginning to feel that old familiar sinking feeling yet again.

'So where is this Akway?' he whispered, as loud as he dared. There was an air of the sacrosanct about this little island, one that he wasn't quite sure about spoiling, not yet.

Mayut rumbled from behind him. 'Clear as day, little warrior.'

Merion made a show of looking about again. 'I don't see a soul.' The chief shook his head solemnly. 'Not one soul. Three.'

Merion threw him a quizzical look, and Mayut pointed a finger at each of his eyes, then back at the tree. 'Look into the tree. At its heart. You find your answers.'

Merion looked, eyes straining towards the rippled trunk, trying to dig out whatever it was the chief was talking about. Anything: patterns, words, faces ...

Faces.

His eyes caught it, and Merion almost yelped with shock. The face was huge and gnarled, made of knots and creases. Embedded deep in the trunk, it must have been the size of a banquet platter, and terrifyingly enough, it was now grinning at the young Hark.

It took barely a second for Merion to spot the second face, almost conjoined with the first, hanging from its chin. It too was comprised of broken bark, though this one lacked eyes. The upper half of its face had been swallowed up by a mossy growth.

Then the third and bottommost face twitched. It wrinkled its knotted brow and took a breath, making a sound like fingernails dragging across sun-baked driftwood. Merion took a step back, doubting his nerve for a moment.

'Fear not,' Mayut advised him, in barely a whisper.

The other two faces were coming to life now, blinking and twitching as the magick crept into their wizened, ancient features. The tree itself began to quiver. Around Merion's feet, the tangled roots started to squirm among the rocks. Rhin, now out of the pack, and as fascinated as Merion, hopped away from them, feeling the magick burning in them. This was old, older than anything Fae. Merion realised what Lurker had meant, back on the shore.

The topmost face smacked its lips together, clunking, and stared at him with eyeless sockets trapped in the whorls of the wood. The dark holes sent a shiver up the boy's spine as they took a fix on him. 'Smell like the sea,' came a deep croak, impossibly old, yet in perfect common.

The middle face sniffed, the mossy growth quivering as he did so. 'Like old houses and pines,' he rasped, in a higher voice than his companion. The roots quivered as he spoke. Merion's eyes widened. *The tall dark pines around Harker Sheer.* He stayed silent, even though he ached to blurt out his questions. The faces prattled on.

Bottom stuck out a tongue that looked like a sliver of bark. 'And blood too. Seen his share.' Here the face squinted his empty eyes. His voice made the stones shake under Merion's feet.

Middle piped up again. 'For one so young. Come far to find the truth.'

'You can help me?' Merion couldn't hold his lips shut for a moment longer. He took a step forward.

'Answers, we have,' rumbled Top.

'Answers, we can give,' added Middle.

'Answers for questions yet unasked,' boomed Bottom.

'For...' Merion stumbled over that. 'What do you mean?'

Middle sighed and sniffed some more, bunching up his wooden cheeks until they cracked. The branches began to droop then, falling inwards at a gentle pace, like an umbrella closing. The leaves were rattling. 'You come with questions. But not the right ones.'

'What should I be asking?' Merion furrowed his brow. The faces replied in turn, stealing the ends of each other's sentences as if one mind owned them. And yet somehow they seemed separate—three old seers, frozen in wood and time.

'Questions are for creatures ...'

'... Other than us.'

'Answers are our ...'

'... skill. You must ask.'

'And we must tell.'

'So I can ask you anything, and you have to tell me?'

There was a loud creaking as each of the faces grinned. 'That depends on the question, Merion Hark.'

Merion felt like scratching his head, too confused to realise he had never introduced himself. He looked at Rhin. The faerie was expressionless. He just sighed, shrugged, and turned his eyes back to the Sleeping Tree. 'Right,' Merion said, before taking a deep breath. 'I want to know who killed my father.'

'That ...

'... is not the right question.'

Merion started forward. 'How can that not be the right question? That's what I came here to find out!'

'Have you no more?'

Merion's heart threatened to jump out of his chest. He was an inch from fuming. 'Fine. Then *why* was my father murdered?'

'For money.'

'Money?' Merion felt the blood in his cheeks, felt how sweaty his palms were. The great Bulldog, slain for money. *How cheap. How despicable.*

'Will I ever catch my father's murderer?' Merion asked.

Bottom nodded, the wood around his face creaking. Still the branches lowered, they were almost touching Mayut's back now. 'You shall,' rasped Middle.

The boy's heart soared. He could have hugged the tree at that moment. 'Then how do I catch him? When?'

'One question …'

'… At a time!' hissed Middle.

Bottom rumbled as he cleared his throat. The branches shook as he did so. A few leaves sailed down to grace Merion's shoulders. 'You will learn in time.'

'That's not an answer!' Merion spluttered.

'It is the only answer,' Top corrected him haughtily. Under the drooping branches, the air was growing thick, and heavy.

Merion pinched his nose between finger and thumb and screwed up his eyes. He wondered blithely if there was an axe to hand. 'Fine!' he snapped, making Mayut hiss. 'Tell me why he sent me here. In his last will and testament.'

Bottom threw him a wide smile, showing off his splintered teeth. 'That is a good question.'

Middle chuckled, rasping like wood being twisted and crushed. 'Because Karrigan had a secret that he wished you to learn.'

'A power.'

'A power in the blood.'

'Your blood and his.'

Top closed his eyes tight and bared his own broad grin. 'And in the blood Lilain Rennevie draws from the veins of her dead.'

'What?' asked Merion.

'What is not a question, Merion Hark,' growled Bottom.

'What power?' Merion growled. The faces rattled off their answers like a Gatling gun, spitting moss and splinters.

'Any and all ...'

'... powers can be found in blood.'

'Your aunt collects.'

'Your father drinks.'

'The power comes from the belly.'

'Speed.'

'Brawn.'

'Not alone, was your father.'

'Neither are you.'

'Are you saying he had ... I have ... some sort of magical power?' Rhin looked at him sharply, but he continued. 'You can't be serious, tree.' Mayut nudged him with a foot. 'Akway,' he corrected himself.

'We say many things,' Top grinned.

'But we say no more,' rattled Middle.

Bottom rumbled, almost pensively. 'Our power is drained.'

Merion stumbled forward. 'Wait, I need more than that! Do I have a power? Can it help me get home?'

Middle was sniffing again, as if scenting the future in the air. 'In time. Though we see hardship. Toil.'

'Loss.'

'How do I get home?'

The branches were drooping so low that Merion had to fend them away. The faces were becoming sluggish. Middle mumbled away as if dozing off. The roots shivered gently to the sound of his voice. 'Family. Come blood ...'

'... or come mud ...'

'Thunder and fire.'

'And stolen words in ink.'

Merion felt like tugging out his hair. 'What does that mean?'

'Fight for family, Merion Hark.'

'Spill blood for it.'

And that was that. The Sleeping Tree fulfilled its calling and fell into a deep slumber, letting its branches bend and droop like a willow's, its faces freezing solid. Bottom was the last to speak, barely a whisper wrapped around his tongue. 'Watch out for rats.'

Rhin pricked up his ears at that.

Cold, flat, and grey was the boy's face, like the shy pebbles lurking around his feet. Merion staggered backwards, his shoes trampling the Sleeping Tree's dead leaves. His fingers felt numb. He flexed them over and over as they hung dead at his sides, but still nothing. His blood, it seemed, had retreated to his heart, and there it pounded, over and over, until he felt sick from it.

'Merion,' rumbled Lurker, but Merion shook his head. Not a word fell from the boy's mouth. He climbed down the warped rocks and back into the canoe. He sat there in silence, with arms folded and shaking with rage, fear, confusion, or perhaps all three, Lurker couldn't tell. He lingered beside the tree. The faces were still snoring away at each other. He scowled.

'You knew,' Mayut said. He had been watching the prospector closely.

Lurker sniffed. 'When a truth ain't yours to tell, I say don't tell it,' he replied.

Mayut shrugged. 'Truth is truth, no matter who tells it. Akway have no right to truth, but I let him tell boy anyway. You could have told him. Days past.'

Lurker shook his head firmly. 'I promised his aunt.'

Mayut drew a spiral in the air with his calloused finger, and spoke slowly. 'You trust them too much, friend. Noose tightens. Blade falls. I said before. If iron rails go further into our lands, we fight. Take the boy, aunt, and leave. Not want see you there, on that day, John.'

Lurker looked back at the boy sitting in the canoe, still shaking. 'You won't, don't worry.'

Mayut clasped the prospector by the shoulders. 'Then we leave Akway to sleep.'

★

'Merion, please speak to me,' Rhin pleaded, and not for the first time either.

It was an hour past sunrise, and Merion had not parted his lips for anything but water the entire night. Not a word, not to the faerie nor to Lurker. The war party had just arrived back at the camp, and in the dawn light, the boy looked haggard, exhausted from the ride and from the thoughts bouncing around his head. Rhin knew that feeling. Merion shook his head. He quickly dismounted and began to pick his way through the sleeping and snoring bodies, head swivelling back and forth as though looking for something.

There had been another feast. The merrymakers had fallen asleep in the circles in which they had sat. A few here and there were still awake. Some were very awake indeed, and Merion could not help but stare as he tiptoed past the writhing, gasping bodies.

Rhin tried a different tactic. 'What are you looking for? Can I help?'

Merion shook his head. It was a start. Rhin pushed his luck.

'I've got the better eyes, Merion. Tell me what it is and I'll find it,' the faerie whispered.

The young Hark's throat was so dry that his word came out as a crackle, like sand being rubbed over stones. 'That drink, the chief's drink.'

'And you think that will help you somehow?'

Merion snorted. 'It will help me sleep. Ah!' he hissed, spying a clay jug lying in between two skinny Shohari women. Merion reached out a curled finger, aiming for its curved handle. He gritted his teeth as he stretched out to hook it. Every one of his muscles ached from the ride.

'You're acting like an old drunk who's just found a bottle of wine amidst the rubbish heap,' Rhin told him, as he climbed from the rucksack and into the dust. Merion waved his free hand, ordering him to be quiet.

When the jug was firmly in his grasp, Merion headed away from the tangle of bodies and into the darkness of the camp. He found a spot between two of the tall Shohari tents and sat cross-legged on the earth. With his teeth, he uncorked the jug, spat it to the sand, and then took a long, deep gulp. It tasted even better than he remembered.

'Look at you,' Rhin said again. He stood barely a foot from Merion, arms crossed and purple eyes narrow.

'I'm sorry, were you or were you not present today while my life was being slowly but surely turned on its head? Did you nod off? Get bored and go sharpen your sword?'

'I was there all right,' Rhin replied. 'But what I saw was a young boy get told he has more than just his father's name, or his eyes, or hair. More than just blood. You're magick, Merion. Why are you angry, and not excited?'

Merion chuckled drily. 'See I distinctly remember a young boy being told that his father was murdered over money, and also that he had lied to him his entire life. You must have missed that part.'

'Yes, well ...' Rhin said, stepping closer. 'You wanted the truth, now you've got it. Mayut did warn you. The truth does hurt.'

'Hmph,' Merion growled, taking another swig of the sho'aka. Rhin shook his head. Merion's pupils were starting to shrink. His face had begun to droop.

Rhin grabbed the jug from Merion's slackening fingers and took a big gulp of his own. 'Look,' he said, wiping his mouth. 'Getting bad news is like shitting yourself. What's done is done. All you need to decide is whether you want to go and clean yourself up, or sit in your own filth and stew. Don't stew, Merion. You're going to burn yourself up from the inside out. Sun's already doing a mighty fine job on the outside as it is. Do you understand me?' Rhin stared into the boy's glazed eyes.

'Understand?' the faerie repeated, giving Merion's face a little slap. The boy nodded and blinked blearily.

'Don't shit myself.'

'You've got the gist. Now,' Rhin said with a sigh, 'go to sleep.'

Merion merely blinked at him, his face emptier than a beggar's belly.

'Fine.' Rhin put a hand against his chest and whispered something under his breath. Merion teetered backwards and his head hit the sand with a thump. 'There,' said the faerie, 'you've had enough.' He lifted the jug to his lips and took another sip. 'Mm,' he hummed. 'This *is* good.'

Rhin saw the strange liquor to the bottom of the jug before joining Merion on the sand. The faerie stared up at the blue sky and let his eyes swim in it. The sho'aka was strong, that was for sure, stronger than he cared to admit. Rhin let his eyes droop. Shadows moved in the corners of his eyes, shadows and shapes Rhin had thought he had left far enough behind. They were shapes with glowing eyes, pale smiles, and hissing wings. *Like rats.* They whispered to him, and amidst the snoring and grunting of the Shohari around him, Rhin heard their fell words, and felt their breath on his mottled cheeks.

The Hoard! The Hoard! Rhin struggled and thrashed, but his sluggish body translated his fear into nothing but weak twitches. His head spun as the sky grew black, a dripping, oozing black that sought to swallow him. It was a fitful sleep that took the faerie.

CHAPTER XVII
A DYING ART

'Merion's growing fast. It was his birthday, whatever that is, today. My my, what a productive afternoon of sneaking. Harker Sheer was packed with guests, and such informative guests. Lord Karrigan wants to move against Lord Longweather and his referendum. Lord Dizali is not so convinced. Lady Knutshire wants to ensure her place at the new table. Karrigan has other promises to keep, it seems. Secrets are a wonderful business.'

19th May, 1867

'Well, Mister Khurt, here we are,' Lilain muttered to herself as she propped the cart's handles upon the steps. The body upon its planks did not utter any sort of complaint. It just lay there, gawping at the sky with a mouth that was in serious lack of a jawbone. This was the third railwraith attack in a week.

Rubbing her sweaty palms on her smock, Lilain went to unlock the door. Her heavy ring of keys chimed. The air inside the house was cool, so she shut the door to keep it in. It was not as though the late Mr Khurt was going to wander off, nor was it likely anybody would be stealing him. The dead never fetch a good price. She felt her way down the curving stars to the darkened basement. The air down here was even cooler, cold even. Lilain sighed at the touch of it on her grimy neck and hot, wood-chafed hands.

Moving through the darkness, she reached for a lever and opened a door with it, exposing a little alcove. Then, with a few tugs of a rope, a trap door slid open and blinding daylight poured in. A table sat at the bottom of the alcove, repurposed as a lift for the dead and the fallen. There were ropes and pulleys hanging above each corner, and Lilain set to them with a dogged determination. The table inched upwards with every grunt. It was hot work now that the sun was on her once more. The cool of her crypt was no match for the midday desert sun. *Maker if it wasn't hot today.*

Once the table was at ground-level, she tied off the ropes, rubbed her hands, and wandered back up the stairs to her new client. He was right where she had left him.

'Let's get you in the cool, before you smell even worse, shall we?' she chatted idly to the corpse as she wheeled it around the side of her house. 'If that's possible.'

Mister Khurt had followed in the footsteps of many of Lilain's visitors to her table; he had soiled himself in his last moments. Lilain didn't blame him. She highly doubted she'd perform any differently, if she were to spend her last few breaths in the arms of a railwraith. Lilain sighed, as she always did. Such is the life of an undertaker.

As Lilain rested the handles of the cart on the ground, something caught her eye. She straightened up and turned to see two figures treading the dusty path, their forms dancing in the heat haze. Lilain mentally checked where her rifle was.

In the kitchen.

Underneath the table.

Where it had been since Lord Serped's arrival.

Lilain bided her time to let the two figures come closer. One was on horseback, she could tell that much through the heat. The other walked. The hills were dark behind them, the ground a rough patchwork, making it harder to see their faces. Lilain reached for her tools, balanced on the tip of the cart. A knife found its way into her hand. If things turned ugly she could jump down into the basement. All she had to do was cut the ropes of the table …

The strangers came on slowly. They seemed weary and their heads were bowed. Definitely not the look and feel of bandits or rogues. The one on horseback wasn't riding a horse at all, but a pony. A piebald one at that. It was then that she noticed there was something perched on the shoulder of the walking stranger. Something like a bag, or a bird, or …

'Lurker!' she yelled, the blood rushing to her cheeks. Seven days, they had been gone. Seven days she had worried and fretted, punched cabinets, kicked stones. Her boot had even found a mangy dog one morning, she was ashamed to say. But now here they were, waltzing back into town as in nothing had happened. *Maker, did they have a nerve!*

'Merion!' she yelled again, beginning to march. She could see them clearly now, barely half a mile away. The boy's head was up. Lurker's was still down. Neither of them shouted back. *Cowards.*

It did not take her long for her to close the distance, jogging across the hot trail and shaking with anger, the knife still glinting in her fist. If either the man or the boy had wanted to speak first, to offer an explanation perhaps, they would have been sore out of luck. Lilain started ranting at twenty paces' distance, even before they could bumble to a halt.

'Lurker, I ought to knock you to the dirt and thrash ten shades of shit out of you! What the *hell* were you thinking? Dragging Tonmerion out into the wilds? Into the desert? How dare you expose him to such danger! No note, no word, nothing! I was worried sick!'

'Lil—' Lurker tried, but Lilain hushed him with a menacing wave of her blade.

'And *you!*' she cried, pointing at Merion. 'You're more of a fool for going with him and disobeying me! Now you listen here and you listen good. I'm your aunt and guardian, and what I say goes, you understand? No ifs, no buts! I'm your father's sister, not some servant or kitchen slave for you to ignore. Oh, you'll be workin' long and hard to right this wrong, Tonmerion Hark!'

Merion reached up to scratch his nose, nonchalant as can be. Merion looked right back at her, with a gaze as flat as the very desert. He did not seem browbeaten, or guilty, as Lilain had hoped. He was angry, she could tell that much, but he boiled underneath his skin, holding it back for the moment. Lilain glared at him.

'You hear me, nephew?' she snapped.

'I hear you alright,' Merion hissed in reply. 'but I don't care.'

'I beg your p—'

Merion cut her off. 'I know what you were hiding from me now. The Shohari told me,' he said, his voice rising, the way it did when he knew he had the upper hand.

Lilain did not wilt. She was a veritable bonfire of rage. She turned on Lurker and pointed the knife at him. 'The *Shohari?* Well, you're a fucking idiot, John Hobble. A fucking idiot and a liar, and I don't want you in my sight! Get away, until such time as I can stomach to look at you!' Lilain screeched, wrinkling her lip in a way that made Lurker's heart fall just a little, though he wouldn't have admitted it. His only reply was a grunt and a tug of his hat, before trudging off down the path and into Fell Falls, his head drooped even lower than before.

Lilain turned back to her nephew. 'You've got some nerve...' she growled.

Merion wrestled Gorm back onto the trail. 'And so do you. How dare you lie to me, keep me in the dark about secrets like your little vials of blood? Oh yes, I know all about your little hobby now, and why you keep such things.'

Lilain smiled, though it was one that was cold and devoid of humour. 'Whatever they told you, you don't know the half of it.'

Merion smiled right back. Amongst all his righteous anger, his confusion and the disappointment he had spent the last few days trying to ignore, a tiny part of him had doubted the Sleeping Tree and its strange words. It was a talking tree, after all. But there it was: an admission of guilt if ever he had heard one. There was no doubt about this now; the tree had spoken the truth, and with that revelation came a fresh rush of excitement and fear to swirl alongside his anger.

Merion leant forwards in his saddle. He spoke very quietly and very firmly. 'And that's why you're going to tell me every last, tiny, little thing.'

All Lilain did was wave her knife and turn away, stomping back to the house. Merion scowled, He tugged at Gorm's reins and led the pony down the trail and up the rise to the house. He was not surprised to see yet another body lying on the cart. The railwraiths had been at work again, that much was obvious. He wondered how many had died since he had left.

Lilain was by the cart. 'Three,' she said, interpreting his look, her voice still strained with anger. 'In a week, the railwraiths have come three times. While you were off gallivanting with Lurker, going behind my back, I had to do all the work. On my own.'

'I saw one,' Merion said, slowly sliding from Gorm's back. 'On the plains.'

Lilain looked up. 'A wraith?' she asked.

'Big as a house.'

Lilain gave the cart a kick with her boot. 'That damn Lurker!'

'He was trying to help.'

'Dragging you into the desert and filling your mind with nonsense don't help one tiny bit!'

'But it's not nonsense, is it?' Merion challenged her. 'You're lying.'

Lilain grit her teeth and busied herself with the body. 'Who told you? Was it Lurker? It was, wasn't it?'

Merion shook his head. 'No, a Sleeping Tree told me. The Shohari took me to it and it told me everything. About what you do, down in that basement of yours. About what my father was capable of, and how I'm like him. I know it all.' He sounded proud of that fact, proud and resentful.

'And what else did this tree say?' Lilain's tone had abruptly softened.

'That father was killed for money,' Merion answered her. If he wanted the truth, he supposed he had better dish some out as well. Besides, he wanted to see what Lilain would say, see whether he could spy another flicker of guilt in her face. 'But you knew that already, didn't you?'

Lilain sighed. 'Well, he wasn't short of it,' she said, in a quiet voice. There was no flicker of guilt there. Not a trace. Instead her eyes were hard, and Merion knew she was telling the truth. 'No, I did not, Merion. But I suspected it. Karrigan was a rich and powerful man. It always has something to do with money, amongst such men. But to kill him? Somebody was desperate.'

Merion narrowed his eyes. 'And you have no idea who?'

That stern face of hers didn't waver. 'Like I've said before. Not a clue. Just like you, nephew.'

A moment passed, filled with silence, then Merion spoke. 'I want to know about the blood. About what my father could do. What *I* can do. I have a right to know,' he said.

Lilain scowled. 'As I told that magpie-toting idiot last week, you're too young.'

A deep voice rang out from behind her then, unmistakeable. 'He ain't Lil,' it said.

Lilain whirled around, instantly enraged. 'Lurker! Get off my property!'

'I've seen it. He can rush alright, Lil. No doubt about it.'

It was then that Lilain slapped him, good and hard across the face and nose. Lurker took it without complaint. He simply spat in the dirt and pointed at Merion. 'The boy rushed the horse's shade, you hear me? Clear as day, I saw it. He's Karrigan's boy alright.'

'You …' Lilain could barely form words, she was so livid. 'You knew what it could have done to him. You knew, and you did it anyway. Horse-blood could have killed him, stone dead, and you would have been standing here with a dead boy in your arms! Did you even think? Did you?'

Lurker nodded. 'Long and hard, ma'am.'

Lilain leant so close they almost touched noses. 'I said, get the fuck off my property,' she hissed.

'So be it,' Lurker grumbled, and turned his back. For the second time that day, he bowed his head, and set a course for the town.

'What does he mean, *rushed*?'

Lilain waited until her knuckles popped before finally unclenching her fists. 'Maker damn it,' she sighed.

'Are you going to tell me now?' Merion asked. 'Finally?'

Lilain shoved Mister Khurt onto the table before answering. 'I suppose I'll have to.'

Merion's face was a picture of grim satisfaction. He nodded. 'Yes, I suppose you will.'

Waiting for answers can be torturous. Enduring the display of a man being cut open and prepared for burial, whilst waiting for answers, is even worse. Merion had thought himself numbed by now, but here he was, as squeamish as ever. Blood had new meaning to him now. It was not just the gore, but the feral power it hid. Not only did he find himself disgusted by it, but somewhat afraid of it. So it was that he sat on his hands and stared at his aunt's fingers moving as deftly as they always did, cutting and slicing, turning the pieces over and over, drilling down into some imagined core. Lilain was taking her time with this one, stalling perhaps. But he would have his answers.

'Why do you cut them all open? You know what killed them. Why examine them?' he asked. His voice sounded harsh against the silence and the wet squelching.

Lilain sniffed. She too seemed angry, but Merion didn't care. All she had to be angry about was his running away, and Lurker. But he had been lied to. The high ground was his.

'Although we're all made of the same stuff, each one of us different. Science, Merion. Its roots lie in research.'

'So it isn't to do with their blood?' Merion asked. This time Lilain flinched.

'No. I only take their blood as a sign of respect. A burial of sorts.'

'Another vial for your collection.'

Lilain flashed him a glare. 'As I said before, I cannot abide sneaking in my house. Nor anywhere else for that matter.'

'It isn't magick then?'

'Oh, all blood has magick in it, Merion. Human blood is sacred, however. It ain't to be touched.'

Merion leant forward. 'While we're on the subject, touched by *whom*? People like my father? Like me?'

Lilain slammed her open palms down on the table, leaving bloody handprints on her table. 'You really want to know, don't you? Every last grisly detail. You still think magick is something to be gawped at, something exciting and wondrous, don't you? Well, you're wrong. Magick is dirty. It's rough. Raw. Magick isn't pretty, it isn't stars and sparkles. It's blood and guts and vomit, you hear me? All humans have ever done with magick is use it to kill, coerce, and destroy, and that's all we'll ever use it for. So, I ask you Merion, do you really want to pick at this scab? Do you really want to open that door and stare into magick's twisted face? Because if you are your father's son, and Lurker is right, there is no going back. You better be ready for what comes at you.'

Merion scowled. 'Is this the part where you tell me that with great power comes great responsibility? Because I've heard that from my father a hundred times.'

Lilain flashed him one of her mirthless smiles, to let him know she was deadly serious. 'No, this is the part where I tell you that with great power comes a great shitload of enemies, Merion. This isn't a fairy tale, understand me?'

Merion ached to snort at that, but he caught himself. This was a time for answers, not for jokes. 'I understand,' he told her.

Lilain turned back to her corpse. 'So be it,' she said, taking a deep breath. 'Maker, what would Karrigan say if he was here.' The stool creaked as Merion shifted his weight. 'And Maker forgive me,' she whispered under her breath.

Lilain worked as she spoke, perhaps trying to distract herself from her own words. She spoke slowly and calmly, with none of the finesse she usually spoke with. This was not a story. Not tonight.

'Bloodrushing is what it's called. And rushers rush with the help of a little blood. It's an ancient magick, one that we've practised for thousands of years, ever since the first ancestor cracked open his brother's skull with a rock and wondered what his brain tasted like. See? I told you it weren't pretty. Ever heard of Arexinder the Great?'

'I have,' Merion said. There was a painting of him in his father's study.

'He was a rusher. It's what helped him blaze a path all the way to Indus, centuries before the Empire was even a whisper on the wind. When he put the red in his belly, it was that of a lion.'

Merion held up a hand. 'You're speaking in riddles, Aunt.'

Lilain sighed curtly before continuing. 'Rushers drink blood to gain power. Your average rusher can only stomach—and I mean that literally—one shade of blood. If a rusher is lucky, or trains very hard indeed, they might be able to stomach two or three. Maybe four. And by shades, I mean types. Types of animal. Each animal has its own shade, and each animal belongs to a certain vein. Fish, birds, mammals, mythical. These are all veins.'

With every word, Merion's heart beat a little faster. He did not know whether it was fear, excitement, or anger that he hadn't known sooner. In any case, his chest thudded and his skin prickled.

'If you're lucky enough to have the stomach for bloodrushing, and very few bloodlines do in this day and age, then you don't get to choose your shades, or your veins. You are simply born with them. Like your eye or your hair colour. Stuck with them for life. Stronger bloodlines, like ours, are usually lucky. Like Arexinder, we've got a natural aptitude. Harks are naturally stronger than other, lesser rushers, who have to be content with bloods possessing powers that are weaker, or just plain useless.'

'Such as?' Merion asked. He could feel sweat on his brow despite the cool of the basement. Magic was what every boy dreams of, and yet *... what if he wasn't good enough? What if his shade was weak?*

'Pelican blood, for instance,' said Lilain, 'is a shade that allows a rusher to drink seawater in great quantities without dying.'

'And what's a good shade? What does lion blood do?' Merion asked, hoping his would be lion.

'Strength, ferocity, and a hunter's instinct.'

'And others?'

Lilain pushed herself away from the table and went to lean on one of the wooden pillars. 'You understand this isn't a game?'

Merion was starting to realise it. 'Of course.'

Lilain squinted at her nephew for a spell. 'Firefly blood makes you glow. Cuttlefish makes your skin change colour. Horse makes you want to run, gives you stamina. Magpie blood, well, I assume you already know that one.'

'Lurker's shade.'

'His only shade, or so he says,' Lilain replied, visibly fuming at the mention of the prospector.

'They call his kind a goldnose. There's all sorts of nicknames, and not all of them kind ones. Smartbeak, dustkicker, mortscent. The bird vein always has the best ones.'

'And my father? What was his shade? Will mine be the same?'

Lilain held up her bloody hands. 'We'll get to that,' she told him. 'But please, before I say any more, you have to promise me that you will not breath a word of this to anybody. Not a soul, you hear? The people who knew what Karrigan could do feared him. They would fear you just the same, and hate you for it. He was dangerous, and maybe that's what got him killed in the end. I don't want the same happening to you, alright? They'll smile alright, before going behind your back, and melt your insides while they're at it. Not a soul, do I have your word?'

'You do,' Merion said. He resented it—that was for sure, promising this lying aunt of his anything at all; but then again, he was not sure he wanted his insides to melt any time soon. Better to keep a tight lip, for now.

'Good. Now, your father weren't no ordinary bloodrusher. Like our father, he was what we call a leech. Your father wasn't stuck to stomaching one shade, or three, no. He could rush with all different kinds of bloods, all from different veins. For that reason, leeches are very dangerous, both to themselves and others.'

'Does that mean I am a leech?' Merion asked, in a voice a little more high-pitched than he would have liked. His emotions kept swirling.

Lilain didn't look too impressed with that question. 'Your father is one of only three leeches I know of. They're rare, and it's been known to skip generations. You may be just an ordinary rusher, Merion. Don't get your hopes up. Leeches may be able to tolerate different shades of blood, but that doesn't mean to say they can tolerate *all* shades. Some even become more deadly to a leech. The purity of the blood is key as well, and for that you need a good letter.'

'What's a letter?'

'Why do you insist on jumping … Oh, for Maker's sake. A letter is a blood-letter, Merion. A bleeder. A butcher. The person who collects, purifies and sells the blood to bloodrushers. Letters were once prized possessions. Every bloodrushing kaesar of the First Empire had his own personal letter, though they left it out of the history books. Bloodrushing used to be the sport and skill of nobles, and nobles only. A lot of gold was spent and a lot of swords drawn to keep it that way, to keep the magick secret. Letting was no different. It's a dying art now. Shame.'

Merion was starting to read between the lines. The way Aunt Lilain spoke of letting compared to the way she had spoken of Karrigan's leech-powers was noticeably different. Even her posture had changed. From slumped shoulders to a raised chin, Merion could see it now. He went about it delicately, if that were possible for a Hark.

'And what, if I may ask, is your shade, Aunt Lilain?' Merion enquired.

Lilain rolled her eyes and moved to the sink so she could wash her blood-encrusted hands. 'I don't have one,' she replied. It sounded like a confession, the way she mumbled it, almost as if she were ashamed.

'So, you're not a bloodrusher?' asked Merion.

Lilain watched the water drip brown and bloody into the white porcelain sink. 'No, I am not. As I said, it can sometimes skip a generation, or a sibling, in my case. Karrigan got all the powers, whereas I was left with my mind and my hands. If my father couldn't have two rushing offspring, he'd raise a letter instead. That was why he'd surrounded me with tutors since I was a child. I've been doing this since I was your age.'

Merion nodded. 'So I take it you sell the blood you collect? This is your business.'

Lilain snorted. 'Why do you think I'm so keen to bury the cats and dogs of this town, as well as its people? I'm a Hark as well, remember. I too have business in my blood.'

Merion could not help but curl his lip. 'What a business it must be.'

Lilain almost threw her towel at the boy. Instead she took a step closer and stared down at him. 'Let's say you are a rusher. Maybe even a leech. Where are you going to get your blood from, hmm? Just going to strut into the desert and bleed yourself a lion, are we? Or an eagle? What about a bluebuck, or an auk? No, you would go to your letter, and they would give you what you need. For a price.'

Lilain kept her eyes fixed on her nephew as she bent down and pulled a lever underneath the counter. Merion heard a click and a rattle of chain, and before he knew it, the wall behind her was moving. A whole bookshelf was swinging inwards, revealing a dark passageway into the earth. Something glittered in the darkness. Lilain reached for a lantern so she could light the way. Merion, fidgeting with undeniable curiosity, hopped from his stool and followed her into the gloom of her little lair.

Blood. The hidden chamber was full of it, from top to bottom and end to end. A hundred colours shone on a hundred different shelves, captured in vials and bottles of all different shapes and sizes. Some were square, others round. A few were banded with metal as if their contents were struggling to burst out. Each wore a little label on a string, with a strange, spiked pattern scrawled on it. Merion peered at every one in turn as he followed Lilain deeper into the chamber, hoping for a more familiar language. A thousand different hues of red watched him pass, the lantern light splashing their carmine colours against the sandy ochre of the walls. Here and there other colours stuck out: yellows, browns, even blues.

Merion heard the rustling first, ominous in the darkness. Lilain did not seem worried by it, so Merion held his tongue. But then he heard their yowling, their cawing and screeching, and the sweat began to flow. Whatever was making that noise could smell them now, could see the flicker of the lantern, and they sounded hungry. Far too hungry for Merion's liking.

The dull gleam of cage doors assuaged his fears somewhat, but with the doors came the beasts that hid behind them. Merion spied their eyes, some glowing, others merely glinting, staring back at him through the shadows. Their fangs and flickering tongues were not far behind. Their whines and growls rose in pitch, until Merion was almost forced to cover his ears.

Lilain reached for a nearby broom handle and began to whack it against the bars. 'Shhh! Pipe down. Food's coming, food's coming,' she told her pets, or her captives—Merion wasn't too sure of the terminology.

As Lilain paraded around the small half-circle of cages, the lantern-light drew their curves and features for Merion to gawp at.

The cockatrice was old and dishevelled. It seemed happy enough, in its rather spacious cage. At first it seemed too small for the space, but as Merion's eyes moved from its feathered rooster's head to its scaly belly and coiled tail, it was plain to see the creature would have stood at least four foot tall had it the room.

The tiny wood nymph sat cross-legged and tucked up. There was ivy wrapped around the bars of her cage, and moss growing in its corners. The nymph's skin was fractured and frayed like the skin of a birch tree. Her eyes were bright emeralds thumbed into hollows, and they glowed back at the boy as he stared.

His aunt pointed at the next cage along. 'This is a mockinghawk. You can tell from its rainbow feathers and bright eyes. It'll change plumage to mimic any bird it wants. That way it can join a flock and go unnoticed, picking off the weak or young whenever it pleases,' Lilain intoned. 'And this,' she said, pointing at a rather excitable-looking slug-like thing in a higher cage, 'this is a sandworm. Eats rocks like they were butter. Lives off the mould and bacteria.'

'What's bacteria?'

Lilain waved her hand dismissively. 'That's another story for another day. Don't want to give you a headache now, do I? Now, I think you know the others, pretty much. Aside from the stunted huldra over there, and maybe the wampus.'

Merion did indeed. Aside from the huldra, which turned out to be a small shrivelled woman with a long cow's tail, and the feral, cat-like wampus, which was the one apparently making all the noise, the rest were just plain old animals. The only remarkable thing about them was that they were behind bars, hidden under the earth in a strange woman's basement, in this far-flung corner of the world.

There was a young wolf pup with a missing ear, a snake or two, kept behind a grate. There were birds in most of the higher cages, but nothing out of the ordinary. There was even a large bowl full of odd-looking fish, nudging shoulders with a grimy tank full of what appeared to be huge spiders, or maybe crickets.

Merion stuck his hands in his pockets and wondered what to make of it all. 'I take it this is not just your own private zoo?'

'Far from it, nephew,' Lilain replied, running her hands over the bars and letting her beasts sniff and scratch at them if they could be bothered. 'Some shades are pure enough in their natural state. These are just a handful of creatures I've been lucky enough to trap over the years, and as long as they're kept alive and well, I can take as much blood as I please without hurting them.'

Merion stepped forwards to take a closer look at the stunted huldra. Her eyes were sad, her face glum, and her cow-tail flicked back and forth impatiently. 'What can their shades do?' Merion asked. The huldra smiled at him then, and the boy took a step back. It was strange to see such a human smile in such a wild creature. Its teeth, despite its shrivelled appearance, were perfect and white.

'Not as much as you think. The wampus might give you claws, if you're strong. The mockinghawk can change the colour of your skin, but not the shape of it. The cockatrice will spit hot venom, if you poke it long enough. I hear its blood tastes like acid. It can give you a poisonous kiss, however,' Lilain lectured.

Merion turned and took a few paces back towards the shelves. He reached out and plucked a slim vial of dark red blood from its place and held it close to his face. The thick blood clung to the glass as he turned it over in his dusty hands. *Could I really drink this?* he asked himself. *Could he?* There was no denying the little hiccup of bile he tasted in his throat. He looked up at his aunt. 'And what do you suppose is to be my shade?'

With a flick of his aunt's wrist, the vial was snatched away and placed back on the shelf. She kept her fingers on it as she spoke, as if it were a chess piece she had not yet decided what to do with. She narrowed her eyes at him.

'You're too excited by it all, I can tell. You need respect for rushing, and I don't think you have it yet. Your father was wise enough to entrust you to me, and I will honour that wisdom by making sure you don't go putting the red in your belly any time soon. Not until you learn otherwise,' she said, shaking her head.

Merion's face turned fierce. 'That's not fair. I could be a leech for all you know. A rarity.'

Lilain shook her head. 'Or you could be some grubsnout addicted to woodpecker blood and rue the day you ever asked. What a fine little lord you would make then,' she told him.

'But it is my right to choose,' Merion cried.

'Not when you don't have the first clue about what you're choosing!'

Merion bit the inside of his lip, wracking his brains for some magic words to make his aunt change her mind. 'You said there's no going back. I know what I am now, what I can do. Would you rather keep me under your roof, and teach me yourself, or would you rather I run off again, and have the Shohari show me how it's done?' he challenged her.

Lilain rolled her lips inwards and glowered at him. Merion pressed on.

'Surely you know more on this subject than any shaman—'

'Yes, alright! You've made your point, nephew. Maker's hands, if you haven't got your father's wicked tongue.'

'Among other things,' Merion retorted, fighting not to punch the air.

'Yes, well, we shall see. But you listen to me. The moment I decide you ain't fit to taste a shade, you do as I say. I won't be disobeyed on this matter. Not when your life is at stake. Do we have an agreement?' Lilain stuck out a bloody hand and waited for Merion to grab it.

Merion slowly reached out, painfully mindful of the blood still drying on Lilain's palm and fingers. His aunt could see his eyes, and his face twitching.

'Better get used to it fast, Merion. Imagine a bloodrusher who's afraid of the sight of blood,' she said drily, half-hoping he would falter, and give up, decide it wasn't for him after all. Merion grabbed her bloody hand and squeezed it with everything he had.

CHAPTER XVIII

LEECH

'Almost caught again today. Three months since the suitcase and today I decide to let my guard down. Karrigan was in his study. I stupidly knocked a table. Rookie error. The man moves fast, that's for sure. Far too fast for my liking. His fingers must have brushed my wings as I made it to the fireplace. Thank the Roots it wasn't alight.
There's something about him that makes my skin crawl, and I can't figure it. Merion must know.'

19th May, 1867

It was almost three o'clock when Merion strode out into the roasting sun. He had not waited to watch Mister Khurt get sewn up. He had barely waited for his aunt to seal up her alcove. There was an excitement in his heart that failed miserably to understand why he should sit around in dark basements on stools, watching corpses get poked by the needle. For the tenth time in almost as many paces, he readjusted the strap of his rucksack.

'Will you please stop that?' Rhin hissed, flicking him through the fabric.

'Sorry,' Merion said, fingers already itching to do it again.

'All you needed was a dead body to change your tune, I see.'

'That, and a conversation I've been aching to have since I arrived in this cursed little hole,' Merion said, unable to stop his lips from curling and his eyes from narrowing. 'What's that old peasant saying? Where there is a will, there is a way? Well now I have a way, and a will.'

'So, you can rush then?'

Merion stopped dead. 'You don't mean to tell me you knew … all this time …?'

'No,' Rhin sighed. 'I heard Lurker say rushing. It doesn't take an idiot to figure it out. The Fae have always known about humans and your blood-magick. I just thought it had died out with your ancestors.'

Merion moved off, wiping his brow. 'Well, apparently it hasn't. I may be a leech, Rhin, a leech.'

'A blood-sucking parasite?'

'A rusher that can stomach all sorts of different shades,' Merion said, his excitement as clear as a bell.

'You've lost me,' Rhin muttered.

The boy tutted and walked on down the hill, past the houses of the Runnels and into Fell Falls. There was a subdued feel about the town. The saloons were quieter, the crowds thinner. Every worker Merion passed looked hollow-eyed and robbed of sleep. The sheriffsmen wore a little more armour than usual; sported more than the usual number of knives. When he had left, Fell Falls had been a brave outpost jutting out into the wilds. The Fell Falls he trudged through today felt like a town under siege, as though the town had suddenly realised its weakness. Everybody seemed to be mechanically going about their business as if monotony and routine would save them, as if breaking it would admit defeat to their intangible enemy.

Despite the mood lingering about the town, there was an awful lot of activity near the station and around the work-camp. Fresh scaffolding poked at the bright blue sky. The smell of cut wood and pitch was thick in the air. If this town was truly under siege, somebody was making arrangements. Merion suspected it had to do with whoever's coat of arms now streamed from the taller scaffolding poles and weathervanes: a coat of arms displaying a green wyrm coiled around a silver spinning-top. The Serpeds had come to town. Merion was still intent on seeking them out, but for now the Serpeds could wait just a little longer. He had more pressing things to attend to, namely blood, and rushing, and Lurker.

The young Hark knew that the prospector was still in town. He would not leave, not after Lilain had told him to. That was the exact

Leabharlanna Poiblí Chathair Baile Átha Cliath
Dublin City Public Libraries

reason he would stay. Lurker's face may have been a mask of dead emotion most of the time, but he had seen the little twitches in that mask on the road whenever Lil was mentioned. If Merion knew anything of men and their sorrows, Lurker would be seeking out something strong and wet, so to speak. He traipsed through the dust and heat of the streets, one by one, peering into each of the town's saloons as he went. Through each set of swinging doors he found only frowning gazes and leering, lead-toothed stares, the punch of acrid pipe-smoke and the smell of sweat and dust. There were plenty of burly men with hats pulled low over their eyes, and plenty of figures in leather, but none of them Lurker. Merion pursed his lips and moved on. There were some more saloons on the western edge of town, near the railroad and the worker camp.

The boy's path took him through the centre of town. A fresh batch of horses had been driven in from Kaspar in the wake of the Serpeds' arrival. More horses for the rails and the workers—and for the lordsguards too. As the stableboys led them through streets towards the western stables, Merion stood by to watch them prance and whinny. Their eyes were wide, as if they could smell the blood in the sand.

Merion turned left and came to the postal office. With all the news of magick, he had forgotten about the irksome place and its dolt of a clerk. He put his feet to the steps and his hands to the swinging doors. Lo and behold, the pouting face of the chubby clerk swung up to greet him. Whatever barely courteous look he had pasted on quickly crumbled away, and was replaced with a scowl.

'Well, look who it is. I thought you dead, or disappeared, Empire. I see I was wrong.'

Merion smirked. Not even this poltroon could drag him down today. 'Letters. Have there been any for me?'

The clerk sighed. 'Your name again, Empire?'

'Tonmerion Hark, son of Karrigan Hark.'

'Don't care whose son you are, just your name will do.' the clerk muttered as he rummaged underneath the counter and in the square pigeon-holes at his back. He did not make much of an effort, tossing letters and small paper-wrapped bundles aside as he searched. 'No. Nothing for you,' he said, seeming a little pleased with his news.

Merion shrugged off the disappointment. 'Please, look again,' he ordered.

The clerk put his fingers, templed, on the counter. 'I am not a peasant on one of your farms, Empire, to be ordered around as you please,' he said, sternly.

Merion put his own fingers down on the counter. 'No, but I am a customer and you are a clerk, and I am asking that you check again.'

The pudgy clerk spat on the floor. 'I've checked.'

Merion raised a finger and waggled it under the man's nose. 'Just you wait,' he said, feeling the pride of his new power fuel his words. Not that it mattered; his words had ruffled the clerk about as much as a fart. The snotty little man would have his comeuppance, just not today.

Merion stomped back to the rough, dusty street. He sighed as he looked up and down its length: still no Lurker. Just horses carving sickle-moons in the dirt as they stomped around. Just sheriffsmen and lordsguards leaning idly against posts, chatting in low tones. Just working women shuffling about, half-cut and half-caring. Merion sighed once more.

'Maybe he did wander off,' Rhin remarked, voice muffled.

Merion began to retrace his steps. 'No, he has to be here. He has to teach me how to bloodrush. I don't care what my aunt thinks. I need to learn what I can do.'

'Pardon the pun,' Rhin cut in, 'but don't you think you're rushing into this a little quickly?'

Merion shrugged. 'We don't have all the time in the world, Rhin. London isn't frozen, patiently waiting for me to come and thaw it. The quicker I can learn my father's skills, the quicker I can use them to get out of this place and back to the Empire, and my estate, where we belong,' Merion said, laying out his new grand plan, the one he had thought up on the walk into town.

'Where you belong,' Rhin muttered.

'Pardon?' Merion's head snapped around. He may have been wrong, but it sounded as though Rhin had said…

'I said it sounds as though you speak of vengeance,' Rhin hissed.

Before Merion could retort, a harsh cry echoed down the street. A few of the sheriffsmen peeled off from their hushed huddles, and marched towards a saloon with red doors and green windows. Merion began to move, talking as he marched.

'Why shouldn't I? It was the murderer that put me here. He was the one who banished me. I will not take that lying down. I'm a Hark, not a cowa—'

It was not a day for finishing sentences.

An almighty crash split the afternoon air as two men burst from the window of the saloon in a cloud of glass and shredded curtain.

'Lurker!' Merion cried. There was no mistaking the hat and the gloves. The very same gloves that were now curled into fists, busy pummelling the nose of the unfortunate brawler sprawled on the saloon's steps. The sheriffsmen moved like lightning. They dragged Lurker up so quickly that his feet left the floor. It was graceful, for a thin whisker of a second, until Lurker's boots returned to the decking, and the rest of his body followed like a sack of drunken cats.

'He's bladdered,' whispered Rhin. Merion nodded and gawped as Lurker began to, well, *pedal* at the floor. His legs flailed and his boots scraped, but they gained not a scrap of purchase. It was a wonderful impression of a donkey in the grip of a fit.

A crowd of half-drunk workers and whores poured out of the saloon to watch the fight. They brayed and roared with laughter and cheering. Whiskey sprayed. Bottles smashed. Fists jabbed the air fiercely. A good drunken fight can lift even the glummest of spirits.

'Sirs!' Merion called, chasing after the sheriffsmen. They spared him not a glance as they fought to keep Lurker still, and more importantly, upright. 'Sirs! If you please, allow me to take him home.'

One of the men, an officer by the look of his silver braids, threw a quick look at the boy. 'He your father or summin'?' he barked.

Merion shook his head. 'Er, no. A family friend.'

'Some friend you got.'

'Jaaaaake!' Lurker was yowling.

There was a dull smack as one of the sheriffsmen thwacked Lurker across the back with a truncheon.

'Aaaagh!'

'Pipe down!'

'Please!' pleaded Merion, 'I'll see him home. You'll have no more trouble from him, I swear it.'

'No can do, boy. Man's broken a window, so man's gotta spend a night or two in jail.'

'And then what?' asked Merion, suddenly fearing the worst.

'Then he's to pay for the window. With gold or work. Either one will do.'

'I see.'

The sheriffsman quickly tipped his hat. 'Now, if you could kindly shift your ass, we'll be on our way.'

Merion hopped to the side to let the men drag the almost unconscious Lurker off to jail. The boy ran a hand through his hair and puffed out his cheeks. He wasn't quite sure whether Lilain would be pleased or further enraged by this news. Maybe it would be best if he just held his tongue, for now.

'A friend of yours, then?' enquired a voice like bells, high and clear. Merion turned and looked upon the speaker, and his tongue turned into a fat lump of lead.

'Erm...' Merion said, clawing for words. 'Family. Friend of the family, that is.' Merion was painfully aware of how fantastic a first impression he must be making, mumbling like an idiot, with a tongue like sand. The poor young girl was already wincing a little, a half-smile lingering on her blood-red lips. Merion couldn't help but stare at them. He vaguely noted a blue dress in his peripheral vision, and white gloves, maybe. He felt the sweat creeping across his scalp. This was not your average girl of Fell Falls. They tended to be covered in mud and horse shit, with brown, tangled hair. Merion had seen them in the alleys, and in the Runnels. They had giggled at him, and he had scowled. This particular girl was very different. She was Empire.

'I see,' spoke the lips ... of the girl ... the talking girl. *Oh, Almighty.*

'Yes,' Merion smiled like a fool. Then, mercifully, he remembered his manners, and clung to them like a life-raft. He waved a hand in a slicing motion and then bowed low, speaking as loud and as clear as he could manage.

'Might I, er, introduce myself, miss,' he said, 'Tonmerion Harlequin Hark, at your service.'

He wasn't sure what to expect as he straightened, but to his welcome surprise, the young lady curtseyed in return, making her blue dress rustle. 'Calidae Ester Serped, at yours, sir,' she replied with a smile.

Merion beamed. *Serped,* screamed his insides. How had he forgotten? How could he have not guessed? Her dress must have been pure Francian silk. The pearls on her wrist were the second biggest he had ever seen. Her bright flaxen hair was perfectly curled and interwoven with silver lace.

'Daughter of Lord Serped, I presume,' he asked, keeping it formal. It seemed to be the only way of keeping his cheeks from betraying his grin, and it kept his eyes from lingering.

Calidae kept her smile, but her eyes took on a different shine. Curious, they roamed over him, giving her the look of a mouse assessing a lump of cheese. 'Call me Calidae, please,' she said, staring down at his strange shoes. The smile grew. 'My father told me the rumours.'

Merion cocked his head. 'Rumours? Of my shoes?'

Calidae actually began to circle him. It was rather off-putting, to say the least. Merion tried to keep his formal composure as he followed her with his head. It was then that he noted her guards, standing a little further down the street, hands on swords. One wore a black suit and a bowler hat. A pair of darkened glasses covered his eyes.

'Rumours that a lord of the Empire had come to Fell Falls. Well, the son of a lord that is,' she said, slowly.

'A son of a lord without a father *is* a lord, I believe.'

Calidae suddenly grew tired of circling and came to rest barely two feet in front of him, with her hands clasped behind her back. 'Well then, *Lord* Hark, what brings you to such a place as this?' she asked.

Merion decided to play the game. Of course she knew about his father. Perhaps this was her way of being polite. 'I could ask you the same question, my lady,' he countered. 'Ladies first.'

Calidae raised her chin. 'And I would answer that I accompany my father on business. And that the practice of "ladies first" does not apply when the lady has asked the first question.'

'In that case, Calidae,' Merion replied, 'I would answer that in light of my father's recent murder, I now live with my last remaining relative, who for reasons unknown has chosen Fell Falls as her place of residence. I have been here almost two weeks now.'

'My condolences,' Calidae bowed her head. 'To the lost,' she added, raising a hand curled around an imaginary glass.

'The lost,' repeated Merion as he raised his own, though his reach was a little lower than Calidae's. Politeness indeed, he thought, and he warmed to her even more.

When she looked at him next, Calidae had yet another glint in her eye. She leant even closer. 'I will tell my father that the rumours are true,' she said, almost whispering. 'He will want you to come to dine with us, on the riverboat. You must be craving real food by now, and real company for that matter.' Calidae smirked conspiratorially before stepping back to curtsey again. 'I look forward to it, my Lord Hark.'

'And I you ... I mean too,' Merion stuttered, kicking himself internally.

Calidae tittered, turned, and walked away, the guards trailing silently behind her. Merion was left standing alone in the street, part of him wanting to bludgeon himself with a stick, and part of him wanting to dance. The former was winning, for the moment.

Inside the rucksack, all Rhin could hear was the odd catch of a word in amongst a stream of self-deprecating grumbles. 'Stupid ... fool ... *And I you* ... idiot.'

Rhin nudged him through the fabric. 'Easy, Merion. It's girl-magic. Remember Illysa, Junton Korville's daughter? You could barely say a word then, just stared at her and flapped your mouth like a fish.'

Merion huffed, ducking into an alleyway. 'That was two years ago,' he said.

'It's a trick they learn young: the knack of reducing a man to a quivering jelly. We grow immune, in time. Well, faeries do. I don't know about you humans.'

Merion groaned. 'Thanks. As ever, you're a rock of support. What would I do without you?'

'I should start charging you,' mused Rhin. 'And just think: dinner with the Serpeds. Dinner with Calidae.'

Merion did not reply, but Rhin could not miss the little kick in his step.

'I think it may all be coming together, Rhin,' was all Merion said on the walk home.

✯

When they arrived at the house, Merion found a portly man standing outside. He bristled with frazzled red hair. It had obviously been liberally churned by nervous, anxious fingers. The man's eyes were wide and stained red with tears. He had a hat in his hands, and his fingers kneaded it continuously.

'Can I help you?' Merion asked of him.

'My dog,' whimpered the man, staring at the door of the house. 'Ruffian. Big ol' beast. Dropped down dead just last night gone. Healthy hound as well, there were naught wrong with him. Then all a' sudden,' the man paused to whack his hat against his leg, 'dead as tumble-weed. Two little marks in 'is throat. Little cuts,' he said, tilting his head back and jabbing two fingers at his sweaty, red throat.

'My condolences,' Merion said. He had nothing to offer the man, except for: 'A rattlesnake, maybe?'

But the man shook his head, adamant. 'No sir. Too far apart. Little men did this.'

A chill ran through Merion. 'Pardon me?'

The man looked around at the roots of the house, as if making sure no eyes nor ears lurked there. 'Faeries, boy. Little people. Little cuts.' The man jabbed again at his throat.

'Well, thank you,' Merion mumbled, and rapidly made his way indoors. The door to the basement was open; a telltale sign.

After placing his rucksack in his room, telling Rhin to stay precisely where he was, and then shutting the door, Merion plodded down the steps and into the cool of the basement.

Lilain was bent over her table. Her door to her secret lair was open. She looked as though she were almost done. The needle was out. As was the thread, and together they were almost done making the dog whole again. All except for a few bits of meat and a stolen drop of blood or two, lingering in a little vial by the dog's head.

Ruffian was indeed a 'big ol' beast'. This was not a dog. This was a pile of black muscle with four giant paws and a face that looked as though it had been smashed in with the flat of a pan. Amid the wrinkles and drooping folds of its pitch-black snout, Merion could see sharp yellow fangs, poking out at odd angles.

Truth be told, Merion was glad the thing was dead. He jabbed a thumb over his shoulder as he stepped into the light. 'There's a mad man out on the steps. Says he's lost a dog.'

'Aye, that he has,' Lilain answered.

'But this doesn't look like a dog. Looks more like a boulder. With teeth.'

'Swartzhund. Prussian breed. I've seen bigger,' Lilain rattled off. She lifted up the vial and jiggled it between two fingers. 'But it's a pure breed, and that means a good shade.'

Merion took a step forward. 'What can it do?'

Lilain rolled her eyes. 'See? Too eager.' She paused to tut. 'Strength. Strong sense of smell. Fangs, in some cases, though I've witnessed that go wrong many a time. Lips and fangs don't get on. Like I said, magick ain't pretty.'

'Well, I thought you should know that the man thinks that faeries killed this brute of a dog.'

'Hmph,' Lilain snorted.

Merion raised an eyebrow. 'It sounds as though you do not believe in faeries.'

Lilain glanced at him. 'Why? Do you?'

Merion shrugged. He was so used to lying that he did it naturally. 'I'm thirteen. Faeries are for little girls and storybooks.'

Lilain gave him a strange look and hummed. He had passed. 'Don't be so naive, Merion,' she said.

'Anyway, I know you believe. Lurker told me about the three beasts you've never caught,' Merion replied.

A bloody fist clenched and pressed against the scarred table. 'That blasted …' But her words trailed off. Perhaps they were not meant for Merion's ears. 'Well, he's right: dragon, mermaid, and Fae.' Lilain counted each one of them on her fingers.

Merion needed to probe. 'So you believe in faeries, but you don't think they killed this dog?'

'Not for a moment, young nephew. He's probably just drunk on grief.' Lilain prodded the dog in the chest. 'Never said I didn't believe. I just know there aren't any faeries out west. In fact, I reckon there's not a single faerie in this whole Kingdom.'

Merion tried very, very hard to suppress the smile that ached to spread across his dusty cheeks. Thankfully, he succeeded.

'And so, another for the shelf,' sighed Lilain, as she lifted up the vial to stare at it. 'I think I need a new cupboard.' she muttered.

'Maybe I should try it out?' Merion said.

'Ha,' she snorted. 'This shade? It'd melt your insides. That's what happens when you drink a shade that ain't yours. And that's why I haven't changed my mind, Merion. And I'm not going to, so stop pushing me. The only thing you ought to be trying is a book.'

As Merion clenched his teeth and tried to stay calm, Lilain knelt down to pluck a few dusty books from a cabinet. 'Here we are. *The Book of the Leech*, that's a good place to start. As is *Farringdon's Compendium of Shadecraft*. The *Laminus Maleficarum*, let's not forget that. We start studying tomorrow, if the wraiths don't decide to pay us another visit. Or any Fae for that matter,' Lilain said, with a wink.

Merion couldn't return it. He stared at the pile of books balancing in his hands. 'Tomorrow,' was all he said. *Tomorrow I'll go fetch Lurker from the jail,* was what he thought.

'Now,' Lilain clapped her hands, jolting her nephew from his staring, 'I've got to go see a man about a dog.'

'A dead one,' Merion mumbled.

'As a doornail, nephew,' Lilain replied, and then with one nimble movement, slid her arms under the mighty hound and lifted it to her chest. Merion was slightly shocked, it had to be said. Somehow she did not look the slightest bit strained.

'Bodies are heavy. Years of pushing them around on carts will give you a few muscles, here and there,' she told him with another wink. Merion watched as she strode to the stairs, dog aloft. 'I'll be back once I've got rid of Mister Leaky Eyes. You'd better get reading.'

As soon as he heard the *clomp clomp* of boots on the boards above, the books went flying. A simple overturning of his hands, and they fluttered and spiralled to the dusty floor. One broke its spine on impact. Merion bit his lip. He hadn't quite meant to …

'Easy now,' muttered a familiar voice. It was Rhin, shimmering in the nearby shadows.

'Are you *mad*, Rhin? Lilain will be back any second!' hissed Merion.

'And I've been here all the time. I followed you down. Wanted to see what all the fuss was about.'

'You've lost it. I knew it. Baked your brain in the sun …'

Rhin shook his head. 'Your aunt is no fool.'

'That she is not, but you will be, if she catches you. She'd bleed you in an instant.'

Rhin tapped his sword and smirked callously. 'I heard. Let her try,' he said.

Merion stared down his nose. 'That is my aunt, Rhin.'

'Sorry, but that's all the more reason to keep me out of sight.'

Merion had turned a strange shade of red. 'I told you to stay! You wandered down here!'

'Well, now I know to be more careful, don't I?' Rhin said, crossing his arms. Something was worrying him. 'Do you think she's right, about there being no faeries in America?'

Merion clapped a palm to his brow. 'I don't know. I don't care. You shouldn't either.'

Rhin narrowed his gaze. 'I want to know whether I should be watching my back or not, Merion.'

'Watching for who, Rhin?' Merion sighed. 'Nobody knows about you!'

That did not seem to settle the little faerie, and he made no reply.

Merion was too concerned with his books. 'I can't believe she's making me read all of this before I can get my hands on … that,' Merion groused, then gulped as he eyed the vials of blood on the nearby shelf, just inside the lair. Thick, gelatinous, seeping blood. Merion felt a little bile rising in his throat, a little churning in his stomach. He growled them away. A bloodrusher who could not stand the sight of blood? *Unimaginable.*

'Well, why not?' Rhin shrugged.

'How did you learn to swing a sword, Rhin?'

'Well, by …' Rhin saw the point Merion was making. He did not like the idea of making it for him.

'By swinging it, I'll bet,' Merion said, slapping the dirt floor. 'Not by reading books!' He went straight for the first vial his shaking hands could reach. He held it in his palms and gazed at it. The blood inside was the colour of rust. The label was as indecipherable as all the rest, just a row of spikes.

Rhin was not impressed. 'You're a fucking idiot if you pour that down your throat. You heard your aunt.'

Merion glared. 'I'm sorry, I didn't realise you knew all about bloodrushing!'

Rhin stepped forwards and into the dim light. His skin glittered. He had that dangerous look in his eye. 'No, boy, but I've had magick running through my veins longer than you can fathom. Several centuries, by my reckoning,' Rhin replied, voice cold. 'Put it back, Merion.'

But the longer Merion stared at the blood in that little vial, the stronger his certainty grew. Before long, he was gripping the vial so tightly he feared it might shatter. 'I know I'm a leech,' he growled. 'Lurker said it was so. I am my father's son. I know I'm right.'

Rhin was getting angry now. Frantic even. Merion could see it in his lavender eyes. 'You could fill this basement with what you don't know about that vial, Merion. Put it back!'

There was a quiet squeak as the cork came free. Merion stared sideways at him, daring him to stop him, to pounce and wrestle him to the floor.

And pounce Rhin did, for the faerie was in no mood for games or further words. The boy was serious, and the aunt's words had scared him deeply.

Rhin lurched forwards like a cheetah, dirt flying from under his sharp nails. His arms pounded the air, and his wings, now spread and humming, threw him forward.

It took barely a second for Rhin to close the distance and collide with the boy's ribs. Unfortunately, it took only half a second for Merion to throw the vial up to his lips and splash the blood onto his tongue.

By the time the two crumpled to the floor in a cloud of dust and scattered books, Rhin was wrapped around the boy's throat and pressing him to the floor. 'Spit it out!' he was yelling.

The blood had already slipped to the back of Merion's throat. He was now faced with a rending decision. To gulp the cold, sour blood down, or to vomit, or choke, right there with his face pressed into the dirt, Lilain bound to arrive at any second.

Rhin grabbed Merion by the cheeks and knocked his head against the ground. 'Spit it out, I say, before I punch it out of you!' he bellowed. He caught the defiant look in the boy's eyes and shook his head, horrified. 'No! Don't you dare!'

And there it was: that dull silence and then the squelching of the throat; that deep gulping sound that filled Rhin's heart with anger, fear, panic, and all sorts of other emotions.

'You fucking idiot!' Rhin shouted, half strangling the boy.

'Agh!' Merion winced, throwing his hands over his ears and elbowing the faerie aside. The world was spinning like a top. His head felt like the anvil of an angry blacksmith. *Almighty, this rushing works fast,* he inwardly groaned. *There was no going back now.*

Merion cried out and clawed for the table as his stomach lit itself on fire. His throat was filled with burning bile. He clapped his hands to his stomach and instantly regretted his decision. In one single deafening wave, the world seemed to rush into him, a wave of chatter, thunder, rasping and scraping. He could hear every mouse in every wall. Every syllable on Lilain's lips as she tried to extricate herself from the awkwardness of a man blubbering on her doorstep. Every thud of every distant hoof, every rattle of Rhin's armour. Merion heard it all.

'Aaaagh!' he cried. It felt as though his head were going to be split in two.

Rhin was now pacing to and fro, wracking his brains. He could hear no footsteps in the hallway above, no aunt on the stairs, nothing. He had to make some sort of noise.

While Merion convulsed on the floor, eyes rolling back, Rhin cast about like a madman, hunting for some sort of pan, or bowl, or spoon to bang against the sink in the corner. Rhin jumped onto the lip of Lilain's bloody workbench and instantly spied his target. He drew his black sword with a flourish and brought the flat of it down against a bowl full of dog-flesh and sent it spinning across the room. It hit the wall with a clang and a squelch, and that was good enough for Rhin.

The faerie went at it with a will, hacking and slashing at anything metal he could find on the tabletop. Bowls. Scalpels. Pliers. Saws. Trays. They all soared in graceful, tumbling arcs to smash and clatter against the walls and pillars. Merion writhed all the while, yelling and cursing the noise. It looked as though he was trying very hard to stuff his fists into his ear. Rhin kept on swinging.

'Merion?' came the shout, and not a moment too soon. Merion retched in reply, spraying a bloody mess over the books and the dirt. Rhin sent one final implement spinning into the shadows before he too vanished with a hiss of metal sliding into leather. Only shivering air remained. That, and a screaming boy.

CHAPTER XIX

IN WHICH RHIN RECEIVES A MESSAGE

'Spent the day hunting rats in the wine cellars. Merion is with his tutors for the day. His father says he is spending too much time in the gardens, and in the tower. Too much time playing, he says. The man is far too obsessed with his campaign. (The boy's only eleven for Roots' sake.) Every boy needs a little magick in his life, even if it is real.'

22nd May, 1867

It was just after dawn when they let Lurker free of the jail. Some gold had apparently greased the wheels of freedom. Lurker did not mind too much. A little expenditure was worth it. His cell had stunk of piss and the bread they had given him could have dented the bars. So it was that Lurker now stood outside of the jail, on the eastern outskirts of town, trying to shake the smell of three days' worth of piss-stench and sweat out of his clothes. The crisp morning air was doing the job.

The sun had barely begun its climb. The sky was still tinted with reds and swirling orange where brave wisps of cloud dared to face the onslaught of the sun. The streets were empty at that time of the morning. Well, for the most part anyway. Empty, save for the stern face of Lilain Rennevie, crossed arms and all.

'Well,' he rasped. 'I knew you were an early riser, but …'

'Stow it.'

Lurker raised his gloved hands and bowed his head.

'I will have my say, John Hobble, and I will have it first. Let me see, where do I begin? Oh yes, with the luring of my nephew into the desert. Or perhaps you takin' him to the Shohari, knowing full-well your friends and their witch or their tree would tell him everything.'

'I did no such thing as lure the boy,' Lurker protested, but then quickly softened. 'But you're right on the second part,' he admitted.

'You're damn right I am. You could have turned him away. You could have …'

'Lil,' Lurker interjected, 'I'm sorry. But the way I see it, the boy is better off knowin' the truth about his father. Might be all he's got left. Otherwise he'll end up trying something stupid. Takin' chances.

Lilain raised a menacing finger. 'Thanks to you, he's done just that,' she hissed.

Lurker tilted his hat back. 'What?'

'Drank a load of bat blood, all because you filled his head with nonsense.'

Lurker brought his hat right back down. 'How's he doin'?'

'Alive. Thank the Maker. Found him in a patch of his own vomit and shit. I won't be telling him about the latter. He's been asleep since then, pale as a sheet.'

'Can I see him?'

Lilain jutted out her chin. 'And why do you care? Don't often catch you caring about anything besides blood, gold, and that magpie of yours.'

Lurker didn't have to pause to think up a fitting answer. He already had the words on his lips. 'Because I know what it's like to be a young boy learnin' to rush, who's excited because he thinks it can get him out, get his life changed. Or back the way it was, whichever. I know what he's thinkin'. Maybe more than you,' Lurker asserted, his words gruff but firm.

Lilain scowled, wearing that trademark frown of hers. 'You … you just keep your nose out of our business, understand?' she snarled, before storming away from him.

'Lil!' Lurker called out, and she stopped.

'What?'

This time Lurker did have to pause. He spent it toeing the dirt with the edge of his boot. 'I was thinking ...' he began.

'What?' Lilain shouted.

Lurker looked up. 'I was thinkin' about some breakfast?'

Lilain crossed her arms, quick as a flash. 'You're lucky I don't take you back and crack your head open with a frying pan, like my dead husband,' she spat. Then she turned away again, but this time her pace was slower, almost calmer. 'You can cook it yourself.'

★

The first thing Merion felt was pain. His stomach was in a knot, and not just your average sort of knot, but the sort that even sailors spend years failing to tie. And all the while the ropes of it burned with bitter flames. At least that's how it felt. The second thing was the sweat, oozing from every pore. Every drop of liquid in his body ached to escape, like rats from a burning barn.

Almighty if it wasn't hot. His mouth felt like a pocketful of sandpaper. His tongue was a fat slug contemplating the merits of suicide. But it was the vacuum of sound that bothered him the most. Not his stomach, not the dripping of his body, not how parched he was—it was the dull smothering of the world's noises, as if somebody had filled his ears with clay while he slept. If three days of fitting and squirming could be called sleeping.

When he finally prised open his leaden eyelids, he found two shadows standing by his bedside: one, tall and willowy; the other dark, foreboding, and muscled. Merion briefly wondered whether he had died, and whether these two figures were to be his new guardian angels. If that were the case, the House of the Almighty must be sorely in need of new staff. His voice was but a croak, audible only in his head. The willowy figure leant forward, and came briefly into focus: his aunt. The other must have been Lurker. Merion felt himself relax slightly, sagging deeper into the greedy, sweat-drenched sheets of his bed.

'Here,' she said. Merion barely discerned the word. It was an echo within an echo.

He found a glass in front of his nose and a hand behind his head, and with its help he leant forwards to fill his mouth with sweet, cold water. It was joyous. Mountain waterfalls had nothing on this little beaker of water. The sweetest wine could be forgotten. It was the best sip he had ever taken. All until the cold water met the fire in his belly, and fuelled its burn. Merion cried out and rolled over.

'See? Lucky to be alive.' The words came as slow as treacle.

'He's strong.'

'But stupid.'

Merion groaned a little louder.

'Drink it down, boy,' he heard Lurker say. Merion couldn't think of anything worse, but there was the beaker, pressing against his lips, spilling into his mouth. It was all Merion could do not to choke.

Another wave of pain shook him, and another, and another, until finally, when the beaker had nothing left to give, the pain began to ebb away. Mercifully.

'How long?' Merion managed to croak, after a few good minutes of deep, long breaths and copious amounts of eye-scrunching.

'Three days.'

Merion felt as though he had been left out in the sun for a week, like a forgotten shirt hanging from a line. He just groaned, and looked up to find Lilain staring down at him with a questioning look on her face. There was a frown there too, and Merion didn't much like it.

'What?' he asked in barely a whisper.

'Don't you have something to say?'

Merion blinked. 'Erm,' he mumbled. 'Thank you?'

'You're welcome, but that's not what I'm looking for.'

'Lil...' Lurker nudged her, but she nudged him right back with the point of her elbow. He grunted and held his tongue.

Merion looked from Lurker to Lilain and back again. 'Erm ...'

Lilain put her hands on her hips. 'It begins with an S, Merion.'

'Sorry,' Merion muttered. He looked down at his bedsheets. If there was one thing he did not like in this world, it was apologising. *To apologise is to admit mistake or defeat. A Hark trifles with neither.*

And there he was again, his father, keeping Merion's back straight and his chin held high even from the grave.

Merion cleared his throat. 'But I'm alive though, aren't I? That proves something.'

For a moment, Lilain looked as though she would give him a good thwack around the ear. But she didn't, much to Merion's gratitude. Instead she held her breath until she could trust herself to speak rather than bellowing in the stubborn boy's face.

'It proves,' she began, her voice strained, 'that you're nothing but a damn fool and a thief. You could have killed yourself. I've got a good mind to throw you out of this house and see how you do beggin' on the streets.'

Merion sat up. 'You wouldn't dare ...'

Lilain cocked her head to the side. 'Wouldn't I? This is *my* house, and in my house I expect my guests to respect my wishes. If they don't, then I will gladly show them the door, and how it looks from the outside, if necessary. You are nothing more than a guest at this moment, Merion, a guest that is causing me quite a lot of grief. I won't have it. Not here. Not now.'

Merion was stunned. How could his aunt be so callous? So cold? He was flesh and blood, after all. Her *last flesh and blood.* A place in this house was a right, not a gift. 'I said I'm sorry,' he muttered.

Lilain seemed happy enough with that. She nudged Lurker once again and together they shuffled out of the room. 'You sleep for the rest of the day, no arguments,' she ordered.

Merion coughed and grasped at the air between them. 'Will you train me? Please, Aunt Lilain?'

The door hovered an inch from shut. There was a pause, and then a whisper floated to his deafened ears. 'I'll think about it.'

When the door clicked shut, and Merion was alone, he licked his lips and croaked out a name. 'Rhin.'

Nothing. Not a rustle.

'Rhin?' he said again, a little louder. Still nothing.

'Almighty damn it.'

Where on earth was that faerie? Merion wondered.

The faerie in question was currently sequestered beneath the boards of a whorehouse, on the outskirts of the town. Not the most glamorous of places to be sequestered, you may agree, but Rhin did not seem bothered. It was good to be out sneaking again.

He had already spoken to a few horses. They were dumber animals than what he was used to, unlike the wise old carthorses at Sheer Gate, with stories to tell and yarns to spin. Rhin had often crept to the outskirts of the Harker Sheer estate, under the half-moon, to wander through the peasant fields, and chat a while with a horse or two. Animals and Fae had always been close allies, for the most part.

Fell Falls horses, however, had never seen a faerie in their lives. A little stupefaction might have been forgiven, but not whinnying terror. Even after the dull beasts had managed to get over their shock, their words were slow and drawled, all backwards and upside down. They had mumbled of rails and wraiths, but that was all, and Rhin was left to sigh and creep on, in search of brighter beasts to mine secrets from. If there is one thing that is true of all faeries, it is that they love a good secret. Or two.

Further down the road, a crow told him quite pointedly to piss off. In the shadow of an outhouse, a rabbit just shrugged, and kept on munching. But in the garden of a barbershop, he found an old, shaggy dog slumped at the edge of a porcelain water bowl, hot and tired—an old, shaggy dog with a pleasing amount of things to grumble about.

There was talk of a new lady in town, Rhin was told. Smelled awful strange, she did, all silver and flowers. Not from around here. Rhin had a slight suspicion as to who that could be. The rail was moving too, and that was something the dog did not seem happy about. His owner was a foreman, he whined. Out all day on the rail, he was. Forgetful man it seemed too; often forgot to fill the water bowl or let the poor dog in at night-time. Awful shame. The new lord was a sour bastard, now that was for sure. Worked him longer hours, hadn't paid him in a while, which of course meant no food for the dog ... With a sigh, the panting beast went back to his staring.

Rhin wished him good luck and then wandered on, scuttling and darting from building to building, hiding under their short stilts and decks, listening to the feet plod and the tongues wag above him. It was only when he had reached the whorehouse that he had grown bored. The day was becoming sweltering, and his wings were beginning to droop. Faeries are fond of the wet earth and the dark, not dust and sand. Besides, the people there today were dull, mechanical almost.

Rhin got up from his crouch, wincing as his legs creaked. He ran a grey hand across his brow and flicked the sweat away. 'Roots be damned. This *is* a hellhole,' he muttered to himself. His black armour was not helping things. It clung to him like hot pastry, heavy and chafing. Rhin turned to face the way he had come, and then he saw it.

He slid his sword from its sheath, just an inch. More than enough to be deadly in Rhin's hands. The rat was waddling towards him, and not just in his general direction; *directly* towards him. There was a dead look in its obsidian eyes.

'Back, *skindr*,' Rhin hissed in his own tongue, calling the rat by its cursename. Rats do not take too kindly to the Fae, nor Fae to rats. They are old enemies. Rats were actually the reason the early Fae began to wear armour. Giant, gnashing teeth are a very good motivator. 'Back, I say!'

The rat kept on coming. It was a big specimen, brown from nose to rump with bristling, rumpled fur. Rhin had killed more than a few rats in his time, and he was well aware of what a rat on the attack looked like. This one was calm as could be. Docile even, like the dull horses in the stables. He kept his hand on his sword all the same.

When the rat was barely a foot away, it stopped and then did something very strange indeed. It turned to the left and then rolled over on its side, exposing its belly and, curiously, a thin roll of brown paper, strapped to its underside with a ragged length of twine.

Rhin stepped forward, heart beating and mouth souring with suspicion. With each step, he came to new conclusions, ones that numbed his fingers and made him sweat even more. 'Please, no,' he gasped, reaching to cut the twine with the tip of his sword. The rat flinched when the blade came close, but Rhin was careful. The sharp black steel split the twine as if it were nothing. The scroll rolled free, and came to a rest against the toes of his black boots. 'Please,' Rhin said as he bent down.

With fingers that were too nervous for their own good, he slowly unravelled the paper. Rhin barely noticed the rat rolling back onto its legs and calmly trundling back to whence it came, leaving him alone to read his message.

Tonight. The Serped barn. East. The Queen demands it.

The Wit

Every internal organ Rhin possessed dropped like a stone. The Wit. The name was a sharp blade in the gullet. *The Queen demands it.* After all those miles.

Rhin's fingers slowly began to close around the paper, crunching it into an ugly ribbon, then a ball, and then finally, as he gripped and strangled and gritted his teeth, it became dust. He wiped its charred remnants from his burning hands and then clapped them together. And he kept clapping. And clapping. Until his lips split apart and a shout came out. It was no word a human could understand. Old Fae, and there was no translation for it. The meaning is one of pure anger and frustration, with a little pain thrown in; the sort you get when banging a knee against a table. Only in this context, the knee is your bare, beating heart, and the table is made of needles. Once the last ragged gasps of that word had been ripped from his lungs, Rhin fell to his knees. His nails dug at the earth.

It took him some time before he could get to his feet again. And before he did so, he took out one of his knives, and ran a finger along the blade. Three drops of lavender blood painted the dust before the hand was closed and the wound smothered with magick.

His business concluded, Rhin set off, one hand on his sword and the other on a knife, each ready to go to work. But the rat was long gone, and that *caelk* Finrig nowhere to be seen. *Tonight*, was all he could think on the long, lonely walk home.

The house was dead. Lilain was nowhere to be seen. Lurker had gone. Only the soft, laboured snoring of a boy in the front room. Rhin tiptoed through the kitchen and across the hall, and after jumping for the door-handle, he slipped into the room without a sound. A mouse would have been embarrassed.

Merion was drowning in a nightmare. His eyes roved madly beneath their lids. Great beads of sweat were busy making their way down to his chin. His clammy fingers grasped at the rumpled sheets. Rhin shook his head and climbed up to stand on the boy's chest.

Merion awoke with a cough and a start. Faeries might be small, but they are peculiarly heavy for their size. Armour and swords did not help matters.

'So,' Rhin mused. 'You're alive then.'

Once he had regained his breath, Merion eyed him suspiciously. Rhin was paler than usual, and his knees were caked in dirt. He smelled vaguely of dog. 'Have you also come to tell me how much of a fool I am? Because I'm growing tired of it,' he snapped, his voice still as hoarse as a rusty gate on an icy winter's morning.

Rhin narrowed his eyes. 'As long as you're in agreement, I'll hold my tongue.'

Merion rubbed his sweaty cheeks. 'Where were you?'

Rhin looked away and then began to climb down on to the floor. 'Exploring.'

'That's too dangerous, Rhin.'

The look the faerie threw Merion was chilling. 'Don't you dare lecture me on what is dangerous and what is not.'

Merion sighed, but said no more. He left Rhin to crawl under the bed and into his makeshift bedroom. But instead of lying down, or silencing his rumbling stomach with a stolen biscuit, he sat with his knees drawn into his chest, and stared wide-eyed at the door. He did not speak and nor did he move. He just kept thinking the same word over and over again. *Tonight. Tonight. Tonight.*

No matter how hard Rhin prayed for the sun to linger a little while longer in the sky, no god nor daemon nor spirit heard him. His pleas fell on deaf ears, and the sun fell as it always did. The night was now a bruised purple. A sickle moon was peering over the hills in the north. It was a wicked moon, and beneath it, Fell Falls sparkled with candles and lanterns. There was a feast of some sort tonight. Somebody important in the work-camp was having a birthday, or so said the whispers of the uninvited. Hired out the *Bettermost*, and the *Thirty Dead Men*, right across from each other. Lady Caboose has brought most of her girls too. It would be a wild night for Fell Falls.

Rhin couldn't give two shits for Lady Caboose and her girls, nor for birthdays and important men. That's what he told himself, over and over again, listing all the things he had no particular defecatory urges for. The Wit was mentioned more than a few times, as was that damn Queen of his, and all his Black Fingers. Not to mention the accursed ship that brought them here.

He had been safe, and that was the sour heart of it all. He was supposed to be forgotten here. Lost. In all the ways a runaway should be. *Uncontactable*. And yet here he was, sat cross-legged under an old bed and busy sweating, on the cusp of meeting up with the enemies he thought he had left four and a half thousand miles behind him.

How? He asked himself for the hundredth time that day. How had they found him? How had they gotten here? Like rats aboard a merchant ship they had brought plague and pestilence. Though in Rhin's case, plague and pestilence came in the form of thirteen black knives between the ribs. If there was anything Rhin hated in this world, it was the prospect of dying. It just simply did not fit with his plans.

When the sickle moon finally summoned the fortitude to cast its pitiful light across the desert, and when that milk-light slipped like a burglar into the room and trickled across the floor towards his feet, Rhin knew it was time. The moon, even a wicked one, never lied.

Merion was still busy snoring, but peacefully this time. He was beginning to heal, thank the Roots. Rhin stepped out into the moonlight and let his wings crackle. His swords were sharp, his knives deadlier than a fistful of razors, and his magick was running strong. If only his heart would calm itself, and stop trying to burst out of his neck, *that would have been great*, Rhin thought.

'Fuck this,' he hissed at the darkness and the sleeping boy. He knew he had to go. He had to know what the Wit wanted.

Rhin steeled himself and crept out the door and along the hallway. Lilain was asleep with her head on the kitchen table, a big old book resting open under a numb hand. There was a candle, but it was almost done with life. Rhin's skin melded with the darkness and bent it to its will. He crept unseen past the woman and out the back door.

The night was dark and deathly still yet full of whooping and hollering. Even on the outskirts, it was loud. Everybody was in town, trying to squeeze their way into the revelry. Any excuse to have a party is a good excuse, when you live at the ragged, bloody edge of the world. Rhin was glad of parties and excuses. The roads were empty. He found himself striding bravely down the middle of the Runnels, wearing such confidence as a shield against what awaited him, whatever it was to be.

The barn was a few miles east of the town's outskirts. There was a good and open stretch of desert between Fell Falls and the barn. It lurked alone in the distant darkness, like the big ugly child at a party, the one too grumpy to join in with the games.

Big and ugly: that did the barn justice. Rhin's keen eyes roved over its rough angles as he jogged through the scrub and sand. It was a simple square block rising up out of the dust, its only company a curving spur of railroad that reached out from the main line. Its flat panels were bleached white by the sun. Its roof was also clad in wooden shingles, and sported a pair of flagpoles. Their flags hung limp in the night air, but Rhin spied a glimpse of a silver spinning-top in their green folds.

Rhin began to look for a door, or a crack in the wooden panels. Whatever was inside was important; the thick padlocks and chains across the big doors said as much. On the southwest side of the barn he found his way in: a cracked panel that made an archway into the darkness. Rhin stepped into it, and held his breath. No shouts. No arrows. No blades. All was still in the giant barn.

Grotesque shapes squatted in the darkness, pierced here and there by shafts of moonlight, sneaking through the cracks. The machines were monsters of iron and cog and wire. Some were covered in huge dust-cloths, others had been left to taste the air. Rhin spied their greasy chains and riveted skin in the light. Their smith-twisted spars of iron looked like fingers and claws, and their pistons like ribs, or the carapace of some great, mechanical beetle. The smell of all that metal and oil stung his nose. There was something else too, an earthy smell, like that of old blood.

Rhin moved on, wincing as he peered behind every pole, leg and scaffold. His eyes were keener than most, and yet the barn appeared to be empty. No shivers in the darkness. No ripples in the air. Even faerie skin can struggle to fool faerie eyes.

But the Wit had no desire to hide. He stood right out in the open, in a circle of machinery at the far end of the barn. His hands were clasped in front of him, and his trademark black hood was up, but did not obscure his face. His long white hair flowed around his neck and down his chest. He was deliberately standing in a shaft of milky moonlight, so Rhin could see him all the more.

He means business then, thought Rhin, peering from between two cogs. *He means to talk.* Talking was good. Talking meant time.

Once Rhin had swallowed whatever emotion was trying to choke him, he stepped out into the darkness and strode boldly towards his summoner. He had almost forgotten how tall the faerie was, in the months since he had seen him last. Rumour suggested he had a bit of dwarf in him, thanks to some debauched ancestor, long ago. That being said, he still stood half a head taller than Rhin. In the world of the Fae, that was a sizeable difference.

'Rhin Rehn'ar, we meet again,' Finrig spoke loud and clear, a smile on his lips.

Rhin took a stand at the edge of the circle, several feet from The Wit. 'Finrig Everwit. As unpleasant a surprise as last time.'

Finrig's face cracked into a broader smile, one chillingly devoid of humour. 'Did you miss us?'

Rhin cut straight to the point. 'Why have you followed me here, to the edge of the world?' he demanded. 'I told you before, I don't have whatever it is the queen wants. I just want to be left alone.'

Finrig scratched his nose. 'Ah, but now I know what you stole. Something very precious indeed. And that makes it serious,' he replied. 'Serious money for us, that is.'

There came a sniggering from the shadows. One by one, a dozen faeries in black hoods stepped out into the light, each with either a grin or a grimace on their lips. Swords, axes, spears, knives—these faeries bristled with sharp implements. The White Wit and his Black Fingers, every last one of them.

Rhin crossed his arms. 'Like I already said, I don't know what you're talking about.'

Finrig looked at his crew 'You hear that, boys? That's the sound of a guilty Fae spewing horse shit from his mouth.' The Fingers chuckled again.

Rhin wondered at his chances. He was a killer, sure, but a killer in the presence of other killers, and each of the Fae around him looked very used to the sight of blood on their blades. He wondered how many throats they'd slit, how many heads they'd caved in, how many babies they'd stolen and thrown into the darkness. He weighed that up against his own murderous wrongdoings, and found himself wanting.

Rhin put a hand on his sword. 'Make your point or draw your sword, or I walk away. I haven't got all night,' he said.

'Somewhere to be?' hissed one of the Fingers. Kawn, Rhin recognised him from decades before, from guard-duty on the walls of Hafenfol, in the Mole Haunts. Rhin flashed what he hoped was a deadly smile. To his dismay, Kawn just sneered. He had a few more scars since last Rhin saw him.

'Where's the Hoard, Rehn'ar?' asked the Wit.

Rhin shook his head firmly. 'I don't know what you're talking about!' he snapped.

Finrig stepped forward. 'Tell you what, Rehn'ar, you tell us where you stashed it, or we'll cut that boy of yours into little ribbons, so the dogs don't choke on him,' he growled.

Rhin's sword barely made it halfway out of its scabbard before a dozen knives and axe-blades were at his neck. These faeries were fast. Kawn waggled a needle-point dagger uncomfortably close to Rhin's right eyeball. 'Tell us where it is,' he growled, in a voice almost as thick as the sludge between his ears.

Rhin smirked back at him, trying very hard not to move his throat too much. 'Let's say I do have the Hoard. If you kill me, you'll never find it. How do you think the Queen is going to pay for your troubles if you come back to her with only my body to offer, and no Hoard?'

Finrig laughed, as if he were conversing with a halfwit. 'She's the queen. The Hoard is not her only stash of gold.'

Rhin narrowed his eyes. 'Really? Do you think so? Why then is she so keen to get it back, I wonder?' he retorted.

Finrig nudged his Fingers aside with his elbows. 'Where is it, Rehn'ar, you thief?' he spat in his face.

Rhin spoke through gritted teeth. 'I've been wrongly accused.'

'Kawn,' Finrig spoke, as calm as a pebble, 'Take three of the Fingers, three big lads, and fetch that Hark boy. Kill his aunt if she has any objections.'

'Aye, Wit,' Kawn grinned. He stuck his needle dagger back in its sheath and pointed at three faeries, all of them thickset and muscled. Rhin bit the inside of his lip.

'Don't hurt him. I want to do that part myself,' added Finrig, casually.

'Stop!' Rhin shouted, and the Fingers froze. Rhin was going pale. His knuckles were white around the pommel of his sword. Finrig came closer, staring deep into Rhin's fierce eyes.

'Got something to say, have we? Rhin Rehn'ar?' he asked.

'Harm the boy, and I'll never help you,' Rhin snarled.

'Help us then, and we won't have to carve our names in his belly. We'll do it in the old tongue, so it takes longer,' chuckled Finrig. 'Where is the Hoard?'

It took a long while for Rhin to spit it out. It was that sour a sentence, that damning a collection of syllables and sounds. The only small mercy was that Merion was not within earshot. The oldest lies are always the sharpest on the tongue. 'I gave it away.'

Finrig grabbed him by the throat, his arms moving like lighting. 'You *what*? To which kingdom? Which duke? Who hired you?'

'I gave it to no Fae,' Rhin gargled.

As it dawned on Finrig, his grip began to tighten. Rhin struggled and gasped and tugged at his sword, but two Fingers held him tight. His heart felt as though it was about to burst out of his chest and explode. Perhaps he could take Finrig out with him.

'You gave it to a *human*? You gave it to the fucking boy, didn't you?' the Wit hissed.

'No!' Rhin managed to croak. His eyes were slowly rolling up into his skull, their glow fading.

'Don't you lie to me, Rehn'ar ...'

'I swear! He knows nothing!'

Finrig snorted and pushed the faerie away from him. While he had never been the sort for crown and countrymen, while he may have had dwarf-blood in his veins, he was still a faerie, and all Fae loathe the big people. Giving something so precious as the Hoard to one was unthinkable.

'I have half a mind to lop off both your legs and make you crawl back to your beloved boy-child so you can tell him what a thief and a traitor you are, you pathetic bastard. What did we ever do to deserve such treachery?' he said, lip curled repugnantly. Rhin though he would stab him right there and then, on principle alone.

Say what you will of the Wit, the faerie had his rules.

'It's "we" now, is it?' Rhin pushed himself away from the Fingers and brushed himself down. 'I'm nothing like you. Our ancestors would spit if they saw us now. Undering has become rotten, greedy, and it's bred faeries like you and yours, queens like Sift. I fought for my kind in the war and was rewarded with dishonour. All I did was return the favour. The Hoard deserved better than the pocket of a sadistic queen.'

Finrig turned and looked him up and down. 'How many times have you practised that little speech in the flat of your sword-blade?' he replied. 'How many times have you sung yourself to sleep with it, cuddled up to that boy like a mewling whelp?'

Rhin hawked and spat, narrowly missing Kawn's boots. He received a gauntlet to the face in reply.

Finrig was staring up at the cracks in the walls through which the moonlight snuck. 'You have a week to bring us the Hoard.'

Rhin eyes flashed. 'I just told you. I don't have it,' he growled. Finrig just shrugged.

'There must be more than one Hoard in the world, surely?' he said, smirking. 'Are there no banks in town? And I hear there are lords and ladies about. Empire sort. They may have one of their own hidden up their skirts.'

'Humans know nothing of such magick.'

'Oh, I wouldn't be so sure of that.' Finrig winked before delivering Rhin's sentence. 'You have one week to repay your debt.'

Rhin's wings buzzed with frustration. *Time. He needed time.*

'Two.'

'One.'

'Two. Be reasonable.'

'Two then, though you don't deserve it.'

'Then you'll leave me be? And the boy too?'

Finrig nodded. 'Then we'll leave you be. And the boy too,' he said, even going as far to spit in his hand and hold it out. After a moment of seething and glowering, Rhin spat in his own hand and clasped Finrig's tightly. 'Then it is agreed,' said the Wit, wearing that cold smile of his once more. 'Lads, escort this traitor back to town. Don't cut him. Don't bruise him. But don't be too shy.'

As Rhin was dragged from the barn and off into the night, Kawn shuffled closer to the Wit, and muttered in his ear. 'I thought you said Sift wanted him, dead or alive?'

'I know,' grunted Finrig. 'But I gave him hope, and hope is a poisonous thing.'

CHAPTER XX

"THAT'S HOW BUSINESS WORKS"

'Karrigan continues to terrorise the boy with tutors and lessons in business. Merion will inherit an immense fortune. And I don't just mean wealth.

Karrigan's got something, some skill. I just know it. He is too — I don't know — impressive to be normal. He is set to take the seat of Prime Lord after next week's election. He has not been home in some time.'

26th May, 1867

Three days went by, and Rhin and Merion spent them in almost exactly the same way: one beneath the bed, face covered, staring at the door, motionless and pensive; the other in bed, still and pale, also staring at the door, each for completely different reasons entirely. Merion just wanted out. He longed to test out his legs and feel the sun on his back, not through glass and curtain. But he had orders. Lilain's orders. *Stay in bed. Don't move. Don't disturb me.* Merion, to his credit, followed them to the letter. Until the morning of the fourth day, that was.

It was early, and being a Sunday, Lilain was treating herself to a few extra hours beneath the sheets for once, eyes screwed shut against the dawn and dreaming of something other than tables and corpses. The dead could wait on the day of the Maker's rest. Lilain was dog-tired after a week of hard toil. She slept like a stone. Merion, however, was wide awake, and busy standing in Lilain's doorway, staring at his sleeping aunt. A few more steps across the grey floorboards and he was at her bedside, looking down. She looked peaceful enough, but she was as still as a corpse. Merion sniffed.

'Aunt Lilain,' he said quietly. She didn't move.

'Aunt Lilain ...' he said again, louder this time. Nothing.

Merion moved things to the next level. He raised a finger and pressed it to her cheek. She was cold to the touch, and for half a second Merion began to wonder if she were actually dead. That was until Lilain's eyes snapped open and she snorted with surprise.

'Maker's balls, Merion!' she coughed, smacking his finger away. 'What on earth are you doing?'

Merion smiled. 'Today you start teaching me how to bloodrush.'

Lilain rubbed her eyes and then pursed her lips. 'Oh, is it that right?'

Merion's smile grew. 'I've made breakfast.'

His aunt just groaned. 'Now this I have to see.'

If there is one area of expertise the Harks are not well-versed in, it is cooking. The Harks are a very old bloodline, reaching as far back as the Bastard King and the First Empire. However, being such a strong and ancient bloodline, Harks have always had the luck of very large homes, or in some cases, castles. And what comes with large homes? Servants, slaves even, in the past. Not a single Hark in all the bloodline has ever learnt to cook, save for Lilain. And even then, her skills were questionable.

It was a sorry scene that greeted Lilain, as she paced down the hallway barefoot, already wincing at the smell of smoke and char. There were beans in the sink, egg on the ceiling, and bacon on the floor. In fact, it seemed that breakfast was everywhere but on the plates Merion had set out. Lilain watched in horror as he began to serve up his concoctions. She said a quick prayer to the Maker and sat at the table.

To say the bacon was crispy would have been a lie. It was more like a thin slice of charcoal, resting on a bed of something that vaguely resembled a fried egg, though the grey bits in it were slightly worrying.

The beans were nearly black. Lilain's fork danced about, hovering cautiously over the food. 'I don't really have to eat this, do I?'

Merion sagged into the opposite chair. 'It's awful, isn't it?' he sighed.

Even though her stomach was growling, Lilain gently put the fork to rest on the table and pushed the plate away. 'Harks can't cook for shit,' she smiled. Merion sniggered.

It was now Lilain's turn to sigh. She tapped her fingers on the table. 'Can I trust you?' she asked. The talk between them had been scant in the half-week that had passed. Scant and stiff.

Merion tried not to act taken aback. 'Of course you can trust me. Once again, I'm sorry for drinking the bat blood. It won't happen again. I just want to learn is all.'

Lilain took a moment to think, combing her tangled blonde hair with her fingers. 'If we start today, we start my way. No jumping ahead. We have to be careful. We don't want another bad rush so soon after your last.'

'Alright,' Merion nodded. 'We do it your way.'

Lilain drummed her fingers some more, letting her eye wander over to the end of the table, where a lonely slice of bacon lingered in brown paper.

'You know, they say it's never wise to rush on an empty stomach. Why don't you eat that bacon there before we begin?'

Merion followed her eyes to the bacon. 'I don't think I can be trusted with cooking it.'

'No,' Lilain replied, her voice as flat as the tabletop. 'Eat it raw.'

Merion grimaced. 'That's disgusting.'

Lilain raised an eyebrow. 'You afraid?'

'No, I'm just not an animal,' Merion retorted.

Lilain kept on firing questions at him. 'You're a bloodrusher, are you not?'

'Apparently so, but...'

'So you drink blood raw?'

'Well, hopefully...'

'Then you're an animal in many eyes.'

Merion gave his aunt a haughty look. 'Well I'm not in mine, and that's what counts.'

'Eat the bacon.'

'I refuse.'

'It's the same as blood.'

'No, it's slimy and cold, and *meat,*' whined Merion.

Lilain slapped her palms on the table. 'I guess we'll see, won't we?' she said, and with that, she went down into her basement, and was gone for a little while.

When she returned, her hands and pockets were full of vials and she clasped a beaker under one arm. Once she'd lain them on the table, she fetched the water bucket and placed it by her feet. She dipped the beaker into it and brought it up dripping to sit between her and Merion. With finger and thumb, she picked up the first vial. This one was bright red, almost orange. It was filled almost to the cork. Merion involuntarily gulped.

'We're going to go through the *veins* first. All six, until we know the extent of your rushing ability,' Lilain told him, as she examined the vial.

'So do I get to find out if I'm a leech?' Merion asked.

'Yes,' she replied, almost tersely.

Merion rubbed his hands despite himself. He waited patiently as Lilain slid the beaker closer and then uncorked the vial. She tilted it over the brackish water and let a little of the blood spill in. She then swirled the beaker around in one hand, keeping an eye on Merion as she did so, one eye narrow and curious.

She offered him the beaker. 'Here,' she said. 'Put the red in your belly.'

Merion took the beaker and looked into the water. It was even browner than before, but at least it didn't look like blood. This, Merion could do. He put the beaker to his lips and began to gulp the cold water down. If this was bloodrushing, then this was easy. Once the beaker was dry, he set it back down and then spread his fingers across the wood, waiting to feel whatever effects Lilain had chosen for him. His heart thundered away. His stomach began to itch. Gradually, that itch became something fierce. Merion winced, half-expecting pain, but instead he felt something else. Hunger. Ravenous hunger.

Merion's mouth had become a pool, nay, a fountain of saliva. His nails dragged at the tabletop as he cast around for something to devour.

The bacon.

There it was: glistening on the brown paper, all pink and fresh, ready to be gobbled down. Merion snatched at it, hooking it with a finger. He didn't spare it another glance before shovelling it into his mouth, raw fat and all. He chewed like he had never chewed before. His teeth felt like razor-blades. His tongue was an overlord, commanding the consumption of the delicious, salty meat. All too soon it was polished off. Fortunately for Merion, the effects of the rushing were beginning to wear off. His mind began to shrug off the lust for meat. He blinked owlishly at his aunt.

'What happened? Did I do it wrong?' he asked, a little worried, already feeling a little disgusted with himself.

Lilain shook her head, smirking. 'Nothing at all, my dear nephew. How was the bacon?' she asked, while she scribbled a symbol on a scrap of paper.

Merion felt the bile rising. He could imagine the slimy, ragged meat lying in his belly. 'Almighty,' he gagged. 'Did the blood make me do that?'

Lilain lifted up the vial and shook it. 'Hyena.'

'Hyena! Where on earth did you find a hyena?' Merion was stunned.

'Met a Zulu letter in Mocorrow. Sold me that vial for some owl blood if I recall. That's a primary shade in the second vein. Mammals. What the water does is dilute its purity, meaning it takes the edge off it and makes it quicker. See, most shades have a positive effect *and* a negative effect. Sometimes the bad comes out slowly, like an addiction. Sometimes it comes instantly. Sometimes it comes charging on in with the good. Impurity can affect it. So can the rusher's own skills. Some are more susceptible than others, and sometimes you're just darn unlucky. The blood and water mixture flattens the curve and gives me a clear insight. Simple really.

'So this is just an experiment, not actual bloodrushing,' Merion asked. He furrowed his brow. 'And what do you mean by "severe"?'

Lilain frowned. 'Not yet. I'm the best letter in the Kingdom. I know what I'm doing.'

Merion shrugged. 'What's next?'

'Hungry for more, are we?'

The boy's stomach growled, and he clutched it. 'Please, don't use that word.'

Lilain held up the next vial, a little fat-bottomed thing with a red cork. The blood inside was a sickly, putrid yellow. 'The second shade. Insects.'

Merion felt his guts entwine. 'Can I have more water?' he asked.

'Of course.' Lilain refilled the beaker and as before, tipped a little of the blood into the water. Merion put it to his lips. The water smelled acidic. He did not care for it.

'Go on,' Lilain urged. 'We haven't got all day.'

Merion held his nose and drank it down, trying very hard to ignore the bitterness on his tongue.

'Aaah,' he spluttered, 'There, done. What's next?'

'Just wait a moment, Merion. Watch your hands.'

'What about my hands?' Merion held up his palms, already grimacing in unease. And rightfully so: his skin was starting to blister and turn a dark green. He winced as he tried to flex his fingers; the skin was rock hard. Merion knocked his hand against the tabletop. 'It's like I have wooden skin,' he said.

Lilain shook her head. 'That's odd. Merion, look at me.'

Merion did as he was told, and Lilain quickly refilled the beaker of water. 'Drink some more,' she instructed him. 'Now.'

Merion lifted the beaker and caught his reflection in the water. His face was skeletal, his skin drained and grey. Long wrinkles scored his face like the bars of a prison cell. Merion drank as deep and as fast as he could.

'That's a no for insects, sadly,' Lilain muttered, drawing another little symbol on her paper, and a big cross next to it.

'What is that?' he asked.

'Bloodglyphs. One for each vein, and together they make up the Scarlet Wheel of rushing. It's how we letters organise the shades,' Lilain informed him, pointing out her scribbles.

'The script on the labels is Sanguine, a blood language to describe shades. I'll teach you, in good time.'

Merion nodded absently. *One yes. One no.* Though if that was what all insect blood tasted like, then he was glad of the failure. *Putrid stuff.*

The next shade was from the underwater kingdom. Pufferfish to be exact. As well as nearly suffocating, his face ended up so swollen he could barely see.

'It'll be a while before you can handle that vein,' Lilain lectured.

Once Merion's face had deflated, he stuck out his fingers. Three veins in, and only insects had been a disappointment. He had to be a leech. *He had to be.*

The reptile vein was his second failure, bringing it equal. The salamander blood gave Merion the most horrendous nosebleed of his life. In mere seconds, he was saturated in blood. It did not stop trickling for almost half an hour.

When it finally did, Lilain hummed to herself. 'I told you. Magick i—'

Merion thumped an incarnadine fist on the table. 'Isn't pretty, I know. Next,' he said, thumping his fist on the table.

'Birds.' Lilain proffered the beaker. This shade tasted oddly sweet, and not all that unpleasant. He silently prayed for another success. Bird vein. *He could be like Lurker, with a pet eagle or something ...*

'Is something burning?' Merion suddenly asked, sitting rigid in his chair.

Lilain shook her head slowly. 'No, I don't believe so.'

'There's smoke ...' Merion looked around, wondering how it was that Lilain could be oblivious to the thick grey smoke that was now filling the room. He knuckled his eyes, but the smoke only got thicker. Soon enough, Lilain was lost in the haze. 'What's going on?'

The voice wandered out of the fog. 'You're going blind, Merion.'

Merion instantly jumped his feet, sending his chair flying. 'What?'

'Relax, it's not permanent. Cataracts are one of the side effects of the Hunter's Gaze. Eagle blood. Actually, this is rabbit hawk, but their shades are very similar. Can you see me now?' she asked, waving with both hands.

Thankfully, he could. The smoke had begun to fade away. Merion was left blinking and deeply grateful for everything single object in that dingy little kitchen. Pots, pans, peelings, his eyes roved over the lot. 'Well?' he asked.

Lilain tutted. 'Might just be too strong a shade for you. This one's a maybe for now.'

Merion groused away beneath his breath, muttering something about eagles and feathered swine.

'One left,' Lilain said, quietly. She pondered over the vials before reaching for a little tube of bright blue blood. She swirled it around in her fingers. The way in which she did it suggested this was a very special vein indeed. Merion ached to know more.

'Myth,' was all she said, and with great care, she refilled the beaker, right to the top, and then slipped just one drop of the sapphire blood into the water. Merion couldn't help but notice the blood hissing as it met the surface.

'Myth?' he asked.

'Mythical creatures. Also called the magick vein.'

'And what is *that*?'

'Imp essence.'

'Right.' Merion sighed. He was sure there were more glamorous creatures in this vein, that his aunt was just starting him off at the bottom. Entry-level rushing. He couldn't wait to find out what other myths Lilain had hiding on her shelves.

This blood tasted of earth. Not of sand or dirt or old grass, but simply of *earth*. Of something rich and deep and ancient. The taste of deep roots and ageless rocks. Merion could barely taste it all before the beaker was emptied.

'What do you feel?' his aunt asked, chewing on the end of her pencil.

'What do you feel?' Merion echoed. Once again the noises had sprung unbidden from his mouth.

'Any odd sensation? Itching?'

'Any odd sensation. Itching?'

Lilain smirked, and Merion found himself smiling along with her for no apparent reason. *Traitorous lip.*

'I see.'

'I see.'

A mischievous look bloomed in his aunt's eyes. 'Oh how I wish I had a husband!' she proclaimed, quite suddenly.

Merion's eyes went wide. He tried to clamp his lips together but they broke free. All he could do was puff out his cheeks and glare as he shouted. 'Oh how I wish I had a husband!'

Lilain just sniggered. Childish pranks, or rather, *impish.*

Fortunately, this vein wore off more quickly than the others. When Merion trusted himself to speak again, he shuffled his chair forward. 'So?' he asked.

Lilain tapped her pencil against the paper. 'Well,' she mused, 'three veins and one maybe. My boy, it seems you have your father's talents.'

Merion beamed, but that smile soon fell when he noticed how dry her tone was; how little pleasure she had taken saying those words. 'You don't seem all that happy, Aunt Lilain,' he stated.

Lilain folded her hands on her lap and spoke to the tabletop. 'More veins means more danger, nephew. And the more dangerous *you* become. Teaching you to balance the two is not something I exactly relish, to tell the truth.' Here she sighed. 'But it is infinitely better than any alternative.'

'And you promised,' Merion reminded her.

A curse was crushed between her teeth. 'That I did,' she muttered.

Merion's smile returned. 'Tell me then, what's next?'

'Nothing. We'll wait until tomorrow, I think. We need to ease your body into it. Most rushers start young. Most leeches start even younger: seven, eight ...'

'But ...'

Lilain flicked him a sharp look.

Merion relented. 'Alright. Tomorrow. But I want to star—'

It was then that there came a sharp knocking at the door. Lilain moved to get up, but Merion beat her to it. 'I'll get it,' he said.

'Probably Lurker,' she muttered, praying it was nothing to do with dead bodies and railwraiths.

✦

Calidae Serped curtseyed as the door swung open.

Merion had forgotten many things on his way to the door. He had forgotten to smooth his hair. He had forgotten his shirt was encrusted with nose blood. He had forgotten his face was in a similar state. He had even forgotten to wipe some of the raw bacon grease from his chin and lips. Truth be told, he had expected Lurker, and Lurker wasn't going to care about such things, was he? And who else could be calling at this hour?

Merion's face was nothing short of aghast, when he opened the door to find Calidae Serped and three of her finest and tallest lordsguards standing on his aunt's porch. Calidae was dressed in flowing green, and there was a bow in her hair. Whatever smile she had been wearing was slowly but surely melting away, turning into a flat line of uncertainty. The guards stood on the steps with their hands now on their longswords.

'Tonmerion,' she began, 'are you unwell?'

Merion's hands wanted to do a thousand different things. They wanted to plunge into his hair and wrestle it back to normality. They wanted to slap the blood from his face and wipe the mess from his lips. They wanted to grab hold of time and throw it back so that he wouldn't be standing there in front of Calidae Serped, looking like a stray dog who had just eaten its own master. Instead he just closed the door behind him and then clasped his hands in front of him, where he could keep his eyes on them.

'I am indeed,' he answered, bowing quickly, formality coming to the rescue. If he could not look like a lord, then he would bloody well sound like one. 'I am afraid you have caught me at a very unfortunate moment, my Lady Serped. Calidae, I mean. As you can see I am suffering from some sort of desert ailment. Nosebleeds. It must be the heat. Please do excuse my appearance,' he explained, waving his hands about, feeling like an escaped lunatic.

'Not at all, sir,' Calidae curtseyed again. When she arose, the smile had returned. 'I shall not keep you for long. I simply came to invite you to dinner aboard my father's riverboat. Our home here in Fell Falls. Though as I see you are unwell … Perhaps another time?'

'What about next Sunday?' Merion blurted. 'I mean, if that suits? I know he must be busy, but I would be honoured to meet your father. I had hoped he might help …'

Merion felt the door behind him swing inward, and he groaned. 'Help with what, Merion?' asked his aunt, coming to stand over him. 'And who are you, might I ask?' she asked the entourage loitering on her porch. The guards edged a little closer.

'Tonmerion's aunt, I believe, the undertaker? Madam Rennevie, I am Lady Calidae Serped, daughter of Lord Castor Serped,' Calidae announced as she curtseyed again. She flashed her most winning smile, but it splintered into pieces against Lilain's sour gaze.

'Yeah, I know who you are,' Lilain muttered, 'and it's Lady Hark to you. Madam Rennevie died with Mister Rennevie.' Merion flashed her a stern glance, as if trying to press some manners into her.

Calidae clearly did not know what to make of that. 'My apologies, *Lady* Hark,' she apologised. 'Tonmerion, we can talk more over dinner on Sunday. I will have a messenger send the details.'

Merion beamed. 'Sunday, of course,' he replied.

Calidae curtseyed once last time. Before she turned to leave she turned clicked her fingers and looked up at Lilain. 'Ah yes, Lady Hark. My father has a message for you and he has asked me to deliver it,' she said, and then held out a hand. One of her lordsgaurds reached into a satchel and fetched the message.

'And what does he want now?' Lilain snapped, making Merion wince with embarrassment.

Calidae shook her head and handed over the letter, thick paper wrapped in twine and sealed with green wax. 'I'm afraid my father's business is his own. I am simply a messenger,' she offered.

Lilain snatched the letter from her and tucked it into her pocket. 'Yes, I'm sure that's all you are. Good day to you, Lady Serped.'

Leaving Calidae looking stunned and more than a little put out, Lilain veritably dragged Merion back into the hallway and slammed the door.

'How dare you be so rude!' Merion cried, half-hoping Calidae would hear him before angrily marching down the steps to tell her father how unpleasant the Harks could be. Dinner would be cancelled. No help would come from Castor. He would be shunned by the only sort of high society this blasted desert had to offer.

Lilain was already making for the kitchen. Merion followed at her heels like a hungry dog. 'She's the spawn of Castor,' Lilain spat. 'And as far as I'm concerned, that wasn't rude enough.'

His aunt performed a lap of the kitchen table before coming to a halt behind her chair. She gripped its wood so tight her knuckles turned white.

'What could you possibly have against her and her father?' Merion demanded.

Lilain fixed him with a stare. 'Do you really want to pick at this scab? You hold them in such high regard, especially her. I can see it in the way you looked at her. It would be a shame to spoil it all for you.'

Merion crossed his arms and stood as tall as he could manage. 'I think you've already done that, ten seconds ago on the porch.'

'Fine,' Lilain snorted. 'Castor Serped's little railroad empire is built on the backs of dead men, men who are worked too hard, and bought too cheap. But Castor doesn't care. All he cares about is a cheap workforce and more miles of track to bray about back in Kaspar. And he's not short of money. Not in the slightest. Workers get to see none of it. No extra guards to ward off the wraiths. No proper camps nor housing. Serped thinks towns can run off saloons and whorehouses. He doesn't think to build schools or apothecaries or more general stores. Why? Because they won't make him money. That's the sort of lord Castor Serped is, Merion, and that's the sort of father that girl has grown up under. You think she's any different? You want her to help you? Serpeds never do anything for free. You mark my words. If they want to help you, it's because they want something from you. You're different now, the game is different. Don't you trust this girl, Merion, don't you dare.'

Now that her tirade was over, Merion did not quite know what to say. It was his father that answered for him. 'That's how business works.'

Lilain worked her mouth. 'You have too much of Karrigan in you.'

Merion lifted his chin. 'Judging by this morning, I would say that was a good thing, wouldn't you?'

'You may have his blood but you also have his tongue. And it was never a kind tongue, Merion, so don't live your life by your father's words. Look where it got him,' Lilain said, trying to sound as kind as she could manage.

'His tongue didn't put a bullet in his chest,' Merion snapped, and Lilain bowed her head. 'Aren't you going to open that? Merion pointed at the letter.

'Let's see what Lord Serped has to say for himself,' she muttered as she ripped off the seal and untucked the paper from its folds. She read quietly as Merion looked on. As her lips twitched with silent words, her brow began to furrow, deeper and deeper.

'There you have it!' Lilain cried, flinging the letter at her nephew and storming out of the kitchen. 'Read it and see what kind of a lord you're trying to petition. We've just been fired.'

Merion scanned it quickly:

It is with regret that I must inform you that the Serped Railroad Company is no longer in need of your services. From this moment forth, any poor souls that are unfortunate enough to lose their lives in service to the Company will be tended to and buried by Company men, and Company men only. I thank you for your service, and I wish you good fortune in your future endeavours.

Kindly,

Lord Castor Serped of Slickharbour Spit.

'You worked for the Company?' Merion hollered after her, confused.

Lilain hovered in the doorway to the basement. 'I'm the town undertaker, Merion. If a body falls in the dust, it ends up on my table. If it fell on the streets, the town paid me. If it fell on the tracks, the Serped Railroad Company paid me. Paid us,' Lilain tersely explained. 'Looks like it'll just be town corpses from now on. A third of the wage,' she added before she slammed the door.

Merion shouted to her, hoping she could hear. 'When … *if* I go to meet with Lord Serped, I will ask him to change his mind!'

'Don't you dare!' came the angry shout.

Merion was left standing alone in the kitchen. He sighed, and wandered back to his room.

Rhin had not moved and Merion was not surprised. He had not moved, nor spoken, in days. He knelt down to take a peek at his friend. 'What are you so afraid of?'

Merion half-expected Rhin to spit and deny his fear, but instead he just blinked and said: 'Rats.'

'I thought you said rats were no trouble for a faerie like you.'

'These rats are bigger than usual. Sharper teeth.'

'Desert rats?'

'Something like that,' said Rhin, staring past the boy, at the door. His lavender eyes were dull and tired.

Apparently the faerie did not want to be bothered. Merion got to his feet and sat on the bed. It was then that he realised he was still clutching Lord Serped's letter. He scanned at it once more before throwing it on the bedside table.

Aunt Lilain's words had been fierce and heartfelt, but there was something in them that Merion simply could not trust. Calidae had been kind enough to him so far. Perhaps there was an old grudge Lilain had forgotten to mention. Perhaps it was something to do with her being a letter. Perhaps it was just Merion's ache for escape that stirred the disbelief, the doubt. She had blamed Castor for building an empire on the backs of dead men, but what exactly was Lilain's empire built on, if not the same? Lord Castor would help him, he was sure of it. He was the new Lord Hark, after all, heir to a grand estate.

Lilain was right about one thing, however. Nobody, not even Calidae, could know he was a rusher, never mind a leech. He was wise enough to listen to that. Another secret for the pile.

CHAPTER XXI
OF RED IN THE BELLY

'I've been caught. It shames me to say it. Karrigan was on me in a flash. He's got some sort of magick in him, that's for sure. Pinned me right against the wall, pistol in his hand. Didn't help that I was wearing my armour. It took a long while for him to calm down. I had to tell him the truth. Any other story didn't make sense …

He's bloody taken it: the Hoard. He demanded it in return for letting me stay. He almost made it sound like a job. Sift's Hoard in return for letting me stay, for being Merion's guardian. Although I'd do it gladly. (The boy has grown on me.) I never thought I would say that …

You should have seen the look on Karrigan's face: the greed, the possibilities. I didn't have a choice, and now it's all gone. I'm down a Hoard. But I'm up a home, and a friend. I can't decide whether I'm up or down. It hurts.'

1st June, 1867

'Are you quite serious?'

'Deadly, boy. Get some red in your belly, Merion, and be done with it,' Lurker ordered him.

Merion stared at the little thimble's worth of blood in the metal cup and willed his stomach to be quiet. The young Hark cursed himself silently. He had wasted most of the week being cross-examined by

Lilain's *tests*, constantly aching to get some real rushing done. Now that he finally had the real stuff in his hands his constitution was failing him. Miserably so.

Lurker was getting impatient. 'Boy, if you can't drink blood you can't rush, can you?'

'I know that,' Merion snapped back at the prospector.

Lurker was not giving in. 'Ignore what happened last time, and *drink.*'

Merion bit his lip and looked around, hoping for a distraction or a passer-by. He was sorely disappointed; the patch of land Lurker had walked him to was far enough out of town to be remote, and silent. The only eyes watching were those of vultures, and mice. No desert rats.

By the Almighty.

Merion rattled off a quick prayer before throwing the dark scarlet down his throat. Lurker clapped sarcastically. 'Only took you an hour,' he mocked.

Merion was too busy swallowing to pay him any notice. With a grimace, he shoved the blood down into the pit of his stomach and took a long, deep breath.

'Now remember, it'll come on fast, but that means you gotta catch it fast. Tense, when it comes, as Lilain's taught you. In here,' Lurker thumped a hand against his leathered chest. 'Then let it out, slowly, 'til you can bundle it all up and hold it. It'll find its way to your head. You've only had a drop, so it should only last a moment,' he lectured. If Merion didn't know better, he would have said the man was enjoying this tutoring lark.

Merion felt the fire stirring in his belly. It was part hunger, part indigestion, and part fear. He tried to force it all together, and the knotting, twisting of his stomach forced the fire into his veins. Soon enough he could feel the itching spreading to his brain, where it could evolve into magick. Or so Lilain had said. The boy's heart thundered.

Merion tensed as he felt the world increase in volume. Even out in the wild, the world could be deafening. For a moment, he grimaced, fighting the noise, until he remembered to tense, and to push. The volume flickered for just a moment. He strained a little harder, and the noise just died a little. He couldn't help but laugh.

'I can do it,' he shouted. 'I can bloody do it.'

'Now see if you can stand releasin' it, but slowly! Don't want to spend another week in bed, boy.'

'It wasn't a week,' Merion grunted. He relaxed his hold on the magick and let it spread, like sand escaping through knitted fingers. His ears opened wider and the hubbub of the waste poured in, clearer now. Merion winced for a moment, but held tight, trying to ride the pain for as long as possible. Gradually it subsided, and as he turned around, he picked up individual sounds above the cacophony of crickets and rustling, clear as gunshots. A mouse snoring. A vulture's wings purring. The crunching of teeth around a tiny skull in a burrow, not too far from where he stood. Merion's head snapped in that direction. He concentrated on that spot and felt the other sounds ebb away, until all he could hear was the crunching of teeth on bone, of chunks being gulped down into a wet throat. Merion tried to hold onto it as long as possible, but already the blood was fading, trickling away.

The world seemed half-deaf to him now. Lurker's voice was just a low whisper.

'Well, you've conquered bat blood.'

'She's picked these out for me?'

'These are your primary shades, she says, the ones that will burn less but burn brighter. The others may hurt, at first. Or, they will hurt you eventually, if you mistreat them.'

'Addiction?' asked Merion.

Lurker nodded. 'Right.'

'Aunt Lilain's been telling me stories of famous rushers and leeches and what happened to them. If she's trying to teach me how dangerous rushing is, she really shouldn't make their exploits sound so exciting,' said Merion. He was dizzy after the rushing. *His first real rushing after the horse-blood. He had done it!*

Lurker snorted. 'Let me guess: Harolk the Fork.'

'Is it true?'

'I heard that one a dozen times. One of Lil's favourites. And it's true alright. Butchered, cooked, and ate his entire family, all because he drank too much mantis blood. It's a darker shade, and rots your mind if you use it too much. Makes you a monster. Had two wives and six children, did you know that? And an uncle, too.'

'I'll count myself lucky that I can't stomach insect shades then.'

'You do that.'

'And you, can you stomach any other shades?'

'No, just magpie.'

'And Jake doesn't mind?'

'It's what drew him to me in the first place.'

'And have you ever felt it? Addiction, I mean?' Merion's question sounded cold, even though he hadn't meant it to.

Lurker took a moment to stretch his back and grunt. 'No,' he replied flatly. 'I'm not addicted.'

'Is it easy?' Merion asked. He was curious about the entire idea. His father had said addiction was the same as affliction. Some men loved beer a little too much, some men tobacco, some men gold and the women that came with it.

Lurker nodded deeply. 'Very, boy. Got to keep a hold on yourself. It all just gets so easy, with blood.'

Merion rubbed his nose. 'You mean the gold?'

'I do,' Lurker replied. 'It's gotten me gold by the barrows, my skill. But that don't mean I can abuse it. Got to be careful. Now, time for a new shade. Whole vial this time.'

Merion rubbed his hands together. 'Alright. What is it?'

Lurker squinted at the label on the vial. 'Springbok. Slightly diluted.'

Merion took the vial from the man and tried to think of anything except thick, oozing blood. The cork came loose with a squeak and he put the vial straight to his lips. The blood was quaffed in seconds. Merion felt the cold liquid settle in his stomach and began to gag.

'Hold it in, boy, and ready yourself,' Lurker told him. Merion tried and tried but the urge to vomit was proving rather stubborn. He felt that familiar fire, and he had to clamp a hand over his mouth to keep from spewing.

'Tense…!'

Merion gritted his teeth and pushed on his stomach, clenching all of his insides. There: he felt the magick flatten. After taking several slow, deep breaths, he let it trickle out, bit by bit into his veins and up into his head with the subtle flexing of muscles he had never known existed. He began to feel his legs twitching. They were eager to move, like that day in the desert, only this time they wanted to run and prance instead of walk. Merion began to shuffle forward.

'You're feeling it,' Lurker muttered encouragingly. 'Let it go and see what happens.'

A simple crouch and hop turned rather suddenly into a lurching bound across the scrub and sand. He must have cleared ten feet and jumped seven foot in the air before nose-diving into a bush. Even as he lay, mangled in a heap, his legs quivered and pulled at him. Merion was too pained to let them escape again. Thankfully, the magick soon died, and the boy was left drained.

Lurker walked over to help him up. 'Human bodies aren't the same as the ones we drink blood from. You drink from a springbok, you act like a springbok. Your muscles ain't much used to that. Drink too much, and your muscles will think that's how they're supposed to work. I can't smell much now if I ain't on the red.'

Merion had a sudden idea. 'Can I try it?'

Lurker looked through the bottles and vials to see if magpie, or anything similar was there. From his frown, it didn't look as though there was. Lurker then checked the list Lilain had written him. No magpie. Not even a crow.

'What's your aunt said about birds?'

'That it's a vein that I can stomach.'

Lurker narrowed his eyes. 'You sure about that?'

'Absolutely,' Merion nodded.

'Well then,' Lurker said, reaching inside his coat for something. He brought out a small silver flask, like the sort a man would keep whiskey or brandy in, and handed it to Merion.

There was something about drinking from the flask that was easier for Merion. Perhaps it was because he couldn't see the blood, and instead could pretend it was something softer, less foreign. Something that didn't taste like bitter copper.

'Just a drop,' Lurker told him, almost snatching back, as if it were more precious than just a flask.

Merion wiped his mouth, unwittingly smearing a dark red streak across his cheek. Lurker tutted. 'Don't let folks see you like that.'

As Merion felt the heat grow inside him, he smirked. 'I suppose I'm kind of like a vampire, drinking blood and all that.'

Lurker looked offended. He shook his head. 'Don't joke about that, boy. We're not damn vampires, we're rushers. Or in your case, leeches. It's a foolish comparison.'

Merion did not get a chance to reply. It suddenly felt as though his nose had been removed, and all the scents in the world had tumbled into the gaping hole, tickling his bare brain. Half the smells he had no clue about. There was something that smelled like corn. Something else that was sickly and sweet. Sweat. He could smell that on Lurker. So strong it almost made him wince. He could smell his leather too, that tangy, cured meat smell. And the metal. From the buckles to the buttons on Lurker's clothes to the giant gun at his back, it all sang to him like a siren.

Lurker reached into another pocket and produced a tiny nugget of gold. 'You smell that?'

It was like having a bouquet of sweet, oily flowers shoved in his face. Merion sniffed long and deep, drinking it in.

'It's always strongest, the first time. Gives you a little somethin' to chase, really.' Lurker smiled wryly and put the gold back into his pocket. 'You're using it up fast, I can tell.'

It was true. Merion was quickly losing the burn. The world became plainer, greyer, inch by inch and scent by scent.

'That ain't a good vein for you.'

'It's fine.'

'You don't know shit about what's fine, boy,' Lurker reprimanded him.

Merion bowed his head, feeling suitably chastised.

'That's enough for today,' Lurker said, picking up the vials and the paper and stuffing them into a satchel.

Merion moodily picked up his flask of water and followed Lurker, and together the two of them walked north, back towards the bustling town.

It was a busy Saturday afternoon in Fell Falls. Fresh workers were coming in by the trainload, like fresh soldiers, ready to be thrown at the walls of the enemy. These were foreigners, men shipped in from the southern ports, from Cathay, in the far east. Merion watched them mill about in clumps, talking in a babbling, urgent tongue and decked out in Serped-green overalls. They seemed agitated, and what did not calm matters were the coffins being busily traded for live passengers. As the new workers filed out of the carriages, the bare wooden coffins were carried in and stowed on the seats. They were watched with wild and nervous eyes. A fine welcome to Fell Falls, indeed.

✶

When they arrived back at the house, they found yet another visitor on the step. Lurker just tipped his hat and walked on by, leaving Merion stuck with the blubbering stranger. This time it was a woman, a large woman at that, with thick black hair and a dirt-smeared dress. There were great red patches around her eyes where she had rubbed and clawed at them. 'Peter,' was all she could say, 'Peter.' Even the name seemed too much for her; she broke into ragged sobs and shook.

'Excuse me,' whispered Merion, sneaking past her to the door.

Inside, the air was cool. Before going downstairs to see what had become of this Peter, he stuck his head into his room and called for Rhin.

The faerie had not moved in eight days. Not a muscle. He just kept staring at the door as if it were his mortal enemy, eyes narrowed and hands clasped tightly.

'Are you still there?'

'Yes,' came the curt reply, as always.

'For Almighty's sake, Rhin. Are you ever going to come out from under there?'

'Soon.'

'It's about time you did. Shall I ask again, or am I wasting my time?'

'Told you. Rats.'

Merion shook his head. He had never seen Rhin like this. Earlier in the week he had been concerned, upset even, but now he was simply exasperated, and bored of his strange Fae mood swing. *Maybe he was just jealous of his new magick.*

'Rats again,' Merion muttered, on the way out of the room.

Down in the basement, poor Peter lay on the table with a great puckered welt down his front, tied with thick black thread. It seemed that Lilain was almost finished.

'Come here,' she said, beckoning to him.

Merion rolled his eyes. 'Are we not saying hello anymore?'

Lilain was obviously not in the mood. 'Just get over here and look at this.'

Merion grumpily obliged her. 'What is it?' he asked, staring down at the pale skin of the dead man. Peter was also a large man, and wore a mop of jet-black hair. A husband or brother, Merion wasn't sure.

'Look at that,' Lilain replied, pointing to three tiny cuts in the side of his neck. The veins around the wounds were black and swollen. 'See that?'

'Snake?'

'Since when have you ever seen a three-fanged snake?'

Merion sighed. 'Never, but seeing as there are also ghosts in this desert that can rip up rail, I thought I would venture a guess.'

'Well, you're wrong. No snake did this.'

'Then what did?'

Lilain didn't seem sure of the answer. She hummed to herself as she poked and prodded. 'Something small, and something sharp.'

'Like a little knife,' Merion offered. He saw the flicker in the corner of his aunt's eye, and realised he had chosen his words poorly.

'Whilst we're on the subject,' said Lilain, reaching to the foot of the table, where two dented trays and one chipped bowl sat. 'It seems you knocked these over when you took the bat blood. Wise of you to make noise, to get my attention. You might not have survived.'

Merion nodded. He could see where this was going.

'You must have thrown them with a lot of force,' Lilain added. She picked up the bowl and showed him a sharp dent and a long scratch through the enamel and tin. 'Must have hit something small. And sharp.'

Merion tried his best to shrug, but somehow it did not feel as convincing as he hoped. 'I was in a lot of pain. Can't really remember.'

Lilain showed him the two trays next. 'See? Something small and sharp,' she hummed.

Merion wanted an escape, and badly. This line of talk was a dangerous one. 'Corner of the table, maybe,' he tried.

'Maybe,' Lilain whispered.

Merion began to back away, trying to extricate himself from this awkward conversation. 'Well then,' he smiled. 'I will leave you to it. Going to pick out my clothes for tomorrow evening.'

Lilain sniffed. 'Still going then?' she asked.

Merion nodded. He had feared his aunt's behaviour at the door had cost him his invitation, but as luck would have it, the details had arrived that very morning by courier. Merion was still in favour. Castor Serped was only a day's wait away. 'Well, I am still invited. It would be rude not to go,' he replied.

'Yes, rude to ignore Calidae Serped,' his aunt retorted. Merion was not sure if she was angry or disappointed. In any case either would have been unfair. His aunt would have to put her grievances aside for now. He had business to attend to.

'Yes, well,' was all Merion could think of to say. He clasped his hands together, shook them at his aunt in some sort of gesture of summation, and then quickly escaped upstairs, to go bother a moody faerie. With the bedroom door double-locked.

CHAPTER XXII

BLOOD AND IRON

'I haven't left the tower in days. Visitors come and go like farmers around a new king. I imagine Karrigan sitting in his grand study, bathing in the horse shit, smug and smirking. Merion will never become such a man, not if I have anything to do with it.'

2nd June, 1867

No railroad on a Sunday, they'd said. Day of the Maker's rest, they'd said. But Fell Falls had no need of Sundays, it seemed, and the Maker's rest had been well and truly trampled under the cartwheels of ambition and profit. The town was ablaze with activity.

Merion noted the sour faces, looking as though they'd been cheated. Cheated out of a good morning's rest, or one last roll around with the mistress, or one last shot of whiskey, depending on the make of the man. Not a single laugh echoed through the bustling streets. Not a chuckle either. Just that slow leaden grumble of conversation, some in the common tongue, or else in the tangled tones of Cathayan dialects, with a sharp order here and there for good measure.

The whole air of the town made Merion want to tiptoe. He felt out of place somehow, as if the disgruntlement against the Serpeds would at any moment be turned on him, the only other high-born in sight— another gold-plated foreigner, throwing his weight around. Merion had already caught more than a few dark looks that morning. *Better not mention the dinner invitation, then.*

Merion was hunting for Lurker. The prospector had promised to come by at ten to continue Merion's training. It was now eleven, and Merion was already bored of traipsing through the dusty, busy streets and peering into even dustier saloon windows. Lurker, for all intents and purposes, had vanished off the face of the earth. It did not help that the town was full to bursting with people and sweaty bodies. Merion felt drowned.

Lord Castor had almost doubled the population of Fell Falls in just over a week. Safety in numbers, some whispered. More food for the wraiths, said others.

Merion spied a few saloons he had yet to try, a handful which lingered near the end of a long street, where the shining tracks carved a path across the dirt and out into the dust and desert. Merion glimpsed them through the forest of legs and pickaxes. Two of the saloons were bright and cheery affairs—well, as cheery as Fell Falls got with a bucket of lavender paint and a sloppy eye for detail. They were quiet, barely a man or two from empty, but there was no Lurker in sight.

Merion traipsed to the last saloon, a dingy affair with a bowed roof and dark windows. The darkness beyond its pair of lopsided swing-doors was smoky and thick. Merion rolled his eyes. With a hop and skip across creaking steps and boards, he stood at the entrance and peered inside. But the day was bright, and the bar area gloomy, and Merion had a hard time seeing anything besides an array of dark furniture, an equally dark bar, and an assortment of shadowy figures, all with hats and coats and hunched postures.

Once he had stepped through the doors and blinked his eyes, he realised he had about four Lurkers to choose from. They sat at separate tables with their shoulders tucked into their necks and their hats low over the half-empty glasses. Each one could have been Lurker in the right light, until you saw the colour of their skin. Even so, Merion felt like he had just barged in on an official meeting of the Grumpy Old Prospectors-with-a-Fondness-for-Leather Association.

'Hey, no children in the bar!' came the shout of a rotund man with red cheeks and slicked-back hair, obviously the owner.

'He's with me,' replied the real Lurker, who was sat at a stool at the far end of the bar, nursing a large glass of orange liquid.

'Well you keep him quiet, and no drinking,' ordered the barman. Merion quickly moved to join Lurker, lest he changed his mind.

Merion dragged over another stool. 'You're late.'

'I was busy.'

'Busy with what? Drinking?'

'For the most part.'

'Most of the morning, no doubt.'

Lurker took another sip of his strange-coloured whiskey. 'You sound like your aunt.'

Merion lowered his voice. 'You were supposed to come and train me at ten. It's now well past eleven.'

'Well I got distracted,' he said, waving his glass around in little circular motions. 'Anniversaries. They come every year, even when you don't want 'em to. Come to fuck up your day.'

'Anniversary of what?'

Lurker knocked back the rest of the glass and put his hands flat on the sticky bar. 'You don't want to know, boy, and I don't want to waste breath day sayin' it, so let's put a cork in your questions for now.' The look in Lurker's eye was hard and dangerous, one that Merion found very difficult to ignore. 'All you need to know is that you're a welcome distraction.'

'I could have been a distraction an hour ago.'

Lurker swivelled in his seat and then eyed the floor as if it planned to swallow him. 'You brought any shades?' he asked.

'Several.'

'Great,' Lurker grunted. Finally he summoned the courage to stand on his own two feet. He swayed like a pine in a gale, but he stood nonetheless. He took a long, deep draught of air in through his nostrils and sighed. 'Come, we're going for a walk.'

Merion was not so sure they were, judging by the course Lurker plotted through the tables and stools, nudging a few shoulders here and there for good measure. Merion followed him, handing out apologies where necessary. Lurker finally made it through the doors without cartwheeling onto his face, and Merion hurried after his drunk mentor, inwardly groaning about how torturous the next few hours could be.

Little did Merion know, all the best mentors are drunkards. There comes a certain clarity when one is inebriated. While some abilities—

such as the ability to enunciate, or even to balance—fade away and become muddled, one stands out true and strong amid drunkenness's lopsided mire: honesty.

When alcohol loosens both the mind and tongue, the truth, no matter how acerbic it may be, finds it delightfully easy to slip out. It is a wonderful way of finding out what people really think of you. Merion was swiftly learning that. Lurker was a veritable truth-cannon, firing off awkward comment after awkward comment as Merion worked his way through his aunt's shades.

'And it ain't as if I can move on, not with the memories so fresh,' Lurker was muttering. Merion had never seen him this drunk before. 'I'm still a wanted man, you know that? In Denn's Folly.'

'Mhm,' Merion hummed, trying to indicate his disinterest for the tenth time already.

'You slouch too much.'

'Thank you.'

'No, stand up straight when you rush. Helps the red settle,' Lurker waved his hand. He had his flask in the other. 'It's not as if I don't think about other women …'

'Okay,' Merion said, uncorking the vial.

'Squirrel, is it? You look like a squirrel. A blonde squirrel.'

Merion sighed. The vial was hovering near his lips. 'Again, thank you.'

'You ain't going to be a little girl today, are you?' Lurker coughed.

'Excuse me?'

'With the blood. Like a little girl who's just pissed herself, that's you. You were afraid to drink it.'

Merion had flushed red. He narrowed his eyes at the belligerent drunkard. 'It's blood. It's not natural to go gulping it down.'

Lurker got to his feet. 'It's more natural than you'll ever know, boy, unless you open your eyes,' he said, wagging a finger. 'You're rushing for the wrong reasons. It ain't a tool you can bend and break, it's a partnership. It's a bond with something older and deeper than you. When we drink it's with respect for the animal that gave it to us. Every sip is a burial, of sorts. Got to take this serious, Merion.'

Merion had little to say to that. 'I do,' he mumbled.

Lurker sat down before he fell down. 'Now drink up, boy. Shit. It's getting hotter out here. I'm sweating like a glass-blower's ass.'

Merion was too busy mulling over the man's words to take notice of his colourful descriptions. *Every sip is a burial.* What a strange way to put it, he pondered, but it somehow made sense to him. *Drink with respect.* A homage to the dead thing that provided it. Merion held the vial up as if he were making a toast, and then poured it down his throat in one single gulp. He forced himself not to shrink or shiver, instead managing to stand there with just the tiniest hint of a grimace on his face.

'See? Drink like a man now,' Lurker said, waving his own flask and taking more than just a sip of whatever liquor kept inside it.

Merion did not feel any fire growing, but he tensed all the same, just in case it was trying to catch him off guard. He felt a little warmth trickling up his spine, but that was all.

'Now,' Lurker took a deep breath, 'this is what Lil likes to call a wash, or a "base coat" of a shade. Stronger rushers can drink one drop in the morning and feel its effects all day, if they're lucky. Some rushers can develop it over time, becomin' so used to a shade that it becomes a wash. Like me and my magpie blood.'

'I don't feel anything.'

Lurker smirked. 'Squirrel blood, right?'

Merion held up the vial and checked to make sure. 'Squirrel. Yes indeed.'

'Good,' said the prospector. He slid from his rock like a dead man from a saddle and then began to walk in circles, casting around for something. 'Ah,' he announced, snatching a round pebble from the ground, narrowly avoiding pitching heels over nose as he did so.

'Now the thing about squirrel shade is ...' But the explanation never came, just a madly hurled pebble instead, aiming straight for Merion's face. Lurker may have been drunker than a skunk, but he was still a crack shot.

Merion already knew it was too late to duck. All he could do was scrunch up his eyes and throw out a hand in a feeble effort to fend off the missile. That was when he felt the stone, hot and heavy, thwack against his palm. He opened his eyes to find his fingers had already curled around it, gripping it tight.

'It's a subtle little shade, but it works just fine. Known a few Buckteeth in my time.'

Merion probed his teeth with his tongue, confused. 'Buck teeth? I'm not buck-toothed,' he complained.

Lurker shook his head. 'No, but if'n you kept on drinking shades of squirrel, chipmunk, or mouse, then you'd be in for a surprise. Jus' be careful now. When it's a subtle shade like this, you don't know when it's run out. Don't go try catching any bullets later, jus' in case.'

'I'm going for dinner with the Serpeds at six o'clock. I can't imagine any such situation arising.'

'You sure 'bout that? Heard Castor shot one of his slaves once, all 'cause the poor bastard spilt hot soup onto her ladyship's lap.'

'Calidae?' Merion asked.

'No, the mother, Ferida.'

'But Castor doesn't have any slaves. Slaving has been banned by Lincoln.'

'Slavin' may have been outlawed, boy, but that don't mean it's stopped for good. Any servant is a slave, when you look close enough. The chains might be finer, but they're there alright.'

'Well,' Merion began, treading carefully, 'no offence, Lurker, but I am neither. I don't think Castor will be shooting me any time soon.'

'Jus' be careful.'

'You sound like my aunt.'

Lurker snorted. He caught a scent then, on the breeze, and turned to face the giant crowd of workers that toiled in the desert off to the north and west. They swarmed over the silver rail like huge green ants. Steam and smoke billowed from the dozen little engines that chugged along the fresh tracks, ferrying rail and rubble to the construction front. The faint chiming of hammers hitting iron railspikes lingered on the breeze. They caught the sound of horses whinnying too, and men shouting. It sounded like chaos.

'What can you smell?' asked Merion.

'Nitroglycerin. Devil's whiskey. Must be blastin' rock,' Lurker sniffed. He and Merion shielded their eyes with their hands and stared out at the spear of rail reaching out for several miles into the desert. A small group had splintered off from the crowd and seemed to be planning the future path of the railroad. Merion could imagine them pointing and poking and discussing, bending fingers to their underlings and demanding nitroglycerin as if it were a cool glass of water.

Merion's curiosity began to unfurl. 'Can we get closer?' he enquired, longing for a yes.

Lurker shrugged as he took another sip from his flask. 'Should be safe, if we stay south of the rail. Wraiths always come from the north, or the west. Keep your wits about you boy,' he said, in a way that made Merion realise that this was probably not the best idea, and that whatever happened, Lilain could not hear a single whisper of it. That would spell the end of his training.

Lurker had no such reservations. He marched on with the confident swagger of a man with a headful of whiskey. Merion followed like a hound, shaking his head. This was a dark day for the man, he thought to himself. Perhaps a strong coffee and a lie-down would be best, after this little jaunt.

'How close are we going?' Merion asked, half-curious, half-concerned.

'Just a little farther now,' Lurker belched his reply.

Merion quickly rummaged through his satchel of vials, hoping to see something that might help in a tight spot, something that might save the day, if it came to it. He was a leech, after all, and there was no point fighting like a man when he could fight like a leech.

Salmon.

Squid.

Otter.

Fox.

His aunt had written the name in common underneath their symbols. None of those sounded remotely helpful. Where was the bear, the lion, or the shark?

'Hey, Lurker. Is there a blood that makes you turn invisible?'

'Ha,' Lurker hawked and spat. 'Better ask that faerie friend of yours.'

Merion hummed thoughtfully. 'Ah, so that's why Lilain wants to find a faerie …' he guessed. 'Invisibility.'

Where was Rhin when you needed him? Merion cursed the little bastard.

The roar of work and industry was louder now. They were close enough to see the coats of arms on the men's green overalls. The Cathayan workers were busy beating the railspikes into the rock with hammers. They worked at a frenetic pace, attacking the spikes with fast and vicious hammer blows. They did not miss a single strike.

More hammering rang out from the end of the line. Holes were being hammered into an inconvenient rock. Holes for nitroglycerin. When the hammering stopped, there was more shouting, and three slim vials were brought forth by young runners, barely older than Merion himself. They ran with their arms straight out in front of them, legs wobbly. Everybody else in the group took a long step back, then another, and another.

Merion almost wanted to do the same, even though they were still quite a distance away, and standing behind some scrub bushes. Lurker was currently relieving himself on a nearby rock, ambivalent to the fact he was splashing his boots.

Merion kept his eyes fixed on the workers. 'What are they doing?'

Lurker replied in a series of grunts. 'First you drill a hole into the rock. Then you fill it with nitroglycerin. Then you light the fuse and run away.'

'Do you ever use it?'

Lurker looked amused at that. 'Nitroglycerin is for miners who don't know where to look.'

'Of course,' Merion said.

A few more shouts echoed across the scrub as the nitroglycerin was lit. The workers scurried back to crouch behind their barrows or stand solemnly with their grubby fingers in their ears. An itchy moment passed, until stomachs got tired of clenching, and faces began to ache from expectant grimacing. For a moment it seemed that some poor soul would be sent to examine or relight the fuse. A runner was thrust forward, but he had barely taken two steps before the explosion came. A simple, sharp crack that made the ground shiver. Merion wished he had covered his ears. Even from that distance it had still hurt.

When the grey smoke cleared, the patch of rock was nothing but a ruptured hole. For now, the desert was no match for the march of industry. The workers crept forwards again, nodding and congratulating themselves. The work teams moved up then, working in tandem with each other. While one team chipped away at the broken rock, the other paved the way for the rail ties and ballast that would form the spine of the rail. Thick, oily beams were ushered up the lines on the backs of mules and carried into the ground one by one, looking like coffins for snakes. Once the ties were laid, horse-drawn carts dragged up the railspikes and plates, then the rails themselves, and with them the engineers and the Cathayan hammers. They were relentless.

Yard by yard the railroad grew, and quickly too. The sheer weight and force of the workers saw to that. In one hour, they had laid almost a mile of track. Castor Serped seemed to have taken ahold of the desert and wrapped his hand around its neck, thought Merion. Now there was a man who echoed his father, bending the world to his will. That took power.

A flicker of nervousness stole his breath away for a moment. Only a handful of hours separated him from the Serped table. Help was only as far off as a polite conversation with a powerful man. Merion could almost taste the salt of the London docks on his tongue. The little speech he had been practising echoed alongside the sound of seagulls.

My Lord Serped ...

An almighty squeal ripped through his daydream. Merion winced and clapped his hands to his ears at a speed that would have made a hummingbird jealous. There was a dreadful pause, just long enough to make Merion wonder if it had just been a locomotive breaking down, or a cart tipping over. There was to be no such luck. That was a rare thing, in this desert.

Merion turned and found Lurker quickly screwing the cap back onto his flask. 'I think it's time we left,' he said firmly, barely slurring at all.

Drunkenness always flees when there is panic in the air. And what panic there was. The well-ordered teams of workers had descended into a herd of spooked buffalo. They yelled and shouted and hollered as they fled back along the line. Carts were tipped and thrown aside. Tools were flung to the ground. Horses galloped and mules brayed with abject fear. Men fell and trampled each other in their mad rush to escape what they knew was coming.

When a wraith begins to bite the rail, it never lets go. The rails squealed again. Merion could see the metal puckering and bending as if claws were grasping at it. Something was pulling it every which way, wresting it from its spikes and bolts. The metal groaned like a tortured banshee. Then it faded. Silence reigned over the dust and the fleeing, frenzied crowds for a cold moment. More than a few workers snuck looks over their shoulders as they ran, to see if they had the guts to stare death in the face. Merion did. He did not dare look away. His eyes were rooted to the rail, glued there by some kind of morbid curiosity.

With an ear-splitting crash, a forty-foot section of rail tore itself from its ties and shattered into ragged pieces. The screech of rent metal was like a knife through the skull. Railspikes and splinters danced and spun across the dust, twirling around the centre of an invisible maelstrom. Piece by ragged piece, bone by iron bone, the wraith built itself a body. It shuddered as its head and broad shoulders rose up out of the clattering metal and swirling dust. It growled as the wooden splinters and railspikes gave it ribs and a throat to rattle. It grinned as its grotesque, hammer-beaten skull was filled with iron shards—makeshift teeth straight from a nightmare. It clamped its claws together as its arms were forged from lengths of twisted rail.

When the railwraith took its first steps, they shook the ground like thunder. Black oil and grease began to drip from its glittering mouth, and when it roared, it sounded as though an entire brass band had been murdered mid-performance. *Monster.* The word almost came close.

'Don't move,' Lurker whispered.

'I thought you said we needed to leave.'

'Too late for that now. Hush. He's more interested in the workers.'

Merion watched the creature swing its iron head around towards them. He felt his face drain. 'Erm, John? I don't think he is.'

'Fuck the Maker,' Lurker cursed. The boy was right. Horrendously right. The railwraith had spied them in the scrub, and by now they were the closest piece of meat he could see. 'Run!' he barked.

The railwraith charged, and so did they, careening through scrub and dead cactus, vaulting over rock and rut and dragging sand. But the railwraith was fast and full of hunger. Its loping strides pounded the rocks to dust as it swiftly closed the distance.

'What have you got in that satchel?!' Lurker yelled, stuck on the other side of a patch of cacti.

'Salmon. Otter. Er...' Merion's feet pelted the ground like pistons as he fished vial after vial out of the satchel. He was running so hard he thought he might break them. 'Seal? Bat?'

'No bat!'

'Crab?'

'Yes! What kind?'

'It just says crab!' Merion squinted at the vial bobbing up and down before him. His chest was heaving and the corners of his eyes were turning fuzzy. He stared hard. 'No wait, ghost crab!'

'Fine! Drink it!' Lurker was fumbling around at the small of his back now, fishing for his mammoth of a gun.

Merion snatched a look over his shoulder and sorely wished he hadn't. The railwraith was just a stone's throw away, and a weak throw at that. With every giant step it took, its pieces squealed and clanged like dying seagulls hurling themselves at bells. Merion's heart skipped so many beats he thought it had stopped for good.

Lurker's gun crackled like thunder, and a slug buried itself in the wraith's eye socket. It would have killed any lesser beast, but this was a wraith made of iron and wood. The only blood it had to bleed was the grease that oozed from its joints. Lurker was smiling nonetheless. The bullet had done its job of distracting the monster.

Merion was already gulping down the blood. The magic hit him like a locomotive, setting his head spinning. Suddenly his body was lurching violently to the left, his legs moving unbidden and unnaturally, skipping through the sand in a way that made him fear they would snap in two. It certainly felt as if they were about to. The more he tried to push forward, the faster he moved left. Before he knew it he was a hundred yards to the left of the railwraith and tottering on aching legs.

The railwraith was furious. It ground its teeth as it cast around for a prey that had somehow escaped. Merion was already down in the dust. As was Lurker, hidden behind a broken cactus, already spinning the barrel of his gun. The railwraith sniffed. It was so odd, for a being made of iron and splinters to sniff. Beginning to swipe at the scrub, its arms and ragged claws swung in great arcs, ripping dead shrubs and stunted trees from their roots and casting them into the air. Rock and metal sang as they clashed over and over again. With every swipe, the monster came closer and closer to Lurker. Merion lifted his head as high as he dared, wincing with each crash of its claws. He could not see Lurker. Merion pushed himself up a little further. Lurker's gun cracked again and the railwraith screeched with fury.

'No!' Merion cried, as the wraith raised its claws. Filled with a strange and sudden bravery, Merion made to sprint forwards but instead he threw himself to the right. The next time he sprang left.

'Crab!' Merion smacked himself on the forehead and turned so the railwraith was directly to his right. And he ran. Oh, how he ran.

His legs moved so fast they were a painful blur. His hands waggled, frantically trying to balance himself. This shade was both a blessing and a curse, but Merion had no choice. He ran on, straight through the legs of the railwraith and straight into Lurker, crouched beneath the shadow of the jagged claws.

It wasn't pretty, it wasn't clever, but it worked. Merion barrelled into the man and shoved him clear of the falling claws. They buried themselves deep in the sand, barely an inch from Merion's heels. The railwraith roared at them, so close and so loud that flecks of grease spattered their faces. In that moment, they knew they were finished. It was inevitable: as soon as the monster tugged its claws from the ground, they would be cut to shreds. Merion wondered if Lilain would poke inside him like she did all the others. But no end came—at least, not yet.

The railwraith was straining to pull its claws from the earth. They had bitten hard, and they had bitten deep, and now the earth held them tight. It strained so hard that its joints began to pull apart. The young Hark could have sworn he saw beads of oil grace its grotesque brow, as it grimaced with frustration and hunger. Merion stared right into the wraith's iron face and knew he would never forget it until his dying day.

Pang!

A bullet ricocheted off the railwraith's back and buried itself in the sand with a puff of dust.

'Sheriffsmen!' Lurker croaked. The prospector was right. As they set to running, they watched the horses charging.

The sheriffsmen whooped and hollered as they fired their guns. Their rifles were long and their aim rough, and the bullets flew wide and high. Merion kept running. He did not fancy coming to his end because of a stray bullet. *How undignified and pointless*, he thought.

Seeing the railwraith was stuck, they fired and reloaded like clockwork, each one of them eager to get that lucky shot in, if such a thing existed. Bullets shattered and bounced but they kept firing. Another shout came. Another rider was approaching. A lordsguard with a bundle under his arm and an idea in his head, apparently.

He shouted something, but Merion could not discern it. Whatever it was sent the sheriffsmen and their horses running. The lordsguard was left alone to charge the wraith. One of its arms was already free, and it had turned to grin at its challenger.

Merion saw it now—the bundle in the lordsguard's careful hands, and the fear on his face. The wide berth the sheriffsmen had given him was because it was nitroglycerin. The poor fool was either tired of living or aching to be a hero. Only the next few moments would define him. As his horse galloped on beneath him, the lordsguard held up the bundle of explosives and shouted something to the nearest sheriffsman, something that made the man cock his rifle and wedge it into his shoulder.

'Throw, damn it!' hissed Lurker.

He was right: the lordsguard was being too bold, leaving it to the last second. It came sooner than he had expected. The railwraith wrenched its other arm from the earth with a roar and swung it towards the lordsguard, who was now standing bravely in his saddle. An iron fist ripped through his breastplate like a bullet through a tin can. The guard was riding so hard that by the time he finally came to a halt, the wraith had run him through up to its elbow. The guard hung there, legs twitching, staring down at the twisted metal that had replaced his insides with a face of abject horror.

Lurker's gun fired one last time, and never a truer nor kinder shot had ever been fired. It would have been perfect had the muzzle of the cannon not been resting beside Merion's ear. The boy cried out and slumped to the floor, almost missing the enormous bubble of fire that enveloped the railwraith, blasting its iron bones asunder. What was not melted was blown to smithereens. Shards of the railwraith scattered in all directions. One sheriffsmen caught a railspike in the neck and went down gargling a fountain of blood. A long wooden splinter skewered the leg of another. The last had his horse speared by a spar of metal and was thrown unceremoniously to the dust as the beast collapsed.

Merion slowly unfurled from the tight ball he had forced himself into. 'Is it over?'

The man nodded and holstered his gun. 'It's over alright.'

Merion put a hand out to steady himself and found something sticky and wet instead. There was a dark puddle forming under Lurker's right knee. Two inches up, he found the culprit: a slim shard of iron, sticking out of his thigh at a right angle. 'Lurker, you're hurt.'

'It's nothing.'

Merion was aghast. What had Lilain told him once? *Drunk men can very quickly turn into dead men if they open up a vein. Whiskey thins the blood and makes it pour.*

'You're bleeding to death, you big fool.'

With a grunt and a curse, Lurker reached inside his coat to rip at its tough lining. He bound a strip around his leg, just above the wound. He bared his teeth as he knotted it.

'Pull it tight, boy,' he ordered.

Merion pulled. Lurker growled like a dragon.

'We need to get you back to Lilain. If anyone asks, we can say you fell.'

'Drunk again,' Lurker muttered.

'That's the story.' Merion strained as he lifted the big man to his feet. He stank of sweat and gunpowder.

The sheriffsmen were running over, still waving their rifles. 'You,' said the nearest man, as he pointed at Lurker. 'You seem to have an 'abit of being in the wrong place at the wrong time,' he barked.

'Seems that way,' Lurker shrugged.

'What were you doin' out here?' asked another.

'We were just going for a walk,' Merion explained. 'Nothing special. We wanted to see the railroad. We would have been meat if you hadn't have come.'

'Yeah, well,' groused the first man. He looked as though he were desperately trying to concoct some sort of plot or scheme, as if the empty, blood-soaked scrub would suddenly sprout some evidence of a villainous conspiracy. In the end he had nothing to say except: 'Do you need help?'

Lurker grunted a no, and that was that. 'The boy's stronger than he looks,' he said, and the sheriffsmen were good enough to leave them alone, going back to tend to their own wounded and dead. Merion rolled his eyes. He was not stronger than he looked, not by any stretch of the imagination. In fact, to be accurate, he was a great deal weaker than he looked. Lurker didn't seem to care. He leant heavily on the boy, bending him almost double with his weight. Merion staggered and shuffled, still sideways, and led the man slowly back towards the town, where the workers stood in nervous hordes, their conversation a dull roar.

They quietened somewhat when they saw a bloodied man and an exhausted young boy staggering towards them. They had heard the shots, and seen the explosion. The sight of them stirred hushed whispers and narrowed looks. The crowd split right down the middle to let them pass, standing like hedgerows as the two awkwardly lumbered along.

Somebody buried several rows back began to clap. Slowly at first, then faster. Others took up the rhythm. The clapping grew stronger and louder. Merion looked about at the dusty, sweat-streaked faces of the men standing beside them, and met gaze after gaze. They looked pleased, not angry, appreciative, not aggressive. He tried to smile and thanked the Almighty, the crab blood had finally worn off.

When they eventually escaped the applauding throngs of workers and gawping citizens, they began the long walk up the rocky slant of the Runnels. Lurker was still bleeding despite the cloth tourniquet. Every now and again, his pained shuffle would flick a drop of blood on the hot sand. Merion could not help but think of the old treasure maps on his father's study walls, with the paths all marked out by red dots.

The Runnels were quieter than usual if that were possible. Folk had run down to the town when the commotion had started. All except Lilain, that was, who was busy standing on the lip of the hill, stark and black against the blue sky behind her, hands framed on hips. Merion did not need to see her face to know what expression was pasted across it: one of fury, no doubt.

Merion steeled himself. Lurker was getting heavier with every step, and they had already taken quite a few falls. Merion gritted his teeth and pushed his legs on, one after the other. They ached after the crab blood, but at least he still had a little strength in him. *Almighty if he wasn't tired.*

Lilain spat as they came near. If anything Merion had underestimated her expression. She looked livid. 'If you weren't already bleeding, Lurker, I'd be the first one tickling your throat with a scalpel,' she hissed at the big man.

'Lil,' he began, holding up his free hand, 'it weren't like that. Came out of nowhere. We were far south o' the rail.'

'I don't want your excuses, prospector, just get yourself on the kitchen table, so I can fix that damn leg. Even I don't punch cripples.'

Lurker sighed and hopped up the steps one by one. The shade of the porch was welcome after the hot and heavy work of carrying Lurker. Merion slumped onto the wooden bench and exhaled good and hard. He looked at his hands and grimaced at the blood on them.

'What happened?' Lilain demanded of him.

Merion shrugged. 'We weren't even close to the rail. It saw us from afar and came chasing. Lurker killed it.'

'Anyone die?'

'A lordsguard. A brave one. Maybe a sheriffsman.'

'Well, I guess bravery has a price out here.'

'It would seem that way.'

Lilain worked her lips around her teeth as she pondered what to do with all this pent-up energy she suddenly found herself with. Her rage had fizzled out after her nephew's words.

'Don't wander off,' she ordered him, as she strode into the house.

'I won't,' mumbled Merion. He stretched, winced, and then slumped a little more, splaying his legs and arms across the angles of the bench. It was far from the comfiest thing in the world, but right now Merion's tired body did not care. He rested his head against his fist and closed his eyes, just for a moment.

It had been a long day after all, a fractured day, full of excitement and terror.

Merion watched the railwraith in his mind's eye, reliving its shining claws and tortured bones. Even then, safe and sound on the bench, he shuddered. His heart followed suit, and Merion gasped, putting his hand to his chest momentarily.

Almighty he was tired. And lucky.

He had almost died today. Several times. *He'd been a fool.* An idiot. His father would have whipped him for his stupidity. And yet he had survived, by the skin of his teeth, and all thanks to rushing. His father might have whipped him, but he could imagine a little smidgeon of pride holding back the lashes, ever so slightly. Merion clenched his fists tightly and smiled to himself. It must have been tiring work, because it only took a matter of minutes for him to drift off into a murmuring, twitching sleep.

CHAPTER XXIII

DINNER WITH THE SERPEDS

'Fought a dog today. Some Lord's prize spaniel. Kicked its arse halfway across the lawn. Yappy little thing tried to take my head off. It'll walk on by the next time it sees me. If it ever walks again, that is.'

2nd June, 1867

The silence hanging in between the clinks of rings on glasses, between the gentle scraping of silver on fine, gold-rimmed china, was downright painful. Even the candles seemed to cringe, making the dark room even darker at the edges. Merion bunched his face up into another smile and cleared his throat.

'I must apologise again, my Lord Serped, for my tardiness,' Merion offered, his voice thankfully not breaking this time, as it had done a dozen times already that evening.

Merion had awoken at precisely a quarter to six, still caked in blood and dust, and stinking of grease and fear. He had spent half an hour on making himself even remotely presentable, but it took only five minutes to reach the Serped riverboat, the one moored several miles away on the tail-end of the Seragho. Five minutes to travel three miles. Merion quite liked antelope blood.

Before he could wonder again at the sort of trouble he was already in (by now Lilain was sure to have spied the empty space on her shelves and noticed her nephew had vanished from the porch), Lord Castor

Serped looked up from his plate and levelled his gaze at Merion. It was the sort of look that silently asked: 'Who and why is this peasant boy sitting at my table?'

Merion, to his credit, held the gaze, as his father had taught him. Inwardly, he longed to stare down at the spotless black lacquer of the table, at his delicious white fish and buttered vegetables, at anything but this man. But it was for this environment that he had longed for the last few months: society, manners, seven courses, and everything in between. This is what Merion was good at. This was his pastime.

'Do you not own a horse, young Master Hark?' Even though Calidae had introduced him as *Lord* Hark, Castor was insistent on calling him *master* instead.

'No, my lord. Therein lies the problem, I'm afraid,' replied Merion.

'And your family. You aunt. Does she not own a beast?'

Merion shook his head. 'Again no, my lord, My aunt is a skilled worker, but her profession isn't a wealthy one.'

Castor hummed at that. 'I see.' And that was all he said. The lord went back to his fish, attacking it like a battlefield general. The silence returned to haunt the dining room.

Castor was a thin man, and bony, but tall. Almost as tall as Merion's father had been. Castor's face was a sharp arrangement of proud bones, as if somebody had grabbed the skin at the back of his head and pulled hard. His hands were the same, all bones and tight white skin. Merion watched those hands manoeuvre the knife and fork around like his aunt worked her scalpel and prongs. Castor's hair was a slicked-back cap of black streaked with a little silver here and there. It was the only hint of his age; his clean-shaven face, although gaunt, had an ageless quality to it, decades younger than the grey in his hair suggested. His attire was as sharp as his face. Almost military in cut, his suit was a dark green, punctuated with gold buttons and a black trim. He looked quite at odds with the grand atmosphere of the dining room, and the billowing dresses of his female company.

Lady Ferida Serped was also tall, and willowy of frame. Her hair was a very pale blonde, so fair it was almost a silvery white. It was tied back and left to trail down the back of her cream and black lace gown. Though its ruffles and layers splayed out around her legs and over her chair, the gown looked impossibly tight around the waist, so much so that when Merion ever stole a look, he felt short of breath.

Ferida had a soft face, pure and unblemished, save for a single dark mole sitting high on her left cheek. That, and a fine beak of a nose. When she spoke, Merion could not help but stare at it.

Calidae, of course, stole most of his glances. She too wore a gown, though hers was a bright green. Her hair was in curls, which bounced gently as she ate. She was perfectly prim and proper, eating her fish one tiny morsel at a time. Whenever he caught her eye, she smiled, once even daring to wink.

If there was one part of the evening that was going swimmingly, it was the food. There was not a bean in sight, and instead he had been served food he had thought non-existent on the frontier: fish so soft it must have been a pillow in a previous life; vegetables so fresh and green that Merion swore he tasted the Empire whenever he bit into one; and sauce so rich you could have paid men with it. His dusty taste buds were on fire. There was one problem: the wine.

Merion had only ever tried wine several times before, and every time it had turned his stomach sour, and made his head spin. Merion had so far avoided drinking it, taking fake sips when they had toasted the first course. Castor was consuming his at a rate of knots. Ferida sipped hers at a steady pace. Even Calidae was getting close to the bottom of hers. Merion was at risk of looking rude.

Merion reached for his glass, but before he could get it to his lips, Castor spoke.

'How does she move the bodies?' he asked, rather bluntly. He was still busy dissecting his fish. Lady Ferida tutted, but Castor held up a hand. 'How does she move them if she does not own a horse to pull the cart?'

Merion decided truth was the best option here. 'She pulls it, my lord, as do I.'

Castor looked up and pointed a fork at Merion. 'You pull the cart?'

'On occasion,' Merion replied, praying he had not just committed social suicide.

'So you are, in fact, the horse,' Castor surmised. It sounded like a joke, but there was no humour in his face, no little hint of a smile.

'Father ...' Calidae reprimanded him. Castor just chuckled and went back to his fish.

Merion chose his moment. 'My father, Lord Karrigan Hark, always said that an unemployed man is either a broken man, or a lazy man. I am neither, my lord, and so I work for my aunt,' he said. That seemed to have got Castor's attention.

'So you work with the bodies?' asked Calidae.

'Not directly, my lord,' Merion replied.

Calidae looked either intrigued or horrified, Merion could not tell. 'Is there a lot of blood?' she asked.

'Calidae, dear ...' Ferida chided.

'It must be meagre pay. An undertaker's assistant,' Castor said.

Merion decided to try his luck. 'I get a carrot a day, my lord. Fair wage for a cart-horse,' he said, making sure to smile so as not to seem sarcastic.

There was a moment, an awkward moment, where Castor just stared at him and did not move. But then he smirked, and he laughed. Merion bravely laughed along with him, more with relief than anything else. Ferida and Calidae both chuckled as well. Merion had well and truly broken the ice. He sighed to himself as he wiped his lips.

Why not? he told himself as he reached for the wine again. He took a swig, wincing, waiting for the disgusting taste to hit his tongue and the back of his throat. Instead he tasted something sweet and fruity, something altogether different. Merion took another, and another, until he had almost caught up with Calidae.

'Did you hear of the railwraith today, father?'

Castor templed his fingers. 'Of course I did, my dear. It halted work on the rail for over two hours, and cost me one of my best lordsguards.'

Merion kept his eyes on his fish.

'Merion? Did you hear about it?' Calidae seemed excited.

'I did,' he replied, saying nothing more than he had to.

Calidae looked around the table, both her hands gripping the black table. 'One of the biggest yet, they say. Had it not been for that lordsguard, the rail might have been delayed for days, father,' she said.

Castor nodded. 'True enough.'

The four continued on in silence until their plates were clean, with only the bones left on show. Knives and forks were crossed and taken away, and more wine was poured. Merion noticed that some of Castor's servants were dark-skinned like Lurker. *Any servant is a slave*, he'd said. Merion dabbed his lips again.

'How are you finding living in Fell Falls, young Lord Hark?' Ferida asked him, once the second-to-last course had arrived, a steamed pudding and custard, just like the cooks in Harker Sheer used to make. Merion's mouth watered intensely.

'It is rather hot,' Merion said with a smile, trying not to slobber. 'It's taking some getting used to.'

'It does take time,' Ferida nodded.

Merion took a sip of his wine. 'There's not much to do, however. And some of the people aren't too fond of people of the Empire. And of course there is the constant threat of death.' *Perhaps the wine had loosened his tongue a little too much*, he thought. He had meant for his words to sound casual, off-hand, but his voice had cracked on the word *death*, and he had sounded nervous instead.

Merion put his wine glass back on the table and reached for a spoon.

'Not at all like London, is it, Master Hark?' asked Castor, in a low voice.

'No, my lord. Not one bit,' Merion replied, shaking his head.

'Do you miss it?'

Merion sat a little straighter. 'Constantly, my lord,' he replied, noticing Calidae watching him out of the corner of his eye.

Castor just nodded and stabbed his pudding with his spoon.

Ferida scratched her beak and hummed. 'I must say, I think I might even miss the dreaded rain,' she tittered, and Merion couldn't help but agree.

'It must be nice though, to travel by riverboat,' he said.

'It's hideously slow,' Castor muttered.

'But *comfortable*, and refined, Castor,' Ferida patted her husband's hand. 'Calidae and I won't travel this far by carriage. Will we, my dear?'

Calidae shook her head.

'You came to this town by train, didn't you, Master Hark?' Castor asked.

Merion bobbed his head. 'I did, sir.'

Castor threw another question at him. 'And what did you make of what I've built so far?'

'Impressive, my lord. Very impressive.'

'Mhm,' Castor grunted. Merion bit the inside of his lip.

'And fast too,' he quickly added. Castor's eyes shifted upwards. 'Very fast. It only took me several days to get here from Boston. Faster than any carriage or riverboat.'

Castor chimed in. 'Quiet too.'

Merion could not agree less, but his smile and nod did not betray him.

When the puddings were devoured and removed, the cheese course arrived—an absolute cornucopia of varied cheeses, with sweet wine, grapes, apples, spreads, and a giant assortment of crackers and biscuits to top it all off. Even though Merion was truly stuffed, his stomach still managed to gurgle. He was eating like a king again, and he was loving it. As they nibbled at the smorgasbord that had been set before them, they chatted idly of railways and weather, of home and of Merion's family and estates. Everybody at the table, blunt Castor included, kindly skirted the subject of his father's murder. Every time any of them strayed too close, the talk skipped away. Ferida and Calidae talked the most. Castor just devoured the cheese as if driven by a personal vendetta. Merion tried to keep up, but it wasn't long before he had to throw in the towel, or in this case, the napkin. His stomach felt fit to burst.

The chitchat continued on for a time until it died of natural causes, somewhere at the tail end of a conversation about how difficult it is to find good sausages in Kaspar. It was then that Castor Serped leant back in his chair and swilled his wine around in his glass.

'What do you know of the Shohari, Master Hark?'

Merion pursed his lips. *I spent two nights with them, getting drunk at their fires, playing their games, and consorting with their shamans and magick trees.* 'Not a great deal I'm afraid, my lord. Except that they are a nuisance, and are apparently moving south to interfere with the railway.'

Castor raised an eyebrow, and turned to his wife. This time, he patted her hand. 'Not a great deal, says the young man.' Castor fixed him with a narrowed look. 'It sounds as though you know quite a bit, Tonmerion, more than you would let on.'

Merion looked at Calidae, but she made no movement to help him. 'My aunt has spoken of them a few times. That's all I know,' he replied, quickly taking another sip of his wine.

Calidae chimed in at last. 'They are a nuisance, indeed. Now they are moving south, we will have to defend ourselves against more than just wraiths and sandstrikes,' she said, almost as if she were her father's business associate as well as his daughter.

Castor tapped the blade of his cheese knife on the table. 'The Americans have done a fine job so far, to hold them back and keep them in their forests and in their hills, but they grow bolder every season. I received a report just the other day of a raid on a cattle farm north-west of Kaspar. Murdered the whole family and took the entire herd. Found all the animals slaughtered in the next valley, for no reason. They're savages, Master Hark, and must be dealt with. The more we can kill this year, the less we will have to kill the next. Their children will soon learn not to trifle with us.' Castor took a moment to spread a mound of chutney across a slab of cheese. 'In fact, the more I see of these Shohari the more convinced I am that they should all be killed, or otherwise be maintained as a species of pauper—should they make good servants, that is. Don't you think, Master Hark?' Castor peered at him from across the table.

Merion didn't know what to say, so he simply nodded.

Ferida cleared her throat politely. 'Please, Castor. No more business at the table.'

'Mmff,' Castor said around a mouthful of cheese. 'Then we shall find another table,' he said, wiping his mouth with his napkin. 'Merion and I will talk in my study. Have them bring in the good wine.'

'Of course,' Ferida bowed her head. Merion managed to catch one last glance from Calidae. She smiled once again and Merion found himself suddenly reticent to go talk business. He cracked a smile of his own, almost more of a wince, and got up from the table. He bowed and then followed in the long footsteps of Castor, as the lord led him into an adjoining room.

✷

The riverboat squatted like a fat whale in the water. Rhin eyed its huge arching stern and the big wheel that hung from it, half of its paddles in the dark, murmuring water. The river was low, and the dock had been built for smaller boats. The ropes creaked with every wash of current. Sand scraped against the hull.

The faerie moved off, thumbing his nose against the cold air. He had followed Merion as best he could, though following a boy who had antelope blood in his veins had proved rather difficult. Rhin had been forced to track him instead. Night had fallen, and the stars had come out to shine and mourn the lack of moon. It was a perfect night for sneaking.

For the most part, the riverboat was cloaked in darkness. Only a few windows at its centre glowed, and they shone with the sleepy orange of dying candles or crackling fires. A thin pillar of smoke rose up from a spindly chimney at the centre of the vessel. A few men were hunched over at the prow, a few at the stern, and a pair at the gangplank. Rhin smirked.

No problem.

Within minutes, Rhin had found a rope, shimmied up it, and found a door down to the lower decks. Sometimes it was just so easy. Knowing his time was precious, Rhin darted along the edges of a corridor, towards what he guessed might be the living area. His wings were proud and his spell was strong. He barely cast a shadow as he strode past lantern after lantern, each standing guard beside a dozen boring paintings of pompous-looking rich people. The carpet was thick, and the ceiling high. He felt as though he were treading the carpets of Harker Sheer, rather than a riverboat in the middle of an American desert. Rhin shook his head.

His keen ears heard conversation behind one door, and the uncorking of wine behind the next. A door was kicked open and Rhin froze against the skirting board, tensing his spell so that it held strong. The servant was utterly oblivious. He strode past without a single glance for Rhin. The faerie smirked, and crept on. Soon enough, he came across another set of stairs and followed them down into a darker corridor. Like its predecessor, it too was bedecked with painting after painting of jewellery-laden octogenarians. Rhin's eyes glowed as he took each of them in. He eyed their gold frames and sucked his teeth loudly. *Humans aged so quickly.*

His instincts told him to try the door at the end, a room built into the boat's snub-nosed bow. Rhin rubbed his hands. With a nimble skip and a jump, Rhin leapt up to wedge himself between the door-handle and the doorframe. While one hand gouged splinters out of the door to keep him steady, the other slid his thin knife into the keyhole and went to work. Rhin twisted it, jiggled it and cursed at it until there came a click and a snap. He felt the door-handle slip just a little. With his rough Fae hands he gripped and turned it until he heard another click.

Rhin was through the door in a blink. It was a study of sorts, filled with bookcases stuffed with folders and binders and books. It was chaos on the shelves, and on the desks too, one on either side of the room. Going to the nearest, he made short work of the jump to the desktop. He had that sort of nervous energy that can only come from trespassing and poking into other people's business, from being set loose after a week spent sequestered under a bed.

Though he rifled through every sheaf of paper before moving on, he seemed to know exactly what he was looking for. Every folder was opened, every page turned. Rhin's eyes darted over numbers and schematics and tables and coats of arms with tigers and eagles as if they were possessed. It was only when he reached the second desk, the one sequestered at the back of the room, that he found something, something that could very easily have been nothing, and yet which tickled his curiosity all the same: a timetable for a train, a big train.

Rhin started to claw at the numbers scribbled across the timetable, and the scraps of paper pinned to its top corner. He had always found human scrawl to be rough, like the wall-scrapings of bored prisoners. Rubbing his nose, he traced the grooved scrapings of a hurried quill.

'One hundred … and seventy … thousand in…' Rhin's eyes widened as he whispered snatches of words. 'Gold florins … Tuesday … Midnight.'

His nimble fingers ripped the piece of paper from the pin, quickly rolled it up, and stuffed it through his belt. Rhin went back to the timetable and began to examine the small ink-blotched map somebody had thoughtfully etched on the bottom for him. He counted off the stations one by one:

Kaspar
Hell's Boot
Wheatville
Nilhem
Cheyenne
Linger Hill
Kenaday
Fell Falls

The gold was coming straight to him. Rhin stared at that map until his eyes felt as though they were going to bleed, until it had been scored into his brain. They say the Fae have excellent memories, but Rhin was not about to leave it to chance. He licked his lips. It was exactly what he had hoped for.

The faerie hopped down from the desk and began to pace circles around the room, dissecting his ideas piece by piece, trying them out in different arrangements, sewing some together, mentally defenestrating others. His mind was either a playground for lunatics, or a tabletop for geniuses, he could not decide. A week underneath a bed, staring at a door can play havoc with one's perception. Yet there was one thing he was certain of: this train and its cargo could be his chance to rid himself of the Wit, his Black Fingers, and that dreaded queen forever. He just needed to get his little grey hands on it first.

Thump, thump.

Boots stamped on the carpet outside the door, and heavy boots at that. Rhin froze and strained his magick. As the door swung open, and a wave of bright lantern-light spilled into the room, the faerie slid quietly under the nearest thing he could find—a small footstool fringed with ... some sort of fur, or hair maybe. It tickled the back of his neck as he crouched to peer out at the boots, and their owner.

The man was not short, nor was he tall. He did not ripple with muscle, though neither was he plump or waddling, nor a thin bag of bones. The man was average, in every angle a man could be. Even his attire was simple and unremarkable. His clothes were tailored, his seams razor-sharp, and yet the entire ensemble was a lesson in how many shades of grey a tailor could muster. His head was shaved short at the sides, the rest hidden under a black, round hat, similar to a bowler. Only two things separated this character from a shop-window mannequin: his boots and his eyes.

The boots were heavy, over-sized, and over-worn. They had seen long days on the road, on both cobble and sand, but had been looked after. Rhin could smell boot-polish, oils, even the damp on the laces from washing. Here was a military man, no doubt about it, just one stuffed into a suit.

His eyes were another thing altogether. One was a verdant green, the other bright piercing blue, like an arctic wolf's. Rhin caught their colour as the man lifted the lantern up and over the nearest desk. He too was looking for something.

The faerie held his breath as he watched the man move between the desks, his boots skimming worryingly close to the footstool. The man whistled to himself as he rifled through the papers. He emitted a sharp tut and Rhin peered out to see what the man had found: the timetable. The man shook his head, and stuffed the paper into his pocket before continuing to rifle. Soon enough, the man found what he was looking for: a square scrap of yellow paper. It looked blank. Rhin narrowed his eyes as the man folded it neatly together and slid it into his pocket.

As the man marched back to the door, Rhin followed in his shadow. The corridor was bright, but the faerie hugged the walls on the man's blindside, praying nobody else would come sauntering past. He was growing tired. After a sprint up a flight of stairs, the man came to an ornate green door and knocked three times.

'Lord Serped?' he called.

'Come!' came the muffled shout, and the man entered swiftly, far too fast for Rhin.

The faerie was left crouching in the corridor, breathing hard and pondering the situation. So the timetable was not just some idle scribbling, or the erroneous note-taking of a nervous clerk, full of too much coffee. It was important enough to keep safe in Lord Serped's pockets. Rhin could smell the pipe, wood smoke and brandy wafting from under the door. No doubt Merion was in there. Business, outside of business hours. Rhin smiled as he began his escape, though it was shakier than he would have liked. It was bittersweet. His salvation had not been earned quite yet. First, he had to rob Lord Serped of his train.

✦

This room was more brightly lit than the dark dining room, with its silver-washed pillars and dark moss-green walls. There was a chaise-longue at the far end, in front of a window, and several luxurious armchairs gathered around a rug in front of the fireplace. He could smell the woody sickliness of cigars in his nose, the warm scent of leather, and the stink of ash sitting in the grate. Why on earth a fire was needed in this corner of the world, Merion had no idea.

As he perched on the edge of his allotted armchair, Merion wondered how safe it was having a fire on a boat made, as far as he could tell, entirely out of wood. But he did not dare complain.

If Merion knew anything at all about lords, and he had known quite a few in his short time, it was that they loved to broadcast their words from a height. It was though a little strut and stretch would press them a little harder into the ears they were aimed at. His father had done the very same. Castor was no different.

'Why do you think it is I chose to make my fortune here, Master Hark, instead of in the Empire, where many argue I belong?'

Merion racked his brain for the cleverest response, or the correct response, anything that was not a joke about the weather. The wine was gurgling in his full belly. He held his tongue and shook his head.

'Over-crowding,' Castor announced, as he turned to make another circle of the room. 'Competition. Exhausted opportunities. The Empire is full of them. There is one problem with a thousand-year reign and an Empire larger than a map can hold. Do you know what that is? It gathers dust, Hark.'

Merion nodded, half-imagining a horde of red-coated soldiers running about with mops and dusters. *That damn wine*, he chided himself.

'Your father did a fine job of keeping it at bay. He was not shy of this new world.' Castor looked around as if the plush innards of his fine riverboat encompassed everything about this lopsided continent. 'But he did not see its full potential,' Lord Serped added. He turned to look at Merion.

'That is, not to impugn your late father, Master Hark. He was a fine Prime Lord. The Benches will be poorer for his loss, I'm sure.'

Merion decided to be brave. This was the moment for it, after all. 'Do you know the manner of his death, Lord Serped?'

Castor moved to a table topped with elaborate decanters and glasses of all different kinds. Crystal, by the way they chimed against his rings. 'I do.'

It was an empty answer, to be sure. Merion pressed. 'Then you must know that his murderer is still at large, unknown and unpunished.'

Castor returned to the fireplace, a pair of ornate glasses resting in the bony cradles of his fingers. If Merion had hoped for a little mercy in the measure, he was disappointed. *Was Lord Serped trying to get him drunk?* The brandy was a deep red in colour. Merion reached for his and raised it to his host. *Measure to measure. Man to man.* Or so he hoped. He sipped, trying not to choke as the brandy burned a path all the way to his soul.

When Castor finally sat, Merion leant forwards. Castor sat and swilled his brandy around as he mused. 'I am aware of the investigation. And I am aware that it has been fruitless so far. But I hear the Queen herself has called for the murderer's head. You are not alone in your thirst for justice, Master Hark. Fear not.'

'The Queen?' Merion echoed.

Castor sipped his crimson brandy and hummed. 'Indeed. The murder of a Prime Lord is no small matter. A thousand flowers were laid at the Sage Steps, did you know? A silence was held in the Five Parks. Both London and the Empire have mourned your father this past month.'

Merion took all that in. 'I had no idea. I was travelling …' The excuse tasted sour in his mouth. All the known world had mourned his father, and he had not. Not yet. Merion blamed this foul town, and his father's damned will. He blamed his aunt. He blamed the railwraiths. He blamed every chance and circumstance he could, save his own stubborn nature. He even blamed the blasted heat, and the dust.

'Of course,' Castor said as he raised his glass. 'You have been stuck here instead, with only dead bodies for company.' It was as though he had read the boy's mind.

Merion almost missed his opening. 'And a useless postal service for that matter,' he added.

Castor stood again. These words obviously needed height. Business was afoot. Was there a smirk on Castor's face? Was the skeleton cracking? Merion hoped he was. It may have been the brandy talking, but he was liking the feel of this lord.

'And here was I under the impression that Calidae had invited you on a social visit. This feels more like an introduction with purpose to me,' he surmised, narrowing his eyes.

Merion also got to his feet. *Man to man.* 'I confess, I have come to dinner with an ulterior motive, one which I assure you Calidae was unaware of.'

Castor took a moment to raise his nose and survey the whole of the boy. 'I believe you, and I am listening, Master Hark.' And he listened while he sipped his brandy.

'As you can imagine, I'm keen to see my father's murderer behind bars. But I seem to be several thousand miles away, and the postal office in this town can't seem to comprehend the urgency of my situation. I've sent almost ten letters, my lord. Not a single one has reached Constable Pagget in London,' Merion took a breath to steady his eager heart. 'You have given me some comfort this evening, Lord Serped, and for that I am grateful, but I need justice. I need information, news, correspondence. And of course, it is not just the matter of my father. His estate needs managing. *My* estate needs managing, to keep the wolves from the door, so to speak.'

Castor turned to admire a painting hanging on the wall behind him. It was an ancestor no doubt, astride a great horse and holding a sword which was far too large for Merion's liking. Castor spoke as if to the painting. 'I take it you have not heard talk of the election, then?'

'An election?' Merion asked, eyes wide. 'So soon?'

'The cogs of the Empire must keep turning, Merion. The Bulldog is dead. We must have a new Prime Lord,' Castor replied. He saw the boy's expression and waved a hand. 'It's early days, Merion, and for now you need not worry yourself with it. You're wise to think of your house, and your name, as well as your father. It shows a keen mind, Master Hark, one that I admire.'

Merion tried not to let the pride show in his cheeks. He was doing well, he could feel it in the prickles of his skin. 'Thank you, my lord.'

Once again Castor turned away to trace a curve in the carpet. 'Tell me then, Tonmerion, what would you ask of me?'

'If you would send a wiregram for me, to Constable Pagget, I would be forever in your debt.'

Castor narrowed his eyes and took another sip of his brandy. Merion mirrored him, feeling the burn of the sweet, hot liquid on the back of his tongue. 'Be careful offering such terms, Master Hark. There are others in this world less scrupulous than myself. They may not be so kind and cautionary,' he advised.

Merion sketched a shallow bow. 'In that case, my lord Serped, I would be very grateful, and you would have my utmost thanks,' he offered.

'Now those are terms I can accept. I shall have a wiregram sheet fetched immediately.'

Before Merion could protest that it needn't be fetched at this very moment, Serped had already rung a small bell on a cloth rope. Within several seconds, a loud thudding was heard behind the door.

A man entered and bowed. Merion immediately noticed his eyes: one a bright green, the other a piercing blue. The man was wearing a bowler hat, and beneath it, a smile peppered with bright gold. He was dressed in a smart, yet unremarkable grey suit.

'My lord,' he said.

'Tonmerion Hark, might I introduce Suffrous Gile, master of my affairs here in Wyoming.'

Suffrous Gile. What a name. Merion bowed low nonetheless, and made the man's acquaintance.

'A pleasure to meet you, Lord Hark. My condolences for your father. He was a very talented man,' said Suffrous. touching the edge of his hat. His voice was a churning pile of gravel.

Merion had never quite heard the Bulldog of London described as 'talented'. 'Thank you, Master Gile,' he replied, bowing again.

Suffrous reached deep into his pocket and brandished a handful of paper. 'As you requested, my lord.'

'Thank you, Suffrous,' Castor replied, holding out a hand. Merion did not dare to wonder how a wiregram sheet had been fetched so quickly. Castor had not uttered a single order.

As Master Gile placed the papers in his master's palm, he leant forwards to whisper something in Castor's ear. Merion had to fight not to lean forwards. Such was the alluring pull of the whispered word, tantalising and out of reach. Castor slipped one of the sheets into his pocket, and held out the other: a yellow wiregram sheet. Merion's heart thudded as he walked forwards to seize it. His prize, long awaited.

'My thanks, Lord Serped, my utmost thanks,' Merion said, nearly gasping his words.

'I cannot be held responsible for the answer, I'm afraid,' Castor cautioned.

'Of course,' Merion bobbed his head.

'If you manage to write it tonight, I can have Master Gile here run it to Kaspar in the morning.'

'You're very kind, my lord. If you have a pen I can have it written in no time at all,' Merion replied. The weeks of practice at the postal office had paid off. He could write this message blind-folded. A smile crept across his lips.

Castor motioned to a small writing desk tucked away in the corner, and then clicked his fingers at Gile. 'Have the good wine brought in, Suffrous, and my wife and daughter also. I believe our business is concluded here,' he instructed.

'Very good, my lord,' said Suffrous, sketching a bow. The man's great boots twisted a whorl in the rug as he turned and strode away, footsteps heavy and clunking.

Merion had the message penned in under a minute. The ink was still drying by the time he handed the sheet back to Castor, who balanced it on the pillars of his fingers. He blew gently on the glistening ink while his eyes flicked over it.

Castor hummed approvingly. 'Short and to the point, Master Hark.'

Merion beamed like a lantern. 'Thank you, my lord,' he replied, fidgeting with his fingers to keep himself from either yelling, dancing, or passing straight out. *Finally, he had done it.*

Before he could enquire how long he would have to wait for his answers, the sound of heavy boots returned to the door. Gile came first, bearing a tray topped with two carafes of dark red wine and five glasses; the small, skinny sort that looked about as sturdy as a weeping icicle.

Merion found Castor's bony hand between his shoulders, guiding him back to his armchair, and a smiling Calidae holding a gold-rimmed carafe of wine out to him. She had spied the wiregram in her father's other hand. Her quick mind missed nothing.

'Wine, Lord Hark?' she asked, her voice like bells again. There was a glint in her eye that transfixed him, pinning him in place like a prize butterfly in a case. A glass was pressed into his hand by Master Gile, and before Merion could answer, deep, ruby-red blood began to trickle into his glass.

'To the Empire,' Castor announced.

'The Empire!' echoed the others, Merion loudest of all.

Glasses were put to lips, and wine introduced to tongues. It was sweet, almost too much, and it had a metallic taste that numbed his mouth. Merion took a long gulp, not wishing to appear rude. The sweet wine filled his mouth until he was wincing from the sugar and his tongue had become sluggish. It was the sort of wine that flowed upwards, as he had heard Lurker say one night in the desert. *Straight to your head, forget your belly.* Merion felt the wine washing around his skull almost immediately. The room grew a little darker at the edges. If he was not mistaken, the riverboat seemed to be listing to one side. All he could do was smile, hold out his glass to Calidae, and try not to fall head-first into her eyes. This was worse than that Shohari swill.

He sat down at some point, he knew that much. Or did he lie down? In any case he remembered Calidae's hand resting on his arm. He had not dared to move it. Not for anything. At the window, Gile had spoken to him of all the facets of his past: ship-wrecker, smuggler, prisoner, manservant, master of affairs. Merion remembered swaying through the man's whispered stories, squint-eyed and silent, wondering how to get away. Calidae had rescued him. Or had it been Castor? Wine flowed in any case. Merion's lips were smeared red and sticky.

In the morning he would remember nothing of the dancing, nor the singing, nor even the long and hushed conversation with Castor. Merion would remember none of the words that passed, for wine is a double-edged blade. It loves to play the merry prince, but it also delights to play the thief, creeping in when the lights have been turned down, when the mind is drenched. It cheats you of sense and memory, leaving a slice of darkness in their place. The thief was already picking the locks, as far as Merion was concerned. Long into the night, and deep into the morning, two things kept flowing. That damned wine, and Castor's hushed words.

CHAPTER XXIV

A LONG DROP AND A SHORT STOP

'Karrigan caught me again. Wanted to know why I was spending so much time with Merion. Rumours had started spreading. The boy had been heard talking to himself on many an occasion. Told him I was teaching him the ways of the world. Karrigan slapped me. Told me I was a guard, not a tutor. I bowed and scraped, but I won't be beaten. I've never been beaten. I'll just be smarter.'

2nd June, 1867

Merion wasn't sure what he abhorred the most: the cold water on his clammy skin or the hot fingers of daylight prying open his skull by the sockets.

'Almighty …!' Merion managed to choke out some blasphemy before his aunt threw another cup of water on him.

'Your Almighty's got nothing to do with it, Tonmerion Hark. Get out of bed this instant!'

This was worse than the bat blood, he swore. Merion felt as though he had a dozen stomachs, and each of them was trying to crawl out of him through a different exit. And his head, oh his head. He didn't even want to admit it was attached to his body. His swollen brain knocked against the inside of his skull with every twitch and jolt. They say you never forget your first hangover. They are absolutely right.

Merion shuddered as he got to his feet. The confusion hit him almost as hard as the dizziness, along with the very tempting urge to vomit all over his aunt and her bucket of cold water. The wine had made a dark, fuzzy hole of last night. All he could remember was muttered words, scraps of song, and sickly sweet alcohol. Merion tried to piece together their tendrils while his aunt ranted.

'... to open the door for the coachman. Poor man, having to drag you to the doorstep in your state ... And this room! What have you done with my books? Why are they here? And what is that in the corner?' Lilain wrinkled her lip, and thought better of investigating. It was all Merion could do to shrug.

'The nerve of those bastard Serpeds! Getting a thirteen-year-old boy into such a state. It's disgusting! What exactly where they plying you with?'

'Wine.'

'Wine indeed.'

'And brandy, I think,' added Merion. 'Calidae was drinking too ...'

Lilain turned a slightly darker shade of red. Veins had appeared at her hairline. Her eyes were blazing with anger. She said nothing.

'Ouch,' Merion sighed, rubbing a tender forehead.

'Ouch indeed,' Lilain curled her lip. 'You're an embarrassment and a disgrace, Merion. What would your father have said, if he were here?'

Merion flashed her a look that warned of dangerous territory, but Lilain was having none of it. She was too angry for that. 'He would have given you the rod, no doubt. But I have other methods of punishment.'

'Punishment? It isn't as if I wanted this to ...' Merion spluttered.

Lilain whirled on him. 'Did Calidae Serped pour the wine in your mouth, as well as your glass, nephew, hmm? Did they force it down your throat? Tie you to a chair and empty flagons down your throat?'

'No.'

'I thought not. Which means you're just as in the wrong as they are, aren't you?'

Merion nodded in reply. All he wanted was to be left alone so he could die quietly under his blanket. There was to be no such luck.

'What if you had said something in your addled state, have you thought about that? Told them all about your bloodrushing, or Lurker for that matter, or of your time with the Shohari? Did you ever stop drinking to think about where you were and the ears that were listening? I don't think you did. Merion, you are too important and too naive to be getting fast and loose with the truth around people of such power, and connection. Do you understand me?'

Merion did. Shame was piled onto confusion and worry. He bowed his head.

'First, you're going to clean this room. Then you're going to wash yourself. You reek of alcohol and other things I don't want to mention. Then you're going to help me with the two Shohari bodies I've got on the table downstairs. Any questions?'

Merion was too sick to argue. 'No, Aunt Lilain.'

His aunt stormed from the room and slammed the door. Pain erupted behind his eyes.

Merion turned around to stare at his mess. The young Hark scratched his head. *Books*? Why would he, even in his drunken state, pilfer a score of books from his aunt only to throw them about, as if they had displeased him. What could he want with books?

A telltale rustling came from under the bed. Merion bent down slowly to find Rhin sitting lord-like atop a pile of books, twitching back and forth between flea-bitten pages and folded corners.

'What,' Merion sighed, 'are you doing?'

'Reading,' Rhin replied curtly. The faerie was still in his odd mood, albeit a little more frantic than before. Rhin looked nervous and worried, yet driven by something. Merion had never seen him like this before.

'You never read.'

'No, you never *see* me read.'

'Well, what are you reading?'

'Locomotive schematics.'

'Locomotive *what*?'

Rhin growled. 'Don't you have cleaning to do?'

Merion scowled at him. 'I'm not in the mood, Rhin. What on earth is this all about?'

Rhin looked up sharply, and it was a look that told the boy that arguing was not on the cards. 'You're not the only one with problems, Merion,' came the sharp reply.

Merion abandoned his line of questioning and began to tackle his mess. While he cleaned, he stewed over what had happened to his faerie, trying to figure the little beast out. But his mind was drenched in treacle and busy tripping over itself.

'Ugh,' Merion gulped as he trod in the puddle of dark red liquid in the corner.

This hangover lark was despicable.

Simply put, the Shohari stank. By the look of their ripped and ravaged shoulders, and the frayed rope still tied around their bony ankles, they had been dragged back in to town by horses. Merion's eyes roved over their colours, and not just the bruises and bloody gashes. Their metallic war-paint accentuated the contours of their lithe arms and long legs, made their skin shine blue, purple, and shimmering green.

Merion regarded the two Shohari males with a heavy heart. His time in the desert with them had shown him their humanity. He knew they were not the savages the Serpeds and the townspeople thought them. The boy looked at the filed teeth poking out through the broken lip of the taller Shohari. There had been some anger, some feral, human outrage, behind the blows that rained down.

'First, railwraiths. Now Shohari war parties,' his aunt was muttering as her scalpel flicked back and forth.

'Are they getting closer?'

'Bolder and angrier,' his aunt corrected him. 'They believe this is their land. We believe it is ours. This is how wars begin.'

Merion raised an eyebrow. 'It isn't our land, then?'

'Through toil and iron, perhaps. But the Shohari have lived here far longer than us.'

Merion looked again at the broken lips. 'Lord Serped believes they should all be wiped out. Or enslaved.'

'Lord Serped is an idiot.'

Merion pouted at that. 'He is not. He is kind, and generous.'

Lilain laid down her scalpel and fixed him with a glare. 'So it was kindness and generosity that had me fired, was it? Pah!' she snorted. 'He is an idiot, and a cruel one at that. He should stick to his railways, instead of dabbling in genocide.'

But Merion would not hear a bad word spoken of Castor. 'He was kind to me last night,' he asserted.

Lilain snorted again. 'If by kind you mean pouring wine down your throat, then I would agree.'

'By sending a wiregram to London for me.'

His aunt smirked as she went back to her disembowelling. 'So that's why you're so defensive. They threw you a few treats and now you bark to their tune.'

Merion flushed with anger. 'How dare you ...!'

'Don't be a fool, young nephew. There are no favours in high society that come without debt. What did he ask you for in return? What's he making you do?'

'Nothing at all,' Merion replied, hesitantly. He picked desperately at the shadows in his memories. 'I don't remember.'

'Maker's balls, boy,' his aunt cursed. 'I've never met a person so full of poor judgement. It's mistake after mistake with you, Merion.'

Merion scowled. 'My first was coming here.'

Lilain sniffed. 'Have it your way. I've shown you nothing but kindness, put a roof over your head, given you a job, agreed to teach—'

'Alright, alright.'

Lilain rambled on. 'If you weren't blood, you'd have been thrown in the gutter by n—'

'I said alright!' snapped Merion. 'No more talk of the Serpeds.'

'Suits me just fine. Now do me a favour and lift our good friend's arm up onto his chest so I can get at his other side, would you?'

Merion shuddered, as he always did, but he had learnt to suppress it. He pushed the disgust down hard, and reached for the mangled hand. Drinking blood ten times a day tends to whip the squeamish out of you pretty fast. The Shohari's skin was cold and sticky with paint and dried blood. The muscles were loose, as though they had already liquefied. Merion took a firm grip of the wrist and heard a few bones crunch underneath his fingers. As he lifted the arm up and over the Shohari's flayed chest, dark blood dribbled from a wound on his palm. It painted Merion's fingers a dark, reddish purple, and the boy was left staring at it in the lantern light.

Ideas are dangerous things. They sneak up like thieves and take you by the throat. Some spring from the dark unannounced, a crime of chance. Others take their time, following you home in the shadows, waiting for their chance to pounce. An idea had been lurking in Merion's mind for many a day now. Staring at the blood, the thief pounced and the penny dropped, rolling and clattering down to his tongue, where it fell out as a question. His words were slow, ponderous, and as he spoke, his finger inched closer to his face. Closer to his mouth.

'Shohari are mammals, are they not? And humans too?'

Lilain caught the tone in his question and looked up. She froze when she saw the blood, and how close it hovered to her nephew's tongue. 'Don't you even think of it, Tonmerion Hark,' she hissed. She had used his full name, the stamp of gravity. Merion froze.

'What does it do?'

'Nothing,' Lilain replied sharply. 'Nothing at all.'

Merion slowly lowered his hand. 'That's the sort of nothing that is full of something. I know you that well by now.'

'You don't deserve any answers today,' Lilain huffed. 'But then again I don't trust you not to try it as soon as my back is turned ...'

Merion shook his head. 'I promised you, and Harks keep their promises. Just tell me what it is, and why it's so abhorrent to you.'

Lilain scowled darkly. 'Is cannibalism not abhorrent to you then, nephew?'

'Er ... Of course, but ...'

'But nothing. Consuming your own shade is cannibalistic, and the Shohari are close enough to us in blood to count. It's forbidden to rushers.'

'And leeches?'

'*Especially* leeches,' Lilain raised her voice. Her scalpel work became harsher. 'There's a name for those who drink human blood: lampreys. And they're not to be trusted one inch. The human shade is poisonous to us, in a way.'

'Poisonous?' Merion's voice came out a little higher than he had intended.

'Your own isn't. Your own is useless to you. It's the blood of others that's dangerous.'

'How so?'

Lilain sighed, as if she knew her next words would erode her others. 'It prolongs your life.'

Merion almost laughed out loud. 'And how on earth can that be poisonous?'

'Because the life you steal slowly replaces your own life, your own soul, your own skin even. It might take centuries, but in the end all lampreys end up as shells of their former self, twisted and cruel. Lampreys cheat the art of rushing. They cheat life, abusing their own shade as if it's a pinch of sniffspice, or a vintage wine to be gulped down with dinner ...'

Lilain paused then, to fix her nephew with a stare. Her eyes glistened with suspicion. 'In fact, wine is often used to disguise blood's taste and colour. Red wine. Red blood.'

And red brandy. No, surely not.

The pieces of whatever his aunt was hinting were beginning to knit together. Merion raised his chin. 'I hardly think that Lord Serped would serve human blood to his guests,' he said. 'The whole idea is preposterous.'

'Bark, bark,' muttered Lilain. The suspicious scowl on her face only deepened. 'Barely a month ago, you thought the idea of drinking any blood was preposterous.'

'But you cannot seriously believe that Castor is one of these, these *lamprey* monsters, can you? Or Calidae?'

'I'm beginning to,' Lilain shot back.

Merion, despite his own little itching of doubt, shook his head. 'I won't have it,' he said. 'You're just prejudiced. Blinded by hatred.'

'And you're blinded by hope,' came his aunt's retort.

Grinding his teeth did not help the pounding of his head one bit. Finally, he had been given a taste of salvation. Now his aunt was telling him that taste was poison.

'I think I will leave you to your dead Shohari, aunt,' Merion sneered, walking backwards. Lilain was turning that familiar beetroot colour once again.

'You wipe your hands first, nephew,' Lilain ordered him.

Merion held his aunt's eyes firmly as he reached for a cloth and wiped his bloody right hand. When he was done, he threw the cloth on the table. Only then did he break the gaze, leaving his aunt to bow her head, and do some teeth-grinding of her own. The scalpel was seized, and dead flesh attacked.

Merion hovered on the very top step of the basement stairs, staring down at the hand that grasped the doorknob, at the little drop of blood that he had missed with the cloth, nestled between his first two fingers. The boy bit his lip as he lifted his hand. Curiosity pulled at him. He winced, and closed his lips around his knuckle.

The blood had grown bitter in the short time since leaving the house. Thank the Almighty he had only tasted the tiniest of drops. But it was not the taste that was bothering him. It was the fact that his aunt may have been right, and the guilt of what he had done. It had come slowly at first, the tingling. For half an hour, Merion paced about his uncomfortable room, wondering if he would feel anything at all, snorting to himself at how mistaken Lilain was, how much of a fool she had sounded. Then he felt that telltale numbness in his fingertips. The faint burn in his lower stomach. The treacle at the edges of his eyes. It was rushing, but not as he knew it. There was a headier weight to it, a sweeter tang, the tendrils of something altogether different yet vaguely familiar.

And so it was that the early afternoon found Merion huffing as he strode down the dusty road into town, a sole and stubborn purpose in mind. He would find Calidae, or Castor, or even that butler, Suffrous, if he had to, and clear this whole damned nonsense up. He was sure there would be a perfectly rational explanation.

The air was thicker in Fell Falls that day. The town's stubborn resolve had ground itself to a sharper edge. The Shohari were the talk of day. Guns had found more hips to rub against. Swords even made an appearance here and there, and daggers for the children. At every corner and crossing, every other roof paid host to lordsguards and sheriffsmen. Fists were tighter. Brows were furrowed. Every other glance was towards the west. If Merion had not known better, he would have guessed a war had just broken out.

A bell rang out from somewhere between the worker's camp and the town boundaries, where the rail slanted across the main street and out into the rough desert. Merion saw the shift in the throngs of people. Like a tide they swept towards the ringing. Merion followed like a piece of flotsam, listening to the buzz of conversations around him.

Like any young boy, he had a strange and natural ability to slip through crowds with ease. It took him less than twenty minutes to duck and weave his way to the front of the huge crowd that had now amassed on the edge of town. A scaffold had been erected out of poles, rope and rusted lengths of spare rail. Something that could be roughly referred to as a stage had been hammered and nailed together beneath the scaffold's tallest point, some twenty feet above the sand. Men dressed in black stood upon it, standing silently with their arms crossed.

Just as Merion was pondering why a travelling theatre company would dare to travel all the way out to the very brink of civilisation, a grim hush fell over the crowd. Out of the corner of his eye, he saw those around him squeezing their faces into half-smiles. Some nodded to themselves, their teeth clenched. It was then that the crowd began to boo, and hiss and curse. Merion spied the object of their hatred meandering through two lines of sheriffsmen, a figure wrapped in a black cloak and hood, standing a full head and shoulders above their dark brown hats. Purple paint smeared the hood: Shohari purple.

More booing erupted as the figure was directed onstage, led by a portly sheriff and two lordsguards. He was in full view now, standing in the crosshairs of the town's rage. A few pebbles clattered against the wooden boards of the stage. A handful of lordsguards moved in to hold the lines back. Merion was shoved sharply in the back as the crowds shifted.

'Calm yourselves!' the sheriff shouted. His uniform was fancier than his subordinates'. The bright eight-pointed star on his chest glinted in the sun. 'I said calm yourselves! Justice'll be served to this one by a rope, not by rocks and angry hands, you hear me?'

There were a few shouts, but the crowd settled. The mood was like a bow at full stretch, ready to cast an arrow deep into the Shohari's chest. This crowd wanted blood, and it would have it.

Muttering now, as Lord Castor took to the rickety steps. The Shohari was hissing strange words under his hood, straining against the ropes around his wrists. A dig in the ribs from an armoured gauntlet put an end to that.

As if to spite the sun, Castor was wearing a fine leather jacket and draped in a dark green cloak emblazoned with the sigil of his house. Merion tried to creep forward.

'You see before you an invader, an intruder, vermin!' Castor yelled, his voice loud, clear, and harsh.

Cheers came from the crowd. Castor was playing them like a fiddle. As the rope was brought up and slung over the top of the scaffold, Castor continued. 'His kind would have the railway we've toiled so hard to build ripped up and left to rust.' There were more boos and curses. 'His kind would have this town razed to the ground. He would have us left rotting in the sun with blue-fletched arrows in our backs!' There was shouting now. Fists punched the hot air. Merion had begun to sweat.

Castor turned to jab a finger at the Shohari's chest. 'His kind will fail miserably,' he said, and his audience clenched their fists and jaws and nodded even more. A hush fell once again as the noose was lowered over the Shohari's head. The condemned struggled and cursed in his foreign tongue. His rage and fear turned to nought but gurgling as the knot was pulled tight. It could have been the heat-haze, but Merion swore he saw his bound hands shaking as the Shohari was pushed towards the edge of the stage.

'Let this one be a message to any other Shohari that think Fell Falls is for the taking. We will not be so easily removed from our businesses, from our homes. We have a future at the shore of the Last Ocean!' Castor raised his hands and his lordsguards stepped forward. 'Captain Orst,' he nodded to the nearest man, 'put an end to this vermin.'

Then came a shove, a gasp and a snap as the rope cracked taut. The poor Shohari halted with a sickening crunch. He swayed back and forth while his legs kicked. Not a sound came from him. It would have been drowned out by the cheering and yelling of the crowds. He swung like a gruesome pendulum as life ebbed from his reach. Merion did not take his eyes off of him for a second. He could not. He stood like a statue in a roaring crowd.

Three full minutes it took, for the Shohari to stop twitching, and for the crowds to slake their thirst for justice. When they finally began to trickle away, like an angry, swollen lake spilling over its own shores, Merion was left standing on his own, staring at the body dangling from the knotted rope. Life was a strange thing, he thought. All the miracles of the Almighty, swept away by a long drop and short stop. Nothing was left of hopes, dreams, fears, and hates but a bit of meat hanging for the vultures. It was such a fragile line that Merion could not help but be terrified by it.

It was only when he heard the deep voice of Lurker behind him that he turned away from the spectacle.

'Never been one for hangin's,' he said. He touched the brim of his hat, and Merion shrugged.

'I'm not sure if many people are,' the boy replied.

'Watching it I mean. Seen enough hangin's in my time. Your first?'

Merion unfortunately had to nod. 'When they caught the Southmoor Strangler, father delivered the sentence personally. Half of London turned out to see him hang. Sixty-two murders tends to make you quite notorious.'

'I imagine so.'

Merion turned back to the makeshift stage and spied Castor Serped marching southwards with a train of lordsguards in his wake. Gile was there, in his bowler hat. A smaller figure walked beside him, her long blonde hair flowing out from beneath a bonnet.

Merion started running, sparing not a moment to excuse himself from Lurker's side. Answers were more important than manners, on this one occasion. Merion closed the distance in five seconds flat.

'Calidae!' he blurted as he ran. Two of the lordsguards whirled around, hands already at their sword hilts. Suffrous Gile tipped his hat with a wink of his brown eye. Merion brought himself to sharp stop and bowed low. 'My Lord, my Lady,' he said.

'Relax, gentlemen,' Castor ordered. 'Master Hark. What brings you out into the hot sun to ogle at such a spectacle?' There was no condemnation in his tone, just a slight quirk of curiosity.

Merion looked over his shoulder at the swinging body, buying himself time to dig out the right answer. 'Justice,' he replied, when he turned back.

Castor raised his chin, possibly to hide the tight smile that had appeared on his thin, pale lips. 'And rightly so,' he said, and then waved to Calidae. 'The coach awaits, daughter. A minute, no longer.'

'Yes father,' Calidae nodded, her bonnet bobbing. Merion's heart thumped.

After a moment full of the rattling of light armour and stamping of boots, they were alone. Calidae stepped forwards to smile at Merion. His face instantly mirrored hers, only his was a little toothier and crazed than he would have liked. He felt his cheeks begin to rosy up.

'It was very good of you to come last night, Merion,' she said, sketching a little curtsey.

Merion's cheeks were beginning to ache. *Stop smiling, you buffoon.* 'It was my pleasure, honestly. And I have you to thank for that. Your father sent a wiregram to London for me, to Constable Pagget,' he said, his words rushed and short of breath.

'Then you'll have news within the week,' Calidae chimed.

'Hopefully so,' Merion nodded enthusiastically.

'It would appear that you are in my debt then, Merion Hark,' she replied, a little coyly if Merion was not mistaken. He had to agree, and tried a coy smile of his own.

'I suspect you're right. And what exactly would you have me do?' Merion felt the corner of his mouth tugging upwards. Something daring held the puppet strings.

Calidae looked up at the blue sky and hummed to herself. 'I think I will wait and see,' she replied, before fixing him with her widest and brightest of gazes. 'You never know when I might need you.'

Merion could only bow. He would not trust his face not to betray his silly, boyish blushing. When he arose, praying he wasn't the colour of a beetroot, he stepped forwards and lowered his voice, even though they were standing alone in the dust. 'On another note, erm ... This might sound slightly odd, Calidae, but ...'

'What is it?' she asked, tilting her head.

Answers must be had. 'Was there blood in the wine last night?'

A horrid, heavy moment passed where his breath hovered somewhere behind his tongue.

'*Blood* ...?' Calidae echoed, her face slowly scrunching up into something very close to disgust. Merion began to sweat.

'Not that would be wrong, of course. I completely understand. My aunt, you see, she has this theory that if you drink blood you can ... I mean you ... Erm. Have you ever heard of a lamprey?'

There it was. The full mask of disgust and horrified confusion. Merion's hands began to quiver. 'I'm sorry. Wait ...' he said, a last ditch attempt to grab onto something before tumbling over the cliff-edge of social suicide.

'Have you been drinking this morning, Master Hark?' No Merion this time. *Almighty.*

'No, not at all! I just ...'

'Well then you must be sun-baked, because otherwise you wouldn't honestly be suggesting that my family and I are some kind of savage, blood-drinking *beasts*, now would you?'

Merion shook his head as fast as he could. 'That's not what I was implying. I know all about ...'

Calidae did not bother to curtsey before walking away. 'Disgusting,' she said. 'After we invited you into our home, after my father showed you such kindness ...' She sniffed imperiously. 'Good day to you, Master Hark. Put on a hat, before your brain boils any further.'

Merion was left standing alone and drooping, his jaw hanging slack with utter bewilderment and abject horror.

'I've ruined it,' he told himself aloud, his words slow and sludgy. 'I've bloody ruined it.'

He watched until the carriage disappeared behind a general store. His salvation was no more; whisked away by the crack of a whip and a clatter of wheels. That, and his cursed tongue.

And his cursed aunt. Yes.

This was all her fault, not his.

Merion felt his knuckles creak as he clenched his fist. 'She ruined it.' He said it louder this time.

'Ruined what?' said Lurker behind him.

Merion twitched. 'And you wonder why they call you Lurker,' he snapped over his shoulder.

A creak of leather as the man shrugged. 'Why's your face all red?' he asked.

Merion literally growled. 'Because I'm an idiot, that's why, for listening to that godforsaken aunt of mine!'

'What's she done now?'

'Filled my head with shit and nonsense about lampreys and cannibalism, that's what! And I had to go blurting it out to Calidae.'

'Those lampreys?' Lurker pointed in the direction the carriage had gone.

'You too?' Merion was glaring so hard it felt as though his eyes would seek their freedom and pop out of his face at any minute.

Another creak. Another shrug. 'I've always had my suspicions.'

Merion raised his fists and held them shaking in the air. He gritted his teeth and let out a strangled snarl.

Lilain was on the porch when he returned to the house, sweaty and caked in dust. She had her arms crossed and was leaning against the doorframe. She looked as though she had been there some time.

'Where did you go?' she asked.

'To watch something die,' Merion snapped back at her as he climbed the steps.

'Ah,' she lowered her head and poked at a splinter with the toe of her boot. 'The hanging.'

'Excuse me, please,' Merion said. He wasted no time bowing or scraping. He stared at the thin gap between Lilain's elbow and the dark of the house, wishing it was wider, wishing he did not have to ask.

'Alright,' she replied, and moved aside. 'I thought we could make amends.'

'I'm tired,' came the mutter of a reply, shortly before the bedroom door slammed.

Lilain sighed as she turned back to stare at the world beyond her porch. She wondered what exactly she had done now.

CHAPTER XXV
A BITTER WIND

'Merion and I made a pact today. He said if he ever gets to be Prime Lord, like his father, that I could be his secret advisor. I almost laughed right there and then. Just the thought of Karrigan's face.

Truly though, the boy has become my friend these last few years. He'll be twelve in a week.'

4th June, 1867

'You know why they say your blood boils when you're angry?'

'I know very well,' Merion gritted his teeth against the surge of power he felt in his hands. It felt good, like the wood to his fire, the chorus to his raging song.

'It's because it does. The angrier you are, the harder you rush, boy. Now that can be a good thing once in a while, but right now it ain't. You'll turn your insides to a pulp if you ain't careful, hear me? This is a tough shade,' Lurker admonished him.

Merion was not listening. He was busy focusing all his pent-up anger, as if he were running a whetstone down the edge of a sword, as he had seen the guards do back at Harker Sheer.

Home. The blood raged within him. For a day and a half he had been left to simmer quietly in his room. A day and a half for his thoughts to tie themselves in knots and chafe themselves to threads. A day and a half of Rhin rustling and poring over maps and diagrams, and whatever else he could get his sneaky grey claws on. He had largely ignored the boy, despite Merion inviting him along to his training sessions. Merion had given up asking what the hell he was up to. It was something big, that was for sure, big, dangerous and possibly nefarious. But although Merion secretly harboured a fear that his small friend was about to get them into an enormous amount of trouble, it was buried under his boiling, bubbling anger.

Anger at listening to his aunt and trying that Shohari blood.

Anger at stabbing his chance of going home through the heart.

Anger at disappointing Calidae.

Anger at disappointing his father yet again.

'Steady, Merion!' Lurker broke him from his reverie.

Merion held his hands out straight and squeezed all of his power into one singular point. The air cracked like a whip between his rigid fingers. Sparks popped and snapped in his palms. Fingers of lightning crawled across his forearms, dancing between the saluting hairs and pimpled skin. Merion pushed harder. The lightning pooled in his cradled fingers, bent and crooked like claws. In each palm, a blue-white orb began to spit and crackle. Even in the late afternoon light, it was blinding. Merion closed his fingers around them, the veins and muscles straining in each of his arms. His eyes had become bloodshot, but still he pushed his fingers closer, compressing the orbs into piercing, burning stars.

When at last his fingers touched, the orbs vanished with another whip-crack. Merion was suddenly and violently bent double as a pulse exploded from him, breaking like a wave from every inch of his body. The wave swept outwards. Lightning crackled across the dust, throwing rocks aside and snapping the dead shrubs from their roots. Lurker cried out as he was sent tottering. He would have fallen had he not found a boulder to hold himself against.

'Fuck me,' he gasped, twitching involuntarily.

'I would rather not,' Merion replied, equally breathless. He fell to his knees and tried to shake the tingling from his arms and chest. His heart had either stopped or was beating so fast it had become a dull drone.

'You're a natural-born crackler if I ever saw one,' Lurker said as he brushed himself off.

'A crackler?' Merion panted.

Lurker tipped his hat. 'That's what they call rushers who put the red of an electric eel in their belly. Met a couple in the south, back in the old days, 'fore the war. Though I ain't ever seen one do that.'

Merion grinned, and Lurker took a step back. 'And it looks like that ain't the only thing you can do,' he said, grimacing and pointing at his own teeth.

Merion raised his tingling hands and gingerly probed his mouth. His teeth were razor sharp, filed to points. That took the edge off the rage; that was for sure. It took a full minute for the shade to fade, and for his teeth to return to their normal selves. Merion was relieved to say the least. He did not take his fingers off his teeth for a long while.

'Rhin would have loved to have seen that,' the boy muttered.

'Where is that faerie anyway?'

'Hiding underneath my bed, refusing to come out. Something's spooked him, but he won't tell me what it is. Another problem to add to the pile.'

Lurker sighed. 'Look, boy, so you ain't the Serpeds' favourite flavour at the moment. That ain't to say you ruined this forever, Merion. You need to calm down, or you'll end up burning yourself out. I'm talking about you, mopin' around, glarin' at everything, fists clenched all the time. You're angry. We get it. Do something about it instead of tryin' to boil away to nothin',' Lurker said.

'You don't understand.'

'Oh,' Lurker wagged a finger. 'Being shackled in a place you don't want to be? I know all about that, boy.'

Merion had forgotten himself. A trickle of ice-cold guilt ran through his hot veins. 'I'm sorry.'

'That you are,' Lurker nodded, before raising his head to the western sky, where the burning sun was busy sinking. 'And look who decides to finally show up. Lazy corvid.'

Merion felt a wing brush his ear as a piebald shape flew past him. He flinched, and as he did so a spark flashed across the back of his hand. Merion winced and rubbed his skin. Jake croaked as Lurker stroked the obsidian feathers under his beak.

'This is why you can't get too angry. Don't do no good, boiling blood when you're rushing. Soaks deeper into your heart.'

Merion hadn't a clue what that meant, but he agreed that it did not sound like the best idea in the world. For the first time in a day and a half, he took a deep breath and tried to push his anger back for a while.

'Come,' Lurker waved a hand, 'let's try another shade, before that sun sets.'

But Jake was having none of that. He hopped from Lurker's shoulder to his arm and squawked long and loud before jabbering away. Merion got nothing from the cackled words, but Lurker was listening intently, and as he did, his face began to fall, and the muscles along his jaw began to clench.

'What's the bird saying?' Merion asked.

'Let's get back to the house. Now,' Lurker ordered as he reached for that cannon he called a pistol, letting it dangle by his side. Jake croaked once more and fell silent.

Merion did as he was told. He got the most distinct impression that this was not a time for discussion.

Darkness fell like a sheet over a corpse. Merion jogged alongside Lurker, weaving through stables and outhouses to avoid the main streets. Merion listened to the music spilling from the taverns, the yells from a dozen fights in the workers' camp, even the shrieks of fun from the windows of a nearby whorehouse. He shot a glance at the bruising sky. No matter how hard he squinted, he could not spy a single star, not one glimmer. Even the moon was absent tonight. Something about that was terribly ominous.

There was a breeze too, one that made Lurker look over his shoulder when it first blew. Merion turned as well, but all he saw was an empty row of fenced-off gardens, and a pair of scrawny pigs licking at a trough. The breeze tasted sweet, as though it had come straight from a meadow. But there was a bitterness mingled with it, as if that meadow hid a pride of starving lions, waiting to rip you to shreds.

'There aren't any stars,' Merion mumbled. 'You can normally see stars.'

Lurker did not reply. He just quickened his pace.

The house was dead and dark save for one tiny candle on the porch, fluttering its last breaths. Its orange fingers barely illuminated the figure standing in the doorway, arms crossed and slouching. She must have noted something in their pace, Merion thought, for his aunt was already halfway down the steps before they had a chance to take a ragged breath and shout. The air was still hot, despite the bitter breeze. Merion's brow was heavy with sweat. The growing sense of fear did not help.

'What is it?' she asked, skidding to a halt in front of them. Lurker tipped his hat despite the urgency of the situation. Merion had to hand it to him. Manners came first. Death and destruction could wait.

'Shohari war party,' Lurker rumbled, 'Jake saw them to the west, just over that scraggy pair of hills. Their shamans must have calmed the wraiths,' He cocked a thumb back towards the town.

'How far away?' Merion piped up, not sure whether to be terrified or excited. His thoughts instantly turned to Rhin, even despite the faerie's recent behaviour.

'Not far enough,' Lurker hissed. Jake cawed sharply twice and Lurker nodded. 'Mayut said this day would come. We got an hour, maybe less. They'll wait until the night's good and dark before comin' in, like a trident.' Lurker jabbed the air with three fingers.

'A what?'

'Like a big fork, Merion,' Lilain told him.

'Worker's camp in the middle, town either side.'

Lilain shook her head. 'How do you know?'

Lurker grunted. 'It's what they always do. Why change something if it works?'

That seemed to throw a shiver down Lilain's spine. Merion felt it too.

'In the house, now,' Lilain beckoned to them. Her voice betrayed just the faintest hint of fear, as if her mouth had been pulled tight at the corners. 'I want you inside and the door locked, and no arguments.'

'Yes ma'am,' Lurker bobbed his head. Merion said nothing.

Only once the key had rattled in the lock did Lilain scratch her head. 'We'll be safe, if you're here, right?' Lilain asked of Lurker.

Lurker shrugged. 'Maybe, but there ain't no guarantee. They might just shoot or fry us on sight. Or set the house afire without even knockin',' he muttered.

'*Fry* us?' Merion whispered, his face aghast. He had quickly ducked into his room to warn Rhin, but the faerie had just shrugged and patted his sword. Merion shut the door tight behind him, and Lurker gave him a knowing look.

'Figure of speech, Merion,' his aunt interjected.

'Magick, boy. The most dangerous kind.'

'Lurker! Will you stop it?'

Merion narrowed his eyes. 'I'm not scared,' he asserted.

'We'll get on the roof,' Lilain said. 'They won't look up there, if they come looking at all. We're on the opposite side of town, thank the Maker. I knew there was a reason I bought a house in the Runnels,' Lilain rambled.

'Get Long Tom,' Lurker said in a low voice.

Lilain scowled at first, but then, with a bite of her lip, her face softened, and went sliding back to well-restrained agitation. Just a twitch, here and there, to show she was human.

'And give the boy a gun too,' Lurker added, half-hiding behind a cough.

'I don't want a gun,' Merion replied flatly, but Lurker dismissed him with a wave.

'You need a gun, Merion. You're ain't fighting grade yet,' he said, before bending a knee so he could talk up rather than down. Somehow, that was more patronising. 'You don't know what magick is until you seen a shaman on the loose. It ain't pretty, but fuck me if it ain't impressive. And loud. And hot. A leech you may be, but right now you need a gun, like a real man of the west,' he said.

Merion was adamant. 'I don't want a gun,' he repeated, chasing them up the stairs as the two of them galloped to Lilain's study.

His aunt hissed down the stairwell. 'Take a gun, Merion. Better to have one and not need it, than need one and not have it. That's what my father, your grandfather, always said.'

Merion caught her at the door to her dishevelled study. He lowered his voice to a growl. 'And it was a gun that killed my father, your brother, and I will not consort with the horrid things. They're ugly. And evil!'

Lilain moved to put a hand on her nephew's shoulder, but Merion shrugged himself away. He stood there, defiant, and watched her face fall, and made no apologies for it. Perhaps she was sorry, and by all rights she should be. If she wanted to pat shoulders, then maybe she shouldn't make a habit of ruining lives.

When finally she had caught herself, she shook her head at him. 'The gun is as evil as the person who holds it. It's a machine, not a monster.'

But Merion was adamant. 'No, I want some shades instead. Electric eel, or a sprite.'

'You're not ready for sprite.'

Merion stamped his foot. 'Yes I am!'

'Yes, he is,' Lurker murmured from the study. He was busy unlocking a chest buried under a stack of books.

'Lurker!' Lilain snapped. 'You just said …'

'What? He is,' he said, and waved his hands in surrender. 'Better to have it and not need it, right?'

Lilain sighed. It wasn't like her to give up so easily. 'Alright,' she relented. 'Give him The Mistress. I'll fetch some shades.'

'The *what*?' Merion asked.

There was a loud click as Lurker's key found its teeth. 'Ah,' he said, grinning, 'here she is.'

Some men love guns more than they love women. Lurker was one of these men. The way he held a gun was evidence of this fact: the way that at one moment he might be caressing its sides, and then the next he was hefting it onto his shoulder, or whirling it around. Certain parallels could be drawn here.

Merion scowled as Lurker held her up. The Mistress. If she had been of the female species, she would have been a tremendously ugly specimen. A revolting lady, all bolts and sharp edges, with a long grey pipe for a snout and copper teeth for a smile.

Merion held her in both hands and sneered. 'This isn't a mistress.'

'Not *a* mistress, boy, *The* Mistress,' Lurker corrected him. He was loading his own gun, Big Betsy, and Lilain's long, twisted-barrelled rifle, Long Tom. It had some sort of skinny telescope just above the trigger.

Merion looked down at his gun and wondered why his was so special. It looked as though it had been stretched out, and instead of six barrels it had just the one, with a revolving breech near the wooden grip. A hammer-like protrusion sat just above his thumb when he held it.

'Six shots. Every time you shoot you crank that back. Don't put your finger on the trigger 'til you're sure you want to pull it, unnerstan' me? And number one rule: keep that hammer forwards when you're not shooting. Even if you don't manage to shoot one of us dead, you'll bring the whole war party down on our heads. Keep that in your mind,' Lurker lectured him. 'Now, on the roof, boy.' Lurker pointed towards a window, and Merion gulped. Was this really happening? Was there really about to be a war?

Could this week get any worse?

The breeze had turned colder, taking the sting out of the hot night. Merion found himself shivering as he climbed on all fours to the apex of the roof. The gradient was hardly steep, but the wooden shingles wobbled under every step. All Merion could think of was how heavy the gun was at his hip.

When he reached the apex he put his back against the rickety chimney and faced south and west. The desert was black like the sky, and where they touched, they almost became one. Merion could not remember ever seeing a night so black, so devoid.

The only light was from the town itself, bleaching a garish hole in the darkness with thousands of lanterns and torches and candles. Light glowed like a river of lava through the jagged edges of sign-boards and rooftops, splashing against the tall cranes of the worker's camp and the spikes of pitched tents. Every few seconds a lonely shout, or a smashing of glass, or the squeak of a fiddle would catch on the breeze and come floating to his ears, muffled and malformed.

There was a shadow in the west. Even in the dark he could see it, and see it moving too, padding silently across the sand, or so Merion imagined.

In his mind's eye he could picture the braids trailing in the wind, the colours of the war paint beginning to catch the light of the town, inching nearer with every thud of tough heels. He could see their long spears, blackened with soot as Lurker had told him, held low but ready, their flint knives, dipped in poison, and their arrows, dipped in the blood of whatever animal or poor soul they had killed last. He could imagine their fierce eyes, unblinking, their rigid cheeks cutting the air.

'I can see them,' he whispered.

'Mhm,' Lurker grunted. 'Nothin' we can do now 'cept raise the alarm. Give these poor bastards an equal chance.'

'But the Shohari …' Merion started to say, but then he thought of Calidae, and of Castor, and what should happen if the town were overrun. 'An equal chance,' he said.

Lurker pointed his six barrels at the sky and emptied each one. When he was done, he hunkered down to reload and watched with a grim expression on his face. Shouts grew loud on the fell breeze. Lights burst into being on each and every rooftop, and suddenly the ground became as bright as the night sky had failed to be. A single, lone gunshot rang out in answer to Lurker's, and then a scream that sent a shiver through every single person who heard it. The shadow in the west galloped on. Bugles sounded now, from the lordsguards. The shadow had been spied. Bright torches burnt away the night, revealing the monsters it had been hiding. The war cries began to rise. Drums began to sound.

Lurker pressed a small spyglass into Merion's hands, and the boy put it eagerly to his eye. He could see them now: lithe, lanky figures, swarming into the light like a horde of locusts, right into the sheriffsmen's firing range. Their spine-chilling undulating war cry was momentarily drowned out by an explosion of fire and smoke from the guns. Bullets flew like hornets. The night began to crackle. All around the edge of town, puffs of pale smoke began to rise, dribbles of grey on an otherwise black canvas.

It felt wrong to think of fireworks, but Merion was guilty as charged. He recalled a night when he had been very young, standing on a box to peer out of Harker Sheer's highest window, his father's steady hand on his back. They had looked down upon the fringes of London, watched it sparkle and shimmer. Fell Falls looked the same, only this time there were no children duelling with sparklers, no popperkins or Jack Flashes being thrown in doorways, only bullets and powder, and the hack and slash of sword and chipped stone. No laughter or giggles, just the screaming of men and Shohari being shown the colour of their insides.

A great spout of flame burst up from the work-camp. A tent soared into the sky with wings of fire. There was more screaming, and this time the frenzied whinnying of horses. Something moved amongst the Shohari, even less human than they were. It screeched like a tortured wolf. Its shape, painted black as pitch against the fire, was nothing short of terrifying.

'Hear that?' Lurker asked. Merion nodded. The whole town had heard the creature. He could imagine children shivering under their beds at the sound of it.

'Lupus,' whispered his aunt, crawling up the roof behind them. She had Long Tom slung across her back. Merion had never seen her so menacing.

'The Norsemen first told tales of them, stories from a time when they braved the ocean to settle here in America, a thousand years ago or more. More desert wolf than Shohari—a twisted bitch of a creature. Only ever see the females, never the males,' she lectured.

'My vials?' asled Merion.

Lilain reached inside her pocket and brought forth three long vials. 'Eel, sprite and roadrunner, just in case. Rather have you running than fighting.'

Merion held onto them as if they were solid gold.

'It's customary to pay your letter,' she said, with a hint of a smirk.

Her attempts to lighten the mood were not working. Merion turned back to the battle, filling his ears with the rattle of constant gunfire. He wondered how many bullets it would take to win the night—or how many spears, for that matter. There came a rally of fire from the work-camp, and more screeching pierced the sound of battle. Merion caught the faint echo of a cheer on the ill breeze.

'If this town survives the night, that lupus has an appointment on my table,' Lilain muttered to herself.

There came a chattering cry from above. It was Jake, circling the rooftop. Lurker wrapped his hand a little tighter around Big Betsy, his finger sliding almost imperceptibly down to the trigger.

'What is it?' Merion asked.

'Shamans,' Lurker grunted, and lifted a hand to point to a new kind of terror, emerging out of the darkness. 'Fuck,' he added, just for good measure.

Lilain unslung her rifle and lay down so she could rest it on the roof. Merion pressed the spyglass harder against his eyeball, as if it would bring the action any closer. There is a terrible fascination to war: part horror, part hope.

The two shamans were glowing white hot when they broke through the hastily-made barricade of dead bodies and cartwheels. Bullets melted inches from their skin. Guns grew too hot to hold. Powder caught inside casings. Soon enough the edge of town was a drumroll of gunfire, pitted only with screams and the shamans' slow, ominous chants. A third joined them on the dusty battlefield, which was now swiftly turning to glass. Lightning crackled from his fingers. Merion sat up like a meerkat. The fighting pressed deeper into the town. A thick crowd of Shohari had gathered behind their Shamans.

Bottles trailing heads of flame began to rain down from the rooftops. They exploded in deadly flashes of hot blue and spitting green. Shrieks and wails filled the air as Shohari were consumed in flame. Alcohol never failed to solve a problem in Fell Falls.

'Moonshine,' Lurker mumbled. It was a fine tactic. The blinding, searing clouds of fire halted the advancing Shohari and the shamans long enough for the lordsguards to bring up their rifles and Gatling guns, and for the sheriffsmen to shore up the flanks, pouring into the alleyways and side streets. There were more bullets, and more screams. Merion drank it all in through the bulbous eye of his spyglass.

As soon as the flames had cleared, the guns began to fire. Wave after wave of bullets met the Shohari ranks. All that could be heard above the thunder of rifle-fire was the deep, rapid pounding of the Gatlings. Rounds spat from its mouth like water from a gargoyle in a storm, shredding the iron bones of the Shohari to splinters and making a sordid memory of flesh and skin.

Bricks and boulders chased the flaming bottles, pouring into the bloody chaos. One caught a shaman square in the forehead. He sank to his knees as the blood began to pour. His hands clawed at the air, wrapped in hot magick. Bullets melted inches from his fingers like raindrops striking a window. Hot metal pooled around him in glowing puddles. As he raised a hand to wipe the blood his eyes, his spell began to falter. His skull must have been split in two. The bullets crept closer. Flecks of hot metal kissed his bare skin and black cracks began to show in his white-hot skin. When the bullets finally met their mark, the shaman was consumed by the very magick that had kept him alive. He vanished in a burst of scarlet flame, and all throughout the town, in the streets, in the bedrooms and in the basements, every single scrap of flame burnt scarlet too.

It was a moment forever to be remembered by whiskey-slicked lips in saloons, whispering of how the moonshine flames had turned blood-red. Merion saw it with his very own eyes. It was a massacre. Straight and cold.

The lordsguards and their Gatling kept firing until the cries of the Shohari signalled utter defeat. The warriors scattered in every direction, only to be met by sheriffsmen waiting in the dark, or sniping from outhouses. The ferocity of their prey had shocked them, that much was clear, and now the carpet of their own dead littering the centre of town proved too much. Even the Shohari are not immune to the claws of fear.

Horns and drums sounded in the desert as they fled. Merion watched the dark shapes scurry across the fire-painted desert, their own shadows nipping at their heels. Merion frowned. He did not know whether to feel pride or sorrow as the cheers began to ring out across Fell Falls.

'They fought bravely,' Lurker hummed as he watched the Shohari disappear.

'Some aren't done fighting yet,' Lilain whispered.

Lilain was right: the fire still burned ferociously in the main street, but only in one place, in amongst a pile of fallen Shohari. Before anybody could stifle the cheers or raise a shout, lightning began to flicker through the dead. Searing blue tentacles reached out to probe the bodies and their oozing bullet holes, as if searching for a soul that was still alive. It soon found one.

A scream cut through the cheering like a sword through butter. Guns began to sing again, but not a single bullet could make it through the curtain of heat and electricity. Two figures rose up out of the dead, shrugging limbs and shattered spears aside. The fire shaman burned fiercely, pressing the lordsguards back and turning one side of the postal office to charcoal. Bricks rained once more. Planks began to spin down through the air. Even sandbags were being tossed, but still their magick raged. The Gatlings were melting; Merion could hear their mechanisms screeching. For a brief moment, it looked as though the shamans would tear a path straight through town.

However, if there was to be one saviour of men above all that night, it was once again the humble vial of nitroglycerin. Merion was starting to notice a theme. The shamans did not see the spinning vials until it was far too late. Two explosions bludgeoned the street, one after the other, like a double-punch straight to the ribs of the town. Every lordsguard fell flat. Two entire saloons met their demise. Even in the Runnels, they felt the wind on their faces.

The splinters were still tumbling when victory was blown on the bugles in true lordsguard style. Merion was the first to blow a sigh of relief. Lurker took his finger off his trigger and chewed his lip.

'I'll—' he began to say, but then stiffened like a cat spying a bird. His finger grazed his trigger once more as he shuffled to the edge of the roof, staying as low as he could manage. Ignoring Lilain's avid gesticulating, Merion followed him, sliding up next to the prospector. He held out the Mistress and pointed it down into the street, just like Lurker.

'Take your finger off the trigger, boy,' Lurker hissed. 'I know what I'm doing.' He pointed with the nose of his huge gun. 'There,' he whispered.

Merion spied the shadow peeking out from behind a fence, betraying its owner. A scrawny Shohari man, painted green, purple, and now red. This Shohari must have been out of his wits with fear. He had no eyes for the rooftops, just the streets. He had a broken tomahawk in his left hand, a lot of blood on his right. There was a cut across his collarbone, from a lordsguard sword.

'Jus' a boy, not much older than you,' Lurker whispered. Merion squinted, and saw that Lurker was right. It was just a skinny boy. Taller than Merion by far, but still a boy.

'What was he doing in the fight?' Merion breathed.

'Fighting for his land, jus' like the rest.'

'But he's no older than I am ...' Merion couldn't understand.

'We all got our own fights. And we fight them in our own ways,' Lurker replied and then he put a leather finger to his chapped lips. The boy was creeping closer.

Merion pondered whether he would have the stomach to wade into battle, if the tables were ever turned. He doubted he would. *But what if it was a battle to his avenge his father, or a fight for a ticket home? Would he charge into battle for that, kill for that?* Merion gritted his teeth.

If that's what it would take, then perhaps.

It was then that the Shohari froze, barely a stone's toss from their front door. He raised his head slowly, until he met the eye of Lurker and Merion, and their gun barrels. They held each other's gazes for a moment. When that moment became too long and uncomfortable, Lurker made his move: a gentle, slow raise of his gloved hand, and a touch of the brim of his hat. The Shohari nodded, and then turned to run towards the darkness of the desert, dripping a trail of blood in the dust.

Lurker sat up. 'You two go on inside. I'll keep watch for an hour or so.'

'Come, Merion. We have a busy day tomorrow,' Lilain beckoned her nephew. She was already halfway to the window.

Merion rankled at the prospect of anything busy. He had work to do, work repairing the mess she had caused. 'I'm afraid you're on your own,' he bluntly informed her. 'I have bridges to rebuild, a lord and his daughter to pacify. I'm not going to let you ruin this chance for me.'

'Will you just come inside, and stop hissing at me like a goddamned viper?'

Merion shoved the gun through his belt and moodily clambered back into the house, mumbling to himself resolutely with every step.

Lilain was waiting for him in the study, hands on hips. But when she spoke, her tone was far from stern; it was softer, more pleading. Merion had never heard it before. 'Look,' she began, 'you can mutter and curse to yourself all you want. You can ignore me, snub me, shy away from me, even run away, Merion, but no matter what, I'm still your aunt. You're stuck with me,' she told him, almost managing to squeeze in a chuckle at the end. 'We're bonded with blood, and that's something you won't share with any friend, or girlfriend, or dog, cat, anything. So can we please stop hating each other for just a moment, and try to get along instead?' Lilain held up her hands and pressed them together. 'I am sorry if I ruined any plan you had. I should have chosen a better time to tell you about what I thought of the Serpeds.'

Merion instantly cut in. 'You should ha—'

But Lilain held up her hands. 'I should not have accused Lord Castor,' she paused here for a spell. This was choking her, Merion could see it. *At least she was trying.* 'Of being a lamprey, or anything at all. From now on, we'll put Lord Castor Serped in a box alongside your father.'

After a great deal of biting his lip and screwing up his dusty face, Merion nodded. 'Fine.'

Lilain wisely resisted the urge to hug him, but Merion allowed her hands to rest on his shoulders. 'I would appreciate some help tomorrow, if you have the time.'

Merion rolled his gaze around on the floor, searching for a better answer than 'I'll help.' But sadly there was nothing besides books and dropped bullets, so he gave in and said it.

'Thank you. Now go to bed,' she said, shooing him out of the door.

Merion nodded and trod the creaking stairs back to his room. He suddenly found himself exhausted. Both the battle and the day's training had beaten it out of him, and now all he could think of was bed. He could give the Serpeds one day to cool, he thought, as he collapsed into his bed. The darkness of his room was so very welcome. Castor would be busy with the town, in any case. One day, and then he would beg their forgiveness. Even in the darkness he practised his best smile, though he had no audience save for the shadows. Merion flipped over to the side of the bed, narrowly avoiding hitting his nose on the wooden frame.

'Rhin,' he said, as he slid to the floor. 'Are you there?'

Nothing. Not a faerie in sight. Words would be had with that damned faerie.

CHAPTER XXVI
THE DEAD AND THE ALMOST

'I saw a shape in the pines today. I couldn't be sure, but I would swear blind it was Fae. The way it rippled, it wasn't just a shadow. I told Merion. I want him to stay out of the woods until I know I was wrong.'

5th June, 1867

It's strange how alive a barren desert can become when there is something dead to nibble on. Rhin swatted at yet another pesky fly. To a faerie, flies are huge: melon-sized, with red and bulbous compound eyes; wings the length of your forearm; and dangling clawed feet; not to mention their slavering, sucking jaws. Rhin punched another square in its grotesque face and watched it fall into a buzzing heap in the dirt. He wiped its rank spittle from his gauntlet.

Rhin heard a sharp shout on the breeze. He looked up and sniffed the rancid, rotten air, instantly wishing he hadn't. The dead turn bad very quickly in the Wyoming sun. Rhin had learnt that shortly after dawn, somewhere near the work-camp. The fallen had been piled into heaps in the night: one for men; one for Shohari. Rhin had watched the men kneeling in the dust, some scratching their heads, others weeping quietly. They might have won the battle, but they had lost hundreds. When the hot morning sun reached them, it did not take long for the bloody mess to start festering. The warm westerly breeze made sure the stench was pushed all the way into town.

Rhin ducked his head so he could measure the progress of the unlucky souls charged with clearing the streets of bodies. It was now some time past nine, and already the sweat poured from them. Every now and again he could hear somebody retching, or crying, but the latter was rarer.

The men and women stalked to and fro, already thoroughly browbeaten by their labour. With one hand they clamped dirty rags to their mouths, and with the other they hauled the broken corpses across the dust and into their allotted piles. The Shohari pile was considerably larger than the other. Perhaps that was what drove the workers on through the raw heat, the stench and the gore, with their rags and their bloody hands. Even though what drove them was how high they could pile their dead enemies, Rhin had to admire their tenacity. *We won. They didn't.* That was enough.

Rhin crept on, keen to be rid of the flies. He shimmered into nothing as he approached the edge of the house, pausing just the same in the brink of its shadow, looking left and right and left again before hopping across the alley, into the shadow of the next house.

It was wonderful how these Americans built their houses, almost as if they were too precious to touch the earth. Either that, or they were afraid their houses might be roasted alive by the hot sand. It was cool enough in the gaps beneath them. Even in full armour.

A corpse was lying half under this house, face-down in the dirt with its arms spread out, almost as if surrendering to the dust. There was a rather large chunk of its skull missing, just behind its right ear. Rhin wrinkled his lip.

As Rhin looked out into the street once more, he heard a whistle, though not that of any man. Human lips can't whistle like Fae lips can, never just a single note. Rhin felt his heart sinking.

'What brings you out here, Rehn'ar? Picking the corpses of their loot? I had expected a bigger Hoard than that,' The Wit called out. He and three of his Fingers stepped out from behind the corpse, arms crossed and looking cheery. 'I think you've got a lot of balls wasting our time like this.'

If they were in the mood to play games, Rhin could be too. 'I don't like the idea of you thinking about my balls. Rather forward of you, Finrig,' Rhin sneered. It was a cheap joke, but it found its mark.

The Wit sneered right back. 'You'll be the unnatural one, when I set to yours with my dagger, Rhin,' Finrig offered. 'Maybe I'll keep 'em as a trophy. I'll get a little glass case, all velvet inside, and show them around at parties when *she* makes me a lord.'

Rhin knew he should not laugh, but then again he had never been any good at saying no to things he should not do. 'And I hope those silk-clad fawners poison you on your first day in court, Wit,' he chuckled.

'Enough,' spat Finrig. 'Where's our Hoard?'

Rhin tensed his jaw. 'I don't have it yet.'

'It's been two weeks, Rhin.'

'I just need a little more time. I have a plan.'

For a moment, Finrig looked as though he would walk around that broken head and stab Rhin in the chest, but he restrained himself. 'We want our gold,' he snarled.

Rhin held up his hands. 'And you will get it. I'm going to bring it straight to the barn.'

'When?' Finrig snapped.

'Tomorrow night. Be at that barn of yours and you shall have your Hoard.'

The Wit pointed a sharp finger. 'We had better, Rhin, or—'

The faeries shivered and vanished as the corpse between them began to move. Formless as heat waves on a horizon they became, utterly invisible to the squinting eyes that came to peer under the house.

'He ain't stuck or nothin'. Mus' just be a heavy one,' somebody drawled.

'Shit. Give me a hand.'

'And one, two ...'

With some grunting, the body began to slide out from under the house, leaving a bloody trail in its wake. The faeries stayed right where they were, visibly only to themselves. Rhin stared at Finrig until the shattered skull had been dragged past them. Only then did he see the knife in Finrig's hand. Its point weaved a little figure-of-eight in the air.

'Or it won't be just your balls I take. Figure I'll get me some lungs too, and a heart.'

Rhin tried to swallow whatever was stuck in his throat. 'You'll get your gold, Wit. Tomorrow.'

The knife came up to aim at his face. Finrig smiled. 'We'd better,' he said, his voice cold as steel, and just as hard. His Fingers chuckled between themselves as they passed by. The Wit made sure to knock Rhin with his shoulder before he left, armour clanking on armour.

'Don't forget about us,' he hissed, before strolling away with a whistle.

Rhin waited until their chuckling and whistled faded, and then waited some more. It was almost lunchtime when he finally decided to move. His body flickered with anger, jumping in and out of visibility as he ground his teeth together and muttered dark things to himself. Promises of blood and the Wit's head on a pike were churned out under his breath. Sometimes it just helps to be angry, to feel your face flush with rage and savour the taste of your own burning. Men can do mighty things when they are full of hate. And so can faeries. Robbing a train would take something mighty indeed. So Rhin let himself burn, let himself churn his hate over like the coals of a forge, hoping it would give him what he needed. It had seemed to help Merion, after all.

'No lupus.' Lilain sighed. 'No lupus. I guess she was first to the torch.'

Merion nodded. They had watched the black smoke rising over a brisk lunch, before getting back to the bodies. Bodies. There was an entire graveyard of them down in the basement. Those that were not lucky enough to have a table or plank to rest on were laid on the floor. The lift had rattled on for hours, up and down, up and down, with Lurker busy at the ropes. The carts had kept on coming, ever since dawn.

Merion was tired of dead things. He kept his eyes on Lilain or Lurker whenever he could, just to know that something was still alive in this world.

There is a certain power in a corpse. If you handle enough of them, you start to feel like one of them, become one. Maybe it is the hungry pit left by the soul that draws us in, or maybe it is the horrific holes and missing bits. Maybe we're just too empathetic, and the task too grisly. In any case, Merion was under the spell of the dead, and his limbs felt sluggish and cold, even though he had not stopped sweating since sunrise. Were he shown a mirror, he imagined he would look grey. He had to keep pinching himself to prove he wasn't going numb.

Scrape, thud, scrape, squelch went the tune of his work. He bent down to seize the broken ankles of the next body and heaved. *Scrape.*

'Heavy one, that!' Lurker called down.

'He is indeed,' Merion grunted. The body came free of the lift and slid onto the floor of the basement. *Thud.*

'How many is that?'

'Thirty … nine, with two more on the lift.'

'By the Maker, I know it's wrong to think of the gold at this moment in time, but …' Lilain looked up to wink. 'Think of the gold.'

'Battles sure are good for business,' Merion said, echoing her morbid pragmatism. Jokes kept the gloom at bay. He dragged the body to the back of the basement. *Scrape.*

'Sadly, I doubt that will be the last,' came the reply. Lilain had foregone her usual investigation with these bodies. She was simply preparing them for burial, removing the splinters and bullets, sewing on the wayward bits if available, sewing up the holes if not. Then, with great deliberation, she would carve a small cog-like symbol on the forehead—to mark them as the Maker's workers, ready for the great forge in the sky.

'Are we safe?' Merion asked. It seemed a very fair question to him, but Lilain looked a little shocked. He watched her think as he rolled the body onto its side. *Squelch.*

'Of course we are, Merion. Serped has filled the town with lordsguards. Sheriffsmen are coming up from Kenaday—mercenaries too, if Jake is right. There's a war on now. There's fighting to be done. Their numbers make us safe, for now.'

'It's the "for now" bit that worries me, Aunt,' Merion said whilst wiping his hands. 'What if they come from another direction next time? Or bring more shamans?'

'They'll have more of that clockwork weaponry coming down from Kaspar, you can be sure of it. This town will be a fortress in no time. I've seen it before.'

'And it doesn't worry you?'

Lilain shook her head. 'Nephew, if this town showed any signs of falling, and falling for good, I'd be the first one runnin' along the train tracks to the next town, believe me. And you'd be there beside me. Lurker as well, if his old backside could keep up.'

That seemed to satisfy Merion. Perhaps it was the taste of corpse he had on his tongue, or the lead-weight limbs he now dragged across the dusty floor, but Merion didn't much fancy being a corpse for real. When his aunt turned back to her body, Merion reached up to pat the three vials sitting in a little cloth sling across his chest. They were hidden under his shirt, and Merion had a mind to keep them that way. An idea had struck him in the night, as he danced along the edges of sleep. What if he showed Calidae what he could do? She would understand he was like them, and trust him. She would tell her father it was a misunderstanding, keep it a secret, and he would be back in the fold, quick as a flash. Merion had let that plan roll around in his head for most of the morning, testing the edge of it. With every hour that passed, the more he liked the sound of it.

'Are we done?' Lilain called to him.

'Lurker?' Merion called up the lift shaft. 'We done?'

'This fella says we are. The rest of the bodies are goin' to be burned.

'Easier for me,' Lilain shouted.

'Then I say it's time for a drink,' Lurker proposed.

Merion felt how rough his parched tongue felt against his mouth and was inclined to agree. 'Water?' he asked.

Lurker popped his head and hat over the edge of the hole and smiled. 'If you're meanin' firewater, then yes sir.'

There was a sickly air in the saloon. The swinging doors did nothing to keep the stench of the dead at bay. It roamed freely, heavy and sour. The crowds of tired workers, sweaty and bloody from their work, did nothing to quench it.

Merion looked around the busy saloon, at the dirty bodies that had wandered in to drink their sorrow. He saw the same look on their faces as the one he imagined he himself wore. The dead had cast their spell on them too, and now they were here to drown it with beer and whiskey.

Alcohol: that bosom that humans adore to nuzzle in, that slippery mistress—part solution, part just another problem. Merion was currently at the solution stage. He sipped at his beer and savoured the feel of it trickling into his empty stomach. The warm buzz in his face was more than welcome, as was the bubbling in his belly. It made him feel like one of the living again, and the more he drank, the more alive he felt.

Lurker had sat them at the bar, in the far corner, where the polished wood curved into the wall. From there, backs to the wood and plaster, they watched the comings and goings of the workers, and got lost in half a dozen fractured conversations.

Merion was fine with listening. His tongue was too busy with sipping beer, and besides, all boys like to listen in, when they can, and glean what nuggets of precious information they could: the location of a treasure map perhaps; a bawdy tale fit only for sailors' ears; talk of the Lord and his daughter maybe. Merion closed his eyes and let himself melt into the loud hubbub of conversation. This was a strange place, and he wanted to hear strange things. Somebody was whimpering at a nearby table.

'All I know is I can't count that high, okay? Too many there were, dozens and dozens.'

'Took us half the day.'

Another whispered by the stairs, thinking they could not be heard. A woman it was this time, young, and urgent. Merion could imagine her curls bobbing as she talked.

'Brigan said he's got one in 'is basement.'

'A live one?' said a man with a deep voice, possibly portly.

'Course a live one. What sport would a dead one be?'

'None, I suppose.'

'You want in?'

A pause. Merion held his breath.

'What time.'

'Sunset. You know the place. Bring coin.'

Merion shuddered at that. So cold.

'So I say to him, Lenni, if you don't put that rifle down right now, it'll be bedtime and no supper.' A weasel-voice man was holding court to his right.

'And what he do?' asked another, in an earnest tone.

'Shot me right in the knee, little bastard. But it got me in the 'firmary nice and easy. I was on the other side of the town when the savages came. Stayed tucked up in my bed all night.'

'Same,' snickered the second voice. 'Though I was at Shell's not too far from the jail. At the bottom of the Runnels. Got myself a young redhead, and not a peep 'til dawn.'

There was a clink as glasses kissed.

Merion turned his head to make sense of the low mumbling he heard from further along the bar, barely a few yards away. There were three voices, all of them low and conspiratorial. Merion leant forward, straining his ears.

'If we don't get paid soon, Serped's going to have a riot on his hands, that's all I'm sayin'. We ain't fighters. We're rail workers. Leave the fighting to the Sheriff and his men. And those damned lordsguards,' said a sharp voice.

'They wouldn't have won without us.' This speaker had a voice almost as deep as Lurker's.

'Day after tomorrow, foreman said. We'll get paid.' A third spoke up. His tone was older and gravelly.

'There's talk of a union,' said the first man, quieter now.

'A union of what?' asked Deep-Voice.

'Us workers. To campaign against Serped. Get more money, see?'

'They'll shoot every last one of you,' said Gravel.

'They wouldn't dare. They need us.'

'You think there's a shortage of workers out here, Nate? You think we work for cheap? If you go marching over to Castor's riverboat, he's going to line you up and shoot you. And while you're all lined up there, sweating and shittin' yourself, you'll be watching the newest train come in, full to the brim with slanty-eyed Cathayans. They'd have your boots off your feet before you stopped breathin'.'

That seemed to shut this Nate up.

Deep-Voice spoke slowly and thoughtfully. 'If they want us to fight, then we should get extra. We don't owe no allegiance to this town or its people, just our wallets. If we don't get extra, we leave. Let the town drown in its own blood if'n that's what it takes.'

Merion's eyes cracked open then, just a tiny bit, so they could wander the room and put faces to the voices of brigands, cowards, and thugs. If you ever play the game of guessing faces from voices, you will know precisely how jarring it can be when the truth is revealed. Merion was experiencing that this very moment, as he spied the fat, toothless woman with scraped-back hair and a loose, patchwork dress. Or the pair of sheriffsmen huddled around a table, still in their blackened leathers, sniggering to themselves. And of the three at the bar, Gravel was indeed old, yet his face was like that of a hatchet. Deep-Voice was a barrel of a youth, blonde, and with quick, narrow eyes. Nate was a rat-faced runt, all limbs, buck-teeth, and greasy hair. He was currently fiddling with a skinny cigar.

Merion looked back at his beer and found a hair in it. He fished it out with a pinch of his fingers. One of his own from the colour, and far too long. His hair was now long enough so that if he gave it a second chance it would hang down and pester his eyes for hours. It might have been annoying, but there was always something unbound about growing hair, something very brink-of-civilisation.

Now that his ears were tuned, Merion found he could not ignore the grumbling from along the bar. His eyes flicked between the beer and the rail workers. Gravel was holding court, and Nate seemed bored of it. He rolled his beady eyes around the tavern until they came to rest upon Merion, who flinched, coughed, and made a show of swilling his half-empty beer around.

As he watched the golden liquid swirl itself to bubbles and foam, he tried to wager whether it was safe to look up again. Gravel's talk was becoming heated. Deep-Voice growled along.

'They ain't got no right to use as their army, when it suits 'em—' went the grumbling.

Merion felt his eyes moving before he could stop them. Eyes were like that sometimes, even more curious than the brain they were tethered to. Nate was still looking right at him.

'Problem, boy?' he spat, slicing Gravel's current sentence in half. With the squeak of stools and the creaking of tired bones, Gravel and Deep-Voice both turned to see who Nate was staring at.

'Who are you …? Well, fuck me,' swore Gravel, smirking, when he saw the leathery lump of a man sitting next to Merion. 'If it ain't ole Lurker. How's business, prospector?'

Lurker had been sitting with his eyes-half closed and dazed, staring at the dusty chandelier that hung lopsidedly from the wooden ceiling. He seemed confused that anybody besides Merion would be talking to him. After a bewildered glance at the boy, he turned to Gravel and his friends. Several of the creases on his forehead deepened at the sight of them. Something in that expression made Merion want to hide behind his beer, to peek through the glass. Nate was still staring.

'Slow,' replied Lurker, raising his glass.

'Well, ain't that a shame?' Gravel said. There was no smirk this time, but he nudged Deep-Voice and Nate. 'You remember me?'

'I'm sorry, I don't,' Lurker lied.

Gravel sighed at that. 'Kass is the name. This is Big Brint and Nate. You know 'em?'

'No.'

That made Kass tut. Big Brint and Nate shook their heads. 'Maker's Dick. Last year? I'd just arrived from Iowa. Drank a whole bottle of Whore's Kiss? No? Ah, never mind.' Kass waved a hand. 'Prospectin' type, ain't you, Lurker? Got himself a magic magpie they say. Can sniff out gold like nobody can.'

'Gold you say,' Nate sniffed. 'Could do with a bit of that, couldn't we? Where's this magic bird of yours, then?'

'Haven't seen it in days,' Lurker said to the bottom of his glass. He signalled to the barman for another round, and an extra three to keep the peace.

It seemed that Kass was not too interested in free beer, much to Nate and Big Brint's apparent disappointment. 'And who's the boy? Can't be your son,' he asked.

'Family friend.'

Nate chimed in again, eyes still on Merion. 'He's got some nosy eyes on 'im.'

Lurker ruffled Merion's hair. 'He didn't mean no harm, did you, boy?'

'No sir.'

'See? Boys stare at everything, you know how it is.'

Kass decided that it was time for them to get a little closer. Stools scraped as they stood and sauntered over. Nate relit his cigar while Kass and Big Brint came to sit uncomfortably close to Lurker. He did not move one muscle.

Kass pointed at Merion. 'He doesn't look like he's from around here.'

The beers came and Lurker slid a pair of coins across the bar. The jingling in his pocket was painfully obvious. Merion saw Nate's eyes shift for just a moment. 'He ain't,' replied Lurker.

'Looks Empire to me,' rumbled Brint.

'Like one of those Serpeds,' hissed Nate, beady eyes narrowing.

Kass nodded. 'That he does,' he rasped. 'What brings you here, boy?'

Merion drew himself up on his stool and raised his chin. 'Death,' he said, in a vain attempt to sound ominous. All they did was chuckle at him.

'There's plenty of that 'round here,' Big Brint told him. 'Come to the right place.'

Nate was getting twitchy now. 'So how many you take down last night, hmm?' he asked Lurker, mouthing the words around his cigar. It smelled like burning paper, acrid and cheap. Nothing like the cigars his father had kept in that golden box of his. They had smelled like toffee, and mahogany.

'How many what?' Lurker replied.

Nate puffed out an impatient cloud of smoke. 'Take down. Kill. Hack to bits. Shoot between the eyes.'

'Shohari, man,' Kass added.

Big Brint swelled that barrel chest of his. 'I got a dozen myself.'

'Fourteen,' Kass boasted.

'Sixteen,' Nate said, garnering a look from Big Brint that screamed *bullshit*.

'I don't talk about the men I kill,' Lurker replied with a wrinkle of his lip, as if his beer had turned sour.

Kass shook his head. 'They ain't men. They're animals. Beasts.'

'Fuckin' savages,' Nate spat.

Their talk had pricked the ears of a few nearby patrons. The conversation in the rest of the saloon had lulled. Eyes turned in their direction. The barman had retreated to the far end of his bar to polish glasses. Merion could feel the tension building.

It was at that moment his fingers began to slide under his shirt, surreptitious and slow, lest he catch the attention of Nate and the others. But they seemed fixated on Lurker now, and nobody saw Merion unclip something from under his shirt, and slide it into his pocket. He was not quite sure what he intended to do with it, but something within him itched to find out.

'How many?' Nate asked again.

Lurker took another sip of his beer, not caring an inch for the foam that stuck to his grizzled lip.

'How many?' This time a prod accompanied the question. Lurker slowly pushed his beer away.

'None,' he said, eyes burning into Nate's. 'Not a single one. And so what? Don't make me a coward,' Lurker asserted. He had turned slightly, placing himself between the men and Merion.

'Oh that's right, I remember now,' Kass said. 'You got somethin' for 'em haven't you?'

Lurker's face was that of stone. 'Don't be ridiculous, friend,' he replied.

Kass's tone had turned hard. His voice was louder now. 'I ain't your friend.'

'Friend of the savages more like.'

'Yeah, I 'eard about you,' Big Brint was nodding. 'Folks say you got a Shohari wife or somthin'.'

Lurker's lip twitched. Only Merion noticed. 'Ain't got no wife,' he growled.

'Sounds like we got a traitor here, gentlemen,' Nate hissed.

Murmurs rippled across the saloon. Talk of a traitor had been heard, and in a town still bleeding from the night before, nothing lifts the spirits like a noose around a traitor's neck. The intrigue was spreading like a bad smell.

One man got up and quickly slipped through the doors. The two sheriffsmen were slowly rising to their feet. If felt as though the faded walls of the saloon were slowly inching inwards. Merion could feel the sweat gathering on his brow. His thumb rubbed pensively against the cork of the vial in his pocket

'I'm no traitor,' Lurker asserted gruffly. 'I fought for this country.'

'Spy!' a lonely shout rang out, cold and yet hot with rage at the same time. It is easy to tell the ones who are still reeling from loss. The first stones always come from their direction. There were more murmurs now. Teeth chattered, and fingers pointed. The walls inched ever closer.

Two things happened then, and in rather quick succession. First, Lurker's fist plunged into the bridge of Kass' nose, shattering the cartilage and reducing his face to a bloody mess. Secondly, Merion learnt a very valuable lesson about the importance of striking first and striking hard. It was all in the shock, he realised, as he watched Kass disappear behind the lip of the bar, and the extra few moments it bought.

The vial was at his lips before the cork touched the dusty floor. He sucked the warm blood back, caring not a smidgeon for the taste. Fists had already begun to swing. Chairs and stools screeched in unison as the saloon surged forwards as one. Merion just prayed he had reached for eel. Nate was already around the corner of the bar and heading straight for him. There was violence in his rat-eyes. His cigar glowed furiously in the corner of his mouth. Merion backed away, shoving the stool between them. Nate batted it away and kept on coming. The boy drank in a deep breath as he tensed. He felt the blood begin to surge, making his extremities tingle and his face grow warm.

Nate's hands seized him by the collar and slammed him back against the wall. His head struck the wood hard and he blinked away stars. Nate was leaning close, the glowing cigar creeping closer and closer to Merion's cheek. He could feel the heat of it already. He struggled, even though he felt the power rising in him. *Come on come on come on!* screamed his brain. Alcohol slowed it; he should have remembered. *Come on!*

'You know what we do with traitors, before we hang 'em? Hmm?' Nate snarled in his face, spit flying. 'We brand 'em!'

Merion felt the power swirling and bulging inside his head. This shade was strong, but it was not eel. He could feel his skin prickling with heat. It was nothing short of intoxicating, rushing as he'd not yet known. With it came a defiant smile. He surprised himself as the strong words stampeded out of his mouth. It is a marvellous thing, the upper hand.

'My father always told me smoking was bad for you,' he grunted, as the rushing reached its apex.

The cigar in Nate's mouth sputtered with fire. In seconds it was ablaze, and devilishly hungry. The fire surged into his mouth and crawled over his face, its crackling joined by Nate's howls and screams. He fell to the floor and clawed at his face like a man possessed.

Merion felt his consciousness tugging at the corners of the flames. He reached out and pinched them, dragging them from Nate and onto the boots of Kass, still writhing on the floor as Big Brint and Lurker danced over him. The flames did as they were bid, tumbling across the floor to lick at Kass' boots, much to Nate's relief. Kass set to screaming almost immediately. The fire was hungry indeed. Merion dealt Nate a hearty kick in the ribs, as hard as he could manage. The man doubled up in pain. *Always kick a man when he's down*, as Rhin had always opined. *That way they don't have a chance to get up.*

As Kass crawled a hasty retreat to the other end of the bar, still flailing at his burning clothes, Lurker took a hefty blow from the barrel that was Big Brint. He reeled into the wall beneath the stairs. Brint leered, and turned his sights on Merion. Any other boy of thirteen might have quailed in the man's presence. Or worse, vacated their bladders. But Merion was not your ordinary thirteen year old boy, or so he was quickly discovering. This boy was a leech. He met Big Brint's leer head on with a wide smile of his own.

What the barrel-chested, blood-spattered rail worker failed to notice was the speck of blood on Merion's lower lip, and the hand sliding an empty vial into his right pocket. Big Brint lunged with an angry yell.

The bloody fists raised up, ready to come hammering down with full force, right onto Merion's unfortunate head. But the fists never met their mark. They met nothing but thin air and embarrassment as Merion darted out of reach. He had done it so swiftly, he had almost become a blur. The crowd gasped collectively. It was almost comical. Big Brint swung again, and again, but Merion was always faster. He even got a few of his own punches in: one to the ribs, and two to the face. Brint's whirling arms couldn't keep up with his eyes. He took a knee and swung his arms in vicious circles, hoping to get lucky. It was embarrassing to watch. In the end, Lurker put him to bed with the thick end of a bar stool.

Now it was just them and the angry yet rather confused crowd. The sheriffsmen took a few cautious step forwards. Merion and Lurker took twice as many back.

'There's another way out,' Lurker whispered, eyes flicking to a curtained door behind the bar. Merion nodded, and eyed the blood streaming from Lurker's lopsided nose, and a deep cut in his lip. The prospector suddenly looked very tired.

'Want me to carry you?' Merion asked.

'I'm fine,' Lurker sniffed, and then winced. 'On the count of three...'

There is always one in every crowd—the inciter, the instigator, that shit-stirrer that has the uncanny ability to turn a crowd into a riotous mob with nothing but a lungful of panicked twaddle. This crowd did not disappoint. It was the man who Merion had heard crying. He smashed a bottle against a table and waved it in the air.

'Get 'em! Traitors!'

The crowd surged forwards with an angry roar. Merion was up and over the bar in the space of a blink, dragging the still-smouldering fire like a wall behind him, keeping the crowd as bay as best he could. Lurker went a little slower, but he was still through the curtain before the fists and broken bottles came crashing down.

'Note this building here, milady, with the scorched side. We can have that fixed within an afternoon,' mewed the dwarf of a foreman. He was terribly short, without doubt the runt of whatever litter he had been born into. He was sweating rather profusely, constantly having to dab his face with a cloth that did nothing except get dirtier with every dab. 'Shall we add it to the list?' he asked, turning around to face her with a weak smile.

Calidae paused her fan-waving to ponder the half-burnt saloon for a moment. Its grimy windows made it looked surly and quiet. She could not tell if there was actually anybody in there. However, before she could say 'Add it to the list', her answer came in the form of an explosion of glass and a man being violently defenestrated from the saloon. He crumpled to a heap against the charred railings, out cold.

A muscular dark-skinned man all clad in leather came next, flying head first out of the shattered window, though this time he had something to break his fall. A boy came next, with a river of blood sprayed down his shirt. Others were trying to scramble out of the window after them, yelling something about traitorous scum.

'Tonmerion Hark,' she whispered to herself, with a shake of her head. 'Whatever have you gotten yourself into?'

Merion and his friend had already slid over the railing and into the dirt of the hot street. Her two lordsguards were already moving in, swords drawn and glinting. Merion was oblivious, trying his hardest to help the man to walk. Calidae fanned herself for a moment while she shaded her eyes with her hand, thinking. Merion's movements were strangely fast, as if he were having some sort of fit. Something about that gave her eyebrow a barely noticeable lift.

'Wait!' she ordered her guards, who were already striding forward. 'I would speak to him,' she said.

'Calidae?' Merion spluttered, his mouth a mask of blood. Somebody had whacked him in the face, it seemed. Not only was his nose streaming with blood, but it looked as though he'd bitten his lip in the process as well. He looked atrocious.

It was then that the angry mob broke out of the swinging doors and came spilling onto the street. The sight of the two lordsguards in their livery and armour halted them somewhat, especially when Calidae ordered the man and boy to be arrested.

'Get back inside,' barked one of the sheriffsmen, who mere seconds before had been baying for blood as loudly as the rest of them. He straightened his jacket and strode forwards to bow to Calidae. She curtseyed in return.

'I do not think my father would wish to see a riot in the streets, sir.'

'No ma'am, I mean, your ladyship. But these two are traitors, spies even. For the Shohari.'

'Nonsense,' chided Calidae. 'Surely it was just a brawl?' she asked, turning to look down at Merion. He was slowly shaking his head, eyes silently pleading. He looked very mature all of a sudden. Perhaps it was the blood, the dust on his face, or the tousled hair, or maybe it was the glint in his eye, a steady look she had not seen before.

'The boy there ain't normal, your ladyship. He's got the magick in him.'

'And how much have you had to drink, sir?'

The other sheriffsman stepped forward. He had been hovering between them and the disintegrating mob. 'It's true, milady,' he told her.

Calidae looked Merion up and down, testing him. The glint in the boy's eyes refused to fade. Her eyebrow climbed even higher.

'You can have the man. I will have the boy taken to my father,' she said.

The sheriffsmen exchanged a look, then a shrug, and nodded. 'Of course, milady,' said the second, bobbing up and down like a chicken with indigestion.

Merion struggled. 'No, he's done nothing wrong, don't take him!' he exclaimed, as Lurker was seized by the sherrfismen. 'I'll get you out!'

'Guards, bring him with us,' Calidae told her protectors. As Merion was hauled up, and Lurker seized by the sheriffsmen, she began to walk away down the street, leaving her dwarfish foreman to wipe his sweaty face and marvel at the howling coming from the arrested man.

CHAPTER XXVII

A LETTER FROM LONDON

'That boy's a stubborn one, that's for sure. And yet he has the gall to call me stubborn in return. All because I wouldn't tell him more about Sift and the Hoard, and why any faeries would still be chasing me. Bloody hell. At least there's been no signs of more.'

5th June, 1867

'My father has told me that I am not to speak to you,' she curtly informed him as she walked. Her guards manhandled Merion along next to her.

Merion panted. The rush had faded quickly, along with his adrenaline, and all they left behind was a numbing ache from tip to toe. The lordsguards' grip was like iron.

'Calidae,' he said, 'I can explain …'

'And now I hear talk that you're a traitor to this town, Merion Hark,' she said, turning to pierce him with a frosty yet strangely curious gaze. 'A shaman of some sort.'

'Look,' Merion said, trying desperately to hold onto the confidence and defiance he had felt in the saloon. 'There is something I need to explain to you. It will make everything right, I promise you, but you have to listen. And I need to tell you and you alone,' he told her, forcing himself to meet her eyes. He shrugged in the guards' grip.

'My lady …' the one on his left began to say.

Calidae had already made up her mind. 'I will hear him out,' she said, holding up a finger. 'You are to stay here.'

The guards looked nervous, but they did as they were instructed. Merion led Calidae down the street and out of earshot. They stood alone between the cart-ruts and drying blood, a little island of secrets amid the bustle and dread of the battle-scarred street.

'This may sound very strange,' Merion began, catching his breath, 'or it might sound very familiar. I'm hoping it's the latter, and if it is then I want you to know that I understand and that I do not judge you, nor your family. And I can keep a secret too. Nobody will ever know.'

Calidae crossed her arms. 'Do you have something to tell me? Or are you just wasting my time? Because I'm hardly in the mood for riddles.'

Merion just let the words fall out of his mouth. He had not planned to tell her so much, but he could hardly bring himself to stop. 'Calidae, I know there was blood in the wine and brandy that you poured for me. I know what it does and why you drink it. I know because I do the same thing, only with other types of blood. I'm a rusher, Calidae, just like my father, and I don't care what my aunt says about lampreys, or whatever they call you, because I know that we can be … friends.' he almost tripped at the end, catching himself before he said something more heartfelt.

Merion was left waiting for an answer for quite a while. He had played his hand, or opened a vein, he was not sure. He stared at her, watching for any flicker or glimmer of something good in her eye, so he could stop his heart thrumming and know that he had fixed it. *All he wanted to do was fix it.*

'Show me,' she said. It was barely an answer, but it was better than nothing.

Merion reached under his shirt and pulled out a third and final vial. He uncorked it and slipped a quarter of it into his mouth. He swallowed hard, making sure to show her that he could do it. If he was hoping to glimpse a reflection of his own pride in her expression, he was sorely disappointed. Calidae's face stayed frosty, and her arms stayed crossed.

'It takes a moment or two,' he whispered, straining.

'I've got all day,' she replied.

'Good.'

Merion looked down at his hands and bent his fingers into claws. As he felt the tingling grow in his stomach he put his fingertips together to make a cradle. He took a breath as the magick made his head spin. He forced it down into his arms, deep into his bones. Blue light began to flicker around his grubby, blood-stained nails. Sparks flickered. Lightning began to flow. It lasted barely half a minute, but it was enough to show that he was not lying. Merion let his hot hands hang loose and watched Calidae's face, seeking his verdict.

'Electric eel,' he added, quietly.

'Your shade,' she said. Those two words had more weight than a thousand. A spark of vestigial lightning ran down his spine, making him twitch.

She knew. She bloody well knew it all, Merion inwardly panted. *Had he done it? Had he fixed it?*

But Merion would have to wait for those answers. Calidae hollered to one of her lordsguards. 'Canton, the wiregram from Master Gile.'

That only set Merion's heart to beating harder. A wiregram meant only one thing. A reply from London. *Precious news.* Truth be told, Merion felt a little faint. He had not expected to be answered with this, and now it was all he could think about. All he wanted was to hold that piece of paper in his hand and know that there was something beyond this ring of dusty hills, with its murder and war and its hardship. Merion practically snatched it from the guard when he came near enough. His eyes devoured the words, sitting neatly on the steam-printed lines.

Dear Tonmerion Hark,

I regret to inform you that the investigation into your father's untimely death has been closed. Despite the generous aid of Her Majesty and the Honourable Second Lord Dizali, we have been unable to identify any culprit or villain, nor the reason for your father's death.

I wish you well in the New Kingdom, and may we see you return safe when the time comes.

Regretfully,

Constable Jimothy Pagget, Esq.

The paper crackled as Merion's fingers closed around it. A moment ago he had felt as though he had been shot out of a cannon and was soaring like an eagle. Now it felt as though he had been shot by one, and the eagle was picking at his remains.

'Untimely death …' he whispered.

'I am so very sorry, Merion,' Calidae said, a little emotion creeping into her tone. She even went as far as to step closer.

Merion just stared at the crumpled ball of paper in his hands. 'They couldn't even say murder.' He had not dared to dream of such a response. It had not even crossed his mind.

'Perhaps they didn't want to offend,' she offered. A lace-gloved hand landed lightly atop his, and Merion snatched at it, like a drowning man reaches for a pole. All talk of magick was thrown to the wayside. 'Calidae, listen to me. I need to get back to London. I need to finish this, to find my father's killer and see him hanged for what he's done. I need to go home,' he said, as he slowly took her other hand. 'Can you help me? Can your father help me?'

Calidae took a moment to withdraw her hands, slowly, but surely. Merion wanted to hold on, but he knew he could not. He stood there alone. They say no man is an island. Well, they must not have met Calidae. She stepped away, and in one small movement, marooned him in the centre of the street. Merion had never felt so awkward. Salvation seemed a mountain climb away.

'Please,' he said. He could count the number of times he had begged in his life. He reckoned this was probably the third, but the occasion called for it. *If that was what it took.*

'Tomorrow night,' she said at last. 'We will expect you for dinner. A carriage will come at seven, or it won't come at all.' With that, she turned and walked away, back to her business.

'Calidae,' Merion called to her. She looked over her shoulder as she left. 'What of my friend?,' he asked. 'He is no more a traitor than I am. Please…'

She sighed, and waved a hand. 'I will see what my father can do for him.'

'Thank you,' Merion mumbled.

'I haven't spoken to my father yet,' she replied, and that was that.

And there Merion stood, for a few minutes maybe more, adrift in a sea of dust, blood, and bullet casings, weighing up tenacity against cold despondency, and wondering which one he should give in to. It was only as the sun began to plunge itself into the ragged horizon that Merion found his answer. The town had been hiding it all along. Merion stared at the flea-bitten horses, and the brow-beaten workers pouring oil on the piles of dead, and the way the whores had begun to come out with the stars—just because every last scrap of beauty had to be perverted and crushed in this torrid, sunburnt little hole—he chose tenacity. Merion took a breath, and shook his head. *Whatever it took.*

'Fuck this place,' he said, turning on his heel.

'What on the Maker's good earth happened to you?' Lilain gasped, when a blood-streaked Merion walked into the kitchen.

'Today happened to me,' he sighed, as he took a seat at the end of the table, shoulders hunched. There was something hard in his eyes, like flint. Lilain could see it.

'Shit,' she cursed. 'That sounds about right. Let me clean you up.'

Merion nodded, and let his aunt fetch water and cloth. She set up a stool beside him and gently began to dab and wipe the crusted blood away. It barely took a moment to turn the cloth and water bright red.

'Who did this to you?'

Merion stared straight ahead. 'A man in a bar. Took offence to Lurker and I for some reason. Obviously upset over the battle last night. We ended up fighting.'

'You drunk?'

'Not in the slightest.'

'Lurker?'

'No more than usual.'

'And did you rush?'

'I wouldn't be that stupid,' he lied.

'Good.'

Merion winced as the cloth uncovered a cut across his nose.

'Looks like he had a ring on,' Lilain surmised.

'Calidae managed to convince the sheriffsmen to let me go, but Lurker's been arrested as a traitor. He's in jail. I've asked her to get Lurker out, but ...' Merion said worriedly.

Lilain's flinch was barely perceptible, a momentary halt in her dabbing, a stumble in her progress. Merion caught it. 'And what was she doing there?' asked his aunt.

'She was with a foreman, surveying the town I think.'

'Mhm,' hummed Lilain. 'I'll talk to the sheriff in the morning. See if I can clear it up. He'll be safe for now at least, out of trouble,' she sighed. 'So she's talking to you again? That's good.'

'She had news from London.'

Lilain stopped altogether. 'Oh?'

Merion turned to face her. He cut an odd look, with one side of his face clean and the other masked in dark, crumbling blood. 'They've given up on the investigation. They barely acknowledge it as a murder.' Merion tossed a crumpled ball of paper onto the table.

Lilain made quick work of the message, and when she finished she ripped it in two and threw its halves back onto the tabletop. 'Idiots,' she muttered.

Merion was a little shocked to say the least, when her arms wrapped around him. Hugging had not been a common practice in Harker Sheer. He gently rested his arms on his aunt's shoulders, and waited until it would be polite to pull away. Lilain smelled like dust. He could feel the angles and edges of her bones far too easily. She was also strangely warm. Merion took a little comfort in that, knowing somebody else was burning as hot as he was, for whatever the reason. His was rage. He wondered about hers.

The bloody cloth was soon at his face again. 'I'm sorry, nephew. You need to put it to rest. There's nothing you can do it about it now, so just ...'

Merion interrupted her. 'The Serpeds have invited me to dinner again. Tomorrow night.'

Another flinch. 'Everything seems to be patched up then,' she murmured, barely audible.

'I hope so. They may be able to help me.'

'I see,' came the reply, just something to fill the space of an answer, betraying nothing but disappointment. Merion could feel it. But then she sighed and said, 'It's your decision, Merion. I can't stop you.' Her words were surprising, but more than that, they were welcome, and warming. Finally, somebody other than Lurker understood. His aunt, of all people.

'Thank you,' Merion said.

They were interrupted by a rattle from down the hallway, something falling maybe, something small but heavy.

Lilain was instantly on her feet. Merion chased her. 'Did it come from the basement?' he asked, hoping to draw her away. Rhin must have returned. Merion cursed the clumsy little fool.

'No it didn't,' Lilain replied.

Merion gulped when her fingers wrapped around the door handle of his room. He could say nothing, lest he arouse suspicion. He hoped the faerie had heard the sounds of heavy boots and voices.

Lilain paused in the middle of his room, staring down at the edge of the bed, next to the bedside table. 'What is it?' he asked, trying hard to hide his breathlessness. The lone candle on the windowsill was half-dead or dying, and the room was dark. She bent down to get a closer look, and Merion wanted to put his fist in his mouth. The books. The notepads. The schematics. She would see them all there. That would be it. Rhin would be caught.

'Nothing,' she shrugged, straightening.

'Just an old house, creaking,' Merion suggested. His insides were squirming, but his face was empty, expressionless, innocent as a babe. 'Well,' he said, 'I think it's time I went to bed.'

'Have you eaten?'

'Yes,' Merion lied. Tomorrow would come quicker if he went to bed now. He had no time to waste on food.

'Alright, well, probably for the best. Sleep well.'

'I will,' Merion replied, and gently shut the door.

He listened to the sound of boots receding into the kitchen, and a door quietly closing. Only then did he dare to speak, and in a low whisper.

'Rhin?'

'Here,' said a little voice, over in the corner of the room. A little form shivered into being, all dressed up in armour and with a sword held low.

'What the hell are you doing?' Merion asked, striding forward.

Rhin shrugged. 'Hiding as usual, of course,' he replied. 'By the Roots, what happened to you?!'

'I got into a fight at a saloon.'

'I …' Rhin didn't know what to say, so Merion just said it for him.

'That was the first time that you weren't there to help. I needed you, and you weren't there. Just like the last two weeks,' Merion said, flatly. 'Lurker's been arrested too.'

Rhin drew himself up to his full height. Merion could see the shame in his eyes all the same, but there was something else there too, something stronger than shame or guilt, something overriding. 'I have been busy.'

'With *what*, Rhin?' Merion hissed. 'It's like you've gone mad! Watching the door for days on end. Stealing books, schematics, the silent treatment. There's a war going on, if you haven't noticed! What is wrong with you?' he demanded. 'I want the bloody truth, and I want it now!'

Perhaps Rhin felt he owed Merion, after he had quite obviously failed him as a friend and sworn protector. Maybe he was tired of holding onto his secrets. Whatever the reason that dragged the words out of him, it was plain it tortured him to do so. Rhin laid it all bare.

'This is going to sound a little strange,' the faerie began, as if that were how all good stories should start. 'When you first found me, in the bushes, I told you I had been wrongly accused, and that I had chosen exile and been chased from the kingdom, right? Well, that wasn't exactly true.' Rhin paused to scratch his head.

Merion took a seat on the bed and put his fingers to his temples. *As if the day could not get any worse.* Now he was discovering his best friend had lied to him. 'If you don't keep talking I'll call for my aunt so she can gut you like a fish.'

'I wasn't wrongly accused; I was actually very accurately and correctly accused. I stole the Hoard. Sift's Hoard.' Rhin faltered again, and Merion started to notice the streak of cowardice in him.

'Rhin!'

The faerie glared at the floor. 'A whole fortune in a purse. It made it rather easy to steal. Power goes to the head, they say. I say power reaches for the nearest knife. Sift was maniacal, and I didn't want anything to do with it. So one day, while the Queen was hunting moles with her royal entourage and half the Coil guard, I decided to steal her Hoard. To teach her a lesson and start my new life over.

'Made it halfway to the park before the bells began to sound. I lost them in the woods for a while, but had to fight my way out. When they caught me at the riverbank, they stuck a few blades in me, along with an arrow. But I managed to swim away even with my armour on. Thank the Roots for paying extra for a blacksmith's blessing.

'It took me three weeks to find safety, to find you at the edges of the garden. I was just thankful you weren't another dog. I had no idea that I would stay, that we were going to become friends, or come here to Fell Falls,' Rhin's voice was low and sombre. He looked up to see if Merion had cracked slightly, there was nothing in the boy's face besides an expectant look that demanded he continue.

'Because it had been so long, I assumed I was safe, but a few weeks before your father died ...'

'Was murdered,' Merion corrected him.

'...before your father was murdered, some old friends paid me a visit in the woods by the north wing. Finrig the White Wit and his Black Fingers: assassins, thieves, and mercenaries, the lot of them. It was fitting that Sift should send Wit after me. I worked with Finrig in the old days, I'm ashamed to say, during the Bloody Uprising, in Ti'firi, when the weasels had come out to play. He demanded I return the Hoard, otherwise he would kill you, and then me. I said I didn't have it.'

'You lied to me?'

Rhin fidgeted, then shook his head. 'No, I told the truth. I lost it long ago.'

'How the hell do you just lose a fortune?'

Rhin waved a hand. 'It's a purse, Merion, it's a lot easier than you think. The Wit was having none of it. He said that if I gave it back, Sift might pardon me. Leave me in peace. I told him to go fuck himself and that was that. They left, thinking I would crumble, and we left for America shortly after,' Rhin said, his gauntlet creaking as he clenched his sword hilt.

Merion looked him up and down. 'So what's the problem?'

Rhin sighed. 'The problem is that the Wit followed me here, and now they want another Hoard, or we have to pay it in blood. Yours. Mine. Your aunt's. They'll kill us all unless I find them a pile of gold,' he confessed, voice cracking slightly at the end.

Despite the fact his faerie had lied to him, Merion had never seen him look so apologetic in all the time he had known him. 'As if I didn't have enough to deal with ...' Merion whispered, his voice tight with strain.

Rhin stepped forward. 'But I have a plan, Merion, and it will work. I've found the gold we need. Wit will take it and leave us alone for good.'

'Where? How?'

'Tomorrow night, there's a train coming in from Kaspar filled with gold. Workers' wages, long overdue. It's a Hoard, as true as any. I'm going to rob it and deliver it straight to the Wit.'

Merion was quick to his feet. 'A train robbery?! That's what you've been planning?' he hissed, incandescent. 'And a *Serped* train! Why must everybody insist on sabotaging my one and only chance to get out of this place! You, of all people, Rhin! This is absolutely unbelievable!'

'I'm trying to save our lives!' Rhin hissed right back. Cowardice can quickly turn sharp, when it is goaded.

Merion pushed a finger in Rhin's face. 'You are robbing from the only people that can help us out of here! I forbid you to rob that train! We can deal with this Wit together.'

'You have idea how dangerous he is, Merion!'

'And so? I fought off three men today with nothing but my magick. I can handle a dozen faeries.'

'No, you can't!' Rhin asserted. 'This is the only way Sift will ever leave me alone. Leave *us* alone. Then we can stay here and be safe!'

'I DON'T WANT TO STAY HERE!' Merion roared. Soon enough, the boots came thudding. Rhin vanished in a blink. Merion threw himself onto his bed, face-down and fists in his pillow.

Lilain swept into the room brandishing a dirty fork in one hand. 'Merion? Whatever's going on?'

Merion rolled over to look up, blinking as though tears were assailing his eyes. 'Nothing, Aunt. I just knocked my nose on the table.'

Lilain squinted at him before nodding. 'Well, be careful. Don't want you bleeding all over my sheets,' she said, and left.

The door clicked shut, snuffing the dying candle in its wake. Merion listened to the sounds of Rhin returning to his place under the bed, to his open suitcase and hidden books. A dark question hovered on his tongue, one that was burning to be asked.

'Tell me the truth, Rhin. Did these faeries kill my father?' Merion whispered to the shadows.

Rhin rustled underneath him. Merion could hear his mouth flapping, could imagine the cogs whirling in his head. His fingers began to throttle the threadbare sheets as the silence stretched and stretched.

'No,' came the answer from under the bed. 'No, they didn't.'

Merion released the sheets and let his heart get its beat back. 'You will not rob that train, do you hear me?' he ordered the faerie.

No answer came this time, just more rustling.

'Rhin? You hear me, damn you?'

Under the bed, Rhin sat cross-legged with his head buried in his hands. Tiredness and guilt tugged at him in equal measure. He could almost feel the pressure pushing him down into the collection of rags he called a bed.

Merion spoke once more before he too gave into sleep. 'Don't you dare ruin this for me,' he murmured.

Rhin waited until he heard the soft raspings of snoring before he answered. 'I think I already have,' the faerie said to himself. 'I think I already have.'

★

If you have ever known the inside of a jail cell, then you will know how singularly uncomfortable they are. Lurker was sure that was the point of it all, but this one excelled in ways he had never known, and he had seen plenty of jails in his life. Maybe this one was reserved for traitors only. It barely had a place to lie down.

Lurker's only distraction was the thin whisker of moon, hovering just over the rooftops. As he stared at the moon's pockmarked curve, he counted the number of ways his situation could turn out. He sniffed at the cold night air. He had been lots of things to lots of people, but never a traitor, and he didn't much like the idea of hanging for something he wasn't. Thumbing his nose, he pressed his forehead against the iron bars, rough with rust.

That was when he heard it; a familiar cawing noise, a cackling almost, as if the night itself was laughing at him. Lurker moved this way and that, swivelling so he could stare into the shadows of the streets beyond the bars. Nothing moved. His heart almost burst with shock when a black shape flapped wildly against the bars. It was Jake. Lurker grabbed him quickly, pinching his beak shut as he wiggled him through the bars.

'What is it? Is Lil alright? Merion?' he asked.

Jake did a sort of shrug before chattering away, as quietly as a bird can manage. To any eavesdropper it would have sounded like the conversation of a madman. Lurker fired question after question as the bird croaked and cawed.

'Another? When?'

'When?'

'How many?'

'Shit. Where are they now?'

'Shit. That's far too close.'

'Well I can't do anything 'bout that, can I?'

'Can you find Merion? Or Rhin? He can unnerstan' you. Gotta warn 'em, Jake before they strike again. This town won't last another night. I know Mayut and his pride. He won't stop now.'

The magpie flapped and Lurker stroked his head. After a little squeezing and pushing, Jake flapped back into the cold night, hunting for a boy and his faerie. He uttered one last lonely croak before he melted into the dark sky. Lurker reached up to touch his hat, but found nothing but empty air. He grunted. *Where was his darn hat?*

Such was the way of men and problems, always using the little ones to distract them from the large and looming ones. It works, for a while.

CHAPTER XXVIII
"STORM'S COMING"

'All quiet on the faerie front. It's been a few months since I last saw anything. I'm starting to think I was wrong. My eyes must be getting old.

Speaking of old, that boy grows up faster and faster every day. He's still got too much of his father in him, but I like to think I've tempered that, just a little bit. I'm teaching him all the troll names. He's got a mind like a blade. Shame he doesn't use it more, and give his heart a break.'

6th June, 1867

Days always move like treacle when you're in a hurry. The sun inched across the sky with a terrible, torpid pace. Morning dragged and the afternoon was lethargic. Merion was painfully aware of each passing second, sat as he was on the roof, with a wooden-cased clock he had pinched from the kitchen. Its ticks and tocks were like the unsteady tapping of a drunken cripple on old crutches and wet cobbles. More than once throughout his vigil on the roof, Merion considered tossing the damned thing over the edge, to be done with its infernal slowness. Night was what he needed, not this blasted day. The day had no opportunities to tempt him with.

The roof was the only place he felt remotely comfortable. The day was stuffy. The house was even more so. Clouds had gathered at the corners of the world, grey fingers groping at the blue sky.

The basement was still awash with corpses, as it had been since yesterday. Lilain had worked through the night. Men had come to take them to the pits and pyres. They had offered him a few silvers to help with the digging, but Merion had politely informed them that he would rather dig out his kidneys with a spoon. He'd had enough of the dead and their cold touch.

His room was soured by the presence of his stubborn faerie. Rhin was busy blackening his armour and putting an even finer edge on his blades. He meant business, and Merion was infuriated it. Rhin's business would ruin his, and yet the faerie refused to empathise. They had argued again that morning, and neither had come away remotely content.

Merion felt as though he was running out of time, and yet he had plenty to spare. It was a perplexing situation to be stuck in.

It was halfway through the afternoon when Lilain popped her head out of the window, hollering his name. 'Merion? You out here?'

'I am indeed.'

'Why, might I ask?'

'Nowhere else to be.'

'You're going to get burnt to a crisp.'

Merion reached into his pocket and showed her an empty vial. 'Lungfish,' he said, flicking its label.

Lilain raised an eyebrow. 'You're learning your Sanguine fast. And you've also been sneaking into my store without asking.'

'You were busy with the men. I only took the one vial.'

Lilain shrugged. 'Fair enough.'

'Any word on Lurker?'

'I spoke to the sheriff. He's far from pleased, and demanded a fistful of sil'erbits for the saloon owner. Seems your Calidae put in a word after all. Lurker's going to be kept behind bars for a few days to "teach him a lesson". Nobody's being hanged just yet,' she replied. 'I'd put my trust in the prospector, Merion. He's managed to line many a pocket in this town with gold over the years, payment for this and that. That might count for something.'

Merion breathed a sigh of relief. At least there was some good news to be had today.

His aunt took a moment to look around at the town and the desert. 'What are you looking at?'

'Anything,' Merion sighed. 'Just passing the time. I've seen three work parties head out west to clear the line. I watched the sheriff arrest a few wastrels over by that Serped barn. I've seen sixteen carriages rattle in from two different roads. Three trains come and go again, one vulture, and a beggar selling roast rat on a stick. Wandered past just a moment ago.'

'You've been busy then,' she smirked.

'Not as busy as I would like to be.'

Lilain couldn't resist trying to cheer him up. 'This is the problem with dinners. They happen in the evening. You should have asked to come to lunch instead,' she chuckled for a moment, but at the sight of Merion's unimpressed face, she fell to silence, busying herself by picking sand from between the tiles.

'Storm's coming,' she said, nodding over at the clouds in the north.

A storm. *Great.* 'When?' he asked.

'Tonight maybe. Or in the morning. Serped's not going to be happy. The rail hasn't moved in two days.'

'And apparently none of the workers have been paid yet,' Merion informed her. 'I overheard some talk at the saloon yesterday. Shortly before it all went to shit.'

His aunt clipped his ear lightly. 'You mind your tongue, nephew. I hear too much of Lurker in you for my liking.'

Merion shook his head. 'This is all happening too fast. The Shohari. Lurker. Rioting. Rain. All I want to do is go to dinner and put an end to it all.'

Lilain had nothing to say to that. Perhaps she did not trust her tongue with an answer. Merion would not have listened anyway. His heart and its path were set.

'What time?' she said at last.

'A coach will come at seven, or not at all,' Merion replied, echoing Calidae's words.

'Well, good luck,' his aunt said quietly. He knew she was trying her hardest to mean it, but in truth he didn't care either way. The simple fact she had said it at all was enough to bring a little glow of warmth to his otherwise icy, impatient mood. He could not remember the last time somebody had spoken to him just to be kind.

'I will see you off,' Lilain said, ruffling his hair before getting up to leave. She had a few more bodies to tend to, and the sun was hot on her face.

Merion listened to her leave before sighing. His aunt's kind words may have been refreshing, but they'd done nothing to shove the sun along its way. He rolled his eyes, and slumped against the chimney.

✸

Six finally rolled around the clock and it found Merion back in his bedroom. Faerie or not, he had to wash and change. At least Rhin had the decency to keep his mouth shut. If it had not been for the nervous, intermittent buzzing of his wings, and the occasional rustle of paper, Merion would have thought himself alone.

Six-thirty came, and Merion had run out of things to wash and press and button and comb. He sat on the bed and twiddled his thumbs, all the while fighting a growing urge to say something, to have one last swing at knocking some sense into this moronic faerie.

A quarter to seven, said the clock, perched on the bedside table, its ticking as gelatinous as ever. Merion could not fight it any more. He stamped his foot and pushed himself off the bed.

'I won't let you do it. I can't let you do it,' Merion hissed.

'I have to,' Rhin sighed, after a moment.

'You *don't* have to. You can wait here until I secure us a ticket home, and then we'll deal with those faeries together.'

There was a grunt and a curse as Rhin rolled out from under the bed. 'If you had listened to a single story I've told you, you'd know there would be a long cut across your throat before you even caught a glimpse of the Wit or his Fingers! They make a living cutting throats, Merion. You make yours manhandling bodies onto carts. Your rushing won't save you. Just trust me!' he shouted.

'This is not my living. It's over the sea, back in London! You call yourself a friend? A friend would know how much I hate this place. A friend wouldn't knowingly rob me of that. But I guess you are a thief, after all,' Merion spat.

Rhin flickered with anger. 'Serped has more gold than the desert has sand, Merion. You really think he'll blame you? Cast you in irons? He'll have another train in town by the weekend, and you and I will be as safe as houses.'

'The town will bloody riot!' Merion was struggling to keep his voice down. Lilain was only in the kitchen.

Rhin snorted. 'Let it riot! What do you care?'

'They could hurt Castor and Calidae. The Shohari could attack, and they'll refuse to fight. Then where will we be?'

'I don't know, but we won't have a band of murderous faeries on our tail.'

Merion tore at his hair in frustration and stamped his feet. 'By the Almighty!'

Boots in the corridor once more. The door-handle rattling.

Lilain peered into every nook and cranny the room had to offer. 'What is it this time?'

Merion paused his hopping to point at his foot. 'Stubbed my toe.'

'Are you ready?' she asked. 'It's almost seven.'

Merion shot a glance under the bed before he answered. 'I am,' he replied. 'Let me just comb my hair.'

Lilain wore a suspicious look, but she said nothing more than, 'I'll be on the porch.'

Merion nodded and let her leave. He ran his fingers through his hair before kicking the frame of the bed. 'I have to go. You do this, and you're dead to me.'

'If I don't do this, you're dead anyway,' Rhin grunted. 'Simple as that.'

Rhin's words put a chill in the boy's chest. 'So be it,' Merion whispered. He did not need this thief of a faerie, this liar. He could fend for himself from now on. Merion had his rushing now, and Lurker, and Lilain. And the Serpeds, Almighty willing. He would be the master of his own destiny, not a selfish, twelve-inch tall beast with shit for brains. *To hell with him*, Merion told himself.

'Tonmerion, the coach is here,' came the shout from the porch.

The young Hark sucked in a deep breath. He took one last moment to pinch his collar tight and check his shoes before leaving Rhin to his madness.

The darkness, ushered in by the advancing clouds, was slowly sucking the light from the day. It was still hot but a breeze had come to stir the dust on the porch and to make the weathervanes rattle. Merion sniffed it cautiously, and was glad to find it was not as bitter as the last breeze he had tasted. The coach sat awkwardly in the middle of the street, one wheel halfway into a rut. A lordsguard sat on the cab, and the driver was waiting at the open door. Merion glimpsed shoes inside, and the telltale frills of evening wear. He would not be riding alone, it seemed.

Calidae appeared in the doorway. 'It seems you owe me yet another favour, Master Hark. My father will have you to dinner,' she said, as if it were casual chit-chat in the street. It was then that she turned her attention to Lilain, as if only just noticing her. 'Madam Rennevie.'

'Lady Serped,' replied Lilain, without a single hint of a curtsey or bow. She did not bother to correct her on the title.

'The pleasure is all mine,' smiled Calidae. 'Merion?'

Merion made for the steps, but Lilain caught him lightly on the shoulder. 'Be careful,' she whispered, before letting him go. Merion nodded, not quite sure what to make of that, and headed for the open door of the coach.

'Your hair has grown far too long,' said Calidae, as he sat down opposite her on the plush seats.

'I heard it suited me,' Merion could be heard saying, before the door cut him off and the coach stole him away to dinner.

'Get up, Rhin,' whispered grey lips. 'Get up.'

If the sword hilt was a neck it would have been snapped long ago.

'You can do this.'

Rhin counted down from ten, but seemed to get stuck around five when another wave of emotion washed over him. He was sweating in places he did not know he could sweat, and there was a dangerous tremble in his legs. The sort of emotion he had not felt in several hundred years. Not since his very first spear had been pressed into his soft hands. He swiped the sweat from his forehead. Now those hands were rough and weary, shaped from murder and battle. Was this murder, or battle, he was going to tonight? Both, he realised. They seem very similar when compared side by side. It was the battle for his own safety, to save the skin of his only friend. And yet it was the murder of that very same friendship. Rhin rocked back and forth as the guilt came again.

'I owe him,' Rhin snapped at himself, chiding the doubt away. 'And that is why I have to save him.'

With a snap and crackle of his wings he was up and ducking under the frame of the bed. One hand was still firmly glued to his sword, the other to his chest, to marvel at how fast his heart was beating. He was halfway across the floor when he heard the almost imperceptible squeak of a door-handle.

✮

Lilain stayed on the porch until the coach had disappeared behind a row of houses. After a hearty sigh, she went inside and closed the door with a click. The door to Merion's room was shut, as always. An idea sprang up to bite her, and before she knew it, she was creeping across the hallway, pressing each heavy boot to the floorboards as if it were a feather being rested atop a house of cards. She narrowed her eyes as she reached for the door-handle. She knew what she was hoping for, what her wildest suspicions were taunting her with, but she also knew that she was most likely being absolutely delusional.

Her hands wrapped around the handle, silencing any rattle that would betray her. Gently she twisted it. She was almost at the full turn when the blasted thing squeaked at her. Not loud, just the coughing of a mouse, but still enough to make her curse. Lilain lunged through the door, springing into the middle of the room with her hands wide and eyes even wider. Nothing. Just as she had suspected. The room was dead and empty, just as Merion had left it.

Lilain rolled her own eyes at herself and shook her head. She was being fanciful, silly even, to suspect that Merion had been hiding something strange in his room all this time, something he'd brought from London that caused him to shout and argue…

'Nonsense,' Lilain told herself, before chuckling.

Rhin had to smirk at that, as he crept through the door which Lilain had conveniently opened for him. His boots tread softer than wind blowing. His armour was silent, its edges muffled with cloth and magick. His spell was strong. It always was at twilight; a time that human eyes have never grown used to, despite being born to it, all those thousands of years ago. Lilain was utterly unaware. He had to smirk. It kept his mouth from quivering.

CHAPTER XXIX
THE HEIST

'Another year, another birthday. Merion is thirteen now. It snowed today. Early, even for London. He played in the snow until his face turned blue. Karrigan had the servants give him some of his best brandy, and for a moment I thought a little differently of him. But then he bellowed at the boy for staying out too long in the cold. Made my blood boil. A son should never be scared of his father.'

6th June, 1867

It was cold under the charcoal clouds, far colder than a desert should rightfully be. The advancing storm had torn the heat from the day and used it selfishly, building and building itself until a colossal anvil lurked on the skyline, bound due south to come soak the scorched earth of Fell Falls. Rhin eyed its brutish, bubbling shape, clear as it was against moonlight and stars. Ash streaks of cloud spread their fingers across the sky, like furrows in a field. Or messengers of the approaching tempest, Rhin thought. If there was one thing Wyoming did well, it was a good storm.

He flicked a nail against the track once more and listened to it sing. He wished it would sing longer, anything to distract him from his impending task. A faerie, robbing a train. Even when size difference was taken out of the equation, the idea was still laughable. Hysterical, some might say, the stuff of fairy tales. Rhin rolled those words around in his head until they dragged him to his feet. His knees ached from kneeling for so long. His fingers ached from constant wringing.

'Come on, Rehn'ar, you've stolen bigger hoards than this,' Rhin chided himself, trying to work the knot out of his throat. 'What's the plan?'

Rhin's week spent under Merion's bed had not been spent in vain. Yes, there had been many long hours of staring at doors, sharpening swords and biting lips, but the rest had been spent poring over schematics and pictures and maps.

Faeries may have been of the old world, but their minds worked just like the scientists of the new. They can see patterns just as easily as you can say the word. They can absorb information like a sponge, and most importantly, if there is a weakness in something, a faerie will find it. Rhin had been studying maps and plans for centuries. A good soldier always does, after all. Those who do not quickly find themselves in a cage with a rabid mole, or dead.

It had taken him a week to find it, that little gem in the crown that was his scheme. The secret of mastering technology is not to examine the alignment of gears and valves, nor the ingenuity of its torque and thrust, nor its multi-chamber boilers and cow-catchers. All that is needed is to master the man who already masters it—in this case, the driver and his brakeman. All Rhin had to do was make them do his bidding. The edge of a sword and the sight of a faerie might just do it. *Humans. They were technology's perpetual shackle.*

Rhin sniffed, tasting the night air. There had been one other problem of course: boarding a train travelling at around forty miles an hour. One schematic had put the weight of the locomotive alone at almost one-hundred thousand pounds. Rhin weighed about two. Solving that had taken far less than a week.

Rhin spied the light on the horizon and felt his stomach begin to churn. The faerie took a breath and uttered his plan, blow by blow. Somehow it calmed him, set his mind straight and clear.

'Last bend, five miles.'

Rhin drew his sword with a flourish and held the blade low.

'Light the fire,' he told himself.

His striking stone rasped across the blade and poured sparks on the kindling splayed across the tracks. He thanked the Roots and all their gods for keeping the storm at bay. Fire had been his only option, besides building a house on the rail.

His kindling was dry as a week-dead bone. It took to flame in seconds, and it was not long before Rhin had to step back and cover his face. He had built a fire that no train driver could miss. It had taken him an hour, but in the end he had covered the area of a sizeable dining table with sticks and brush and twigs. It was well and truly ablaze now. Rhin shimmered into nothing and stepped aside.

'Twenty-six and a half feet, and ten for luck,' he ordered his legs.

Rhin hopped from boot to boot as he counted out the steps in sharp breaths.

'Six ... seven ... eight ...' Each hop was a foot, more or less. Moments couldn't be wasted on having to catch up or to run, not at times like these.

'Eleven ... twelve.'

Past the bogie now, and its cow-catcher. Their diagrams were etched into his mind, and now he could almost see them drawn against the night and the dully-shining rails.

'Eighteen ... nineteen.'

Past the second axle now, in the shadow of the engine's bulbous boilers, all wrapped in iron, with valves jutting into the sky in a trio. Never mind the humongous smoke-stack, standing proud and over-sized on the locomotive's nose.

'Twenty-six...'

Now here he was at the back half of the engine, with the bigger wheels and their multi-cogged centres spinning madly.

Now the cab, where the driver and his brakeman took shelter from the soot and steam of the iron beast, and shovelled coal. They were the brains of it, and Rhin couldn't wait to meet them. Rhin jogged on

'Thirty-six,' Rhin hissed. He could spare the half, he decided.

He heard a screech in the far-off night, and not of any owl or dying thing. *They'd seen his fire.* The locomotive was breaking now, gentle and curious of the blaze in its path. Rhin could see the wake of its lanterns and fire-grate glowing against the sand. It was barely a mile away now and closing fast.

More screeching, and a stammer in its heavy chuffing. Even the clatter of its iron changed. It was not about to risk the Lord Serped's gold by charging through a fire.

'Just as planned,' Rhin smirked, as he rested his sword blade on his shoulder.

Now for the hard part.

✭

Nobody offered but a scrap of talk over dinner. The food may have been piping hot and as delicious as before, but the atmosphere was even colder, and the expression on Lord Serped's face nothing short of terrifying.

Merion placed his spoon and fork neatly in the crystal bowl and chanced another glimpse at his host. There he was, stern as a statue, as he had been for the whole meal. His face did not speak so much of anger as it did intense scrutiny, as if Merion were being sized up for the final course.

With a cough, Lord Serped broke his vigil and got to his feet. It was as if he had heard Merion's thoughts as clear as a bell.

'I think we shall retire to the sitting room tonight. We have much to discuss,' he stated, his voice rough and deep, as if sleep had escaped him the past few nights. 'Gile?' he nodded to his servant, who bowed. He had been standing in a corner, quiet as a rock. One blue eye, one green eye, both staring.

'Yessir,' he said, before scurrying off into another room.

'Come,' ordered Castor, and Ferida, Calidae, and Merion all stood up as one.

The sitting room was warm thanks to the fire. Merion pulled at his collar as he walked into the room, already feeling the heat. Nothing like stewing your prisoner before you question him. Merion took a breath to steel himself. *His destiny, his hands.*

Merion was pointed to an armchair right by the fireplace, a deep red thing that looked like a yawning throat. Merion perched on its edge to avoid being swallowed.

'Brandy, Merion?' asked Castor, and there it was: the test.

'Please, Lord Serped,' replied Merion, without a moment's hesitation. Although his stomach churned, his face remained a mask of utmost politeness. He caught Calidae's eye and smiled. She barely returned so much as a pout, much to his dismay. 'I must thank you, first of all, for your help in keeping my friend Lurk ... John, from the gallows,' Merion said.

'I have spoken to the sheriff,' Serped commented as he poured. 'Your friend shall be kept locked up for now. Until I say otherwise.'

'He is no traitor, my Lord,' Merion urged.

'A drunkard and a brawler, from what I hear,' he replied. 'Be that as it may, he will stay behind bars for now.' Castor took an own armchair directly opposite Merion and placed Merion's brandy on a small table that sat between them. He did not remove his fingers from it. 'So, my daughter tells me you have a theory about our beverages, Master Hark. Is that so?'

So Calidae had told him. No secrets after all.

'It is, my Lord. I believe I know a little something about what's in that glass,' Merion nodded to tabletop. 'I'm not such a stranger to the practice myself.'

'And what *practice* is this, pray Master Hark?' Ferida queried him, two chairs to his right.

'Blood, my Lady,' he replied flatly. *Might as well get it out there.* 'Drinking blood. In this case mixed with brandy, or wine.'

Ferida snapped her head to glare at her husband. 'So it is true, Castor. He believes us to be vampires. Savages.'

Merion inched forwards on his seat. 'Not at all, my Lady. I would not dare reduce it to something so crass as nonsense such as vampirism. Please, you must believe me when I say I am the same. I understand what you do and why.'

'And how exactly?' Unlike his increasingly distraught wife, Castor was calm and collected. It somehow made him seem more threatening.

'Because I drink blood also. I'm a bloodrusher, like my father, sir.'

Castor put his hands on the arms of his huge chair and leant back to think a while. He left the brandy alone on the tabletop. Stranded and masterless.

Merion had come this far, he might as well go the whole distance, he decided. The young Hark reached for the glass and brought it slowly to his lips. It smelled as strong and as sickly he remembered. Merion took a liberal swig and cradled the glass in his lap as he swilled it about his mouth. He could feel every eye upon him, making sure he swallowed. He did not disappoint them.

Merion felt the blood bite in an instant. It kicked him hard and made his head spin. This was far stronger than the last batch he had tasted. He winced and squirmed as the blood crept from his stomach to his head to his heart and back again. His skin tingled, as though it was trying to dance. So this was what being a lamprey felt like. Merion did not dare trust himself to enjoy it. His aunt's words echoed in his head. *Cannibalism. Poison.*

Castor had raised an eyebrow. 'Now, you understand,' he said. Calidae and Ferida sipped their drinks, and to Merion's dismay they did not bat an eyelid. *Practice indeed.*

Ferida had dropped her mask of indignity, and instead now wore something of a coyer nature, as if she had just revealed a dark and wonderful secret to the room. Calidae was expressionless, staring ahead at the fire. Merion wondered what she was trying to avoid.

'I do, Lord Serped,' he replied. The blood was settling now, but the buzzing in his extremities still remained.

'Come then, show us this rushing of yours, Master Hark,' Ferida demanded, raising her glass. 'If it is true.'

Merion shook his head. 'I'm afraid, my Lady, that I haven't brought any shades with me. I didn't expect to—'

'Shades?' Castor cut in, that eyebrow of his crawling higher.

'Surely you mean shade, Merion?' Calidae asked. 'Electric eel?'

'That's right,' Merion nodded. He patted his pockets. 'But sadly I have none with me.'

'Electric Eel …' Castor mused, before shouting for his manservant. 'Gile!' he yelled.

Suffrous must have been waiting behind the door. He was at the lord's side in the blink of an eye. Merion swilled his brandy around. 'Definitely stronger than last time,' he muttered under his breath.

'Master Gile,' began Serped.

Gile bowed. 'Your lordship.'

'Would you happen to have the blood of the electric eel on your person?' asked Serped, as casually as if he had just asked for the time.

Gile grinned, showing a few gold teeth dotted around his smile. Merion felt a little shiver of nervousness. *Surely not ...*

'Why as it so happens, my Lord ...' He paused to unbutton his jacket and pull it aside, revealing an astounding collection of vials, all sewn into little pockets that filled the inside of his jacket. As Gile wiggled his coat around to make them dance, Merion could see their colours licking at the corks; brown, red, orange, yellow, green. Even blue. Lilain would have tackled him to the ground already, were she here. Merion had no doubt.

Merion gripped his glass tightly. Was this Gile a leech perhaps? His mind raced. It made perfect sense and yet none at all. The perfect bodyguard. But with so many vials, he could have also been a letter. What if he was Castor's letter, and Castor was the rusher? A leech *and* a lamprey? Almighty. Merion's thoughts tumbled down the slopes of what ifs, and all the while he fought to keep his face from betraying him. He had come here with a purpose. He would ride this wave of theirs and see where it took him.

'Ah,' said Gile, selecting a dark red vial from the bottom of his jacket. 'Here we are. For you, sir?' Gile was looking directly at Merion, as if this had all been staged and rehearsed.

Merion didn't falter. 'Indeed sir, thank you,' he replied, catching the vial awkwardly with one hand. It clinked against the brandy glass. Merion took a deep yet surreptitious breath as he got to his feet. 'I better make some room,' he said.

'What in shitdarn is it, Hosh?'

'I ain't got a clue. Let me have a look,' replied a blustered Hosh. Red in the cheek and large in the belly, the locomotive driver was smeared from tip to toe in coal dust and engine grease. He looked as though he had just crawled out of an inkwell.

'Bring us in to about ten feet, Jaspar. Ten feet and no more. Don't want to set light to the thing do we?'

Jaspar nodded and worked his brake levers, gently squeezing the train to a halt, almost exactly ten feet from the smouldering fire that had been lit for them.

As Hosh leant out of the cab and put a greasy palm on the railing, he felt a tap on his shoulder. Jaspar wiggled the handle of a gun in his face. 'Take it,' he said. 'Looks suspicious.'

'Right you are. Keep her hot, just in case.'

'Aye,' Jaspar nodded again. He didn't say much, did Jaspar, though he loved to curse and spit when the mood took him. Hosh throttled the little two-shotter and manhandled himself down the steps and into the dust.

Chuffing just like his very own steam engine, Hosh waddled forwards until he stood at the edge of the crackling fire. He scratched his head. He couldn't make head nor tail of it, and after some more scratching and sighing, he decided he would tell Jaspar just that. Hosh hurried back towards the cab. They were already late. The Serped men would be waiting to unload their precious cargo, tapping their feet and checking their papers. Hosh wiped his sweaty bald head and hurried on.

'Can't make head nor tail of it, Jaspar, I—' Hosh froze halfway up the steps. Jaspar was on his knees, and there was some sort of huge insect on his shoulder, wrapped around his neck. He knuckled his eyes with his dirty hands, but the thing was still there, all black and grey, with wings and a horridly human face.

'What in hell is—Want me to shoot it, Jaspar?'

'Shit no!' Jaspar hissed.

'What he said.' The insect thing spoke, and Hosh almost fell backwards off the locomotive.

It spoke again, and Hosh started to suspect this might not be an insect after all. Was that a sword he spied? Was that armour? His sooty eyes were getting confused.

'Now be a good man and drop that gun of yours. Not in here, on the ground. Now,' it ordered.

Hosh opened his mouth, but nothing came out. His jowls just hung loose like a bulldog's.

'Now. Or your brakeman here will soon find out what black Fae steel feels like,' the thing threatened. It moved, turning its hand, and a blade became visible at Jaspar's throat. There was already a little smudging of blood.

The gun thudded onto the sand.

'Good man. Now. I want you to back up this engine, and drive straight through that burning brush, and then do exactly as I command. You will drive the locomotive. Mister Jaspar here will do the braking. That sound hard to you?'

Hosh was still trying to figure out what the blasted thing was when he realised it had spat a question at him. 'Er … no?' the reply came breathless.

'And you, Jaspar?'

Jaspar shook his head despite the blade at his throat. He wasn't the cleverest of sorts, was Jaspar.

'Good boys. Now, if you please. Get this locomotive running, not too fast but not slow enough to bring people running. If you do what I say, your throats will remain unsliced, and when we're all done here you can go back home to your wives, or your dog without a mark on you. Well, almost,' the thing shrugged, wiggling the blade at Jaspar's throat again.

Hosh had both a wife and a dog, and he suddenly realised he would very much like to see them again. He put a sweaty palm to a sweaty throat. He liked it how it was.

'What are you?' he asked as he clambered back into the cabin and began to paw at valves and wheels.

The thing had released Jaspar, but now he was standing directly behind him, its sword pointed straight at the back of his skull. Hosh was no surgeon, but he knew that was a nasty place to get stuck. His uncle got shot there once. He lived, but never walked again.

'Fae,' the thing uttered with a grey tongue. 'You call us fairies.'

'A fairy?' Hosh could hardly believe his ears.

Jaspar was muttering something foul under his breath. The creature nicked his ear with the blade and the muttering soon stopped.

'I'm the real kind,' hissed the fairy. 'Now plough through that fire, and let the track guide you. Do not deviate.'

Hosh was even more confused now. 'You want us to go into town?'

The fairy shook his head. 'We aren't going into town, my good fellows, we're making a little stop first. Just follow the track and do as I say.'

If Hosh had looked over his shoulder, he would have seen the fairy smiling. Hosh did not know it, but they would be sidling up to the Serped barn in a matter of minutes. All it had taken was a stout sword and a hard shove to move the lever that controlled the track direction. So easy, even a faerie could have done it.

✗

When the clapping stopped, Merion let the magick seep into his bones and scurry away. He had only rushed a little, but he had still impressed his judges.

Castor rubbed his hands together and turned to Gile. 'Would you like to try your hand, Gile? Put the red in your belly, as you call it?'

'Indeed I would, your lordship,' he said, and then winked at Merion. The boy stood where he was and folded his hands behind his back. This he had to see.

With great ceremony, ruined only by the beaming, gold-spattered smile across his face, Suffrous Gile reached into the other side of his jacket and brought forth two vials. What was curious about these was that they had been tied together with what looked to be a mile of twine, wrapping them close so that their mouths touched. There was even a little cord attaching the two corks. Suffrous hooked a finger underneath it and tugged. The corks came free with a simultaneous pop, and Merion was left with his mouth hanging slightly agape, despite his best efforts, wondering why nobody had told him it was possible to blend shades, and why Suffrous needed it all to be so convenient, so quick. That wave of theirs was building.

Suffrous threw his head back and emptied the twin vials into his mouth. One was dark red, almost brown, and the other an arsenic yellow. Merion was dying to know what they were. There was a moment of excitable silence as the man concentrated his efforts into controlling the shades. He was quick, Merion had to give him that. Like Merion, he too held his hands out like claws; a cage to pour the magick into.

The man's fingers began to glow with a bright yellow light. It seemed to drown the room of all other colour as it pulsated and grew between his fingers. Soon there was a throbbing cloud of light stretched across his hands. He raised them up, puckered his lips, and blew gently on the light. It fluttered. Suffrous tensed, blowing harder. Thin trails of fire began to flit through the strands of yellow light, turning the room the colour of tangerines. More fire sparked, and from where Merion was standing, he could see the air in front of Suffrous' lips shivering.

It was then the fire caught the light, and became one. Suffrous threw his head back as the cloud of light became an orb of fire, and he held it out, as if offering to Merion. The young Hark tried to smile as politely as he could, despite the burning jealousy within him.

Castor must have seen it, for he held up a hand and called for Gile to stop. The manservant squeezed his hands together and clapped out the flame, just like that. *Such control*, Merion marvelled.

Castor clicked his fingers. 'Do you have the papers, Master Gile?'

'I do sir. All like you asked.'

'The newspapers, first.'

First. A minute slip from Castor. There was architecture here, Merion could feel it. He was being bricked into a corner. Merion fought the urge to swallow. Whatever Castor had in mind, what mattered was whether it aligned with Merion's. Merion retook his armchair, and leant over the table as Castor spread the papers across the table.

'The front page will tell you everything you need to know,' Castor instructed, turning it around to face the boy.

Merion scanned the headlines and felt a sweat growing under his collar.

Dizali Takes the Benches by Queen's Word Alone! said one.

A New Prime Lord Announced! Cobalts Keep Control! crowed another.

Dizali: The New Hand of the Crown! said yet another.

Understanding was nailed home. Not only had his father suffered an untimely death, he had been replaced. Forgotten. Merion felt as if he were holding that wiregram again. The wave was curling over, and Merion was swimming right in its shadow.

'As you can see, Lord Hark has a successor. Second, Lord Dizali has become the first Prime Lord in history to ascend in the wake of a predecessor's murder. There is no precedent.'

'Impressive,' whispered Merion.

Castor reached for another piece of paper. 'What you might not find as impressive, Master Hark, is what his first move is,' he said. He held it to his chest and waited for an answer, even though he hadn't asked for any.

'And what is that?' Merion gave in, like a condemned man asking to examine the noose.

The paper landed in front of him. It was a letter from a minor Lord to Castor. He spoke as Merion read. 'On behalf of Victorious, Prime Lord Dizali has petitioned the Benches that while there is no eligible heir, your father's vast estate be placed under the protection of the Crown and the Palace of Ravens. To keep it from withering, or turning rotten at the core of the Empire,' Castor informed him.

The wave came crashing down, foaming fangs and all. There Merion was, washed up on the shore, numb and breathless. 'But they have no right,' he croaked. He took another sip of his brandy to distract himself from the confusion and anger.

Ferida seemed put out by his words. 'It is the Queen's right, young Hark, and you would do well to remember that. She is law.'

Castor nodded as he spoke. Calidae hadn't even blinked yet. 'The Hark estate may be yours in name, but until you have come of age, you are merely a bystander, with power of signature alone. The Queen and Crown sadly do not need your signature to take it under their wing, if they deem it vital to the ongoing success of the Empire. Unless ...' Castor paused here to take a sip of his own.

'Unless what?' asked Merion, numbly.

Castor sat on the edge of his armchair and leant forward. 'Calidae informs me you came here tonight to ask for my help. I had it in mind to turn you away, and yet, despite my doubts, you have somewhat proven yourself and your word to us. I am prepared to help you if I can. And I believe I have a way of keeping your estate out of the Queen's hands.'

Merion could not make his mind up whether Castor was being earnest or theatrical, but at that moment he did not care. 'I'm open to suggestion,' he replied.

Castor snapped his fingers again. 'Gile,' he said, and another sheaf of papers was pressed into his hand. Castor gave it straight to Merion. 'If your estate, in its entirety, were to be transferred to another, more suitable, ward, then the Crown would have no right to take it, unless by force, and that would have the Benches up in arms.'

'And who would be suitable?' Merion still hadn't looked at the paper.

'A Lord of the Benches perhaps, or one with a business history comparable to your father's. A man who could run your estate well and keep it waiting for you. A man who can be trusted to hand it back over when the time comes.'

Merion was starting to see the face of this man already. It was sitting right across from him, and staring hard. Silence reigned, save for the crackling of the bothersome fire.

CHAPTER XXX

BLOODSUCKERS

'Today I managed to sneak aboard the royal barge. I don't even think that needs an explanation. Merion is furious, but I know he secretly finds it hilarious.'

6th June, 1867

'Nice and easy,' whispered Rhin, tickling the back of Jaspar's neck with the tip of his sword. The man kept flinching away, making the locomotive squeak and lurch.

'Easy, I said,' Rhin reminded him, with a sterner jab. He turned to Hosh. 'Do what you need to do to turn this engine off. It'll coast from here.'

'Aye,' Hosh said. He was an obedient sort, now that Rhin had got through that thick skull of his. Hosh's hands moved over the valves and levers again, cutting the chuffing of the engine to a loud hiss, loud enough to wake the dead. Rhin flinched and accidentally stabbed Jaspar a little deeper than he would have liked. The brakeman cursed and clapped a hand to his neck to feel the blood dripping.

'Bring it up to the barn door, brakeman, like I said,' Rhin ordered. Jaspar nodded, not wanting to get stuck again.

The barn door was open a foot or so, just wide enough for a faerie. As the locomotive hissed again, drawing to a halt, an evil baker's dozen of faeries traipsed out to greet them. The Wit stood at their head, arms crossed and eyebrows raised.

Rhin pressed his hands to the back of Jaspar's neck and a jolt of magick flew through him. Light flashed, and Jaspar curled into a heap on the floor. He managed to mumble a quick 'fuck off' before unconsciousness swallowed him. Hosh followed, barely moments later. Rhin jumped down the steps and strode across the dust and sand to confront Finrig. The look on the Wit's face made him grin.

'You've brought us a train,' Finrig surmised expertly.

Rhin nodded. Steam leaked from the beast like wine out of an old skin. It gave their rendezvous a rather dramatic air. 'That I have. Loaded with Serped coin,' he replied, chest swelling.

Finrig pointed to the bodies lying in the cab. 'And two useless sacks of meat. They saw you and they saw us. Here. You've made yourself a pair of witnesses, Rhin. And I don't like witnesses.'

Rhin shrugged. 'Nobody will believe them. They'll think they're mad, or covering up an inside job.'

Finrig sniffed. 'Slim chance. Serped will come looking for his gold.'

Rhin narrowed his eyes. 'Not if you're long gone by then. As promised.'

Finrig spat, missing Rhin's boot by a whisker. 'In a rush, are we? We'll look at the gold first, before making any rash decisions,' he said, his voice as hard as nails. He whistled sharply, and the Fingers moved towards the two cars tethered behind the locomotive's coal tender. They made no sound. Neither did Rhin and the Wit, as they followed in the shadows. The night was muggy, and it was making Rhin sweat.

The heavy padlocks were no match for tough Fae steel. The lock fell away in two disappointed halves, thudding into the dust. The sliding doors were yanked back, and the faeries looked upon their spoils. Rhin's heart somersaulted when he saw it.

Lord Serped had not disappointed.

The first car was stacked floor to ceiling with bundles of coins. Rhin walked forwards to ogle some more. There was a queen's ransom stacked before him, and this was only the first car.

Another shredded padlock hit the dust, and more doors were wrenched back by strong faerie muscle. Rhin went to see what else this train had to offer.

To his heart's delight, yet another pile of coins. Not as big as the first, but still sizeable, sharing its space with medical supplies and fresh tools.

Rhin turned around to the Wit and rubbed his hands. 'Didn't I promise a Hoard?'

Finrig spat again. He was impressed, and he didn't like it. That dream of mounting Rhin's body parts in viewing cases was starting to fade very quickly. 'We'd better ask our very own Hoarder. Baelh? What do you think?'

One of the Fingers stepped forward, a lithe, long-haired fellow with a rapier rested on his shoulder. He bobbed his head from side to side. 'Twenty, thirty tonnes, I reckon, if that first car is full to the brim, Wit.'

'A Hoard if ever I seen one,' Rhin asserted. 'Sift will be pleased.'

Finrig stewed in his disappointment for a while before snorting. 'Baelh, get to work. You lot, help him. Rest of you, with me.' Finrig clapped a heavy hand onto Rhin's shoulder and walked him back to the cab. 'Let's see to your two witnesses, shall we?' he asked, almost jovially, as if a little murder was just what he needed.

'I promised them they could go home alive,' Rhin growled, shrugging him off.

Finrig gripped him by the collar and threw him forward. Two of the Fingers were on him before he could protest. 'Well, you shouldn't make promises you can't keep, Rhin. Didn't your mother ever tell you that?'

Rhin did not reward him with an answer. He did not like the way this evening was turning out.

Finrig waved to the two limp bodies. 'Grab 'em by the legs and drag them out. Let's put them in the barn with the other guests.'

Rhin's stomach churned. 'Others?'

Finrig flashed him a wink. 'Oh, you'll like this, Rhin, you really will.'

While the Fingers set to work manoeuvring the men onto the ground and into the barn, Rhin watched the Hoarder go to work on the spoils. The Fingers split the bundles and let the coins pour on the ground. Gold and silver poured onto the dust like the sloughed scales of some dragon. It may have looked insane, to those who have never seen a

Hoarder's magick in action, but there was plenty of method in this madness.

Baelh knelt down, the coins still pouring from the car like a metallic waterfall. His hands spread over the coins at his feet, making them jiggle and twitch. He pointed at one particularly fat gold coin, and flipped it on to another without touching it. The two stuck together, melded in some way, and became one, no bigger nor smaller than either had been before.

Thieves' magick, it is called; the ability to hide away loot by shrinking it down and folding it into itself. It is a dirty magick, but it has its uses—such as now.

Baehl's quivering hands set off a chain reaction. They waved over the pile and let the coins rattle and conjoin, chiming and rattling musically.

'Stay close now, Rhin. Wouldn't want you wandering off and missing the best bit, now would we?' Finrig smirked, pointing the way towards the barn door. Rhin saw only darkness inside.

As they walked, the Wit leant close to whisper in his ear. 'Remind me, Rhin, where's that boy of yours tonight?'

'At home, with his aunt,' Rhin lied, quick as a flash.

They got to the door, and Finrig slammed his arm against the wood to block Rhin's path. He stared him right in the eye, noses almost touching, that infernal smirk still plastered across his lips. 'Now if there's one thing I dislike more than witnesses, it's lying, Rhin. Don't come this close just to blow it. My knife will be tickling your lights before you know it.'

Rhin said nothing.

Finrig narrowed his eyes. 'A dinner is it? At the Serped abode?' he inquired.

Rhin had to force himself to nod.

'Right,' Finrig mused. 'Strange people, don't you think? The Serpeds? Wouldn't trust them with Merion. Not with a hair on his precious head,' he chuckled.

'If you know something …' Rhin growled.

Finrig stepped back and gestured towards the darkness. 'See for yourself, Rehn'ar. You've got eyes, haven't you?'

Rhin scowled as he stepped into the darkness. His faerie eyes adjusted immediately, turning the world a palette of grey and maroon. He instantly wished they hadn't.

✭

'You want me to sign over my father's ... my estate to you, for safekeeping?'

Castor nodded for a third time. 'Yes I do,' he said. He reached into his pocket and produced a pen. It was placed on the table, atop the dotted line of the very long and very incomprehensible contract.

Merion stared at the pen and tried to decide whether it held all the salvation in the world, or whether it was a knife for the slitting of his own wrists. Something about this made him itch intensely. He scratched his head, and as he did so, he caught a glimpse of Calidae's sideways glance. There was something in her eyes that urged him on, willing him to pick up that pen and scrawl his name. Something that said she owed him.

Merion stammered. 'I can't just ... I can't sign the whole ...'

Castor leant even further forward. Merion half-expected him to fall off his chair at any moment. 'My daughter tells me you are eager to go home, Merion,' Castor said, and Merion had to nod. 'If you sign this, I will have to return to the capital to assess your father's estate. There will be new business for me there. You could return with me.'

Merion's heart soared. There they were: the magical words he had been praying to hear ever since his shoes had first met the cursed dust of this hellish town.

But what price had he been willing to pay for them? His whole awaited empire, with the flick of a pen? The weight of the decision was a heavy one, and it pushed Merion deeper into the armchair.

'Calidae will come, of course. Gile could even train you, should you have the time. I will need an assistant of course.'

Castor was laying it on thick. The pile of prizes was mounting, getting more tempting by the minute. Merion would have bitten his lip if it had not looked so childish.

'Perhaps I should speak to my aunt. Or even have the estate handed to her. That way…'

'Merion, the Crown won't respect a woman like your aunt.'

Merion raised an eyebrow. 'What do you mean?'

Castor's stern face broke for the first time. A little curl of his lip, that was all, but it might as well have been fireworks exploding from his eyes for all the expression that he had ever offered. 'Come now, Merion. Your aunt is not a lady of the courts. Far from it.'

Ferida began to titter by her husband's side. She was on her third glass of brandy. Merion narrowed his eyes at the two of them.

'She is still a Hark,' he asserted.

Castor waved a hand. 'By name only. I am a lord of the Empire. Your aunt is a struggling undertaker, Merion, a loner and a self-made exile, playing with bodies all day long.'

'Not to mention divorced,' added Ferida.

'She …' Words failed Merion, much to his own disgust.

Castor leant forward. 'Do you know why she left Chicago? Has she ever told you that story? I did not think so. It's not one for a nephew to hear.'

'Tell me,' Merion shot back, rigid in his chair now. Any pleasantry was well and truly evaporating. All sense of business etiquette and protocol crumbled. Castor had just sharpened this into something very personal.

'She tried to open a clinic for the poor of the city. I imagine she thought she would try her hand at a little charity, apply her skills and scalpels to some live bodies, instead of corpses. It was an unmitigated disaster, Master Hark. In three weeks, her clinic had a higher death toll than a battlefield. The police finally closed her business, and threw her out of the city. That is why she has come here,' Castor's finger pressed into the arm of his chair, 'to Fell Falls, to eke out a living burying the dead of the desert and the rail. Is that a life you want, to be a disgrace, like your aunt?'

The penny dropped, and with it Merion's hopes, dashed to splinters on Serped rocks.

Merion got to his feet. 'I think, Lord Serped, that I've outstayed my welcome,' he said, voice cracking ever-so-slightly.

'You will sit,' Castor demanded, the sharpness of his tone almost bending Merion's knees by force alone. 'We are not finished here.'

Merion took a breath. 'I cannot sign my father's empire away, even to you, sir. If there is another way that will get me home, of you representing my estate without signing it over, then I would be happy to discuss that,' offered Merion. *Hell, he would rush in circuses if he had to, if it paid for a ticket home. Whatever it took.*

Merion stared at the pen and shook his head. This legacy was all—besides his magick—that he had left of his father. How could he be expected to give it away to a man who kept a leech in his employ, who worked men to death on the rail, and sought the genocide of any Shohari within a hundred miles? Perhaps his aunt was right, he thought, and it stung him. *No*, this man was not worthy of what his father had built.

'That will not work, Master Hark. Ownership must be clear cut!' Castor was becoming angry now. His carefully laid plan had collapsed, and he knew it. He had cut too deep and now he was left covered in blood. 'The Crown wants your estate, Merion, and where there is a will, there is a way, to be ever so blunt.'

All his words did was make Merion walk quicker, even though every step meant a little more crushing disappointment. His heart slumped painfully in his chest as he turned and walked to the door. He was dizzy from wine and insult.

'I will see myself out,' Merion grunted, fighting back the waves of emotion now churning within him.

'Tonmerion Hark, I *demand* you sign these documents. For your own sanity, boy! For your father!' Castor yelled. His white face had turned a beetroot red. His finger was a rigid spike, waving furiously at the contract on the table.

Merion laid a hand on the door-handle and paused to think of some witty reply that would cut the Lord to the bone, and show him exactly how far over the line he had stepped. But nothing came. He chanced one last glance at Calidae before he made his exit. She had a disdainful grimace on her face. Even she was in on it, he realised, and that crushed his heart just a little bit more.

'I have never like being called "boy",' he said, before slipping through the door. 'I bid you all a good night, and a farewell, no doubt.'

'Hark! You leave now and this deal is off. The Crown will find a way around this, and Victorious will feast on your father's empire like a vulture feeds on a corpse!' Castor was still yelling.

The Lord Serped's only answer was the firm click of the velvet-clad door. Merion had gone.

Gile stepped forwards. 'Want me to go fetch him, your lordship?' he asked.

Castor sat back down and drummed his nails on the armchair. 'No,' he hummed, and then thought for a while. When his eyebrows raised, so did his finger, and he wagged it Gile. 'The aunt. Pay her a visit and bring her here, to me,' he whispered.

'As you wish,' Gile replied. He sketched a quick bow and hurried out of the other door, already cracking his knuckles and rolling his shoulders.

'We'll see where that boy's allegiances lie,' Castor thought aloud. Nobody dared answer him.

✶

Rhin had walked over his fair share of broken battlefields in his long years, and seen more than enough of gore and slaughter than he liked to admit—bones broken through skin, soldiers howling, insides splayed across a rock or a patch of grass. He truly believed he had seen every disgusting thing the world of bloody murder could offer him. He was wrong. Rhin let his mouth hang open as he took in every last grisly detail. The Serpeds had been busy.

The insectile machines hiding under dust covers had been put to use since Rhin had last visited. Their covers now lay on the floor, and their spider-like limbs were left bare for him to gawp at. Rhin was gawping, sure enough. His eyes wandered over the bodies in their clutches, over the tubes and syringes, and the way the ribs had been peeled back on the bodies, so that the heart could be drilled and tapped. There were seven of them, some Shohari, some human, each in their own machine, cradled within its claws and held aloft like meat left to cure. Tube after tube punctured their skin as their blood was slowly drained away, at a horribly precise rate. It was not enough to kill these poor souls, just enough to turn their skin grey and puckered like old leather, to make their eyes hollow and milky. They were still very much alive.

Rhin counted two women, one girl, and two men, one young, one old. The other two were Shohari scouts. One of the men wore the blood-smeared uniform of a sheriffsman. The women and the girl had the remains of servant attire wrapped around their bony ankles. Their nakedness was stark, and harsh on the eyes.

'Haven't the Serpeds been busy? Blood suckers, the lot of them,' Finrig sighed, staring up at the naked, open bodies, and the sleek curves of metal that held them.

'Monsters, more like it,' grunted Rhin. He could not tear his eyes away. Something cold and prickly unfurled within him, something that made him shiver.

Finrig spoke his fears aloud. 'Just think: your boy is having dinner with those monsters at this very moment. His throat may have already been cut, Rehn'ar.'

Rhin made to leave, but Finrig caught him by the arm. 'And where exactly do you think you're going?'

'You've got your gold. We had a deal and it's done. I need to find Merion,' Rhin spluttered.

Finrig tutted. Rhin felt the Fingers closing in around him. 'I've changed my mind,' Finrig said with a shrug.

Rhin struggled against the strong grip of two black-clad faeries. 'You swore you'd leave Merion alone!'

'And I will. It's you I want. As a prize for Queen Sift.'

'You backstabbing fuck!' Rhin yelled, showering spittle on Finrig's face. The Wit took a moment to grimace and wipe the mess from his face, leaving Rhin to struggle and strain.

'A hoard like that won't satisfy our good Queen, but your head might, and that means I get to keep mine where it is.'

Rhin was turning blue. 'I'll cut it off myself if you don't let me go!'

Finrig waved a hand dismissively. 'You are in no place to be giving orders, Rhin. We leave tonight, once Baelh is finished.'

'Half-done, Wit!' came a shout from the door.

'There, see?' Finrig patted Rhin on the cheek. 'We'll be leaving very soon. Want to get an early start. It's a long journey back to London.'

Rhin panted like a racehorse. His blood veritably boiled with outrage and panic. He could not leave Merion to those monsters. Not now. Not after all he had done to the boy already. Something inside of him, he did not know what or where, snapped. And it snapped hard. Rhin rammed his forehead into the nose of the nearest faerie, and used his crumpling weight to throw the other over his shoulder. The Wit already had his blade free, but Rhin was closer, and faster. He whipped his sword up so that the flat rested underneath Finrig's chin.

'I honour my bargains,' Rhin spat in his face. 'You honour yours. You leave alright, but you leave without me. On that condition I spare you.'

The Wit held up his hands and dropped the knife he had been spinning between his fingers. 'Alright, Rehn'ar,' he said, 'you win. See him out, boys.'

The Fingers cleared a path to the door and beyond. Rhin tasted freedom in the hot, muggy breeze. He used his sword to steer Finrig out of the barn, away from its terrible machines and out into the night. Baelh was almost done; the pile of gold was shrinking down, coin by coin.

'Off you go, Rhin, before it's too late,' the Wit spat.

Rhin drew a bloody line under his chin. He didn't flinch. 'If I see you again, I'll kill you,' he threatened.

The Wit just smiled. 'We'll see.'

And then Rhin ran. He ran as if hounds were chasing him. His wings powered his long, loping strides. His sword flashed in the lights of the town as it swung by his side. He had to get back to the house before it was too late, whatever in hell *it* was. Rhin only knew one thing. He had to get to Lilain.

CHAPTER XXXI
OF CLEVER BEASTS

'That damn boy, leaving the door unlocked. Maid almost walked in while I was showing him how to use a sword. Damn it if he hasn't got a tongue though. He convinced the old woman he was practising his waltz. Gods love him. I never thought I would count a human as a close friend. Roots, as my only friend.'

6th June, 1867

Breathless, the faerie sprinted. He could run for hours. He could run for days. He could probably run for weeks, and yet this handful of miles between the barn and the Runnels dragged and stretched and crawled past no matter how hard his wiry legs pounded the sand, no matter how hard his wings heaved and thrust him forward, no matter how many boulders he bounded or corners he whittled down. He kept his eyes on the house and its cheap yellow lights. Each glowing pinprick wore a sleepy aura in the rising mist. Rhin hung onto their paltry glow as if they were ropes to haul himself forwards on. The back yard was quiet and dark.

Words were nowhere to be found, neither on his tongue nor in his throat. He had hoped a few might have materialised by now, but all he tasted was dust instead, and the constant, cold vanguard of the storm. He could hear its rumbling in the distance, testing its voice for the evening's performance. Rhin rumbled also, clearing his throat of the sand and dry spit, and tested his own voice on the shadows.

'Lilain ...' he whispered with a wince. 'It's about Merion.'

'Merion's in trouble.'

'I'm a friend of ...' Rhin wondered whether that was too much of a lie.

'This is going to sound strange, but ... shit,' Rhin wrung his hands. 'It's all gone to shit!'

With that cry, a chill of fear and failure swept through him like a winter river bursting its banks. It nearly floored him, driving his hands to his stomach and his chin into his chest. He felt sick, and yet all he had to vomit was a strangled sob. Rhin spat his frustration on the floor and forced himself forwards towards the doorstep. This night was not over yet.

The kitchen was dark at its edges, the candle in the window, old and withered. Battered pans sat like battlements along the countertops, stubborn suds still clinging to their lips. The table was strewn with old paper and cloths. Spotless vials hung upside-down to dry on little spikes. Worried hands always find tasks to busy themselves with. There was no sign of Merion's aunt at the table, nor in the hallway. Merion's door was dark and no lantern hung outside in the road. Only a dim sliver of orange light crept out from under the basement door. Rhin took a breath. Why was he so scared? He had just robbed a human locomotive, for Roots' sake.

'And look how well that went ...' he muttered to himself.

The door inched open with a loud creak, and Rhin had to fight to hold back his invisibility, second-nature to him as it was. This all felt tospy-turvy, to be prowling in full and open view. Even in the hallways of Harker Sheer, Rhin had always crept unseen. But now here he was, on his way to break another promise, to reveal himself to Lilain, a letter no less, with his blood on her brain. He would have to be quick with his words instead of his magick for once. And still his tongue felt like sandpaper.

Perhaps it was the faerie's fear that distracted him, or his task, or just the simple fact he was not used to throwing a shadow. Fae magick wrapped light around itself. Shadows become obsolete with practise. As Rhin strode deeper into the room, and past a little candle sitting on the bottom step, his shadow crept with him, splayed on the wall, all haggard and monstrous. Had his eyes not been glued to the empty shadows at the end of the wall, he might have noticed. He also might have noticed the heavy blanket, the sandbags, the ropes, maybe even the huddled figure hiding between two bodies, waiting for just such a shadow to come creeping down her stairs.

The first thing Rhin noticed was the pain in his head. If felt as though a swarm of wasps churned between his ears. He could feel their wings and jaws scraping the meat from the inside of his skull. The second thing he noticed was his inability to move. Something cold and tough was wrapped around his wrists and ankles, even his waist. His muscles flared but he could not feel them move. The third thing was the fingers probing his bare stomach and pinching his legs. These were the coldest of all, and with every prod came a little mutter.

'And to think, you've been here all along,' somebody said.

Was he in Sift's dungeons? Was he in the corner of a rail car, with the Wit standing over him? Was he still in that rhododendron, half-dead and bleeding, dreaming this whole life up? Something sharp tested the back of his hand, and his eyes snapped open. He saw a wooden roof painted orange by a dozen candles. A shadow that was not his, jagged and bony, danced across it. Somebody was tinkering with something down by his waist. He tried to lift his head but found a strap of wire across his forehead, pressing deep into his skin.

'Lilain,' Rhin croaked.

There was a clearing of a clenched and excitable throat, and then:

'It speaks. Apparently in the common too.'

Rhin heard a scratching of a nib on paper. *She was taking notes!* The scratching was a little more frantic than necessary. Something in her handwriting was excited and nervous.

'I'm not here so you can bleed me, woman, I'm here about Merion!'

Silence. Rhin felt her fingers upon him again. She had removed his armour; that was clear. He could feel her clammy hands on his legs, his hips. It made him squirm to feel such foreign fingers upon his skin. Faeries do not like to be touched, especially by humans.

Rhin tried again. 'I know you've been waiting for this moment for a long time, Lilain, but it is not the right time! Merion's in trouble!'

'Has a deep understanding of the language. Voice, deep. Accent, slight. Unknown origin. Attempting to gain freedom with emotional response. Clever beast.'

'Woman, listen to me! I went to the Serped barn. They bleed people dry with these machines of theirs! Merion is in danger and you have to help me!'

The probing fingers retreated, shaking a little. A little worry mixed with the excitement.

'Faeries are well known for their trickery,' said Lilain. Rhin could see her shadow fall away from the table. *Was she speaking to him, or still stubbornly taking notes?*

'Yes, we are,' Rhin said. No point lying about it now. 'And for our lies, and our games, but we are also known for our loyalty.' That was less true, but at this moment, he would chance anything to save that boy. He sighed. 'And Tonmerion Hark is the finest friend I've ever known. He may not feel the exact same way at the moment, but if he's in danger, he must be protected. That's all I have ever tried to do.'

Lilain did not answer for what felt like an age. She just stood there, peering down at her prize and wondering whether it should be picked apart or let loose. The latter would crush her of course, but not as much as the death of her nephew. Lilain sighed, and reached for the ties around his arms, but not his legs. Rhin instantly sat up, but a wave of dizziness knocked him back down again. He rubbed his swimming eyes and contemplated retching.

'It's the chloroform. It will wear off soon,' she said.

That explained the throbbing in his head. A quick glance behind his captor, at the pile of sandbags lying in the dust, explained the rest. 'A little clichéd, isn't it?' he mumbled.

'Got a sharp tongue, haven't you?' asked Lilain, now wielding both a pen and a scalpel. The scalpel ventured closer than the pen.

'And you've got a sharper blade. Care to put that away?' Rhin pointed at the scalpel. He could already feel the burn from the little wounds on his legs where it had already kissed him. Rhin felt naked without his armour on. In truth, he pretty much was naked. Only a single strip of cloth protected his dignity.

'Until I know what's going on here, it'll stay out,' Lilain raised her chin. 'From the top, faerie, before I change my mind and see what colour your blood runs.'

✪

The trail was dark and wreathed in curling fingers of rising mist. Merion kicked at every single stone and shrub he came across on the path to the muddled lights of the town. He had left the riverboat alone and on foot, with barely more than a nod to the lordsguards at the dock. Something rumbled in the distance, as if the starless night was hungry. Merion didn't care for it; he had his own emotions to churn and stew.

Disappointment.

Anger.

Disgust.

Sorrow.

He tasted them all. Each burnt him, in their own strange ways, and yet he relished how they flared and rushed, how they made him sweat and clench, or twitch and ache. He used every scrap of emotion the Serpeds had given him and channelled it. Into what, he did not yet know, but he held a slight suspicion it might salvage his night somewhat. His hopes might have been dashed on rocks, but even rocks are bitten away by time.

The shock got to him more than anything. Shock that Castor would ask such a thing. That he would be so bold as to ask the highest price for a ticket home. That he would play such an intricate game to win his prize. It had been cold business, and that cut him even deeper. Part of him had hoped he would call Castor's bluff by leaving, if there was any to call. Another part imagined Calidae running after him, begging him to reconsider. With every step he took, those scenarios dwindled away to nothing.

The towering horizon rumbled again, and Merion swore he caught a flash of blue light in the upper reaches of the black sky. This storm was getting closer by the minute. He could feel its cold, vanguard breeze on his cheek, and the weight of the air as the storm postured and flexed.

There was more rumbling then, but not from the storm. Merion's heart leapt a little. A quartet of wheels could be heard crunching over the stony trail behind him, along with the sound of hooves, fast and heavy.

Merion turned with a half-smile, half-expecting to see Calidae leaning out of the coach window, waving her handkerchief to flag him down. No handkerchief. No open window. No Calidae. Just a darkened coach flying down the path, heavy in the axle and groaning loudly. The horses' mouths ran with frantic spittle. Merion had to step off the road to avoid being struck down. Not a shout from the driver, with his tall hat low and his face covered. Merion stared, open-mouthed, as the coach rattled past. He glimpsed a familiar face at the window, staring out from between the curtains. Gile, with a curious smirk on his face.

Merion did not move, not until the coach had careened around a curve in the road and disappeared from view. They were not headed for town. Not that Merion could tell. It almost looked as though they were headed straight to the Runnels. It was a deep worry that settled like a lump of ice in his heart. Merion began to walk, his strides starting out short and slow, but quickly became quicker and longer, until he was jogging after the coach. Before he knew it, he was sprinting after it, dust spurting from his frantic heels. Somehow he knew it. Somehow he knew he would be too late. He just did not know what he would be too late for.

'So these faeries have come here for what, for you? For Merion?' Lilain asked, walking in tight circles.

'For gold. For me,' replied Rhin, through gritted teeth.

'What does any of this have to do with the Serpeds, and Merion?'

'Because the faeries are hiding in the Serped barn, a few miles outside of town. That's where I saw their machines and the bodies, like I said.'

Lilain looked as though she wanted to wave her fist in the air, but instead she held herself back and crossed her arms. The scalpel was still in her hands. 'Lampreys.'

'I don't really care what you call them. Lamprey or not, they torture people in that barn of theirs. I've never seen machines so ugly and evil. And the people they held: young, old, women, children. They were still alive, kept that way so they could get every last drop of blood out of them. I won't let Merion succumb to that horrid fate.' Rhin spat what little saliva he had on the tabletop.

His vehemence seemed to satisfy her, for a moment at least. His fingers ached from making fists out of frustration. He did not know what else he could say or do to convince her. But if he failed to, it would be the feel of excitable, clammy hands and the cold steel of a scalpel. Lilain was about to reply when there came a thud that echoed through the floorboards above them.

Her head snapped to the faerie. 'Your friends?' She shot him a dark look.

Rhin shook his head, staring up at the ceiling. 'They aren't my friends, and no—that was a boot, or the butt of a gun, not a faerie. The Fae do not thud.'

'Lurker, maybe,' she suggested. 'Perhaps they let him out already.'

'Untie my legs, and I can go look,' Rhin said.

'Or run away. Don't take me for a fool, Fae,' Lilain hissed.

Rhin stood up as straight as his shackles would allow and stared Lilain right in the eye. 'There's no more running to be done. I ran to the other side of the world, to the very edge of civilisation, and still they came sniffing, still found me.' Rhin growled.

Lilain furrowed her brows and clicked her tongue. 'I know that feeling all too well,' she said, and then sighed. 'If you truly are Merion's friend, then, you're a friend of mine.'

'And you aren't going to bleed me?'

Lilain raised the scalpel above him and narrowed her eyes. 'Not yet, anyway,' she muttered, before teasing the shackles free and setting the faerie loose. Rhin slowly got up and stood with his arms crossed, as if to prove he had no intention of running.

'My armour?' he asked.

'The bowl,' she whispered. More thudding came from above, along with more boots on her floorboards. Lilain gently put down her scalpel and tiptoed over to a tall cupboard in the corner. Her gun hid inside it. Long Tom's cogs and levers glinted menacingly in the lantern light, like the complicated fangs of some skinny monster.

Rhin tottered over to the bowl in question and quickly pieced his armour together, from his legs to his shoulders. The cold metal felt good against his hot skin. He winced as he grazed one of the cuts Lilain had made. There came a loud crash from the kitchen, and Lilain looked at Rhin.

'Serpeds,' she growled, and the faerie nodded.

'My blades?'

Lilain reached for a nearby container. 'Don't let me down, Rhin,' she warned him as she crept forward, lowering the muzzle of her gun at the foot of the stairs.

Rhin's fingers strangled the hilt and haft of his sword and knife. *Maybe tonight was the night he would make amends*, he silently told himself. *Tonight he would put an end to all this nonsense.* They crept towards the dusty stairs, faerie and letter, each with their ears tingling with the sounds of banging and crashing. The intruders had moved upstairs, to Lilain's room and the study. The sound of crashing bookshelves and hurled boxes became constant, just like the pounding of heavy boots.

Rhin closed his eyes and tried to count them. Six, he guessed, picking the ruckus apart with his keen ears. Six men, and no doubt armed. No orders or voices. These were professionals, and they were looking for something. Rhin's mind began to churn. He gripped his sword tighter, conscious of how sweaty his hands were. He bit his lip and tried not to taste the fear at the back of his throat.

One by one, the boots fell silent on the floorboards. The only sound was Lilain's heart, beating like a war drum. There was a sheen of sweat on her brow. Her lips were tight and pale, and yet she held that gun of hers as steady as a rock, as if she were holding a new-born made of glass.

There was a creak as the door to the basement yawned. Shadows from the hallway skittered down the steps. Vague shapes of heads and arms. Lilain cocked her gun as quietly as she could. Rhin took a step towards the shadows at the edges of the room, sword and knife dancing back and forth to hide how much they wavered. He could feel his magick tingling in his fingers and in his stomach, ready and waiting. Nobody breathed. Not Lilain. Not the faerie. Not even the six men poised on the stairs, clubs and knives raised and waiting to fall.

Boots hammered the stairs like elephants galloping. An almighty thunderclap deafened the basement as Lilain fired too soon, spooked by a shadow. A chunk of wall exploded under the shot, half-blinding the first man down the stairs. He cried out but kept on coming, a heavy wooden pole in his ham-sized fist. Lilain frantically worked the levers of her gun as she reloaded. Just as the man raised the pole to strike, as the muzzle of her gun came close to poking the man in his belly, she fired. A gaping hole appeared in his stomach, blown right through him, and he reeled backwards, blood spraying like a fountain. Shouts and cries filled the air.

The other five charged forward, spreading out like hungry fingers. They knew speed was their ally. Rhin raised his sword and let his magick flow. His form shivered and faded as he darted towards the first challenger. Black Fae steel made quick work of his Achilles tendon, even through his thick boots. The man howled as he bit the dust. He fell silent when a sword was buried in his left eye, right to the hilt. Rhin snarled in his own tongue.

If the men were shocked to find a murderous faerie amongst them, they did not show it. Two of them began to circle the shimmering shape, their wooden poles and clubs banging the ground in unison, flicking dust to keep him visible. Rhin hissed at them, but they kept on coming, forcing him back into a corner. A club clipped him in the ribs as he tried to roll free, and he was sent spinning into the wall.

Rhin snarled again, cursing their mothers and fathers and every generation through time. He swung his sword as one man came too close, drawing a bloody line down his arm, but that did not deter him. Another swing, and Rhin took a chunk from his leg, baring his arteries to the hot air. This time, the man slumped to his knees and began to growl with pain. Rhin smirked, but his victory was short-lived; a wooden pole caught him square in the back and he sailed across the basement, leaving a neat hole in a wooden crate.

Lilain was faring no better. The remaining two men had managed to snatch Long Tom from her grasp, but not before one last thunderclap. The bullet ripped a hole in the dusty floorboards above, showering them with splinters as they struggled. Lilain fought like a caged demon let loose. She scratched at eyes and bit at fingers, kicking and screaming all the while.

For a moment it looked as though she would fend them off with her wild thrashing, but then a seventh man strode down the stairs. The way he strolled across the room, so casual, hands in pockets and whistling audaciously, was bizarrely threatening. This man had no mask nor hood, just a simple black bowler hat and a smart coat. He didn't even have a weapon. Lilain began to scream for help as the two men pinned her down on the table. The man in the hat came to look down on her as she thrashed and spat and screamed.

'No point yelling, ma'am,' he said, in a worryingly polite tone, the tone of a man who enjoyed his ghastly job far too much. There was something in his two-tone eyes that Lilain recognised. He was a rusher, pure and simple. That glint, that fire in his gaze was unmistakeable. 'Nobody can hear you down here. And even if they did, I doubt they'd care,' he added, with a gold-toothed smile.

'You can tell Castor to go fuck himself.'

The man smiled again, and tugged at the brim of his hat. 'Why,' he said, curling his hand into a fist, 'you can tell him yourself, ma'am.'

With speed that defied the eye, his fist shot out and struck her square in the face. Lilain sprawled on the tabletop, her rage suddenly and deftly extinguished. As she mouthed half-words and gurgled blood, the man leant forwards to whisper in her ear.

'And that was only a drop of mantis-shrimp blood. Imagine what a whole vial could do. Food for thought, letter,' he told her, as Lilain slipped into darkness. He sniffed, and pointed to the two men holding her. 'Take her to the carriage. If she struggles, beat her, but keep her alive. You two, tear this place apart and then burn it,' he ordered. The men obeyed him without a sound. Lilain was hauled away by her arms, dribbling blood across the dust and up the stairs. The other two slipped metal bars from their coats and proceeded to turn the basement into kindling and splinters.

From the shattered hole in the crate, Rhin watched bleary-eyed. The table was overturned and had its legs broken. Bottles, vials, and syringes were smashed to diamonds. The sink was kicked free and sputtered brown water onto the floor. Even Long Tom was broken in half and cast aside.

The man in the bowler-hat stood by and watched, hands once again tucked into his pockets. He waited until they had found the door behind the bookshelf, before whistling sharply. He strode forward, already unbuttoning his coat.

Rhin waited a long time for the man to return, and when he did, he was holding a cluster of vials in his hands. There was a smile on his face. 'Very nice, Hark. Very nice,' he was muttering. He turned to his cronies. 'Destroy it all,' he ordered, casual and cold.

They needed no further encouragement.

With his work done, the man strolled back to the stairs. Rhin's vision was becoming hazier by the second, but before darkness overtook him, he could have sworn the man caught his bleary gaze, and winked.

CHAPTER XXXII

OF CRIERS AND COWARDS

'I'm almost certain of it now. Somebody is stalking the grounds, right from the pines down to the lake. I've twice seen a shiver in the shadows, and this time I think they saw me. I swear I heard a hiss before they vanished. Found the footprints too, in the snow. Definitely Fae.

Three years. Three bloody years, and now they decide to come after me. I need to protect Merion.'

6th June, 1867

Merion saw the pillar of smoke clear and stark against the looming storm. A thin streak of ash-grey, painted against bruised grey-black. His stomach had already been in his mouth. Now it practically perched on his tongue. Merion wanted to vomit, but he forced his legs to run harder, faster. He could see the first edges of orange flame between the buildings, ugly and sore against the misty night.

Merion sprinted up the rise in the road and skidded to a halt in front of the house. Flames belched from the windows on the northern side, while the south oozed smoke through every crack and seam. The front door was broken and splintered. Merion's face hung slack and aghast. Even though it had felt like a borrowed home, it was the closest thing to a home he had, and now it was going up in flame and ash.

But Merion did not have time to wallow in horror and misery. His aunt could still be in there. That blasted faerie too. The boy sprinted around the side of the house, shielding his hands from the heat, and darted for the hatch to the basement. The latch was hot, so he used his shirt sleeves to slide it aside. Smoke poured from the spaces around its hinges. Merion yanked open the doors with a cry, and a cloud of black smoke billowed forth. The young Hark retched as he tried desperately to knuckle the sting out of his eyes.

'Aunt Lilain!' he yelled, but there was no answer. Merion slid his feet over the side and pushed, landing hard on the platform stuck halfway down the shaft. He had to wriggle into the basement on his belly, choking on the thick, acrid air. All he could see was a swamp of black and orange, thick with smoke.

Merion's face met the dust, hard, and he wheezed as the air was driven from him. 'Rhin!' he shouted hoarsely.

'Merion!' came the shout, somewhere to the right, in the darkness. By the Almighty it was hot, skin-peelingly hot. Merion winced as he felt the burn on his back.

'Where are you?' he cried.

'Over here,' said a shape, tottering out of the inky shadows.

'What the hell happened?'

Rhin waved his arm back and forth and flapped his mouth like a fish, but no answer came.

Merion knelt down to grab him. Rhin batted him away and almost fell over in the process. 'Where is my aunt? Where's Lilain?'

'They took her! Serped's men! They've only just left.'

Merion must have missed them on the turn to town. He had been too fixated on the smoke. He was frozen to the spot, half-choking, half-burning, and gawping at the new world he was suddenly party to—a world where houses were ransacked and burnt; friends beaten; family kidnapped; a world filled with lies and murder; magick and mayhem. They had taken his aunt hostage, to force him to sign the contract. She would be hurt, tortured even, until he did. *How could Castor behave so despicably?* Merion felt the rage surging within him. He buried his chin on his chest, trying to fight the tears that were rushing to his eyes. *Real men cannot be seen to cry*, came the words, echoing in his head over the crackle and snap of the fire behind him.

Merion let the rage loose. He scrambled for what was left of his aunt's bookcase, ducking the flames that were licking hungrily at the walls. 'And why didn't you stop them from taking her, Rhin? Tell me that! Too busy with your train robbery?' he shouted, as he dug through the broken, blood-soaked mess that was once Lilain's proud collection.

'I …' Rhin yelled, 'She and I were coming to find you. They burst in before we could leave. We killed two of them, but one knocked me out and sent me flying. I saw them take her, but … I couldn't help.'

Merion burst from the doorway with an armful of bottles and broken glass. He wasted no time in sprinting for the stairs. He barely spared a glance for the faerie as he hurried past, curling his lip in disgust. 'You coward, saving your own skin again.'

Rhin stamped his foot, and his wings buzzed angrily. He chased the boy up the stairs. 'I tried to help!'

'You should have tried harder!' Merion screamed. 'Now she's in Castor's clutches. Almighty damn it!' He looked around the hallway for something to kick, or punch, or strangle, something to destroy. He almost went for Rhin, but he did not want to waste any more time on the useless creature.

'What are you going to do?' asked the faerie, his face was hollow and miserable. His world had also just come crashing down, as any man's or faerie's will, when you recognise that streak of cowardice in your veins.

'Whatever it is, I'm doing it alone!' Merion shouted, heading for the bedroom. Rhin was left standing alone in the smoke-choked hallway, frozen and crushed by guilt. Rhin wondered if he should just let his legs crumple, and wait for the fire to take him. After all he had done, every wrong decision turned sour, it was probably for the best. Do the world, and the boy for that matter, a favour.

But that's what a coward would do, Rhin thought, and that put a kick in his bones. 'Merion!' he yelled.

Rhin sprinted into the bedroom. The fire hadn't yet eaten its way to this room, but the smoke surged nonetheless. The air was black, and Rhin could feel his lungs starting to seize up. He put a hand to his chest and wheezed.

'What are you doing?'

Merion reached under his pillow and brought out a gun, the Mistress that his aunt had forgotten to ask him for. Merion had hidden it there praying he would never need the ugly thing. He held it aloft and glared at it for a moment, even though his lungs were wracked with smoke and the life ebbing out of him with every single breath. He nodded to the weapon. 'What needs to be done. Castor Serped needs to learn what we Harks are capable of.'

Rhin stepped forward, hands clasped. 'We can argue about this in a minute, but we need to leave, Merion! Before the house comes crashing down around our ears!' he rasped.

Merion barked out his words between the clinking of vials and bottles. 'You can leave whenever you want, Rhin. I'm doing this alone. I have to save my aunt from Castor, and protect my father's name.'

'But that's suicide! I saw what Castor's men are capable of. You didn't. You're a fool if you go,' Rhin spluttered.

'And you haven't seen what I'm capable of,' Merion replied. 'And better a fool than a coward.' The coldness of his words managed to shock Rhin more than he liked to admit. He reeled.

'Merion, please ...' he said.

But Merion would not be convinced. He shook his head, stuffed the handful of unbroken vials into his pocket, and set a brisk course for the front door. 'Don't you dare follow me,' he spat, as he kicked his way through the broken panels.

Rhin ran for the back door with his hand clamped over his soot-smeared mouth. He slipped easily through a hole in its lower half.

The faerie stumbled across the dirt towards the outhouse, retching and coughing into the clean night air. He was suddenly aware of something pelting him on the back and shoulders, of how his feet dragged against the ground. It was beginning to rain, and rain hard. The mighty storm had finally arrived.

Rhin dropped to one knee so he could soak up the cool drops that battered him and the soil around him, which had already turned halfway to mud. Great clouds of steam began to pour from the blackened ribs of the house, and Rhin found himself letting loose a huge cry of relief. At least the weather gods could find it in their hearts to be kind, Rhin thought.

The faerie pushed himself back to his feet and looked around. The night was awash. Clouds rumbled overhead. And Merion was gone, marching towards death or victory at the Serped riverboat. Rhin bit his lip. Of course he was going to follow. Merion had called him a coward, and by the Roots, if that wasn't a challenge to prove him wrong, Rhin didn't know what was. He would see his sins washed away tonight, even if it killed him. He may have been a coward, he may have cheated, lied, and murdered … and here Rhin paused to look at the raindrops exploding at his feet … but even a coward can find redemption in a hero's actions. Rhin drew his sword with a ring, and set his own course south, for the town and its shadows, for a jail and a certain occupant incarcerated within. If anybody knew something about redemption, it was Lurker.

✶

'What's goin' on?' came yet another shout from the crowd.

The lordsguard held up his hands once again and called for calm. The crowd was multiplying, he swore, growing bigger every second. There must have been five hundred of them already, a sea of green overalls and stern faces, staring right at him. What a shift to pull.

'Please, gentlemen. I've been informed the locomotive is running late, but that it should be here at any moment. Now, I want you to form ten orderly lines in front of these tables here, ready to collect your wages,' shouted the lordsguard, so that everybody could hear.

'How late?' came a question, hollered from the back of the crowd.

'Half an hour at most,' lied the lordsguard. The station master hadn't a clue. He was busy being useless, peering into the gloom to see if he could spy anything on the tracks.

'We want to be paid!' somebody else bellowed.

'And you will! Just a little longer!' The lordsguard snapped his fingers to his lieutenant and beckoned to him. The younger man came closer and threw a quick salute.

'Yes, Captain Orst?'

'I want you and the men to move slowly outwards around the crowd. Form a perimeter, but do it gently and quietly. I don't want any trouble. This crowd will be hungry for blood if they don't get their coin, hear me?'

'Yessir.'

Orst waved him away and turned away to mop the sweat from his brow. This was going to be tough work if this blasted locomotive didn't turn up.

Something struck him in the shoulder, and Orst turned to glare at the crowd, half-expecting to see vegetables, kitchen implements, or tools flying towards him and his men. Nobody had thrown anything. He felt another on the back of his hand, and realised what was happening. The heavens were opening their floodgates.

'Great,' Orst muttered himself. He beckoned to the station master. 'News?'

'Nothing at all on the tracks, sir,' he whispered over the drumming of the rain and the grumbling of the growing crowd. 'Something tells me it may have run into some trouble.'

'Mechanical?'

The station master bobbed his head from side to side. 'Possibly. Or somethin' criminal.'

Orst felt a little something stab him in the gut. 'Bloody hell,' he muttered, before straightening his hat and turning back to the crowd.

'Gentlemen! Workers! It seems the locomotive has had some trouble ...'

The crowd erupted in angry words and shouts.

'What kind of trouble?'

'Is it lost?'

'Are we ever goin' t' get paid?'

'Listen to me!' Orst bellowed, going some way to quelling the outrage. 'It isn't lost. It may just have been waylaid ... *delayed*, that is to say ...' Orst felt like biting his traitorous tongue off right there and then. He watched the crowd inch forward. Fists began to punch the air.

'Waylaid?'

'As in *robbed*?'

The magic words. There's always one in every crowd.

Orst held up his hands as some of the workers began to inch forward. He could see the panic-stricken looks in the eyes of the guards as they crept around the simmering crowd. 'No, that's not what I ...' he tried to explain, motioning for his men to move in.

'Where is our money?'

'They've lost our money!'

'How long do we have to wait now?'

Orst began to back up. Some of the workers had reached the platform and were already busy climbing up. Orst put a hand on his sword hilt and tried to wave them back. 'Now listen to me! I am an officer of his Lord Serped, your employer. This is not my fault. Not if the train got robbed! Stay back, I say!'

One particularly burly man with a slick of ginger hair and a smattering of freckles stepped out of the small group that had now assembled on the platform. The station master had legged it, and Orst could already hear the shouting of his men as they were overrun. The burly man cracked his knuckles and shrugged. 'Well his lordship ain't here, so seeing as you're his officer, we'll have to take it out on you, won't we?' he said.

'Back I say!' Orst yelled, swinging his sword out of its scabbard, but steel was useless in the face of the pure anger of a mob. Many things are.

'Back!'

As Orst fell back under the heavy blows, his head cracked upon the platform and his mouth hung open. He could not help but taste the raindrops, and taste how sour they were. Like acid.

Then again, it may just have been the blood.

No matter how hard Merion tried to avert his gaze, his eyes kept creeping back to the gun held firmly in his hand. It was too heavy for his liking. His arm already felt weak, and it had only been half an hour since he had left the burning house.

The rain he was glad for, but not the mud. It turned his journey into a slog, hindering his need for haste. Over and over again he asked himself what exactly he was doing, what he hoped to achieve. Doubt ran through his mind like a cockroach scurrying from the lantern light— doubt mixed with fear. He was about to walk into the snake pit, so to speak. Merion knew that all too well. Memories of Suffrous and his display flashed before his eyes, mimicking the sporadic lightning that darted across the angry sky. Could he fight him? Would a quick bullet to the head suffice? Questions plagued him with every step.

Thunder rolled in the wake of a lightning flash, and Merion found himself wishing for a coat, or an umbrella. He was already soaked to the bone, and there was nothing he could do about that. All he could do was shelter the Mistress and hope that rain wouldn't jam it. Looking down at it again, Merion wondered whether he could use it, were he pushed. Could he stoop as low as his murderer? He imagined the sight of his aunt tied to a chair, bloodied and beaten, would certainly be enough to throw him over the precipice. If murder had to be committed to protect her, then so be it. That was the truth in its basest form. Merion felt the hot flush of that simplicity through him. It steeled him, and stirred something monstrous inside of him. He let his blood boil, and it felt good. It felt powerful. That rage shouted down the doubt and fear enough to keep his feet moving through the slick mud.

Merion threw a quick look over his shoulder to make sure Rhin wasn't following him. You could always spot him in the rain. The droplets clung to whatever cloak of invisibility he wore, making his shape easier to see. It was the one flaw of that particular Fae magick. The road behind him was empty, as it should be. No sign of the coward.

Merion did not regret a single word he had uttered to the faerie. It was how he felt, simple as that. Rhin had let him down time and time again, and this time, now that he had stood by while his aunt was kidnapped, was the last straw. Merion let that new anger swirl with the current, and together they helped him burn.

With a wet hand, he rummaged through his pockets and checked his vials. Some of the labels had been blackened or smudged with other blood, but as far as he could tell he had quite a selection, despite the odds.

Ox.

Blue whale.

Pigeon. *Useless.*

Mongoose.

Bobcat.

Flamingo.

Turtle.

And electric eel. *Thank the Almighty.*

Merion prayed that these would be enough, and as he smudged the labels with his wet fingers, he wondered what combinations he could make, and whether he dared to.

It was then that he heard a squawk from behind him. Merion whirled around to find Jake flying right at him. Merion threw up his hands and Jake flared his wings, coming to a stop on the boy's left arm. He winced as the magpie's claws sunk in. 'What is it?' Merion asked, staring into the beady eye of the bird.

The magpie chattered something utterly incomprehensible, and Merion shrugged.

'I don't understand, I'm sorry,' he apologised.

Jake chattered again, this time flapping his wings and bobbing his head. Merion kept his eyes fixed on the bird's good eye and poured all his concentration into it.

'War,' Merion said. Just one word, like a bell chiming in his head.

Jake nodded his head eagerly. The claws unfortunately sank deeper. Merion gasped. 'I can't do anything about it,' he said. 'What am I supposed to do?'

Jake cawed loudly in his face.

'Jail? You mean Lurker? I don't have time. They have my aunt!'

The magpie screeched at him before launching himself back into the rainy sky. He circled once, cawing something disapproving, and then flapped back towards the town.

'I'm sorry,' Merion shrugged. Lurker could not help him now. He was in jail, surrounded by sheriffsmen and steel bars. Ox blood would do it, but he needed that for Castor, and his guard dog Gile.

Merion looked down at the gun once again, and let his finger trace the curve of the trigger—practising, almost, for that moment when he would put a bullet in somebody.

There was just one other factor that he had not yet considered, partly because he refused to, and that was Calidae. What side would she choose, when his aunt's blood was spilled, and Merion's gun fired? He let that question hang unanswered in the dark parts of his mind, stowing it away for later. He hoped he would not have to ask it of her. The last thing he wanted was Calidae as an enemy.

⋆

Lurker sniffed at the cold air, and the droplets of rain that splashed through the bars. 'Don't smell right,' he murmured. He looked up at the night to watch the downpour and the lightning playing in the storm cloud's canyons and valleys.

'Don't smell right at all,' Lurker shook his head. 'Sheriff!' he yelled, pressing his face up against the bars of his cell. 'Sheriff! I need to talk to you.'

There was a bark of laughter and cursing from the room along the hall, and then a sigh. A shadow moved against the brick, and sure enough, one of the sheriff's lackeys ambled down the hall.

'If you've shit yourself, I swear to the Maker, I'll break your—'

'I don't shit myself, man, it's the Shohari!'

The sheriffsman crossed his arms and put his head on a slant. 'What about 'em?'

'They're goin' to attack again. Tonight,' Lurker said.

That seemed to put a little kick into the man. He straightened up and came a little closer. 'How'd you know, traitor? You tip them off? Feeling guilty all of a sudden, are we?'

'No, I mean, yes. You have to warn somebody,' Lurker urged him.

The sheriffsman snorted. 'And what if that's exactly what the Shohari want us to do? Huh? What if this is a little plan of yours, you and your painted monster friends. Nice try, traitor.'

The man began to turn away, but Lurker reached through the bars and grabbed his sleeve. 'Please, you got to—'

Lurker had seen many strange and horrible things in his time, but this one had to take the prize for both categories. Before Lurker could finish his sentence, a hazy, rain-soaked shape jumped onto the sheriffsman's shoulders and sank a glass-like blade into his throat, cutting a neat crimson stripe across his skin, and opening his veins to the air. Lurker grabbed his other arm and held him upright against the bars so he could clamp a hand over his mouth. The eyes of the sheriffsman were wild and frantic as the blood dribbled

'What the *hell*, Rhin, you demented bastard? They'll kill us!' Lurker mouthed.

'They won't have time to notice. The town is rioting over late pay,' hissed the faerie, materialising out of the air. 'In about ten seconds they'll be out of that door and we'll be left alone to deal with him.' Rhin held the sheriffsman's head as he struggled.

'Rioting? Shit.' Lurker pressed his forehead to the bars. He suddenly didn't care about the blood any more. 'The Shohari are about to attack for a second time.' Lurker sniffed then, and said: 'And you smell like gold. Lots of gold.'

Rhin frowned and shook his head. 'None of that matters right n—'

There was a bang as the door at the end of the corridor flew open. Two lordsguards burst in and hollered at the top of their lungs. 'The workers are up in arms! There's a damn riot on Main Street! We need your help!'

Another chorus of cursing began as the sheriffsmen scrambled for the door. One of them called out to the dying sheriffsman. 'Iker, get a move on! There's a riot going on!'

Lurker acted quickly, shouting out on behalf of the unfortunate Iker. 'I'll be right there! You go on!'

'Well, hurry up!' came the reply, but the man was already halfway out the door.

'See?' shrugged Rhin. 'And you even did a reasonable impression, too.'

Lurker let the man slump to the floor, but not before relieving him of his keys.

'You were saying?' he asked as he unlocked his cell door.

Rhin took a breath. 'It's Merion. And Lilain. The Serpeds have taken her and Merion is on the war path. He's taken a gun and is marching on Castor's riverboat right now. We have to help, or he'll get himself killed.'

Lurker looked as though he were having a hard time processing all of that information at once. He scratched his shaved, scarred head, wondering how long he had actually been in jail. 'How?' he croaked.

'It's a long story and one we don't have time for.'

Lurker took one last look at the dead sheriffsman, pulled a wry face, and then nodded. 'I need my hat. It's raining,' he said as they jogged down the corridor.

'I don't know about that, but your gun is hanging on that wall,' Rhin replied, managing to keep up with Lurker's loping strides.

Lurker had already spied it, and was currently tucking it into his belt. He also took a spare rifle from a rack. He was about to leave when he noticed a hat hanging from a peg. It was rounder, and sandier in colour than he liked, but a hat was a hat, and he couldn't go without. He grunted, and slipped it onto his head.

'You done?' Rhin snapped.

Lurker nodded, pulling the brim of his new hat low. 'Lead the way,' he growled.

The house was a smouldering, hissing wreck when the Wit and his Fingers arrived. He stood in the middle of the muddy road, crossed his arms, and tapped his feet. They stood in plain sight. The town's thoughts were on the riot that had abruptly sprung to life, and was raging through the streets. Doors in the Runnels had been tightly locked, and windows shuttered. If a house fire could not gain their attention, then a gang of thirteen heavily armed and armoured faeries would hardly cause a stir.

The sky rumbled and Wit shrugged. 'Let's see what we've got,' he ordered, and his Fingers swarmed forwards as one. He strolled behind them as they picked their way through the blackened, sodden wreckage of the front door. The downpour was showing no signs of letting up, and though fortunate for a burning house, it was a terrible inconvenience for faeries on the hunt for other faeries. The Wit was in a foul mood now. There was knife-work to be had, and his fingers itched for it.

His eyes fluttered as they illuminated the smoky, wet darkness for him. Everything was black. The upstairs was gutted, and the kitchen had fared no better. The Wit could still feel the heat in the floorboards beneath him. The rain had a job left to do. As the Fingers prowled and poked about in the corners and under fallen beams, Finrig moved to the right, to the one room the fire had failed to turn to charcoal, some sort of bedroom.

The Wit stood in the doorway and let his eyes wander, as they had a habit of doing. He drank in every grubby little detail, every crease and burn, every corner, every … There was a mound of something under the bed. Finrig moved forward, hands creeping onto his knife, eyes widening to take advantage of what feeble light the stormy night had to offer.

Then came lightning. The night froze, drenched in haunting blue light, and in that blinding flash, the Wit saw his prizes, strewn across an old and dusty suitcase, wrapped in old clothes. Bending underneath the frame, he began to pick through the moth-bitten detritus: a whetstone that fit his hand perfectly; a fork far too small for any human; shoes made of thick leather, just short of the Wit's own; and paper—reams of paper covered with crude and tiny diagrams written in stolen ink. This was a faerie's den, just as sure as the Wit was a bastard.

But Finrig did not seem at all happy. He let his wings rattle angrily. Rhin was nowhere to be seen. The Wit pulled out his knife and poked around in the mess, looking for something to assuage his dark mood and itchy fingers. There was a dull thud as the knifepoint found something unyielding. He flicked a cloth aside to uncover a small but thick book, bitten at the edges and yellower than a beggar's teeth.

'What do we have here?' The Wit whispered to himself. Faeries were great keepers of books, but the road was not a joyous place for those with heavy packs. If a faerie carried a book with him, there was bound to be an important reason for it. His knifepoint tickled the corner of the book and made it yawn. The Wit sank down to peer at its scrawled words, like the barely legible scribblings of a shivering child.

The Diary of Rhin Rehn'ar.

The Wit did not need to read any further than that to make him smile. He reached down to seize the diary and then backed out from under the bed. His Fingers were standing, waiting.

'There ain't nothing here, Wit. Not a sniff of the boy or Rehn'ar,' spat one of the Fingers.

Finrig smirked, tucking the heavy diary under his arm. 'I think there may have been a falling out of the houses, lads,' he said.

'Trouble in paradise?' chuckled another.

'Looks like we've got some more walking to do.'

'Which way?'

Finrig looked around at the blackened walls. 'To a finer house than this, that's for sure. Might even get some loot out of it, once we've wiped our blades,' he grunted with a grin.

The murmuring of eager anticipation that followed would have chilled any bone in your body, and sent your soul scarpering, had you been unfortunate enough to witness it. The Wit sheathed his knife and pointed to the door. 'Let's get to it,' he barked, and the Fingers did his bidding with a will.

CHAPTER XXXIII

TRIGGER FINGER

'The fucking Wit. Of all Fae, Sift sent him, and his Black Fingers, all twelve of them. They stepped right out of the bushes at the foot of the tower, as if they were out for a stroll. It was a miracle they weren't seen. I thought I would have to fight my way out, but Sift had sent him with an offer — an offer of truce if I handed back the Hoard. I couldn't tell him I had given it away, especially not to Karrigan. They threatened to cut Merion's throat if I didn't. And mine. Roots damn it! After all these years!'

6th June, 1867

Hearts are treacherous things. At times they can beat so proudly it feels as though they will burst from your ribcage at any moment. They can drum a tune to run to, or fight to, or love to. But they are not to be trusted, for every heart will skip or slump, sickeningly so, and always when you need it not to.

Merion cursed his quietly as he stood, dripping, on the rise above the landing. His feet were numb blocks, his hair a matted, swimming mess, his clothes chafing strips of cloth, and his legs dead and buried. But his heart was the true criminal, slinking away, deeper into his chest, purged of all vim and vigour.

The riverboat sparkled through the thick curtains of pouring rain. A hundred lights glittered along its side, yellow, white, some even red.

Smoke scattered from a half-dozen chimneys, chased by the storm. She looked altogether too awake for Merion's liking.

Merion gripped his gun as tightly as his numb fingers would allow, and gritted his teeth. He stirred up every dark thought, every desperate mental cry, every flash of emotion he had borne to that muddy rise, and brought them to the boil again. He felt the heat spread from his face to his chest. Slowly his heart began to lurch and obey. Slowly his blood began to simmer again. Lurker had told him that boiling blood was a fine thing every once in a while, and that time was now. The young Hark bared his teeth and set off down the hill, keeping his gun low and slightly behind him. Two hooded figures stood at the riverboat's gangplank, guns on their shoulders, and looking entirely too miserable. Merion racked his brains as he marched through the mud, as the lightning flickered around him, bleaching the night into terrible starkness.

They had seen him. He was only a hundred yards away now. Even the rain couldn't hide him in the orange glow of the riverboat. Merion slipped the vial of ox blood from his pocket and set the glass to his lips. He could smell the copper stinging his nostrils as he flicked his head back and drank it down, putting the red in his belly. The vial was thrown to the mud and crushed underneath his shoes as he marched.

Confidence was his ploy, he had decided somewhere about halfway down the hill. That, and the innocence of youth. Merion pasted a sad and desolate look on his pale, rain-streaked face as he approached the two men. They were already signalling him to halt. One had raised his rifle. Merion kept the Mistress out of sight, carefully turning it around so he could hold her by the barrel.

Twenty yards now, and already he could feel the hot blood coursing through his veins. Now his heart wanted to thunder, that was for sure. He had to strain hard to keep it from bursting into pieces. As the blood entered his skull his vision swam, and for a split second he faltered, almost tumbling into the mud.

'Stop there, I said!' shouted one of the lordsguards over the hammering of the rain. He was peering out from under his hood, trying to get a gauge on this bedraggled wastrel. *Was it just a boy, just a young lad?*

Merion held himself hard against the magick as it yanked at every fibre in his scrawny body. This shade was strong indeed, but then again, oxen do have a reputation for strength.

The lordsguard was now jogging to meet him, holding his hands up. 'Just hold it there! Damn it, boy. What are you doing out here in the —Ooof!'

Merion swung that gun as though he were trying to shake off a tiger. The handle caught the man square in the jaw, and Merion winced at the wet, squelching *crack* he heard as most of the guard's teeth were ripped free of their sockets. The lordsguard flew backwards and collided heavily with his awestruck comrade. There was a shocked cry, then a *bang*, and then an even louder cry as the two men landed in the mud. The second guard had shot himself in the foot, and now half of his boot was missing. Sprinting over to the man, Merion drove a fist to the side of his head, knocking him out cold. Merion grunted as his muscles screamed for more. His legs felt as though they were going to gallop off without him at any moment. He was wise to follow them.

With a grim face, and thoughts of what he had just done ricocheting around his skull, Merion marched for the gangplank. Those men probably had families to feed. Now they had lost their teeth and a foot. Merion had done that to them, and it made his teeth chatter.

'Whatever it takes,' he growled at himself, repeating it over and over until each syllable became a stamp of the foot. He was rushing the blood of an animal four times his size. It felt as though there was an ox trying to explode out of his own skeleton. It took everything he had to contain it.

The door shattered in two kicks, and suddenly Merion was standing inside the plush atrium of the riverboat, alone and bewildered, breathing like a locomotive at full speed.

There were no lordsguards in sight. There were no bells, no sirens, or shouts. Just the drumming of the rain on the windows and hull, and the repetitive groaning of thunder. The storm had drowned out his approach. Merion headed right, following his earlier route, though this time he had no servant to guide him.

Up the stairs and right again.

Merion found a guard at the top of the stairs. The man was already unslinging his gun from his shoulder, a curious look on his face at the sight of a bedraggled, mud-splattered boy running at him at full pelt.

'Halt!' he cried, just before Merion barged him into the opposite wall, breaking a picture in half and leaving a man-sized dent in the woodwork. The noise was horrendous. Shouts came from down the hall. Merion's brain was still being overridden by the blood and his anger, but whatever they were doing, he was happy to go along. The boy grabbed the nearest thing he could find: a small table, and lifted it above his head. With a grunt, he threw it just as two guards rounded the corner. The table caught them in the faces, one after the other as it span through the air. There were more cries, and more teeth skittering over the floor. Merion gulped, but somehow he knew he had to fall a little deeper into hell, before he could climb back out.

'Better press on,' he growled to himself. His own voice managed to scare him.

Hearing further shouting, Merion decided to dip into the nearest room, to sneak through the inner doors until he founded that blasted, roasting sitting room the Serpeds insisted on frequenting. If they were expecting him, that's where they would be, sitting smugly in their armchairs while his aunt was tied to hers. He would smack the bloody wine glass right out of Castor's hand, Almighty help him.

Merion made sure to rush hard before he stepped through the door into the next room. Feet fell outside his door and clattered on, leaving him alone in the dark, ornate study he had found. The room beyond that was a little brighter—a smaller lounge with windows looking out onto the river. Merion scowled at the luxurious chairs and sparkling decanters lining the shelves.

Merion put a hand to the next door and took a breath. If he was right, this was the infernal sitting room. The door handle certainly felt warm enough. Merion put a hand to his chest and tested his magick, letting it dizzy his head. He was about halfway through, he could feel it. He would have to make this quick, whatever the hell *this* was. Raising his gun, he cocked it as quietly as he could manage. The single click of the mechanism sounded like a thunderclap. Merion put his hand on the door handle. His palms were slick with sweat and his fingers shook. A twist and a push, such a simple movement for all the weight and danger it carried.

The light inside the room was hot and blinding. Every candle shone, every lantern blazed, and the fire crackled defiantly in its place. Merion blinked as he strode into the room, waving his gun in wide sweeps until his eyes adjusted.

'I'm insulted,' said a voice, rasping like a file. Unmistakeable. Merion rubbed the stars away from his eyes and saw Castor standing near another door, Gile in tow, and grinning gold as always. Castor wore a venomous glare. 'To bring a gun into my house. How positively common of you. Can we not settle this like gentlemen?' he asked, raising open hands.

Merion could taste the poison in his tone. He shook his head, disgusted. 'Gentlemen do not play sadistic little games,' he growled, waving his gun between the two of them. His finger ran along the trigger, itching and yet cowardly at the same time. The blood raged, urging him on, begging him to rip their arms from their sockets, but something held him back. 'And lords don't dirty their hands with kidnapping. It seems you are neither, Serped. You should be ashamed of yourself,' spat the boy.

Castor was unarmed, as far as Merion could tell. There was no gun at his hip, no dangerous bulge hiding under the folds of his perfectly tailored dinner suit. Gile was half-hidden behind his lord, arms crossed and twiddling his fingers, waiting for something.

Castor looked as though he were eager to get this over with. 'Have you heard the saying "All's fair in war and business"?' he asked.

'Where is my aunt, Castor?' Merion cut to the chase.

Lord Serped sneered. 'Waiting for you to save her, Hark.'

Merion was trying. 'Then give her to me,' he said. 'No more men need to have their faces broken tonight.'

'Her release is not conditional on how many jaws you break, Hark,' Castor snapped. He reached inside his pocket and dragged out a tightly rolled scroll of papers. 'Sign your estate over to me, and she will be yours to take.'

'And if I don't?' Merion had to ask.

Something hungry twinkled in Castor's eyes. 'Then Mister Gile here,' he gestured to his associate, who had the sick audacity to wink, 'would be happy to help you stuff her broken body into a barrel and shove it overboard. Wouldn't you, Mister Gile?'

'More than happy, your lordship,' Gile breathed.

Merion lurched forwards, spit flying from his bared teeth and his gun pointing straight at Castor's forehead. 'I will shoot you, if I have to. Make no mistake about it. Don't push me ...' Merion threatened, still wondering whether he could or not.

Castor cut him off with an unnerving laugh. And there it was, the difference between man and boy, carved in the air between them. Merion was rash and angry and hot, Serped calm and devious. That laugh rattled the young Hark deeply, blood or no blood. He felt the tremor in his hand, tried to stop it creeping to the muzzle. Castor and Gile were already smirking. He wouldn't give them the satisfaction.

As Merion tried to rush his blood back into a frenzy, Castor walked around him to erode his authority. Merion tried to keep the gun on him, but Gile was already creeping forwards, fingers delving into his coat, his strange eyes narrowed.

'What did you think would happen here tonight, Merion? You thought bringing a gun and a handful of vials to my door would break me, did you not? You thought you could save your aunt with force, with intimidation, with a little spark and gunpowder, am I correct? Thought Mister Gile and I would just capitulate, fall to our knees with a few harsh words, is that it? Pah!' Castor sneered, the very definition of belittlement. 'You have no idea of the hands working behind the scenes, or the power they wield. This is not about you, or I, but about the Empire. If some must die for the preservation of the many, then so be it. This isn't one of your fairy tales, boy. There are no happy endings here for y—'

Nobody was more surprised by the gunshot than Merion. He had to look, just to make sure he had fired the bullet. There it was: his own finger was wrapped tightly around the trigger, holding it against the wall of its tiny metal cage. Merion's mouth hung agape. His traitorous heart slunk away into his chest. His legs began to wobble.

Gile was dumbfounded. All he could do was hold Castor as the lord fell back, a horrible, twisted grimace on his face and a hand clamped tightly to his chest. Blood seeped from between his white fingers.

'You bastard, Hark!' Castor cried, between tight lips. 'You fucking bastard.'

Merion could do nothing but croak and gag at the smell of gunpowder pouring from his gun. He wanted to see it fall to the floor and be done with the horrid, murderous thing. But his finger would not let go. Something inside Merion held on, something ruthless and daring—the very same something that had pulled the trigger just a few short moments ago.

'Aagh!' shouted Lord Serped as Gile dragged him to a nearby armchair. Suffrous had turned a bright shade of red, a crimson storm cloud brewing in his cheeks. His hands were shaking too. Castor was already pointing at Merion with a crooked finger. 'Get that boy! I want him tied up next to his aunt. And I want a bloody doctor too, Gile!' he screeched.

Merion darted for the door as Gile reached inside his charcoal coat. Though not for blood; that would be too slow, even for a man like him. He reached for a gun instead, a stubby, six-barrelled pistol with hammers that curved like claws. Gile moved like lightning, and as Merion wrenched open the door, the gun began to thunder. Merion dove headlong for the safety of the corridor. Bullets burst through the door, ending in explosions of splinters and varnish. One after the other, they pounded a viciously neat line into the wood. Several zipped through his clothes without a scratch, but the very last clipped his ear, and sent him sprawling on the floor in a shower of blood.

The pain was searing. Merion clapped a hand to the side of his face and ran for the stairs. The boy knew where his aunt would be, where any self-respecting lord would keep a prisoner: away from prying eyes, in the hold.

The ox blood was dwindling now. By the Almighty did he feel weak. Maybe it was the blood, pouring from his head, or the fact that he had just shot a man. Merion could only shrug and hurtle on. This was about Lilain, not he, and that was the first time he could ever remember knowing what selfless meant. He was not quite sure he liked it, if this was what it took.

'Tonmerion!' came a howl. He couldn't tell whether it came from Gile or Castor, but he was not waiting around to find out. He ran on, barging two guards into opposite walls as he sprinted around the corner. The ox blood was not quite done yet. The rolled-up eyes of the fallen man were testament.

'HARK!' somebody screeched. It sent a shiver down Merion's spine but still he kept running.

Two more lordsguards stood at the bottom of the spiral stairs, but two swift kicks saw them both out cold and bleeding. Merion's legs were beginning to ache, as if he had run a marathon to be there. He needed to rush again, before he collapsed. He sprinted on.

The first door led to a cupboard full of brooms. The second unleashed a cacophony of engine noise. The third revealed a row of bunks, mercifully empty. The fourth, however, was a cargo hold, and drenched in darkness. All save for the feeble glow of one tiny candle, sitting in the centre of the dark cavern. A shadow sat next to it. Merion shut the door behind him and weaved his way between the crates and support struts and ropes. There, in the middle of the hold, at the centre of a circle built of boxes, sat his aunt, tied to a chair with only the candle for company. Her head lay heavy on her chest, and her legs were at awkward angles from each other. Droplets of dried blood polka-dotted her bare and muddy arms. Her long hair was tangled and matted.

Merion took a deep breath to keep from crying out. He clicked his fingers in front of her face and tapped her lightly on the shoulder, but she did not stir. He shook her, gingerly, as if he were worried her head would come loose and fall into her lap. 'Please, be alive ...' he prayed. He shook her again and elicited a moan. Faint, but a noise nonetheless. Merion rocked her from side to side and pressed a hand to her knee.

He got more than a moan this time.

'Faaaahh!' Lilain wheezed, eyes wild and bloodshot. She struggled against her ropes as she bit down hard on her lip.

Merion looked down at his hand and realised what he had done. Her kneecap was completely shattered. Blood had seeped through her trousers and turned them a deep crimson.

'Fucking Castor,' Merion cursed.

'Fucking Castor indeed,' Lilain whispered hoarsely. 'Water?'

Merion shook his head, feeling suddenly guilty. 'Only blood.'

'There.' Lilain nodded to a nearby crate, where a skin of water had been left draped over a corner.

Merion grabbed it and pulled the cork. He sniffed it and pulled a face. 'It's wine.'

'Screw it,' Lilain rasped. 'I need something.'

Merion obliged her. She coughed and she spluttered, but she managed a few gulps, gasping as the sweet wine met the cuts on her split lips.

'They've ruined you,' Merion mumbled. He had pictured it with every muddy step on his way to the riverboat, but now he was here, he just wanted to be sick.

'Thanks,' she said, trying to wink with one puffed-up eye.

'Was it Gile? A man named Suffrous Gile?'

Aunt Lilain nodded. 'Most of the time. Castor too, when he was bored of watching.'

Merion pressed his fists to the floor.

'And your Calidae too. She was here,' Lilain sighed. 'Watching just like her father. Not a trace of emotion in that bitch's face.'

'Aunt, please.'

'You have to know, Merion. In case I don't make it out.'

Merion was about to protest when shouting echoed through the hold, muffled but closing in, accompanied by the heavy thumping of boots.

Merion emptied his pocket of vials and spread them on the floor. 'I'm not done yet, Aunt. I came here to rescue you and that's exactly what I intend to do.'

Lilain smiled, or winced, Merion couldn't tell. 'Ever your father's boy,' she said, with a pained gasp. 'And what happened to your ear?'

'Bullet from Gile. Protect the family name and all that,' Merion said, trying to sound nonchalant. His voice cracked instead. He looked to his vials.

'Blue whale. Mongoose. Pigeon. Turtle. Eel. Bobcat.'

'Drag me over there, between those two tall boxes. Careful now, and I'll tell you what to do,' Lilain told him. Merion thanked the Almighty for the last few scraps of blood. He rushed them hard and fast, letting them swirl around his head.

But this was no time to dabble in euphoria. He seized the back of the heavy chair and pulled, letting Lilain's feet drag on the floor. She bit her lip and screamed in her mouth. Merion scrunched up his face and pulled harder, faster, remembering what his old nurses had told him of bandages and ripping them off quickly.

'The quicker it's done, the sooner it's ...' Merion paused to lift the chair over an uneven floorboard before stopping. '... over.'

Lilain was on the verge of passing out. Her head swung back and forth and she moaned in one continuous stream of delirious pain. Her legs were twitching. Merion tried not to listen to the crunching of her cracked bones.

'Bastards,' Merion hissed, and in that moment the horror felt from pulling that trigger was forgotten, and his finger itched for it again, ruthless, and daring. 'I'll kill every last one of them. They'll die just like Castor.'

That seemed to wake his aunt up. 'Are you saying you ... *killed* Castor?' she squeaked.

'I didn't mean to ... I ...'

'Good.' Lilain spat a purple gob of spit on the floor. 'About time somebody did. But you aren't a murderer, Merion. Just get us out of here.'

'Just one more then,' Merion said quietly. There it was again: that inner voice that scared him deeply.

'Gile.'

Merion listened to the shouting and banging for a moment. 'He's a leech, like me,' he replied.

Lilain looked at him then, through the matted strands of her hair, and Merion saw something sad in her eye, something beaten. 'Read out your vials again, nephew. Let's see what we can do.'

Merion ran back to his vials. He rattled them off as quick as he could. 'Blue whale. Mongoose. Turtle. Eel. Pigeon. Bobcat.'

Lilain took a breath and closed her eyes. 'Blue whale. If you can stomach it, gives you the ability to create shockwaves by clapping your hands. Or fins, if you're unlucky. Mongoose. Fast reflexes and sharp teeth. Bobcat, again sharp teeth but a ferocity that will be hard to stomach. Turtle. Protective magick. Hardens your skin to a shell. Not your shade, but maybe, if you're strong enough ... Pigeon. Used for homing. Can increase concentration ...' Lilain took a moment to wince and shift in her seat.

'Can I mix any of these?' Merion blurted. He could hear banging at the end of the corridor. His heart thudded, almost painfully.

'You're not ready for that,' Lilain gasped. 'We don't know what shades you can mix.'

Merion spluttered. 'Gile can do it. How am I supposed to ...'

'Pigeon,' Lilain exclaimed.

'Pigeon?'

'Pigeon!'

Brooms clattered on the floor. Engine noise blared.

'Mix it with the mongoose, quickly!' his aunt urged him. She was shaking in her bonds, eyes constantly flicking between him and the faraway door. 'They'll hit you both like a brick, so hold on and concentrate.'

Merion nodded, and as he walked slowly back to the centre of the dimly lit circle of boxes, a candle his only ally, he uncorked the vials and knocked them back. *Putting the red into his belly*, Merion muttered to himself, as he felt the sour sting in his throat.

CHAPTER XXXIV

"ROTTEN AS THE REST OF THEM"

'I knew I had to take it Karrigan. I had to ask him outright, and show him I was serious.

He saw me in the shadows of his fire before I had a chance to call out. I told him of Sift and the Black Fingers' visit, told him of the White Wit and who he'd threatened. Merion. I asked him for a Hoard to pay them off. He told me no. With barely a thought. I asked again. He told me it was impossible. He ignored my pleas. His face was like stone. I see why Merion fears him the way he does. I saw then why they call him the Bulldog.

His fucking son, I told him. And if that wasn't a reason to pay them, I didn't know what was!'

6th June, 1867

The blood kicked him like a mule, never mind a brick. Merion fought the urge to double up as his stomach roiled, just as the door to the hold burst open under the force of boots and rifle butts. The hinges shattered and the door lay flat with a loud bang. Merion flinched. His hands were shaking. It felt as if every strand of muscle in him shivered uncontrollably. Merion winced, trying to work it into some sort of fearless grin as four lordsguards rushed inwards.

Merion stood his ground, unmoving. He stared down the barrel of each rifle in turn, daring them to crackle. The rushing blood and swirling magick made him bold. And then in walked Calidae, small gold pistol in her hand and a vicious glare on her pretty face. Her hair was coiled up in a tight bun, and she wore a slim black dress with frills at the bottom. Merion narrowed his eyes, wondering whether she was a friend or foe. He desperately hoped it was the former. Gile came next, holding a very pale Castor under his arm. Ferida was there, glowering just as darkly as her daughter. She too had a gun, though she was too busy making sure her husband could stand to wield it. The whole family had come out to play.

Merion felt very alone in the centre of his circle. His eyes flicked from one Serped to the other, and then to Gile. He could see it right away, the way his eyes jittered and flickered, the way a glimmer of sweat sat on his brow, the way his knuckles burned white: he was rushing, though Merion had no idea what.

'So here he is, the murderer,' Castor sneered, his voice a hoarse rattle. His coat was soaked with dark blood, and despite Ferida's dabbing, the wound continued to ooze. Castor would die, but not before he'd seen his murderer die at the hands of his manservant.

'The monster,' Calidae spat. The viciousness of it made Merion wince again.

'And yet you're the ones who kidnap an innocent woman, tie her to a chair, and beat her senseless,' Merion retorted. He had never spoken to Calidae like that, and the shocked look on her face confirmed it. Her gun rose up an inch or two. So did Merion's. If Calidae had chosen a side, then so be it. Her wiles would not work on him anymore.

'Did you think you could get away with this, boy?' Castor wheezed. 'Come into my home, shoot me, and steal my prisoner? Audacious, Hark. Foolishly so. Just like your dead father.'

'He was a fine leech, it must be said,' muttered Gile. His wild eyes had not yet left Merion. The young Hark stared right back, letting them wax lyrical and threatening. Merion just wanted to get on with it, whatever it was. The blood surged in him, waiting to pounce. The mention of his father had made him boil.

'And my father would be doing the same thing, were you trying to cheat him instead of me.'

'We're trying to help you, Merion,' Calidae hissed.

Merion sneered. 'You're trying to rob me, Calidae, all of you. Thieves. I expected better from a lord of the Empire,' he goaded them.

'How dare …!' Castor gasped, as he struggled to stand straighter. 'You foolish little boy, you dare to lecture me on being a Lord? You are nothing, Hark, not even a shade of your father. You have no idea what it requires, and no idea how lost you are out here. Alone. Forgotten. There will be nobody to bury your corpse when Gile is finished with it, nobody to write home and apologise to. Your estate will be divided up and carted away. Dizali will see to that, as will her Majesty. They will be most pleased, when I present them with your signature.' Castor cackled. 'Calidae?'

Calidae raised her gun, saying nothing. Merion steeled himself, but then he realised that she was not aiming at him, but rather, just past his arm, at his aunt.

'No,' he said, instantly standing between them. 'Leave her out of this.' Merion raised his gun up to match hers. His finger shook. Castor was one thing, but Calidae …

'She's one of them,' Lilain hissed at him. 'Don't you dare hesitate.'

Castor held up the contract, surprisingly untouched by his oozing blood. 'Sign it, boy, so we can get on with burying you.'

'Sign the contract, Merion, or I'll shoot her,' growled Calidae.

'You'll have to shoot me first,' he said defiantly, hoping there was some vestige of fondness in her, hoping it hadn't all been an act. 'I won't move.'

'Calidae …' Castor urged.

'Just sign it, Tonmerion,' she told him. 'There's no way out.'

Merion's eyes darted back and forth, looking for any hint of a twitch in her aim, or a crack in her cold voice, like winter ice meeting spring. No matter how hard he looked, there was nothing. Not a sliver of the humanity he had glimpsed there before. Like her father, she was nothing but false promises and deceit. He had been duped by her fluttering eyelashes and little smile, and now that all else had been burnt or cut away, he could see her true self. It was as rotten as the rest of them.

He drew himself up to his full height. 'Go to hell,' he said, before swinging his gun to the left and opening fire on Castor, and Gile, the guards, the whole lot of them. Merion didn't aim; he was too busy pulling the trigger, and wondering how many bullets this contraption had in it. He just wanted to keep firing until all of these people were gone, and he was alone.

Five was all it sputtered. Merion looked up from the pounding hammer of the gun.

Castor was sliding down the doorframe, leaving a bloody smear on the wood. Ferida was splayed on the floor and still as bone. Gile was somewhere behind the boxes, saving his own skin. One lordsguard clutched a knee and howled. The others were shouting and throttling their guns, ready to fill the young boy with lead.

So was Calidae, Her mouth hung agape, and her eyes raged with fire. She stared down at her shoe, and her mother's hand that rested on it, limp. Lifeless. Calidae looked up at her father, and found him pointing at Merion with a weak and crooked hand. 'Kill him, daughter!' he croaked.

Calidae needed no further encouragement. She too opened fire, marching forwards with each wrench of the trigger. Merion felt the icy cold flush of fear as the gun was levelled at him, but he had forgotten his blood. It surged through him, pouring magick into his muscles and tendons, making them quick. The first bullet flew at him, and Merion watched it fly past as he ducked. The next came, and it too slid past him without a scratch, Merion marvelling at how it spun as it flew, the air rippling behind it.

Four bullets came at him and four bullets slipped past him. He was so enraptured by this strange new ability, that he didn't notice Calidae bearing down on him. Only when she pressed the barrel of her gun against his chest did he notice. Before even he could react, there came a horrifying click that froze them both. Her gun was empty.

Merion moved like lightning. He knocked the gun aside and brought his own down on the side of her head, just above the jaw. She was out cold in the space of a blink. Almighty, if this mongoose blood wasn't fast.

'Gile!' screeched Castor, somehow still clinging on, even though blood now oozed from his stomach as well as his chest. Merion had aimed true. Fate seemed to want Castor dead as much as he did.

Suffrous Gile emerged from behind a crate with murder in his two-tone eyes. He held his hands out flat and upturned so his fingers could curl like claws. Electricity jumped between them, crackling, sparking and making Merion take a step back. He needed something to attack with.

'Blue whale!' hissed a voice from behind him. Merion delved into his pocket and fumbled for his vials. Gile was entering the circle.

As Merion knocked back the whale blood, Gile pounced. He put his hands together and reached out for Merion. Lightning shot from his fingers. Merion dove for cover, the mongoose blood still working its magick. Gile swung the lightning after him. Lilain cried out as a finger of it caught her across the chest, searing its mark on her skin. Merion kept scrambling. He could feel the heat snapping at his heels, but the mongoose blood kept him just out of reach.

'It's always a shame, killing another leech,' Gile said, as he let his magick die away for a moment. 'Aren't many of us left.'

'And there'll be one less after this,' Merion spat. He was panting. His blood may have boiled but his body was still that of a very tired, and very burnt-out boy. His muscles screamed.

But the magick was swirling again, pounding in his chest and surging into his skull to dizzy his eyes. Merion crouched low, a smaller target for what it was worth. Gile stood his ground on the other side of the circle, smiling his golden smile as always.

'Come on. Let's see what you've got,' he coaxed the boy, taunting him.

'With pleasure,' Merion snarled, as the whale blood reached its apex.

Clap your hands, his aunt had said, and the young Hark did so with a will. He slammed his hands together and let the blood pour into them. A wave of magick burst forth with an ear-splitting boom of thunder, rippling the air as it rushed towards Gile. He tensed himself, but it was no use. The wave hit him hard, throwing him through the row of crates behind him.

Merion was instantly on his feet and striding forward. He held his hands poised, but it was his tongue that stole the moment. It felt itchy, eager to move. Merion opened his mouth as he felt the magick surge up his throat, as if he were about to be sick. Merion's tongue curled against the roof his mouth and then hammered down against the back of his teeth. Ordinarily he would have been rewarded with a satisfying click, but the whip-crack that ripped from his mouth instead was a lot more interesting. Merion watched as the crate next to Gile's heard burst into a thousand vicious fragments. Gile cried out as splinters punctured his skin. He lashed out with a fork of lightning, sending Merion reeling back and clutching his arm, where the skin was suddenly ripped and raw.

'Nice try, Hark,' chuckled Gile. The man was terrifyingly casual. Merion backed away again, wincing at the pain. He clapped again, taking Gile's legs from under him. He aimed a kick but the man grabbed his foot and twisted, sending Merion spinning to the floor with a cry. Gile was instantly upon him, raining blows down on his shoulders and ribs. Merion tried to scramble away, but Gile had him pinned.

Merion's tongue came crashing down once more. The sound wave rebounded from the floor, snapping several of the boards, and threw them both into the air. Gile landed on his back, while Merion spun into a nearby crate, a sharp splinter of wood cutting a neat line across his temple. He reeled, blinking furiously as the blood came pouring down.

Gile was putting a vial to his lips. 'No,' Merion coughed as he struggled to stand.

'Have you ever heard of the archer fish?' Gile queried, as he tensed his muscles for the rushing.

Merion wiped the blood from his eye with the back of his hand. 'No,' he sighed, trying to stop his head from spinning. He raised his hands to clap again, but he was having trouble focusing the rushing magick. It was too slippery.

'A fish from Indus,' Gile intoned. He kicked open a nearby crate with a heavy boot, and several bottles wrapped in twine rolled onto the floor. Something clear sloshed around inside.

'Merion …' Lilain croaked.

'It's known for its mighty clever ability to spit water like an arrow. Knocks insects down from branches and so forth.'

'How interesting,' Merion replied.

'Turtle, Merion!'

Merion reached into his pocket and felt around. *Only four left.* He flicked the cork away with his thumb and shook the vial into his mouth. This blood was sourer than the rest. It stung his aching mouth like acid.

Gile was already swigging the water down, gulps and gulps of it, until the bottle was completely drained. When he was finished he hurled it at Merion, catching the boy off guard as he concentrated on controlling yet another burst of magick in his chest. Merion fell to the floor, the bottle glancing off his thigh and making his leg go numb. Merion crumpled to the floor.

Gile took a breath and a step forwards. He pursed his lips together, as if he were going to whistle, and then heaved. Merion rolled onto his back just as a sharp jet of water shot across the circle. It struck him in the dead centre of his back.

Merion took a breath, ready to wail at the feeling of his spine breaking in two. *This was it*, he surmised. He had been bested.

But all he felt was a heavy pounding on his back. No pain, just a violent jolt that pushed him onto his knees. Merion clapped a hand to his neck and felt the ridges of a shell instead of skin through his ripped shirt. He panicked for the briefest of moments, and then grinned.

Gile fired and missed again. The bolt of water left a dripping hole in the floor, barely an inch behind Merion's foot.

Bolt after bolt sprang from Gile's pouted mouth, ripping holes in boxes and turning crates to wet splinters. Merion crawled for all he was worth.

A lucky shot caught his leg, ripping the sole from his shoe and sending the boy spinning to the floor. Another splinter caught him, carving a bloody trail across his cheek. Another bolt pounded into his back. The shove reverberated around his skull. His knee throbbed. Waves of pain shot up his leg. Something was broken, but he had no time to worry. Gile was taking a deep breath, fists clenched and thrown backwards, belly swollen with air and water. Merion scrambled, digging for magick inside his veins. Panic had ripped the edge from his shades. His beating heart had pounded it to dust. The mongoose was petering out, the whale was also dying, and Gile was savvy to it now anyway.

Merion fumbled for his next vial, but his hands were too busy shaking. His body felt like molten lead, slowing him, chipping away at that vicious resolve.

They say the Almighty works in mysterious ways, that there are no coincidences in life, only design, that the sharpest minds are oblivious to whatever architecture lurks behind the scenes of this world. But mysterious was not the word the nearest lordsguard would have used, as he stepped forwards to try and seize the boy from behind the crates. It would not have been a word, but a gurgled scream.

A blur of grey and glinting black steel had appeared on his shoulder. Before Merion could blink, blood was spraying from his neck in a fine crimson jet. Pain and horror came in a wailing, bubbling cry. The guard dropped his rifle, squeezing off a round off in his panic. With the blood draining quickly from his skin, he looked at the small figure hanging from the sword embedded in his neck, at the blood spurting from the artery it had sliced.

'Rhin!' yelled Merion, scrambling to his knees. Gile had been momentarily frozen by shock. It wasn't every day something invisible came to slice your throat. His mouth hung agape as he watched the blood spray a knotted pattern on the wooden floor.

'Don't just sit there!' Rhin shouted in reply. 'Fight!'

A clatter of explosions deafened the hold. The other two lordsguards had opened fire on the vicious, shimmering attacker. Their panic was their downfall. Their bullets ripped straight into the lordsguard's stomach, putting a swift end to his howling. Rhin wrenched the sword free and disappeared between the crates.

'Kill it! Whatever it is!' Gile bellowed at his two men. He took a sharp breath and turned to smite the boy, once and for all. But Merion was not where he had left him. A wave of thunder punched him in the ribs and sent him spinning into a box. The sharp edge caught him in the kidney and he roared in pain.

Merion dug the next vial from his pocket with frantic hands. The whale blood was exhausted now. It was time to kick this up a notch. *Electric eel*, said the label. The blood rushed down his throat and straight into his veins. His body veritably hummed. Merion could already feel his fingers tingling, his bones swelling.

Gile had found his feet, but not for long. Merion threw his hands out like the talons of a diving falcon. Lightning poured from his fingertips in a twirling, blinding stream. Gile dived for cover, but the magick caught his legs and clung on. Gile fell to the floor writhing, grimacing in pain. Merion strode forward.

More shots rang out from the guards. More cries. Light flashed as Rhin cast his own spells. He darted between the cargo as if he had been born here in the hold, flitting in and out of invisibility. Here and there he would jab, or pounce. More cries, more shots.

'If you would like to offer a word to whatever god it is you pray to, the time is now,' Merion spat, as he stood over Gile, fingers clawed and crackling.

'Mercy,' begged Gile, still shuddering. 'Mercy, I beg of you. I'm just a servant, a lackey.'

'You're a torturer and a bully,' Merion spat again, this time almost in Gile's face.

'Castor made me do it …' Gile whimpered, holding his hands over his face.

Merion furrowed his brow, making his lightning flare for a moment or so. Although the blood urged him on, he couldn't help but spare a glance at Castor, still slumped against the doorframe, blood trickling from his mouth. His eyes were glazed, fixated on the floor between his knees. It was not the moment to spare a glance.

Gile pounced like a leopard, slipping a vial between his lips and then striking Merion in the gut. He hit him again in the face as he doubled over, right in the nose. As the blood began to trickle, the lightning burst from his hands. But Gile weathered it, growling as he got to his feet. The boy was reeling from the blows. Gile rained down several more before reaching inside his coat with shaking hands and retrieving a long vial full to the brim with dark, almost purple blood. As Gile gulped it down, Merion spat some of his own on the wood, wheezing.

As Gile reached down to seize the boy, the skin on the back of his hand convulsed and rippled. Merion heard the snapping of cloth as Gile's body swelled and grew, bursting at the very seams of his clothes and skin. His teeth grinned like fangs, gold and bloody. Then he was towering over the boy, heaving and swollen with muscle. His aunt was already screeching at him.

'Get away from him, Merion! Get away!' she warned, but Merion was too dazed and too weak. Gile grabbed at him, fingers spring-loaded and iron-clad, and lifted him into the air.

The young Hark waved his hands frantically as he felt the air being squeezed from him. Sparks shot in all directions, but Gile had taken him by the throat and under his armpit, holding him impossibly tight. His legs flailed like those of a hanged man. Some of the broken crates caught light and began to crackle with fire.

In a stolen breath, Merion briefly thanked the Almighty; the turtle shell was holding Gile's bulging, vein-ridden muscles at bay—even if just for the moment. He could feel it creaking under the strain. Gile roared in his ear as he pressed even harder, driving the boy against his bulging chest. Spit streamed from both their mouths. Their eyes were wild, locked as were their bodies in an even battle of willpower and magick.

But Gile had no intention of playing nice. He whirled around to shout to his lordsguards, baring his cowardice for all to see. 'Over here, you oafs! Shoot him in the chest!' he yelled.

'Dirty tricks!' Merion choked. Despite the shell, Gile's huge arm still pressed against his throat. He could feel the shadows clawing at the edges of his vision, trying to drag him under. His lungs burned.

'This ain't no fairy tale, boy! This is real life, where men will do whatever they must to stay out of that yawning grave,' Gile whispered in his ear. 'You were brave, boy, but a fool. Shoot him, for fuck's sake!'

One of the lordsguards turned to take aim, but something slashed at his leg and he fired into the ceiling instead. There was another cry, and the man disappeared behind a box. Merion gasped.

'I won't let you get away with this!' Merion wheezed. 'I ... can't ...,'

'Accept it, boy. All it takes is one bullet, and then we'll have two lords to throw in the river tomorrow,' Gile snapped. Merion could hear the desperation in his gruff roar. 'Shoot him now!' he yelled again, squeezing harder than ever.

A tear rolled down Merion's cheek, in the middle of all the burning, crackling chaos. It could have been the fact his head was being slowly squeezed to pulp, but Merion knew better. It was his first acceptance of failure, of frailty and the inexorable. He hated himself in that moment.

But hate can make men, and thirteen-year-old boys, do marvellous things.

The young Hark closed his eyes and tensed with all he had—until his hair stood on end, until his ears popped, and his eyes strained to escape, until he felt every single molecule in his body shiver and pull to be free. The blood rushed like a storm through his veins, as uncontrollable as the one that was raging in the sky above, and just as savage.

'SHOOT HIM!' Gile screeched.

The magick burst from him, pouring out in great, crackling spheres. Merion was sure his bones had snapped, that he had come to pieces. *At least he would go down fighting*, he thought. But it was not to be. Not today.

Gile practically melted under the force of the spell. His own magick withered instantly as his bulging flesh erupted and sizzled. His scream was short-lived, but it was ragged and horrified all the same. Merion fell heavily in a heap, just conscious enough to see Gile writhing in a heap of his own, his skin smoking. He clawed at the air like a blind kitten, but it was useless. The hold stank of pork and burnt cloth. Merion retched, sprawling and clawing at the tortured wood.

'Rhin!' he gasped, when he had found his voice. 'Where are you?' His lungs felt as though they were full of gravel. There was no intoxication now. This shade had turned on him; all he knew was pain.

'Get up, Merion!' came a hoarse cry. Merion blinked, wondering if his eyes were damaged or if the hold was slowly filling with smoke. It was the latter, his nose informed him. He could smell burning wood. A flash of pain across his skin told him it was getting hot.

'You need to get up! Come on, you can do it. Just roll onto your front and push yourself up,' the voice instructed him.

Merion did as he was bid, though it felt as though it took him an hour. His muffled, pounding ears heard the crackling of a dozen different fires.

'I'm up,' he breathed, swaying like a young willow. Panic and urgency were as forgotten things to him. He moved like a ghost across a battlefield, searching for its body.

'Untie me, quickly now!' his aunt urged. Merion nodded and began to fumble with her ropes. Rhin was soon at his side, grim-faced and drowned in blood, as if he had crawled through a corpse to get there. The fact that he stood there, broad as day in front of his aunt, did not even factor. War and death have a habit of making mockery of the little things.

'The town is rioting. The Shohari are about to attack. We need to leave,' the faerie mumbled over the hissing of the flames. His black Fae steel made short work of the frayed ropes.

A numb Merion stared down at his aunt, looking at her bruises and cuts. There was a fresh gunshot wound in her shoulder now, from which blood oozed at a steady pace. There were burns on her knees from the waves of electricity. Merion felt a pang of guilt. *As if she had not already gone through enough.*

Lilain tried a half-broken smile. 'I don't think I'll be running out of here.'

'Merion,' muttered Rhin. 'The bobcat blood.'

'Huh?' Merion swayed again. He felt ruined. He had barely even realised he had won.

'The ferocity. You need it.'

'He's right,' said Lilain. 'Drink it.'

Merion was flabbergasted. 'I can't rush any more. Not after ...'

'Yes, you can, slowly but surely,' his aunt encouraged him. 'We need you. You beat him, Merion. You did that, and you can do this.'

They were right. The bobcat blood stoked something up inside him, and brought some of the battered pieces together. Within minutes he was dragging his aunt across the blood-stained, splintered floor and past Gile's burnt and twisted body. He stopped, even though the fire was now raging around them, to stare at his handiwork.

One side of the man's face was a molten hole where his cheek used to be, splattered with gold and blackened bone. One eye was milky white and bubbling, the other vacant and dead, staring at the ceiling. His right arm was withered to a burnt claw. Merion could spy blacked stubs of rib poking through his jacket. He sighed, and kept dragging.

Calidae's dress was already smoking when they reached her. So were the bodies of Castor and Ferida. Castor seemed to be staring right at him, even in death. Merion scowled and reached down for Calidae's arm. He may have been a killer, but he wasn't a murderer.

'Rhin, help me,' Merion gasped under the weight of the girl. The heat was unbearable in the hold. The fire had broken through the ceiling on the far side, spiralling up into the middle decks of the riverboat. 'I can't carry her.'

Rhin obliged, grudgingly, seizing the girl's other wrist and helping to pull while Merion carried his aunt over his shoulder. Lilain wanted to scream, he could tell, but she did not. Up the stairs and through the burning atrium they staggered. Pillars came crashing down around them. The heat was searing. Sweat dripped and poured. No sooner had they reached the riverboat's main exit than an explosion rocked the vessel. The fire had reached the engine room, and its precious flammable oils and lubricants.

'What ...?' Calidae moaned as she cracked open her eyes. At the sight of a bloody Merion and a small black creature wrapped around her wrist, she started to scream.

'You bastard!' she cried, clawing at his arms and leaving long scratches down her arm. Merion gritted his teeth and snarled. 'You let me go this instant!' she screeched.

'I'm saving your life, you idiot. Or haven't you noticed the fire?' Merion shouted.

Calidae had not, but now her gaping mouth and wide, bloodshot eyes said differently.

'My father? Mother!'

'Dead,' spat Lilain.

Calidae seethed as she tottered to her feet. Her hands hung curled as fists at her side. She glared at them, one by one, though her gaze faltered slightly when it came to Rhin, until she could bring herself to speak.

'Then I will die with them,' she hissed, backing away. Merion snatched for her, but she darted away. 'I'd rather die than accept your help.'

Merion growled, baring teeth sharper than normal. 'Don't be a fool, Calidae! You don't need to die for those murderers!'

But Calidae shook her head stubbornly.

Lilain pulled at her nephew's sleeve. 'Let her go, Merion. If she wants to die, then let her. The world will be a better place.'

The bobcat blood told him his aunt was right, but the human clinging on inside him said otherwise. 'I've seen that look in your eye, Calidae. I know you doubted what your father was doing. Come with us. Start over.'

Calidae looked up as the stairs began to fall to pieces, crashing in swirling clouds of sparks. 'You've destroyed everything we worked for …' she muttered. 'Everything.'

'Trust me, I know the feeling, now come on! Please!' Merion urged her.

Calidae simply smiled, waved, and turned to face the inferno. She raised her hands and walked slowly into the centre of the atrium, to feel the world burn down around her.

'Leave her!' Rhin snarled, pulling the boy away. Merion bared his teeth, but he knew Rhin was right. *She was as rotten as the rest of them,* he reminded himself, as he trudged towards the smoking hole that was the main door.

CHAPTER XXXV
THE DIARY OF RHIN REHN'AR

'I stewed for days, hidden in the tower. I put on a brave face for Merion, but inside I raged. Like old times. Dark times. Karrigan had dismissed me as a fool, and coldly condemned his son to cold Fae steel.

'Stop dragging Merion into your tiny little world of lies,' he had said.

That made me boil. I couldn't allow him to do that to me, or to his son. He is a stubborn fuck, and I knew there was only one way to make him listen to me, to get him to understand how important Merion was, how terrible a father Karrigan was and how much Merion needed me. Like he always bloody has.

It didn't take much to get into his study ...'

7th June, 1867

The night that greeted them couldn't have been further from the blazing havoc they left inside the riverboat. Instead of searing heat and thick smoke, they were met with biting rain and a wind that tugged and pulled at their limbs and clothes, trying to steal them away into the darkness. Merion blinked furiously as the rain lashed his face. His eyes were blind from the fire. The night was black and impenetrable. The boy staggered into the darkness, as each lightning flash painted the edges of the world.

Thunder rolled in the wake of a blue flicker, and he saw the trail leading up to the rise only a few hundred yards away. 'This way!' he cried to Rhin, who was already casting around in the shadows, wary and silent. His sword was out and on guard.

Merion sloshed through the mud. He could see his feet now that his eyes were adjusting, now that the fire was breaking out through the windows and doors of the riverboat and giving the desert a faint glow. Oranges, yellows and reds met the bruised black of the night sky. The hot colours played in the puddles around his tattered shoes.

'You said the town was rioting?' Merion asked over the drumming of the rain.

'It is,' Rhin hissed.

'Why?' Lilain whispered. She was getting heavier with every step.

'They didn't get paid,' muttered the faerie.

Merion snarled. 'I wonder why.'

Another lightning strike turned the night into day, and Merion saw the two lordsguards still sprawled on the ground, ruined faces lying in the muck. He bared his sharp teeth again and battled on.

'We'll get to the hill, then we'll take a look at you,' Merion told his aunt. She didn't answer, and Merion shook her, eliciting a groan. He was not about to let anybody else die tonight.

'We need to get Lurker out of the jail,' Lilain breathed.

'I wouldn't worry about that,' Rhin replied.

Yet another fork of lightning split the sky. Merion froze. 'Rhin,' he snapped. 'Stay here.'

'What?'

Merion pointed as the sky flashed again.

Thirteen little figures stood in a line in the mud, a stone's throw away.

Darkness returned, and despite the hot glow of the fire, they had vanished. No matter how hard Merion peered into the curtains of rain, he couldn't see them.

'Friends of yours, Rhin?' Merion asked, pawing at the empty space at his belt where the Mistress had been. She was now lost to the fire and the flame. All Rhin had to offer was a nod.

When the next flash showed the canyons in the clouds above, Merion squinted. There they were again, somehow closer now, yet unmoving, standing still with their arms crossed across their black breastplates, hooded and pale-faced. Merion slowly bent an aching knee and slid his aunt from his aching shoulder.

'What's going on?' she asked, the wet mud jolting her awake.

'Faeries,' Merion hissed.

Lilain squinted through blood and puffed-up eyes at Rhin, standing beside her. 'I only see one,' she replied. Merion gently put a finger against her swollen cheek and turned her head, just as the lightning came once more.

Thirteen little figures were standing all around them, etched in rainwater and cold light. Lilain pushed herself upright as the tallest of them marched forward. His face and armour glowed orange in the firelight. As if they had not already dealt with enough that evening.

'Your handiwork, Rehn'ar? Or the boy's? he asked, bold as brass.

'Who are you? What do you want?' Merion challenged him.

The faerie looked shocked, and batted Rhin a look of disbelief. 'Haven't you told him about me, Rehn'ar?' he said.

Merion raised his chin, eying this intruder up. He had never seen another faerie besides Rhin. Now he was surrounded by thirteen of them. He couldn't help but stare at them, marvelling at the scars, and the narrowed eyes, and their various sharp implements. 'I know who you are. You're the White Wit, aren't you, and your Black Fingers?'

'Ah, so word does get around.'

Rhin waggled his sword-point at Finrig. 'No more, Wit. You've got your Hoard, and that was the deal. It's over. Go back to Sift and tell her it's done.'

The Wit hummed, making a show of picking at his nails. 'Like I said before you sprinted off into the darkness earlier tonight, I think she would rather hear it from you, rather than me,' he sighed, as if the whole situation was a tiresome affair.

'He's not going anywhere with you,' Merion snapped. The faeries around him tensed. One even went as far as to growl. Merion bared his teeth, still sharp from the bobcat blood. He may have exhausted, but seeing as the last hour of his life had consisted purely of gunfire, blood, and death, the prospect of another fight hardly shocked him. Even Rhin cast a glance in surprise.

'Oh yes?' Wit replied. 'Are you going to stop us, rusher? Make a mess of us as you did the Serpeds?'

The Fingers sniggered among themselves. Merion would have taken a step forward, if he had any vials. His pockets were painfully empty.

'We know all about you,' grinned the Wit.

'You told them?' Merion flashed an accusatory look at Rhin.

'Oh, we've been watching you all,' smirked the Wit. He looked between each of them from Merion to Lilain, and then to Rhin as he spoke. 'Watching you go about your training in the desert, or playing with your corpses in your basement, or writing in your diary, under the bed.'

Rhin flinched. His sword tip lowered an inch. Lilain groaned, still slumped in the mud, as if she'd known all along.

'My what?' Rhin breathed in sharply.

The Wit grinned from ear to pale ear, and took a moment to wipe the rain from his white face. He reached behind his back and brought forth a battered old tome from under his cloak, dog-eared and wrapped in a cloth to keep it from the incessant rain.

Rhin started forward, but the nearest Finger raised an axe, and Rhin stopped dead, shaking all the same.

'I've only had a chance to thumb through it on the walk, but by the Roots, it's interesting reading, Rehn'ar. Have you told the boy yet?'

Merion felt a cold chill run up his spine, independent of the rainfall or the adrenalin of the recent fight. 'What's he talking about, Rhin?' asked Merion.

The lightning flashed, and even in its bleaching light, Merion saw it. There was a colour in the faerie's face the like of which Merion had never seen before, and it was not from the glow of the burning riverboat roaring behind them, nor his rain-soaked stubble, born of frantic days. Merion felt the chill climb his spine.

'You don't know, Tonmerion Hark?' The Wit asked, smirking again. Merion wanted to drive his foot into his face, to see if he could boot him over the rise. He let the bobcat burn and roil inside him.

'Spit it out, damn you,' Merion cursed at him, and the Wit shrugged. 'Whatever you have to say, just say it and be done with the theatrics.'

The Wit bowed sardonically. 'As you wish, Lordling,' he said, and then cleared his throat, as if he were a bard in a tavern.

'"I asked again. And again he told me it was impossible. He ignored my pleas, my reminders of our bargain. His face was like stone. I see why Merion fears him the way he does. I saw then why they call him the Bulldog."' Here the Wit paused, flicking his eyes up to linger on Rhin and Merion.

'Keep reading,' Merion ground the words out. His aunt reached up to touch his hand, and he seized it.

'"I told him of Sift and the Black Fingers' visit, told him of the White Wit and who he'd threatened. His fucking son, I told him. And if that wasn't a reason to pay them, I didn't know what was." It really does have a ring to it, doesn't it?' the Wit snapped his fingers.

Rhin felt Merion's eyes upon him. He spat in the mud and pointed his sword at the Wit once more. 'How fucking dare you!' the faerie growled, his voice like a landslide of gravel.

'"I raged for days. He is a stubborn fuck, and I knew there was only one way to make him listen to me. It didn't take much to get into his study … nor to find that little pistol of his. When I took the gun from the closet, I only meant to threaten him. To see how he liked it …" And here it becomes a little scribbly, Merion, my apologies. "It was bastard of a thing. Like lugging a cannon, but the magick held strong. When I met him on the stairs as I had the day before, he seemed surprised. I had never seen him surprised before.'

'You shut your mouth, Wit! Stop reading these lies!' Rhin blurted. 'He's taken bits out!'

'You keep fucking reading,' Merion hissed, hands shaking. His eyes were locked on Rhin, and the faerie could feel the heat of them.

The Wit tugged the top of his hood. 'Be delighted to. "I held the gun and pointed it up at him, but he just crossed his arms. 'Don't be a damn fool,' he told me, as if he were scolding Merion. 'Give me the Hoard,' I demanded of him, but he shook his head. 'It's spent, don't you understand? Put to good use. Bought half the tribes in Indus with that little bounty.' I couldn't breathe. The bastard had spent it all, after agreeing to take his cut for sanctuary, and to keep the rest safe, until I was. Until Merion was older."'

Here the Wit began to pace forward, first towards Rhin, then at Merion. His voice dropped, and his tone was sickeningly earnest. He even had the gall to wave a hand around in the air as he read, as if he were flicking each syllable at them. Merion felt sick to his core. He didn't know which faerie he wanted to kill first, but he knew it had to happen. His fists clenched so hard that his knuckles popped. He felt the blood rushing to his head. The Wit read on.

"'I couldn't believe it, but I did all the same. I didn't remind him of our agreement. I didn't shout and curse. I didn't march away and hand myself in. I just gripped that trigger with my hand and I pul—'"

'Now Lurker!' Rhin bellowed, cutting right through Finrig's performance. As he shouted, he pulsed with a blinding blue light. It was so bright, Merion had to cover his eyes, and reeled backwards. Before he could cry out, the gunshot rang out through the roar of rain and shouting faeries. When he took his hands away, he saw the Wit.

There was a vacant look in his eye, almost as though he were in the midst of deciding whether he had left the stove on. He looked up, shaking, and raised his arms. Merion blinked, and saw two halves of the diary, one in each hand, and strangely far apart. There was a hole where its spine had been, and when Merion looked closer, there was a hole where Finrig's should have been too. He was staring right through him at the mud beyond. Lightning flickered, and drew the edges of the oozing hole. The Wit was being held together by his armour alone.

If he'd had lungs to speak with, he might have finished his sentence, not that Merion needed to hear it. He already knew the truth, but sadly, it would have to wait. The Fingers had realised why their leader had stopped talking, and why his armour smoked and glowed. As one, they began to hiss, rattling almost like snakes. They crept forward, low and dangerous, wings flickering and weapons held low.

'Enough,' Merion grunted, as the pure rage swept through every orifice of his body, chased by the ferocious blood. He'd had enough, he said again, in his spinning head. He didn't want to be lied to any more. He didn't want to deal with traitorous lords any more. He didn't want to see faeries any more. He just wanted to go home.

Through bloodshot eyes, Merion watched himself go to work. Punching, kicking, even biting at one point, whirling, and screaming … the young Hark let the rage drive him. That rage that had been building up ever since he had stared down at the gun in the impossibly clean tray. It had been building with every twist and turn he had taken through this cursed town and its desert. With every lie, and disappointment, it had grown. It surged through him now in equal parts to the rushing blood, and together they boiled into something altogether monstrous— monstrous, and magickal.

Limbs were torn from sockets, swords and spears knocked aside and shattered. The cuts and gashes did not matter. Bodies flew through the air, only to be grabbed and hurled into the mud, stamped until the armour bent inwards. The spears bothered him not. Rhin was in trouble, a blade at his throat and a snarling face in his. One kick saw him saved. Then his fingers found the rock, and the others' black steel did not matter under the furious boy's raging swings.

After the rock in his hand had taken the head clean off the last Finger, he collapsed into a breathless heap. His chest pulsated like the bellows of a forge, and anybody looking would forever remember the sparks of electricity flitting through his matted, drenched hair. He was completely covered in mud, he and Rhin. The only surviving faerie breathed in ragged gasps, staring around him at the battered and crushed bodies of the thirteen finest mercenaries known to the Buried Kingdoms, despatched by a thirteen-year-old boy.

Merion wasn't done yet. With a half-roar, half-sob, the boy rolled over and brought the rock down, aiming for Rhin's head. The faerie rolled to the side, just in time to see the rock plunge into the muddy earth with a bang. 'Merion, stop!' he gasped, suddenly wordless after all these months of practising under the bed, of pinching himself so he wouldn't scream though the middle of the night. 'I never meant …' he croaked.

'YOU DON'T GET TO SPEAK!' Merion bellowed raggedly. His words made him pant. 'You don't get to talk to me … ever … again.'

'I would hold your tongue, if I were you, faerie,' Lilain muttered from behind them. She had only just shaken the carnage out of her swollen eyes. Now they shot daggers at Rhin.

Rhin bowed his head, and walked away, to stand at the edge of the carnage, and hold his head in his rain-soaked hands.

'Maker's balls, Merion!' Lurker shouted as he ran up, coming to a sloshing halt just short of a faerie corpse. Its head was either buried in the mud, or it was missing altogether. Lurker looked up at the boy with a desperate look in his rain-soaked eyes, as if he were trying to find a sliver of humanity in the boy's face, a trace of sanity in those mad eyes.

It was a long while before the boy found himself. Nobody said a thing. Not a sound, save for the tumbling sky and the wet slapping of the hammering rain. Slowly, the human in Merion fought back against the animal. With it his face took on a grave pallor, so Lurker took off his hat and held it over the boy's head, to shield him from the rain.

'How on earth, boy?' Lurker asked, words failing him.

'My blood boiled,' Merion whispered, before reaching up to take the hat. He pulled it down, over his soaking hair. His eyes were closed and his lips trembling.

With equally unsteady legs, he forced himself to his feet and stumbled a few steps down the slope. Lurker reached for him, but Merion waved him away, grunting. Without another sound, he stomped his way towards the inferno that was the riverboat. The shell of the vessel was a skeleton, engulfed in flames. Flames ruled the riverboat, bursting in great towers of red and swirling orange from its windows and funnels. The firestorm paid the rain no mind. It hissed and steamed, but the storm was no match for it. On and on it stubbornly raged, so hot it could have blistered skin at a hundred paces.

When Merion could take no more of the heat, he let his knees kiss the mud, and there he slumped. Every inch of him ached to be closer to the sodden ground. He stared up at the fire and let the light force his eyes to narrow slits. *Real men cannot be seen to cry*, he told himself as the first sob wracked his body. Then came the second, and Merion shook his head. He spoke to the roaring inferno as if it were burning just for him. 'I'm sorry, father,' he choked. 'But I have to let you down.'

Merion watched one of the funnels crash down onto the deck in an explosion of white-hot flame, sparks, and screeching metal. It was almost like an answer.

'I said I was sorry,' he whispered, tears springing to his eyes. 'It's time for me to stop listening to you, and listen to myself instead.'

A dull boom came from the innards of the riverboat, and Merion hung his head, his chest convulsing with every deep sob. The tears came in rivers. Merion would have been powerless, even if he had wanted to stop them. It was a purge, like a phoenix throwing itself into the flames. Merion welcomed every single one of them. When the sobbing became too much for his crumpled lungs to bear, he sagged onto his side. The cold mud sucked at his ear while the rain pelted his cheek. His eyes scrunched up into narrow slits, and through the tears he watched the riverboat burn until it was just a smoking wreck, and a wretched one at that.

CHAPTER XXXVI

WHATEVER IT TAKES

'America, we are headed for America.'

7th June, 1867

The rain stopped as dawn broke. There was no sun, no glowing firebrand in the east, just a gradual lightening of the sky, bruised as it was by the thick and angry clouds. The storm must have feared the sun, for it was soon moving on, skittering away to pastures new and dry, breaking up in its hasty retreat. The dawn light sliced through the storm's scattered limbs and threw strange shadows on the ground. Several thick columns of black, ominous smoke dared to spear the morning sky, leaking from the town to the north.

Lurker took a sip of his water, sniffed, and flicked Lilain on the arm.

'What?' she whispered dazedly, as though she had been half asleep.

'Shall we wake him?' Lurker asked.

Lilain shook her head. 'He'll come when he's ready. He needs every scrap of sleep he can get, after last night.'

Lurker sniffed again. 'What did he do?'

'Slew a nest of vipers is what he did. Pretty much with his bare hands. The boy is …' Lilain paused to yawn and scratch her head. 'I don't know *what* he is.'

Lurker grunted. 'Hmph. Better than his father?'

Lilain's eyes widened as she slowly nodded. 'If he isn't now, then he will be.'

Lurker sniffed once more, and looked up at the sky. 'Going to be a hot day.'

'Yes it is.'

'You heard the guns, right?'

Lilain took a sip of her water, wincing as she lifted her bloodied arm. She had no idea how she was still even conscious, but she wasn't about to question it. 'Ever since the thunder stopped, a few hours ago.' She turned to look him in the eye. 'I know the sound of guns when I hear 'em.'

It was Lurker's turn to nod, and he did so whilst Lilain looked him over. His rippled, shaven scalp still glistened with raindrops, making the ridges of his scars even more pronounced. She watched him sniff, his nose twitching to one side as it always did. She marvelled at how hunched his shoulders were, and yet how somehow it still felt like a giant sat beside her.

Lilain reached out, wincing again, and patted his gloved hand. 'Thank you.'

'Thank Rhin. He's the one who broke me out. Though, it doesn't look like I was needed.'

'Yes you were. Hell of a shot, by the way.'

'Ma'am,' Lurker said, reaching up to tug at a non-existent hat. He frowned and shrugged.

'I can't believe it's all over,' Lilain sighed.

'What?'

'This,' she said, looking around. 'Fell Falls. The Serpeds. My house.'

'What happened to the house?'

'Castor's men burnt it down. Everything's gone.'

Lurker cast a glance at the burnt-out riverboat, lying awkwardly in the grey, oily water. 'Seems to be a lot of that goin' round,' he replied, scratching his nose. 'What'll you do?'

'Move on. Back east, maybe. Or north. And there's always him to consider,' Lilain sighed again, nodding to her nephew, still curled like a foetus in the mud, thirty paces or so away. 'I can't imagine what he's got in his mind right now, after what he heard uttered last night.' Lilain turned her gaze on the small black figure who was also curled up in the mud, over to the left, head resting on a stone. She wasn't surprised to see Rhin's eyes open. They had been like that most of the night. If she hadn't known better, she'd have thought him dead, slain by guilt.

'We'll just have to see,' Lurker sniffed.

Half an hour later, the boy moved—slowly at first, a curl of a finger there, a shrug of a shoulder here, then a tottering to the knees, weak and cold. Merion painted a bedraggled figure, lost in all ways. And yet his eyes, staring out from under his tangled mop of muddied hair, spoke differently. They had in them a fearsome glint, hardened by both storm and cold revelation. He stalked through the mud towards them.

Lurker got to his feet and went to shake the boy's hand. Merion's hand was as wet and limp as a fish. Lurker wrinkled up his face in an awkward gesture, and opened his mouth to speak.

'Spare your words, John Hobble,' Merion rasped, throat chafed from sobbing. 'I know the truth now. That chief was right,' the boy sniffed, his sharp eyes darting to Rhin, who was now watching from his rock. 'Maybe some answers hurt too much.'

'Speaking of Shohari,' Lilain whispered.

'I can see the smoke,' Merion nodded, and the others turned to stare at the black towers. 'I want to go see.'

Lurker shook his head firmly. 'Merion, the fighting could still be ragin'. And your aunt can't walk. She needs rest.'

'We have to walk in any case, Lurker, we can't stay here,' Lilain said.

'I want to see it burn,' Merion stated, folding his arms.

Lurker sighed. 'Help me get her up then.'

The monster, speared by rail and road, had died a violent death. Fell Falls was a blackened husk, with fires still burning between the ribs of broken buildings. Everything was a different shade of char. Only the outskirts had survived, save for the camp. That was a bloody smear in the sand, a wasteland of bones and bodies. From their viewpoint on a rolling hill, they could see the victors stalking the fields of the dead, though this time, they were long of limb and brightly painted. The tide had been turned on Fell Falls. Lord Serped's railway had failed.

To the north, one house, right on the edge of the Runnels, had also fallen victim, a blackened stranger in an otherwise untouched patch of town. It sat alone, half cleaved in by the fire that had died sometime in the night, as the battle raged.

'It's all gone,' Lilain breathed, as she hung from the shoulders of Merion and Lurker. 'The camp, the workers, everything.'

'Wiped off the map,' Merion whispered, his voice as touch as grit.

'You sound almost happy,' Lurker rumbled.

'I don't know what I am,' replied Merion, squinting at the bloody mess below, 'but I know that I'm glad to be leaving. I know what I have to do.'

Lilain's head slumped against his shoulder, and Merion propped her up against Lurker. He stepped away to look behind them, at the lonely, pale figure standing amidst the pebbles, crooked and fearful.

'And what is that?' Rhin wheezed. His ears were drooping. His skin was a deathly white, and all in all, he looked dreadful, a hollow shell of a faerie.

'Trust in my family,' Merion announced, his voice hard, as if this were hard for him. 'Like the tree told me to. I understand now.'

Lilain and Lurker swapped confused glances.

Merion took a breath, and poured out the words he had been chewing all night. 'When I first set foot on this godforsaken continent I was an orphan with a sidekick. Now I have a family, and that means that even though my world has been crushed and ripped to pieces, I'm not standing alone in the ashes. And this may be the most fucked-up family civilisation has ever known, but it is still a family. My family, and that's important.' Merion took a moment to narrow his eyes at Rhin. 'I guess every family has its black sheep, Rhin Rehn'ar, and you are ours.'

'Merion …'

But the boy held up a hand. He did it in a measured, not an angry, way. 'Know that I may never forgive you, for what you have done to me, my father, and to my aunt …' Merion told him, like a judge issuing a sentence. Rhin had already bowed his head. '… but know that in some small way, if you had not murdered my father, I would not be here. And for the first time that is not a regret.'

A silence followed the young Hark's words. From where the wind blew the sounds of the dying town to their ears came a wounded moan, a crash of falling timbers, and the yell of a Shohari who has found a live one. It was Lilain who broke it.

'Your father would be proud of those words, nephew. Trust me,' she said, clasping her hands together. Merion could have sworn he saw something glistening at the corner of her bruised eyes.

Lurker did not try to mask the gleam of pride in his eyes. 'So what's your plan, boy?'

Merion stared off into the wilderness. 'Head east, I suppose. Earn a wage and travel until we hit the coast.

Lurker grinned wryly and snorted. 'You make it sound easy,' he said, before a nudge in the ribs changed his mind. 'But it ain't like we have a choice, now is it?'

'We'll make it,' Merion said. 'Hell, I'll rush in circuses if I have to, whatever it takes. Lilain can help the sick. Lurker, you can pick up a little gold, on the way. If you haven't got a hoard already.'

'Not any longer,' Lurker threw the smouldering town a dark look. 'Not any longer.'

Merion sensed that was a story for another day, and sighed.

'Am I coming?' said a small voice, closer this time. Rhin stood just behind Merion's heel, like a wounded pet. Rhin had a spark of something hopeful in his eye, despite standing as though a weight were slowly crushing him. He was stubborn to the last, as always. 'Because I think I know where I can find us some gold. The train robbery. The Wit would have left it in the Serped barn.'

There was another silence as Merion just looked straight ahead. 'Family, like I said.'

Rhin took a deep breath and stood as tall as he could. 'I will earn your forgiveness, Merion, somehow and someday. I swear it, and a Fae's oath is his bond.'

Only then did the boy meet his wide-eyed and purple eyes, and saw such sadness and determination there that he could not help but soften, if only for a brief moment. 'Take us to the barn,' replied Merion.

'So that's it then. This barn and east it is,' Lilain waved an arm at the desert and the rising sun, and began to totter in its direction.

Lurker scooped her up in both arms to save her the trouble. He barely grunted with the effort. 'With no water, no supplies, no fresh clothes and no blood,' he said, grumbling already.

Merion shrugged. 'But if Rhin is right, what we will have is a hoard of Serped gold. I do believe that is what they call the start of an adventure.'

While Lilain sniggered, the big old prospector sniffed. 'Now, this ain't no fairy tale, boy,' he grunted.

'You could have fooled me,' Merion wrinkled his face into a wry smile, despite it all. He flicked a glance at the weary faerie trudging by his side. He shook his head, sighed, and stared out into the desert that beckoned to them with barren, rocky arms. His future.

Merion held his heavy head up. He could almost feel the gust of wind from the proverbial page turning over. He was free at last. He was heading home.

'Could have fooled me.'

Leabharlanna Poiblí Chathair Baile Átha Cliath
Dublin City Public Libraries

EPILOGUE
A BLOOD MOON IS RISING...

13th June, 1867

London was being roasted alive. The summer sun had come early, and ferociously. The hottest summer since records began, the newspapers brayed.

Lord Bremar Dizali sat stiff in his wide leather chair, presiding over a fine mahogany desk full of papers and folders and all sorts of other important things.

Sweat dribbled down the man's bony chiselled features. Dizali hated the heat. He hated the stench of London's sewers and the swarms of people aching to soak up the precious sunlight, something the Empire's beating heart rarely got to see. Rain was normally the flavour of the day.

There came a rap on his huge doors, ornately carved with a design of the Dizal eagle, dragging a tiger into the cloudy sky.

Bremar sighed irritably. 'What now?'

The handle turned, and in marched Gavisham. Despite his obvious urgency, the man knew better than to leave the door open behind him. He shut it with a bang, and then practically jogged to Lord Dizali's desk.

'What the devil is it, man?!' Bremar hissed. He was not in the mood for theatricals.

Gavisham held a folded piece of paper aloft before letting it fall to the desk. 'A wiregram, Milord. I think you'll want to have a look,' he said, loudly. Bremar couldn't tell whether the man was fuming or burning with excitement. His curiosity was piqued, that was for sure. He snatched the letter from the man and walked to the window. Gavisham followed him like a hound.

'Almighty's sake man, calm down,' Bremar snapped as he flicked the wiregram open and began to read. His green eyes scanned over the message, and with each word they grew wider and wider.

Dizali had barely finished the last sentence when he ripped the letter in two, threw it to the carpet, and put his fists against the hot glass of the window. 'One boy ...' he growled. 'One fucking thirteen year-old boy did this?!'

'Slaughtered the whole lot of them, and burned the riverboat to ashes.'

'No survivors?'

'None, save for the two lordsguards that sent the letter. More's the pity.'

Lord Dizali thumped the glass. 'Damn it! Damn that boy to hell!' he roared. Gavisham simply stood still, hands folded behind his back, glaring. 'Fetch me a carriage!' Bremar snapped at him.

Gavisham clapped his hands. 'With pleasure, Milord. Where to?'

'To the Palace of Ravens,' barked his lordship, beginning to pace around in furious circles.

'And you're sure that's wise, Milord?' Gavisham. 'To tell her so soon?'

Lord Dizali whirled around to face him. He did not speak, he did not deign to reply. He simply narrowed his eyes and glared, daring his manservant to challenge him again, staring deep into those strange mismatched eyes of Gavisham's. Just like his brother's.

One green. One blue.

Ars Magica:

Bloodrushing, or haemomancy, is the consumption and exploitation of blood. There lies a power in the blood of most animals, accessible by those with the ability to rush, or 'stomach' it.

The History:

Bloodrushing is not a new art, nor has it always been called 'rushing'. It has been called many names over the centuries. The Scythians, as they were called by the Greeks, first practised the art a thousand years before the First Empire. It was originally a warrior's sport, consuming the blood of the first enemy killed in battle. The Mongols would consume the blood of their horses. The indigenous peoples of Brasilia, the new-worlders, spilt and drank the blood of their enemies to appease their gods. Bloodletters of the First Empire collected and examined the blood of the sick.

When the Age of Enlightenment dawned, the practise of rushing shifted from that of pagans and warriors to that of scientists, pioneers, and the influential. With influence came coin, and with coin, expansion. As the corners of the world were uncovered, one by one, the opportunity for exotic bloods only increased its popularity. Rushers began to travel the spice runs and trade routes to Indus and Africanus. Bloodetters flourished in every port and city across Europe and Asia. Books were written and rules wrought. In short, bloodrushing saw its first and only golden age.

But all ages must tarnish, and with new passion came thirst for power; for apparent immortality. The rushing of human blood began to increase, splitting rushers into warring factions. Unavoidably, the Church became involved, citing sorcery, demonism, and black magic. Rushers were dubbed as heretics, and many were burned at the stake. Bloodrushing was chased into the shadows, leaving only myth and folklore behind. Vampires and pagans, they were dubbed. It became a secretive art, its practitioners a dying breed, and the knowledge was passed down only through families and dusty books.

The Practise:

Rushers usually drink the blood, ingesting it through the stomach wall. In the past, however, some were known to inject blood directly into veins or arteries. This can only be described as foolhardy as the blood is somewhat filtered, or concentrated, by the stomach acids and digestive juices.

Letters:

Practitioners of the ancient art of bloodletting. Originally healers and surgeons, a modern letter focuses solely on collecting, extracting, and purifying blood of all different types. Also known as butchers, or draugrs in some parts of Europe.

Rushers:

Those who can drink blood and tolerate its effects. Not all humans can withstand the strain of bloodrushing, but those who can are usually able to tolerate between one and three shades. Also known as haemomancers.

Leeches:

A rare form of rusher who can tolerate multiple shades from different veins. Only a few have ever been recorded, as many are forced into secrecy for their own safety. Being a leech is highly coveted indeed.

Lamprey:

The term for those who focus solely on rushing human blood, a practice that was shunned by early rushers from the first Empire, yet adopted later by the powerful as a way of cheating death. Also known as parasite, or vampire.

The six veins of rushing, as ordered on the Scarlet Star:

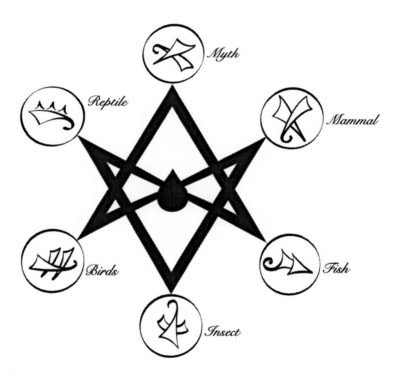

Shades:

Listed below are some of the primary shades within each vein. While not all rushers will experience either the positive or negative effects, they are listed below for reference.

—Birds—

Known as 'Hollowbone' or 'Pinion'

Magpie—Goldnose
Bestows the ability to sniff out precious metals. Increased use can result in short-term memory loss and greed.

Seagull/Cormorant/Puffin
Gives the rusher a heightened passion for fish

Vulture—Mortscent
Rushers are able to sniff out corpses or those near death. Can cause nosebleeds in minor cases, and/or cannibalistic tendencies with continued use

Eagle—The Hunter's Gaze, or Goldeyes
Enhances the sight of the rusher. Can cause cataracts or complete blindness in later life.

Cardinal—Beacon
Flushes skin to a near-fluorescent red colour. Overuse can result in permanency.

Pelican
The rusher is gifted the ability to drink great quantities of saltwater. Causes an incredible thirst once rushing is over.

Turkey
Rusher becomes desperately gluttonous. Often used as a poison.

Roadrunner—Dustkicker
Increased speed and reflexes. Can result in blisters or injury to ankles and knees.

Peacock/Oriole/Bird of Paradise—Colourbuck
Rusher's skin takes on an iridescent quality. This may result in the shedding of skin after rushing.

Mockingbird—Smartbeak
Bestows the ability to mimic any noise or voice. This shade can cause laryngitis with extended use.

Hummingbird—Windmiller
Gives a rusher the ability to move appendages at great speed. May cause sprains and broken bones in extreme cases. Also causes a near-debilitating thirst for sugar after rushing.

Finch—Twitcher
Allows a rusher to adapt to extreme environments quicker than usual, such as the ability to withstand extreme cold or heat. This shade is highly addictive, hence its nickname. Rushers can develop cravings when not rushing, and start to twitch involuntarily.

Duck
Makes a rusher's skin impervious to water.

Is reported to cause massive dehydration

Ostrich—Kickback

Allows the rusher to kick out with powerful speed and force. Weaker rushers may find their knees swiftly dislocated.

Parrot

This shade gifts the rusher with an incredibly strong bite.

Flamingo

Rushers have the ability to withstand strong acid and some poisons, whether ingested or touched. It can cause bright pink skin with overuse.

Penguin—Feathercoat

Rushers are able to withstand desperately cold temperatures, thanks to a thickening of the skin. Unfortunately it can cause weight gain.

Kiwi

Bestows an incredible sense of smell on the rusher.

Woodpecker—Grubsnout

Provides a very strong skull and the ability to move rapidly, particularly when head-butting. Drawbacks include a vicious hunger for tree-dwelling insects.

—Fish—

Known as 'Gillers'

Carp—Barbel

Rushers gain an extra-sensory ability which enables them to feel the presence of other rushers

Piranha—Mumblers

Gives a rusher a mouthful of sharp teeth. Side-effects can often include the severance of a tongue, difficulty speaking, and damage to the inside of the mouth.

Electric Eel—Cracklers

Rusher can electrify the skin and manipulate electricity. An untrustworthy shade, it can resurface at random even without rushing.

Trout

Brings a rainbow-like quality to the skin. Can last for weeks.

Salmon

Gives the rusher a dogged sense of determination Skin exudes a fishy odour.

Anchovy

Rushers can withstand increased pressures.

Shark

Bestows upon a rusher an increased awareness of and resistance to disease. Can last months, but can also make a rusher short-tempered and violent.

Stingray

Both a blessing and a curse, this shade gives rushers poison barbs along the spine.

Squid—Blackmouth
Gives a rusher the ability to spit ink. Can also cause a loss of bone density.

Octopus
Rushers have the ability to bend bones and warp skin to avoid getting damaged. However, prolonged use can permanently alter the hue of the skin.

Archer fish—Sprat
Rushers can spit water with incredible velocity and force. The drawbacks of this shade include loss of teeth and mouth control.

Lungfish
Provides the ability to withstand the heat of the sun for long periods, and an increased lung capacity.

Jellyfish
Gives a rusher rubber-like skin and muscle, and the ability to squeeze or fit into smaller spaces.

Box jellyfish
Gives the rusher poisonous barbs on the fingertips.

Lobster
Gives a rusher an increased sense of loyalty and armoured skin along the shoulders, neck and back.

Lion-fish
Speckled skin, and sharp barbs protrude from the shoulders. Gives skin a speckled or striped quality for camouflage, and spiked barbs protrude from shoulders.

Swordfish/Tuna
This shade increases a rusher's speed and reactions

Cuttlefish
Skin can adapt to its surroundings, altering colour and texture to camouflage the rusher. Overuse can result in loss of muscle control and bony growths on the arms.

Moray Eel—Snapper
This shade sharpens the teeth and gives a strong bite to the rusher.

Mantis shrimp—Hammer
Bestows upon the rusher an incredible punch. Its drawback is strangely colourful skin.

Anglerfish
Rushers are given glowing eyes and increased night-vision

Stonefish
Skin can adapt to surrounding textures, though this shade can cause barbs to grow on the face and skin to become a dark grey colour.

—Mammals—

Bison/Ox/Buffalo/Mule
Provides increased stamina and an oddly strong herding instinct.

Wolf
Increases a rusher's ferocity and overall body hair. Does result is a strange fascination with the moon, and permanence.

Bear—Hulker
Rusher grows in both size and gains enhanced strength. Extended use can cause ailments of the joints, a short temper, and the inability to discern between friend and foe.

Coyote—Scavenger
This shade enables a rusher to survive off a fraction of the food intake they normally would.

Horse
Increases stamina and top running speed. Unfortunately, some rushers can develop hard, hoof-like growths on the soles of the feet.

Fox
Gives rushers improved night-vision, however this shade only lasts for a matter of minutes.

Ram/Rhino—Ironhead
Rushers have a thicker cranium for short periods. Resulting activities, such as head-butting, can result in extensive brain damage

Beaver—Axetooth
Makes a rusher's teeth incredibly strong. This shade can turn permanent, if pushed.

Porcupine
Gives a rusher black spines on arms and legs

Skunk—Stench
Yet another shade which is as much blessing as curse. It makes the rusher able to emit a putrid stench from their pores. The drawback is the actual power itself.

Wildcat/Cougar/Lynx
Rushers experience unstoppable savagery, as well as an increased sensitivity to noise.

Lion—Loner
An incredibly strong hunting instinct. With overuse, this shade can cause antisocial and violent tendencies.

Armadillo—Clinker
A very hard shade to stomach. Results in armoured skin in most cases, however it can result in thick and unsightly calluses.

Deer
Increased awareness of nearby creatures. It can make a rusher skittish and nervous even when not rushing.

Elephant
Rushers using this shade can carry huge loads with no trouble. Skin can become greyer with use.

Bat
Hearing becomes incredibly sensitive. For weaker rushers, this can cause temporary deafness or tinnitus.

Dog—Snuffler
Sense of smell is increased to outstanding levels.

Cat
Sense of balance and agility is heightened. Rushers have been reported to experience furballs.

Meerkat
Heightened reactions and sense of danger, verging on the precognitive.

Panda
Increased strength and the gift of very strong jaws. Unfortunately, use of this shade can result in a complete loss of libido.

Monkey
Enhanced climbing skills and reactions. This shade will cause excessive body hair with overuse.

Tiger
Gives a rusher faintly striped skin and therefore a camouflage ability. Savage

tendencies have also been recorded.

Rat
Rushers using this shade are able to withstand poisoning, and consume almost anything without harm. However, this shade can wear off unpredictably, causing trouble if digestion is not quite complete.

Squirrel/Chipmunk/Mouse—Bucktooth
This shade heightens the reactions of a rusher. With prolonged use it can cause the two front teeth to grow larger and protrude from the mouth, hence the nickname.

Ferret/Weasel/Mongoose—Flitter
Heightened agility and reactions.

Sloth
Gives the rusher sharp claws instead of fingernails. Can cause narcolepsy or extreme tiredness.

Mole—Milkeyes
Another shade that produces sharp claws in rushers, as well as better night-vision. However, claws can instead manifest in the feet instead of hands, and cataracts from repeated use have also been recorded.

—Reptiles—
Known as 'Scalebleeders' or 'Coldbloods'

Rattlesnake—Whisperskin
Gifts a rusher with the ability to rattle skin to intimidate enemies. Also makes a rusher's bite poisonous. The drawback, as with many of the reptile shades, is permanent scales.

Tortoise/Turtle

Gives a rusher leathery armour along their back and shoulders.

Whiptail lizard

This shade gifts a rusher with increased speed. Overuse can cause muscle strains, atrophy, and even permanent damage.

Horned lizard

Rushers have the ability to siphon water out of the air in desert climates. Scales are once again a drawback.

Horny devil

This shade produces multiple, jagged spikes on a rusher's shoulders, arms and back.

Gecko

Rushers using this shade have enhanced climbing abilities thanks to sticky fingers.

Komodo dragon—Dribblekill

The Komodo shade gifts a rusher with mildly poisonous saliva which, over a period of time, can debilitate an enemy. Extreme tooth decay has been recorded as a side-effect.

Asp/Sea snake

These shades give rushers poisonous fangs, but can cause damage to gums and lips

Boa—Wraparound

Enhanced strength, and slightly longer arms for reaching around enemies. Arthritis is a common side-effect of this shade.

Bearded dragon

Rushers grow tough scales instead of skin. Dermatitis has been recorded.

Cayman/Alligator/Crocodile—Sneakfang

Rushers become incredibly stealthy. Teeth also become sharper and more numerous. This can cause gum disease as well as scales in lesser rushers.

Chameleon—Trickskin

Skin becomes reactive to colour and light, changing to adapt to surroundings. Very difficult shade to master.

Cobra—Borer

Rusher's eyes take on a very intimidating quality which is only increased by staring.

Snapping turtle/Terrapin

This shade gives rushers thick leathery skin and stronger teeth than normal.

Salamander—Char

Increased resistance to fire and flame. Permanent blackening of the skin can occur.

Dart frog—Sickskin

Skin becomes poisonous to the touch. Rushers can develop halitosis with prolonged use.

Monitor lizard—Raker

Rusher can grow sharp and long claws. Side-effects can include blisters, ingrown nails, and arthritis.

Gila monster
Gives rushers the ability to spit acid for short periods of time.

Coqui frog—Screech
Rushers can screech at a piercing volume. Laryngitis is a very common condition associated with this shade.

Horned toad
This particular shade bestows the ability to swallow great volumes, and stretch mouth to incredible proportions. Can clause slack jaw.

Bullfrog
Increases aggression.

Toad
This shade thickens the skin, turning it into leather.

—Insects—
Known as 'Blackeyes' or 'Greenbloods'

Butterfly—Flutter
Increases a rusher's overall physical attractiveness. It is recorded that this shade may shorten lifespans.

Waterboatman—Placid
Rushers of this shade can run across water if they are fast enough.

Honey bee
Provides an enhanced sense of smell. Overuse can cause depression if the rusher is left alone too long.

Wasp—Shiv
Gives the rusher a sharp, slightly poisonous sting that protrudes from the base of the palm. Rushers of this shade can develop a nervous disposition

Dung Beetle (nt) Stag beetle—Charger
Enhanced strength, yet can cause blackening of the eyes, like many other shades in this vein.

Mantis—Snapper
Gives a rusher the ability to snap hands together at supersonic speeds, crushing enemies. In extreme cases, rushers also develop jagged fingers. The drawbacks include broken limbs.

Moth
A rusher of this shade can shed a fine, choking dust from the skin.

Glow worm
This shade makes skin glow a bright yellow or green. Bleaching of the skin to a pure white or pale yellow can occur with overuse.

Cicada—Siren
Sirens can screech at a piercing pitch and volume, momentarily stunning enemies or breaking glass. Snapped

vocal chords may occur in lesser rushers.

Firefly

This shade causes the skin to glow or flash brightly for a limited time.

Funnel-web spiders —Silkfingers/ Strangler

Hands produce a sticky, tough silk, which can also provide enhanced climbing abilities. One common drawback is an increased hunger for flies and other insects.

Trapdoor spider

Rushers are able to move in incredible, though short-lived, bursts of speed.

Black Widow spider —The Dead Man

Causes the rusher's fingertips to become poisonous. The drawback, even for strong rushers, is permanence, hence this shade's nickname.

Goliath spider

This shade causes the rusher's body to grow one and a half times larger, and swell with muscle. It can result in dislocated shoulders and joints.

Centipede/Cockroach —Black Knight

Gifts a rusher thick, armoured scales along the forearms, back and shoulders. In almost all cases, it causes a blackening of the eyes.

Stick insect

This shade causes thinning of the limbs and enhanced sneaking ability.

Mosquito—Sapper

Gives a rusher the ability to sap energy from a victim or enemy. This shade should be treated with caution, as it is viciously addictive.

Leech

This particular shade can heighten a rusher's power and ability to rush. The drawback is

once again blackened eyes.

Earthworm

This gifts rushers with an incredibly sturdy digestive system.

—Myth—

The Fae

Invisibility.

Minotaur—The Beast

Increased strength and endurance.

Centaur

Enhanced vision.

Phoenix

Immunity to fire, and marginally increased life-span.

Huldra

Gives a rusher the ability to seduce or coerce people.

Kelpie/Water Nymph
Rushers can breathe underwater for short periods of time.

Dragon
Impenetrable skin.

Elf/Wood Nymph
Rusher becomes extremely light of foot.

Dwarf
This shade grants the ability to bend metal and withstand heat.

Giant
Increased strength and size.

Troll/Golem— Stoneskin
Gives a rusher skin as tough as stone.

Goblin
This shade grants a rusher the ability to see in the dark.

Sphinx
Rushers have the ability to temporarily transfix and stun enemies with a single look.

Banshee
Rushers of this shade can fade the skin and howl in a mesmerising fashion.

Mockinghawk
Rushers can change skin and clothing to imitate almost anybody.

Thunderbird
This shade electrifies the skin and causes it to crackle.

Rainbirds
This shade grants rushers the ability to control and manipulate rain.

Wisps
Rushers are able to manipulate fog, mist and smoke.

Kee-wakw/Draugr
A very special shade that should be treated with absolute caution. Rushers can use other shades for a limited period of time, emulating a leech. Should it wear off whilst rushing a foreign shade, it can have disastrous consequences.

Nimerigar
Rushers can shrink to less than half their size at will.

Piasa bird
This shade turns the rusher's skin colour into a hypnotic, ever-changing rainbow.

Wampus cat
Rushers can growl with intimidating ferocity and volume.

Mermaid
A curious shade that allows rushers to understand the minds of fish and aquatic beasts.

Sleeping Tree/Oracle
These shades give a rusher visions of truth and the future.

Chupacabra
This shade gives certain rushers the ability to steal and empathise another rusher's powers, replacing their own until finding another victim.

Lupus

Turns a rusher into a
creature similar to a
lupus itself, though
decidedly more human.

Sprite

Control and
manipulation of fire.

TONMERION WILL RETURN...

CPSIA information can be obtained at www.ICGtesting.com
Printed in the USA
LVOW06s0921230315

431631LV00003B/212/P